THIS SIGNED EDITION OF

PORTRAIT OF A SPY

BY

DANIEL SILVA

HAS BEEN SPECIALLY BOUND

BY THE PUBLISHER.

PORTRAIT OF A SPY

PORTRAIT
OF
A SPY

DANIEL
SILVA

HARPER

An Imprint of HarperCollins*Publishers*
www.harpercollins.com

PORTRAIT OF A SPY. Copyright © 2011 by Daniel Silva. All rights reserved. Printed in the United States of America. No part of this book may be used or reproduced in any manner whatsoever without written permission except in the case of brief quotations embodied in critical articles and reviews. For information, address HarperCollins Publishers, 10 East 53rd Street, New York, NY 10022.

HarperCollins books may be purchased for educational, business, or sales promotional use. For information, please write: Special Markets Department, HarperCollins Publishers, 10 East 53rd Street, New York, NY 10022.

FIRST EDITION

Designed by Leah Carlson-Stanisic

Library of Congress Cataloging-in-Publication Data has been applied for.

ISBN: 978-0-06-207218-4 (Hardcover)
ISBN: 978-0-06-211392-4 (International Edition)
ISBN: 978-0-06-210693-3 (Signed Edition)

11 12 13 14 15   OV/RRD   10 9 8 7 6 5 4 3 2 1

*For my wonderful children, Nicholas and Lily,
whom I love and admire more than they will
ever know. And, as always, for my wife, Jamie, who
makes everything possible.*

*Jihad is becoming as American as apple pie
and as British as afternoon tea.*

ANWAR AL-AWLAKI, AL-QAEDA PREACHER AND RECRUITER

*One person of integrity can make a difference,
a difference of life and death.*

ELIE WIESEL

PART ONE

DEATH
IN THE
GARDEN

THE LIZARD PENINSULA, CORNWALL

IT WAS THE REMBRANDT THAT solved the mystery once and for all. Afterward, in the quaint shops where they did their marketing and the dark little seaside pubs where they did their drinking, they would chide themselves for having missed the telltale signs, and they would share a good-natured laugh at some of their more outlandish theories about the true nature of his work. Because in their wildest dreams there was not one among them who ever considered the possibility that the taciturn man from the far end of Gunwalloe Cove was an art restorer, and a world-famous art restorer at that.

He was not the first outsider to wander down to Cornwall with a secret to keep, yet few had guarded theirs more jealously, or with more style and intrigue. A case in point was the peculiar manner in which he had secured lodgings for himself and his beautiful but much younger wife. Having chosen the picturesque cottage at the edge of the cliffs—by all accounts, sight unseen—he had paid the entire twelve-month lease in advance, with all the paperwork handled discreetly by an obscure lawyer in Hamburg. He settled into the cottage a fortnight later as if he were conducting a raid on a distant enemy outpost. Those who met him during his first forays into the village were struck by his notable lack of candor. He seemed to have no name—at least not one he was willing to share—and no country of origin that any of them could place. Duncan Reynolds, thirty years retired from the railroad and regarded as the worldliest of Gunwalloe's residents, described him as "a cipher of a man" while other reviews ranged from "standoffish" to "unbearably rude." Even so, all agreed that, for better or worse, the little west Cornish village of Gunwalloe had become a far more interesting place.

With time, they were able to establish that his name was Giovanni Rossi and that, like his beautiful wife, he was of Italian descent. Which made it all the more curious when they began to notice government-issue cars filled with government-issue men prowling the streets of the village late at night. And then there were the two blokes who sometimes fished the cove. Opinion was universal that they were the worst fishermen anyone had ever seen. In fact, most assumed they were not fishermen at all. Naturally, as is wont to happen in a small village like Gunwalloe, there began an intense debate about the true identity of the newcomer and the nature of his work—a debate that was finally resolved by *Portrait of a Young Woman*, oil on canvas, 104 by 86 centimeters, by Rembrandt van Rijn.

Precisely when it arrived would never be clear. They assumed it was sometime in mid-January because that was when they noticed a dramatic change in his daily routine. One day he was marching along the rugged cliff tops of the Lizard Peninsula as though wrestling with a guilty conscience; the next he was standing before an easel in his living room, a paintbrush in one hand, a palette in the other, and opera music blasting so loudly you could hear the wailing clear across Mount's Bay in Marazion. Given the proximity of his cottage to the Coastal Path, it was possible—if one paused in just the right spot, mind you, and craned one's neck at just the right angle—to see him in his studio. At first, they assumed he was working on a painting of his own. But as the weeks ground slowly past, it became clear he was involved in the craft known as conservation or, more commonly, as restoration.

"Hell's that mean?" Malcolm Braithwaite, a retired lobsterman who smelled perpetually of the sea, asked one evening at the Lamb and Flag pub.

"It means he's fixing the bloody thing," said Duncan Reynolds. "A painting is like a living, breathing thing. When it gets old, it flakes and sags—just like you, Malcolm."

"I hear it's a young girl."

"Pretty," said Duncan, nodding his head. "Cheeks like apples. She looks positively edible."

"Do we know the artist?"

"Still working on that."

And work on it they did. They consulted many books, searched many sites on the Internet, and sought out people who knew more about art than they did—a category that included most of the population of West Cornwall. Finally, in early April, Dottie Cox from the village store screwed up the nerve to simply *ask* the beautiful young Italian woman about the painting when she came into town to do her marketing. The woman evaded the question with an ambiguous smile. Then, with her straw bag slung over her shoulder, she sauntered back down to the cove, her riotous dark hair tossed by the springtime wind. Within minutes of her arrival, the wailing of the opera ceased and the window shades of the cottage fell like eyelids.

They remained tightly closed for the next week, at which point the restorer and his beautiful wife disappeared without warning. For several days, the residents of Gunwalloe feared they might not be planning to return, and a few actually berated themselves for having snooped and pried into the couple's private affairs. Then, while leafing through the *Times* one morning at the village store, Dottie Cox noticed a story from Washington, D.C., about the unveiling of a long-lost portrait by Rembrandt—a portrait that looked precisely like the one that had been in the cottage at the far end of the cove. And thus the mystery was solved.

Coincidentally, that same edition of the *Times* contained a front-page article about a series of mysterious explosions at four secret Iranian nuclear facilities. No one in Gunwalloe imagined there might be any connection. At least not yet.

The restorer was a changed man when he came back from America; they could see that. Though he remained guarded in his personal encounters—and he was still not the sort you would want to surprise in the dark—it was obvious a great burden had been lifted from his shoulders. They saw a smile on his angular face every now and again, and the light emitted by his unnaturally green eyes seemed a shade less defensive. Even his long daily walks had a different quality. Where once he had pounded along the footpaths like a man possessed, he now seemed to float atop the mist-covered cliffs like an Arthurian spirit who had come home after a long time in a distant land.

"Looks to me as if he's been released from a sacred vow,"

observed Vera Hobbs, owner of the village bakeshop. But when asked to venture a guess as to what that vow might have been, or to whom he had sworn it, she refused. Like everyone else in town, she had made a fool of herself trying to divine his occupation. "Besides," she advised, "it's better to leave him in peace. Otherwise, the next time he and his pretty wife leave the Lizard, it might be for good."

Indeed, as that glorious summer slowly faded, the restorer's future plans became the primary preoccupation of the entire village. With the lease on the cottage running out in September, and with no tangible evidence he was planning to renew it, they embarked on a covert effort to persuade him to stay. What the restorer needed, they decided, was something to keep him tethered to the Cornish coast—a job that utilized his unique set of skills and gave him something to do other than walk the cliffs. Exactly what that job might entail, and who would give it to him, they had no idea, but they entrusted to themselves the delicate task of trying to find it.

After much deliberation, it was Dottie Cox who finally hit upon the idea of the First Annual Gunwalloe Festival of Fine Arts, with the famous art restorer Giovanni Rossi serving as honorary chairman. She made the suggestion to the restorer's wife the following morning when she popped into the village store at her usual time. The woman actually laughed for several minutes. The offer was flattering, she said after regaining her composure, but she didn't think it was the sort of thing Signor Rossi would agree to. His official rejection came soon after, and the Gunwalloe Festival of Fine Arts quietly withered on the vine. It was no matter; a few days later, they learned that the restorer had taken the cottage for another year. Once again, the lease was paid in full, with all the paperwork handled by the same obscure lawyer in Hamburg.

With that, life returned to something like normal. They would see the restorer in mid-morning when he came to the village with his wife to do their marketing, and they would see him again in mid-afternoon when he hiked along the cliff tops in his Barbour coat and his flat cap pulled low over his brow. And if he failed to give them a proper greeting, they took no offense. And if he seemed uneasy about something, they gave him room to work it out on his own. And if a stranger came to town, they tracked his every move until he was gone. The restorer and his wife might have come from Italy originally, but they belonged to Cornwall now, and heaven help the fool who ever tried to take them away again.

There were, however, some on the Lizard who believed there was more to the story—and one man in particular who believed he knew what it was. His name was Teddy Sinclair, owner of a rather good pizzeria in Helston and a subscriber to conspiracy theories large and small. Teddy believed the moon landings were a hoax. Teddy believed 9/11 was an inside job. And Teddy believed the man from Gunwalloe Cove was hiding more than a secret ability to heal paintings.

To prove his case once and for all, he summoned the villagers to the Lamb and Flag on the second Thursday of November and unveiled a chart that looked a bit like the periodic table of elements. It purported to establish, beyond a shadow of a doubt, that the explosions at the Iranian nuclear facilities were the work of a legendary Israeli intelligence officer named Gabriel Allon—and that the same Gabriel Allon was now living peacefully in Gunwalloe under the name Giovanni Rossi. When the laughter finally died down, Duncan Reynolds called it the dumbest thing he'd heard since some Frenchman decided that Europe should have a common currency. But this time Teddy stood his ground, which in hindsight was the right thing to do. Because Teddy might have been wrong about the moon landings, and wrong about 9/11, but when it came to the man from Gunwalloe Cove, his theory was in every respect true.

The next morning, Remembrance Day, the village woke to the news that the restorer and his wife had disappeared. In a panic, Vera Hobbs hurried down to the cove and peered through the windows of the cottage. The restorer's supplies were scattered across a low table, and propped on the easel was a painting of a nude woman stretched upon a couch. It took Vera a moment to realize that the couch was identical to the one in the living room, and that the woman was the same one she saw each morning in her bakeshop. Despite her embarrassment, Vera couldn't seem to summon the will to look away, because it happened to be one of the most strikingly beautiful paintings she had ever seen. It was also a very good sign, she thought as she headed back to the village. A painting like that was not the sort of thing a man left behind when he was making a run for it. Eventually, the restorer and his wife would come back. And heaven help that bloody Teddy Sinclair if they didn't.

2

PARIS

THE FIRST BOMB EXPLODED AT 11:46 a.m., on the Avenue des Champs-Élysées in Paris. The director of the French security service would later say he received no warning of the impending attack, a statement his detractors might have found laughable were the death toll not so high. The warning signs were plain to see, they said. Only the blind or the willfully ignorant could have possibly missed them.

From Europe's point of view, the timing of the attack could not have been worse. After decades of lavish social spending, much of the Continent was teetering on the brink of fiscal and monetary disaster. Its debt was soaring, its treasuries were empty, and its pampered citizenry was aging and disillusioned. Austerity was the order of the day. In the current climate, no cow was considered too sacred; health care, university tuition, support for the arts, and even pension benefits were all undergoing drastic cuts. Along Europe's so-called periphery, the smaller economies were falling like dominoes. Greece was sinking slowly into the Aegean, Spain was on life support, and the Irish Miracle had turned out to be nothing more than a mirage. In the smart salons of Brussels, many Eurocrats were daring to say aloud what had once been unthinkable—that the dream of European integration was dying. And in their darker moments, a few of them actually wondered whether Europe as they knew it might be dying, too.

Another article of faith lay in tatters that November—the belief that Europe could absorb an endless tide of Muslim immigrants from its former colonies while preserving its culture and basic way of life. What had started as a temporary program to relieve a postwar labor shortage had now permanently altered the face of an entire continent. Restive Muslim suburbs ringed nearly every city, and several countries appeared demographically fated to Muslim majorities before the end of the century. No one in a position of power had bothered to consult the native population of Europe before throwing open the doors, and now, after years of relative passivity, the natives were beginning to push back. Denmark had imposed draconian restrictions on immigrant marriages. France had banned the wearing of the full facial veil in public. And the Swiss, who barely tolerated one another, had decided they wanted to keep their tidy little cities and towns free of unsightly minarets. The leaders of Britain and Germany had declared multiculturalism, the virtual religion of post-Christian Europe, a dead letter. No longer would the majority bend to the will of the minority, they declared. Nor would it turn a blind eye to the extremism that flourished within its midst. Europe's age-old contest with Islam, it seemed, had entered a new and potentially dangerous phase. There were many who feared it would be an uneven fight. One side was old, tired, and largely content with itself. The other could be driven into a murderous frenzy by a doodle in a Danish newspaper.

Nowhere were the problems facing Europe on clearer display than in Clichy-sous-Bois, the volatile Arab *banlieue* located just outside Paris. The flashpoint for the deadly riots that swept France in 2005, the suburb had one of the country's highest unemployment rates, along with one of the highest rates of violent crime. So dangerous was Clichy-sous-Bois that even the French police refrained from entering its seething public housing estates—including the one where Nazim Kadir, a twenty-six-year-old Algerian employed by the celebrated Fouquet's restaurant, lived with twelve other members of his extended family.

On that morning in November, he left his apartment in darkness to purify himself at a mosque built with Saudi money and staffed by a Saudi-trained imam who spoke no French. After completing this most important pillar of Islam, he rode a 601AB bus to the suburb of Le Raincy and then boarded an RER train to the Gare Saint-Lazare. There he switched to the Paris Métro for the final leg of his journey. At no point did he arouse the suspicions of the authorities or his fellow passengers. His heavy coat concealed the fact he was wearing an explosive vest.

He emerged from the George V stop at his usual time, 11:40, and started up the Avenue des Champs-Élysées. Those lucky enough to survive the inferno to come would later say there was nothing unusual in his appearance, though the owner of a popular flower shop claimed to notice a curious determination in his gait as he closed in on the entrance of the restaurant. Among those standing outside were a deputy minister of justice, a newsreader from French television, a fashion model currently gracing the cover of *Vogue* magazine, a Gypsy beggar clutching the hand of a small child, and a noisy group of Japanese tourists. The bomber made one final check of his watch. Then he unzipped his coat.

It was never clearly established whether the act was preceded by the traditional scream of *"Allahu Akbar."* Several survivors claimed to have heard it; several others swore the bomber detonated his device in silence. As for the sound of the explosion itself, those closest had no memory of it at all, for their eardrums were too badly damaged. To a person, all recalled seeing a blinding white flash of light. It was the light of death, said one. The light one sees at the moment he confronts God for the first time.

The bomb itself was a marvel of design and construction. It was not the kind of device built from Internet manuals or the how-to pamphlets floating around the Salafist mosques of Europe. It had been perfected under battle conditions in Palestine and Mesopotamia. Packed with nails soaked in rat poison—a practice borrowed from the suicide bombers of Hamas—it carved through the crowd like a circular saw. So powerful was the explosion that the Louvre Pyramid, located a mile and a half to the east, shivered with the blast wave. Those closest to the bomber were blown to pieces, sheared in half, or decapitated, the preferred punishment for unbelievers. Even at forty paces, limbs were lost. At the farthest edge of the kill zone, the dead appeared pristine. Spared outward trauma, they had been killed by the shock wave, which ravaged their internal organs like a tsunami. Providence had granted them the tender mercy of bleeding to death in private.

The first gendarmes to arrive were instantly sickened by what they saw. Extremities littered the paving stones, along with shoes, smashed wristwatches frozen at 11:46, and mobile phones that rang unanswered. In one final insult, the murderer's remains were scattered among his victims—everything but the head, which came to rest on a delivery truck more than a hundred feet away, the bomber's expression oddly serene.

The French interior minister arrived within ten minutes of the explosion. Seeing the carnage, he declared, "Baghdad has come to Paris." Seventeen minutes later, it came to the Tivoli Gardens in Copenhagen, where, at 12:03 p.m., a second suicide bomber detonated himself amid a large group of children waiting impatiently to board the park's roller coaster. The Danish security service, the PET, quickly established that the *shahid* had been born in Copenhagen, had attended Danish schools, and was married to a Danish woman. It seemed not to trouble him that his own children attended the same school as his victims.

For the security professionals across Europe it was the nightmare scenario come true—coordinated and highly sophisticated attacks that appeared to have been planned and executed by a skilled mastermind. They feared the terrorists would strike again soon, though two critical pieces of information eluded them. They did not know where. And they did not know when.

3

ST. JAMES'S, LONDON

L ATER, THE COUNTERTERRORISM COMMAND OF London's Metropolitan Police Service would expend much valuable time and effort trying to reconstruct the movements
that morning of one Gabriel Allon, the legendary but wayward
son of Israeli intelligence, now formally retired and living quietly
in the United Kingdom. It is known, based on eyewitness accounts
from his meddlesome neighbors, that he departed his cottage in
Cornwall a few minutes after dawn and climbed into his Range
Rover, accompanied by his beautiful Italian-born wife, Chiara.
It is also known, due to Britain's Orwellian system of CCTV
cameras, that the couple reached central London in near-record
time, and that, through an act of divine intervention, they managed to find a somewhat legal parking space in Piccadilly. From
there they proceeded on foot to Mason's Yard, a tranquil quadran-
gle of paving stones and commerce in St. James's, and presented
themselves at the door of Isherwood Fine Arts. According to the

CCTV camera in the yard, they were admitted into the premises at 11:40 London time, though Maggie, Isherwood's latest mediocre secretary, would erroneously record the time in her logbook as 11:45.

Purveyors of museum-quality Italian and Dutch Old Master paintings since 1968, the gallery had once occupied a lofty perch on tony New Bond Street in Mayfair. Driven into St. Jamesian exile by the likes of Hermès, Burberry, and Cartier, it had taken refuge in three floors of a sagging warehouse once owned by Fortnum & Mason. Among the incestuous, backbiting villagers of St. James's, the gallery had always been regarded as rather good theater—comedy and tragedy, stunning highs and seemingly bottomless lows, and always a whiff of conspiracy lying just beneath the surface. This was, in large measure, a consequence of the owner's personality. Julian Isherwood was cursed with a near fatal flaw for an art dealer—he liked to possess art more than he liked to sell it. As a result, he was burdened with a large inventory of what is affectionately known in the trade as dead stock—paintings for which no buyer would ever pay a fair price. It was rumored that Isherwood's personal holdings rivaled those of the British royal family. Even Gabriel, who had restored paintings for the gallery for more than thirty years, had only the vaguest idea of Isherwood's true holdings.

They found him in his office—a tall, slightly precarious figure tilted against the front of a desk piled with old catalogs and monographs. He wore a gray chalk-stripe suit and a lavender necktie that had been given to him the previous evening by his latest love interest. As usual, he appeared slightly hungover, a look he cultivated. His eyes were fixed mournfully on the television.

"I take it you've heard the news?"

Gabriel nodded slowly. He and Chiara had heard the first bulletins on the radio as they were passing through the western suburbs of London. The images playing out on the screen were remarkably similar to the ones that had formed in Gabriel's own mind—the dead covered in plastic sheeting, the bloodied survivors, the onlookers with their palms pressed to their faces in horror. It never changed. He supposed it never would.

"I had lunch at Fouquet's last week with a client," Isherwood said, running a hand through his longish gray locks. "We parted company on the very spot where that maniac detonated his bomb. What if the client had scheduled the lunch for today? I might have been—"

Isherwood stopped himself. It was a typical reaction after an attack, thought Gabriel. The living always sought to find some connection, however tenuous, to the dead.

"The bomber in Copenhagen killed children," Isherwood said. "Will you please explain to me what cause is served by the murder of innocent children?"

"Fear," said Gabriel. "They want us to be afraid."

"When is this going to end?" Isherwood asked, shaking his head in disgust. "When in God's name is this madness going to end?"

"You should know better than to ask a question like that, Julian." Gabriel lowered his voice and added, "After all, you've had a ringside seat at this war for a very long time."

Isherwood gave a melancholy smile. His backbone-of-England surname and English scale concealed the fact that he was not, at least technically, English at all. British by nationality and passport, yes, but German by birth, French by upbringing, and Jewish by religion. Only a handful of trusted friends knew that Isherwood had staggered into London as a child refugee in 1942 after being carried across the snowbound Pyrenees by a pair of Basque shepherds. Or that his father, the renowned Paris art dealer Samuel Isakowitz, had been murdered at the Sobibor death camp along with Isherwood's mother. Though Isherwood had carefully guarded the secrets of his past, the story of his dramatic escape from Nazi-occupied Europe had reached the ears of Israel's secret intelligence service. And in the mid-1970s, during a wave of Palestinian terrorist attacks against Israeli targets in Europe, he was recruited as a *sayan*, a volunteer helper. Isherwood had but one assignment—to assist in building and maintaining the operational cover of an art restorer and assassin named Gabriel Allon.

"Just keep one thing in mind," Isherwood said. "You work for me now, not them. This isn't your problem, petal. Not anymore." He aimed his remote at the television and the mayhem in Paris and Copenhagen vanished, at least for the moment. "Let's have a look at something beautiful, shall we?"

The limited space of the gallery had compelled Isherwood to arrange his empire vertically—storerooms on the ground floor, business offices on the second, and on the third, a glorious formal exhibition room modeled on Paul Rosenberg's famous gallery in Paris, where young Julian had spent many happy hours as a child. As they entered the room, midday sun was slanting through the overhead skylight, illuminating a large oil painting propped on a baize-covered pedestal. It was a depiction of the Madonna and Child with Mary Magdalene, set against an evening backdrop, quite obviously of the Venetian School. Chiara removed her car-length leather coat and sat on the museum-style ottoman at the center of the room. Gabriel stood directly before the canvas, one hand resting on his narrow chin, his head tilted to one side.

"Where did you find it?"

"In a great limestone pile along the Norfolk coast."

"Does the pile have an owner?"

"Insists on anonymity. Suffice it to say he descends from a family of title, his property holdings are enormous, and his cash reserves are dwindling at an alarming rate."

"So he asked you to take a few paintings off his hands to keep him afloat for another year."

"At the rate he goes through money, I'd give him two months at the outside."

"How much did you pay for it?"

"Twenty thousand."

"How charitable of you, Julian." Gabriel glanced at Isherwood and added, "I assume you covered your tracks by taking a few other pictures as well."

"Six worthless pieces of crap," Isherwood confessed. "But if my hunch about this one is correct, they were well worth the investment."

"Provenance?" asked Gabriel.

"It was purchased in the Veneto by one of the owner's ancestors while he was doing his Grand Tour in the early nineteenth century. It's been in the family ever since."

"Current attribution?"

"Workshop of Palma Vecchio."

"Really?" asked Gabriel skeptically. "According to whom?"

"The Italian art expert who brokered the sale."

"Was he blind?"

"Only in one eye."

Gabriel smiled. Many of the Italians who had advised British nobility during their travels were charlatans who did a brisk trade in worthless copies falsely attributed to the masters of Florence and Venice. Occasionally, they erred in the opposite direction. Isherwood suspected that the painting on the pedestal fell into the second category. So, too, did Gabriel. He dragged the tip of his forefinger over the face of the Magdalene, dislodging a century's worth of surface grime.

"Where was it hung? In a coal mine?"

He picked at the heavily discolored varnish. In all likelihood, it was composed of a mastic or dammar resin that had been dissolved with turpentine. Removing it would be a painstaking process involving the use of a carefully calibrated mixture of acetone, methyl proxitol, and mineral spirits. Gabriel could only imagine the horrors that awaited him once the old varnish had been stripped away: archipelagos of *pentimento*, a desert of surface cracks and creases, wholesale paint losses concealed by previous restorations. And then there was the condition of the canvas, which was sagging dramatically with age. The remedy was a relining, a perilous procedure involving the application of heat, moisture, and pressure. Any restorer who had ever performed a relining had the scars to prove it. Gabriel had once destroyed a large portion of a painting by Domenico Zampieri by using an iron with a faulty temperature gauge. The fully restored painting, while pristine to the untrained eye, was definitely a collaborative effort between Zampieri and the Studio of Gabriel Allon.

"Well?" asked Isherwood again. "Who painted the bloody thing?"

Gabriel made a show of deliberation. "I'll need X-rays to make a definitive attribution."

"My man is dropping by later this afternoon to take the pictures. But we both know that you don't need them to make a preliminary attribution. You're like me, petal. You've been around paintings for a hundred thousand years. You know it when you see it."

Gabriel fished a small magnifying glass from his coat pocket and used it to examine the brushstrokes. Leaning slightly forward, he could feel the familiar shape of a Beretta 9mm pistol digging into the flesh of his left hip. Having worked with British intelligence to sabotage the Iranian nuclear program, he was now permitted to carry a weapon at all times for protection. He had also been granted a British passport, which he was free to use for foreign travel, provided he was not working for his old service. There was no chance of that. The illustrious career of Gabriel Allon was finally over. He was no longer Israel's avenging angel. He was an art restorer employed by Isherwood Fine Arts, and England was his home.

"You have a hunch," said Isherwood. "I can see it in those green eyes of yours."

"I do," replied Gabriel, still entranced by the brushstrokes, "but I'd like a second opinion first."

He glanced over his shoulder at Chiara. She was toying with a strand of her unruly hair, a slightly bemused expression on her face. Posed as she was now, she bore a striking resemblance to the woman in the painting. It was hardly surprising, thought Gabriel. The descendant of Jews expelled from Spain in 1492, Chiara had been raised in the ancient ghetto of Venice. It was quite possible some of her ancestors had served as models for masters such as Bellini, Veronese, and Tintoretto.

"What do you think?" he asked.

Chiara joined Gabriel before the canvas and clucked her tongue in disapproval at its deplorable condition. Though she had studied the Roman Empire at university, she had assisted Gabriel on a number of restorations and, in the process, had become a formidable art historian in her own right.

"It's an excellent example of a Holy Conversation, or Sacra Conversazione, an idyllic scene in which subjects are grouped against an aesthetically pleasing landscape. And as any oaf knows, Palma Vecchio is regarded as the originator of the form."

"What do you think of the draftsmanship?" Isherwood asked, a lawyer leading a sympathetic witness.

"It's awfully good for Palma," Chiara replied. "His palette was unrivaled, but he was never regarded as a particularly skilled draftsman, even by his contemporaries."

"And the woman who posed as the Madonna?"

"Unless I'm mistaken, which is highly unlikely, her name is Violante. She appears in a number of Palma's paintings. But there was another famous painter in Venice at the time who was said to be quite fond of her. His name was—"

"Tiziano Vecellio," Isherwood said, completing the thought for her. "Better known as Titian."

"Congratulations, Julian," Gabriel said, smiling. "You just snared a Titian for the paltry sum of twenty thousand pounds. Now you just need to find a restorer capable of knocking it into shape."

"How much?" Isherwood asked.

Gabriel pulled a frown. "It's going to take a great deal of work."

"How much?" Isherwood repeated.

"Two hundred thousand."

"I could find someone else for half that."

"That's true. But we both remember what happened the last time you tried that."

"How soon can you start?"

"I'll have to check my calendar before making any commitments."

"I'll give you an advance of one hundred thousand."

"In that case, I can start right away."

"I'll send it to Cornwall the day after tomorrow," Isherwood said. "The question is, when will I have it back?"

Gabriel made no response. He stared at his wristwatch for a moment, as though it were no longer keeping proper time, then tilted his face thoughtfully toward the skylight.

Isherwood placed a hand gently on his shoulder. "It's not your problem, petal," he said. "Not anymore."

4

COVENT GARDEN, LONDON

A POLICE CHECKPOINT NEAR LEICESTER SQUARE had brought the traffic on Charing Cross Road to a standstill. Gabriel and Chiara hurried through a fog-bank of exhaust fumes and set out along Cranbourn Street. It was lined with pubs and coffee bars catering to the herds of tourists who seemed to wander aimlessly through Soho at all hours, regardless of the season. For now, Gabriel seemed oblivious to them. He was staring at the screen of his mobile phone. The death tolls in Paris and Copenhagen were rising.

"How bad?" asked Chiara.

"Twenty-eight on the Champs-Élysées and another thirty-seven at the Tivoli Gardens."

"Do they have any idea who's responsible?" asked Chiara.

"It's still too early," Gabriel said, "but the French think it might be al-Qaeda in the Islamic Maghreb."

"Could they have pulled off a pair of coordinated attacks like this?"

"They have cells scattered across Europe and North America, but the analysts at King Saul Boulevard have always been skeptical of their ability to carry out a Bin Laden–style spectacular."

King Saul Boulevard was the address of Israel's foreign intelligence service. It had a long and deliberately misleading name that had very little to do with the true nature of its work. Those who worked there referred to it as the Office and nothing else. Even retired agents like Gabriel and Chiara never uttered the organization's real name.

"It doesn't feel like Bin Laden to me," Chiara said. "It feels more like—"

"Baghdad," said Gabriel. "These death tolls are high for open-air attacks. It suggests the bomb maker knew what he was doing. If we're lucky, he left behind his signature."

"We?" asked Chiara.

Gabriel wordlessly returned the phone to his coat pocket. They had reached the chaotic traffic circle at the end of Cranbourn Street. There were two Italian restaurants—the Spaghetti House and Bella Italia. He looked at Chiara and asked her to choose.

"I'm not going to start my long weekend in London at Bella Italia," she said, frowning. "You promised to take me to a proper lunch."

"In my opinion, one can do far worse in London than Bella Italia."

"Unless one was born in Venice."

Gabriel smiled. "We have a reservation at a lovely place called Orso in Wellington Street. It's very Italian. I thought we could walk through Covent Garden on our way."

"Do you still feel up to it?"

"We have to eat," he said, "and the walk will do us both good."

They hurried across the traffic circle into Garrick Street where two Metropolitan Police officers in lime green coats were questioning the Arab-looking driver of a white panel van. The anxiety of the pedestrians was almost palpable. In some of the faces Gabriel saw genuine fear; in others, a grim resolution to carry on as normal. Chiara held his hand tightly as they strolled past the shop windows. She had been looking forward to this weekend for a long time and was determined not to let the news from Paris and Copenhagen spoil it.

"You were a bit hard on Julian," she said. "Two hundred thousand is twice your usual fee."

"It's a Titian, Chiara. Julian is going to do quite nicely."

"The least you could've done is accept his invitation to a celebratory lunch."

"I didn't want to have lunch with Julian. I wanted to have lunch with you."

"He has an idea he wants to discuss."

"What sort of idea?"

"A partnership," Chiara said. "He wants us to become partners in the gallery."

Gabriel slowed to a stop. "Let me make this as clear as possible," he said. "I have absolutely no interest in becoming a partner in the sometimes-solvent firm of Isherwood Fine Arts."

"Why not?"

"For one thing," he said, walking again, "we have no idea how to run a business."

"You've run several very thriving enterprises in the past."

"It's easy when you have the backing of an intelligence service."

"You're not giving yourself enough credit, Gabriel. How hard can it be to run an art gallery?"

"*Incredibly* hard. And as Julian has proven time and time again, it's easy to get into trouble. Even the most successful gallery can go under if it places a bad bet." Gabriel gave her a sidelong look and asked, "When did you and Julian concoct this little arrangement?"

"You make it sound as if we were conspiring behind your back."

"That's because you were."

With a smile, Chiara conceded the point. "It happened when we were in Washington for the unveiling of the Rembrandt. Julian pulled me aside and said he was beginning to think about the possibility he might actually retire. He wants the gallery to end up in the hands of someone he trusts."

"Julian will never retire."

"I wouldn't be so sure about that."

"Where was I when this deal was being hatched?"

"I believe you'd slipped outside for a private conversation with a British investigative reporter."

"Why didn't you tell me about any of this until now?"

"Because Julian asked me not to."

With his edgy silence, Gabriel made it clear that Chiara had violated one of the fundamental tenets of their marriage. Secrets, even undeniably trivial ones, were forbidden.

"I'm sorry, Gabriel. I should have said something, but Julian was adamant. He knew your first instinct would be to say no."

"He could sell the gallery to Oliver Dimbleby in a heartbeat and retire to an island in the Caribbean."

"Have you considered what that might mean for us? Do you really want to clean pictures for Oliver Dimbleby? Or Giles Pittaway? Or were you thinking you could scrape up a bit of freelance work from the Tate or the National Gallery?"

"It sounds as if you and Julian have it all worked out."

"We do."

"Then perhaps *you* should become Julian's partner."

"Only if you clean pictures for me."

Gabriel could see that Chiara was serious. "Running a gallery isn't all about attending glamorous auctions and having long lunches in fancy restaurants in Jermyn Street. And it's not something that should be considered a hobby."

"Thank you for dismissing me as a dilettante."

"That's not what I meant, and you know it."

"You're not the only one who's retired from the Office, Gabriel. I am, too. But unlike you, I don't have damaged Old Masters to occupy my time."

"So you want to become an art dealer? You'll spend your days rummaging through piles of mediocre paintings, looking for another lost Titian. And chances are you'll never find one."

"It doesn't sound that bad to me." Chiara looked around the street. "And it means we could live here."

"I thought you liked Cornwall."

"I adore it," she said. "Just not in winter."

Gabriel lapsed into silence. He had been bracing himself for a conversation like this for some time. "I thought we were going to have a baby," he said.

"So did I," Chiara said. "But I'm beginning to think it might not be possible. Nothing I try seems to be working."

There was a note of resignation in her voice that Gabriel had never heard before. "So we'll keep trying," he said.

"I just don't want you to be disappointed. It was the miscarriage. It's going to make it much harder for me to ever conceive again. Who knows? A change of scenery might help. Just think about it," she said, squeezing his hand. "That's all I'm saying, darling. We might actually enjoy living here."

In the broad Italianate piazza of the Covent Garden Market, a street comedian was arranging a pair of unsuspecting German tourists into a pose suggestive of sexual intimacy. Chiara leaned against a pillar to watch the performance while Gabriel fell into an undignified sulk, his eyes scanning the large crowd gathered in the square and atop the balcony bar of the Punch and Judy. He was not angry with Chiara but with himself. For years, their relationship had revolved around Gabriel and his work. It had never occurred to him that Chiara might have career aspirations of her own. If they were a normal couple, he might have considered the opportunity. But they were not a normal couple. They were former operatives of one of the world's most celebrated intelligence services. And they had a past that was far too bloody to lead so public a life.

As they headed into the soaring glass arcade of the market, any residual tension from their quarrel quickly dissipated. Even Gabriel, who detested shopping in all its forms, took pleasure in roaming the colorful shops and stalls with Chiara at his side. Intoxicated by the smell of her hair, he imagined the afternoon that lay ahead—a quiet lunch followed by a pleasant walk back to their hotel. There, in the cool shadows of their room, Gabriel would slowly undress Chiara and make love to her in the enormous bed. For a moment, it was almost possible for Gabriel to imagine his past had been erased, that his exploits were mere fables gathering dust in the file rooms of King Saul Boulevard. Only the watchfulness remained—the instinctive, gnawing vigilance that made it impossible for him to ever feel completely at peace in public. It forced him to make a mental charcoal sketch of every passing face in the crowded market. And in Wellington Street, as they were approaching the restaurant, it caused him to freeze in his tracks. Chiara tugged playfully at his arm. Then she stared directly into his eyes and realized something was wrong.

"You look as though you just saw a ghost."

"Not a ghost. A dead man."

"Where?"

Gabriel nodded toward a figure in a gray woolen overcoat.

"Right there."

5

COVENT GARDEN, LONDON

THERE ARE TELLTALE INDICATORS COMMON to suicide bombers. Lips can move involuntarily as final prayers are recited. Eyes can have a glassy thousand-yard stare. And the face can sometimes appear unnaturally pale, evidence that an unkempt beard has been hastily removed in preparation for a mission. The dead man exhibited none of these traits. His lips were pursed. His eyes were clear and focused. And his face was evenly colored. He had been shaving regularly for a long time.

What set him apart was the thin tributary of sweat leaking from his left sideburn. Why was he perspiring on a crisp autumn afternoon? If he was warm, why were his hands buried in the pockets of his woolen overcoat? And why was the overcoat—a size too large, in Gabriel's opinion—still tightly buttoned? And then there was his walk. Even a physically fit man in his late twenties will have difficulty feigning a normal gait when saddled with fifty pounds of high explosives, nails, and ball bearings. As the dead man walked past Gabriel in Wellington Street, he appeared unusually erect, as if he were trying to compensate for the added weight around his abdomen and kidneys. The fabric of his gabardine trousers vibrated with each step, as though the joints in his hips and knees were shuddering beneath the burden of the bomb. It was possible that the perspiring young man with the oversized coat was an innocent who simply needed to do a bit of midday shopping, but Gabriel suspected otherwise. He believed the man walking a few paces ahead represented the finale of a continent-wide day of terror. First Paris, then Copenhagen, and now London.

Gabriel ordered Chiara to take shelter in the restaurant and quickly crossed to the opposite pavement. He shadowed the dead man for approximately a hundred yards, then watched as he rounded the corner into the entrance of the Covent Garden Market. There were two cafés on the eastern side of the piazza, each filled with lunchtime patrons. Standing between them in a patch of sunlight were three uniformed Metropolitan Police Service officers. None took notice of the dead man as he entered the market arcade.

Gabriel now had a decision to make. The most obvious course of action was to tell the police of his suspicions—obvious, he thought, but not necessarily optimal. In all likelihood, the police would respond to Gabriel's approach by pulling *him* aside for questioning, wasting several precious seconds. Worse still, they might confront the man, a ploy that would almost certainly cause him to detonate his weapon. Although virtually every officer on the Met had been given basic instruction in counterterrorism tactics, few had the experience or firepower necessary to take down a committed jihadist bent on martyrdom. Gabriel had both, and he had acted against suicide bombers before. He glided past the three officers and slipped inside the arcade.

The dead man was now twenty yards ahead, moving at a parade-ground clip along the elevated walkway of the main hall. Gabriel reckoned he was carrying enough explosives and shrapnel to kill everyone within a seventy-five-foot radius. Doctrine dictated that Gabriel remain beyond the lethal blast zone until it was time to make his move. The environment, however, compelled him to close the distance and place himself in greater danger. A headshot from seventy-five feet was difficult under the best of circumstances, even for a gunman with the skills of Gabriel Allon. In a crowded shopping arcade, it would be next to impossible.

Gabriel felt his mobile phone vibrate softly in his coat pocket. Ignoring it, he watched as the dead man paused along the railing of the walkway to check his watch. Gabriel took note of the fact it was worn on the left wrist, which meant the detonator switch was almost certainly in the right hand. But why would a suicide bomber stop on his way to martyrdom to check the time? The most likely explanation was that he had been ordered to end his life and the lives of many innocent people at a precise moment. Gabriel suspected there might be some sort of symbolism involved. There usually was. The terrorists of al-Qaeda and its offshoots loved symbolism, especially when it involved numbers.

Gabriel was now close enough to the dead man to see his eyes. They were clear and focused, an encouraging sign. It meant he was still thinking about his mission rather than the carnal delights awaiting him in Paradise. When he started dreaming of the perfumed, dark-eyed *houris*, it would show on his face. Then Gabriel would have a choice to make. For now, he needed the dead man to stay in this world a little longer.

The dead man made another check of the time. Gabriel glanced quickly at his own watch: 2:34. He ran the numerals through the database of his memory, looking for any connection. He added them, subtracted them, multiplied them, reversed them, and re-arranged their order. Then he thought about the two previous attacks. The first occurred at 11:46, the second at 12:03. It was possible the times were representative of years on the Gregorian calendar, but Gabriel could find no connection.

He mentally erased the hours of the attacks and focused only on the minutes. *Forty-six minutes past, three minutes past.* Then he understood. The times were as familiar to him as the brushstrokes of Titian. *Forty-six minutes past, three minutes past.* They were two of the most famous moments in the history of terrorism—the exact times at which the two hijacked airliners struck the World Trade Center on 9/11. American Airlines Flight 11 crashed into the North Tower at 8:46 a.m. United Airlines Flight 175 struck the South Tower at 9:03 a.m. The third plane to successfully hit its target that morning was American Airlines Flight 77, which was flown into the western side of the Pentagon. The local time had been 9:37 a.m., 2:37 p.m. in London.

Gabriel checked his digital watch. It was now a few seconds past 2:35. Looking up, he saw the man in the gray overcoat was once again moving at a brisk pace, hands in his pockets, seem-ingly oblivious to the people around him. As Gabriel followed, his mobile began to vibrate again. This time, he answered and heard the voice of Chiara. He told her that a suicide bomber was about to detonate himself in Covent Garden and instructed her to make contact with MI5. Then he slipped the phone back into his pocket and began closing the distance between himself and the target. He feared that many innocent people were about to die. And he won-dered whether there was anything he could do to stop it.

6

COVENT GARDEN, LONDON

THERE WAS ONE OTHER POSSIBILITY, of course—
the possibility that the man walking several paces ahead
of Gabriel had nothing beneath his coat but a few extra
pounds of body fat. Inevitably, Gabriel recalled the case of Jean
Charles de Menezes, the Brazilian-born electrician who was shot
to death by British police in London's Stockwell tube station after
being mistaken for a wanted Islamic militant. British prosecutors
declined to bring charges against the officers involved in the killing, a decision that provoked outrage among human rights activists and civil libertarians around the world. Gabriel knew that,
under similar circumstances, he could expect no such leniency. It
meant he would have to be certain before acting. He was confident
of one thing. He believed the bomber, like a painter, would sign his
name before pressing his detonator switch. He would want his victims to know that their imminent deaths were not without purpose,

that they were being sacrificed in the name of the sacred jihad and in the name of Allah.

For the moment, though, Gabriel had no choice but to follow the man and wait. Slowly, carefully, he closed the gap, making small adjustments in his own course to maintain an unobstructed firing lane. His eyes were focused on the lower portion of the man's skull. A few centimeters beneath it was the brain stem, essential for controlling the motor and sensory systems of the rest of the body. Destroy the brain stem with several rounds of ammunition, and the bomber would lack the means to press his detonator button. Miss the brain stem, and it was possible the martyr could carry out his mission with a dying twitch. Gabriel was one of the few men in the world who had actually killed a terrorist *before* he could carry out his attack. He knew the difference between success and failure would come down to a fraction of a second. Success meant only one would die. Failure would result in the deaths of scores of innocent people, perhaps even Gabriel himself.

The dead man passed through the doorway leading to the piazza. It was far more crowded now. A cellist was playing a suite by Bach. A Jimi Hendrix impersonator was grappling with an amplified electric guitar. A well-dressed man standing atop a wooden crate was shouting something about God and the Iraq War. The dead man headed directly toward the center of the square, where the comedian's performance had sunk to new depths of depravity, much to the delight of the large crowd of spectators. Using techniques learned in his youth, Gabriel mentally silenced the noises around him one by one, starting with the faint strains of the Bach suite and ending with the uproarious laughter of the crowd. Then he glanced one last time at his wristwatch and waited for the dead man to sign his name.

It was 2:36. The dead man had reached the outer edge of the

large crowd. He paused for a few seconds, as if searching for a weak point to make his entry, then shouldered his way between two startled women. Gabriel entered at a different spot several yards to the man's right, slipping virtually unnoticed through a family of American tourists. The crowd was four-deep in most places and tightly packed, which presented Gabriel with yet another dilemma. The ideal ammunition for a situation like this was a hollow-point round, which would inflict greater tissue damage on the target and substantially reduce the risk of collateral casualties due to over-penetration. But Gabriel's Beretta pistol was loaded with ordinary 9mm Parabellum rounds. As a result, he would have to position himself to fire at an extreme downward trajectory. Otherwise, there was a high probability he might inadvertently take innocent life in an attempt to save it.

The dead man had breached the inner wall of the crowd and was now headed directly toward the street comedian. The eyes had taken on the glassy thousand-yard stare. The lips were moving. *Final prayers* . . . The street comedian wrongly assumed the dead man wished to take part in the performance. Smiling, he took two steps toward him but froze when he saw the hands emerge from the pockets of the overcoat. The left was slightly open. The right was bunched into a fist, with the thumb cocked at a right angle. Still, Gabriel hesitated. What if there was no detonator? What if it was a pen or a cylinder of lip balm? He had to be sure. *Tell me your intentions*, he thought. *Sign your name.*

The dead man turned to face the market. The patrons looking down from the balcony of the Punch and Judy laughed nervously, as did a few of the spectators gathered in the piazza. In his mind, Gabriel silenced the laughter and froze the image. The scene appeared to him as though painted by the hand of Canaletto. The figures were stock-still; only Gabriel, the restorer, was free to move among them. He slipped through the front row of the spectators and focused his gaze on the spot at the back of the skull. Firing at a downward angle was not possible. But there was another potential solution to prevent collateral casualties: an upward line of fire would carry Gabriel's round safely over the heads of the spectators and into the façade of the adjacent building. He pictured the maneuver in sequence—the cross-handed draw, the crouch, the shot, the advance—and waited for the dead man to sign his name.

The silence in Gabriel's head was broken by a drunken shout from the balcony of the Punch and Judy—a command for the martyr to move out of the way and allow the performance to continue. The dead man responded by lifting his arms above his head like a long-distance runner breaking the finishing tape. On the inside of the right wrist was a thin wire leading from the detonator switch to the explosives. It was all the evidence Gabriel needed. He reached into his jacket and seized the butt of his Beretta. Then, as the dead man screamed *"Allahu Akbar,"* Gabriel dropped to one knee and leveled the weapon toward his target. Remarkably, the shot was clear, with no chance of secondary casualties. But as Gabriel was about to squeeze the trigger, two powerful hands pulled the gun downward, and the weight of two men drove him toward the paving stones.

At the instant he hit the ground, he heard a sound like the crack of thunder and felt a wave of scorching air wash over him. For a few seconds, Gabriel heard nothing more. Then the screaming started, a single shriek, followed by an aria of wailing. Gabriel lifted his head and saw a scene from his nightmares. It was body parts and blood. It was Baghdad on the Thames.

7

NEW SCOTLAND YARD, LONDON

T HERE ARE FEW MORE GRIEVOUS sins for a professional intelligence officer, even a retired one, than to land in the custody of the local authorities. Because Gabriel had long occupied a nether region between the overt and secret worlds, he had suffered such a fate more often than most of his fellow travelers. Experience had taught him there was an established ritual for such occasions, a sort of Kabuki dance that must be allowed to reach its conclusion before higher authority can intervene. He knew the steps well. Fortunately, so did his hosts.

He had been taken into custody within minutes of the attack and driven at high speed to New Scotland Yard, the headquarters of London's Metropolitan Police Service. Upon arrival, he was delivered to a windowless interrogation room where he was treated for numerous cuts and abrasions and given a cup of tea, which he left untouched. A detective superintendent from the Counterterrorism Command arrived in short order. He examined Gabriel's identification with the skepticism it deserved and then tried to determine the chain of events that led "Mr. Rossi" to draw a concealed firearm in Covent Garden the instant before a terrorist detonated his suicide belt. Gabriel had been tempted to pose a few questions of his own. Namely, he wanted to know why two Special Firearms Officers of the Met's SO19 division had chosen to neutralize *him* rather than an obvious terrorist about to commit an act of indiscriminate mass murder. Instead, he responded to each of the detective's inquiries by reciting a telephone number. "Call it," he said, tapping the spot where the detective had written the number in his notebook. "It will ring in a very large building not far from here. You'll know the name of the man who answers. At least you should."

Gabriel did not know the identity of the officer who finally dialed the number, nor did he know precisely when the call was placed. He only knew that his internment inside New Scotland Yard lasted far longer than was necessary. Indeed, it was approaching midnight by the time the detective escorted him down a series of brightly lit corridors toward the entrance of the building. In the detective's left hand was a manila envelope filled with Gabriel's possessions. Judging from the size and shape, it did not contain a 9mm Beretta pistol.

Outside, the pleasant weather of the afternoon had given way to a driving rain. Waiting beneath the shelter of the glass portico, engine idling softly, was a dark Jaguar limousine. Gabriel accepted the envelope from the detective and opened the rear door of the car. Seated inside, one leg crossed elegantly over the other, was a man who looked as though he had been designed for the task. He wore a perfectly fitted charcoal gray suit and a silver necktie that matched the color of his hair. Normally, his pale eyes were inscrutable, but now they revealed the strain of a long and difficult night. As deputy director of MI5, Graham Seymour bore a heavy responsibility for protecting the British mainland from the forces of extremist Islam. And once again, despite the best efforts of his department, extremist Islam had won.

Though the two men had a long professional history, Gabriel knew little of Graham Seymour's personal life. He knew that Seymour was married to a woman named Helen whom he adored and that he had a son who managed other people's money for the New York branch of an important British financial house. Beyond that, Gabriel's knowledge of Seymour's private affairs was drawn from the Office's voluminous file. He was a relic of Britain's glorious past, a by-product of the upper middle classes who had been bred, educated, and programmed to lead. He believed in God but not with much fervor. He believed in his country but wasn't blind to its shortcomings. He was good at golf and other games but was willing to lose to a lesser opponent in service of a worthy cause. He was a man admired and, most important, a man who could be trusted—an attribute rare among spies and secret policemen.

Graham Seymour was not, however, a man with unlimited patience, as evidenced by his dour expression as the Jaguar pulled into the street. He removed a copy of the next morning's *Telegraph* from the seatback pocket and dropped it in Gabriel's lap. The headline read REIGN OF TERROR. Beneath it were three photographs depicting the aftermath of the three attacks. Gabriel searched the photo of Covent Garden for any sign of his presence but saw only the victims. It was a picture of failure, he thought—eighteen people dead, dozens more critically injured, including one of the officers who had tackled him. And it was all because of the shot Gabriel had not been allowed to take.

"Bloody awful day," Seymour said wearily. "I suppose the only way it could get any worse is if the press finds out about you. By the time the conspiracy theorists are finished, they'll have the Islamic world believing that the attacks were plotted and carried out by the Office."

"You can be sure that's already the case." Gabriel returned the newspaper and asked, "Where's my wife?"

"She's at your hotel. I have a team staying just down the hall." Seymour paused, then added, "Needless to say, she's not terribly pleased with you."

"How can you tell?" Gabriel's ears were still ringing from the concussion of the blast. He closed his eyes and asked how the SO19 teams had been able to locate him so quickly.

"As you might imagine, we have a wide array of technical means at our disposal."

"Such as my mobile phone and your network of CCTV cameras?"

"Precisely," Seymour said. "We were able to pinpoint you within a few seconds of receiving Chiara's call. We forwarded the information to Gold Command, the Met's operational crisis center, and they immediately dispatched two teams of Specialist Firearms Officers."

"They must have been in the vicinity."

"They were," Seymour confirmed. "We were on high alert after the attacks in Paris and Copenhagen. A number of teams were already deployed in the financial district and spots where tourists tend to congregate."

"So why did they take *me* down instead of the suicide bomber?"

"Because neither Scotland Yard nor the Security Service wanted a rerun of the Menezes fiasco. As a result of his death, a number of new guidelines and procedures were put in place to make sure nothing like it ever happens again. Suffice it to say a single warning does not meet the threshold for taking lethal action—even if the source happens to be named Gabriel Allon."

"So eighteen innocent people died as a result?"

"What if he wasn't a terrorist? What if he was another street performer, or someone with mental problems? We would have been burned at the stake."

"But he wasn't a street performer or a mental patient, Graham. He was a suicide bomber. And I told you so."

"How did you know?"

"He might as well have been wearing a sign declaring his intentions."

"Was it that obvious?"

Gabriel listed the attributes that first raised his suspicions and then explained the calculations that led him to conclude the terrorist intended to detonate his device at 2:37. Seymour shook his head slowly.

"I've lost count of how many hours we've spent training our police officers to spot potential terrorists, not to mention the millions of pounds we've poured into behavior-recognition software for CCTV. And yet a jihadi suicide bomber walked straight into Covent Garden, and no one seemed to notice. No one but you, of course."

Seymour lapsed into a brooding silence. They were headed north along the floodlit white canyon of Regent Street. Gabriel leaned his head wearily against the window and asked whether the bomber had been identified.

"His name is Farid Khan. His parents immigrated to the United Kingdom from Lahore in the late seventies, but Farid was born in London. Stepney Green, to be precise," Seymour said. "Like many British Muslims of his generation, he rejected the mild, apolitical religious beliefs of his parents and became an Islamist. By the late nineties, he was spending far too much time at the East London Mosque in Whitechapel Road. Before long, he was a member in good standing of the radical groups Hizb ut-Tahrir and al-Muhajiroun."

"It sounds to me as if you had a file on him."

"We did," Seymour said, "but not for the reasons you might think. You see, Farid Khan was a ray of sunlight, our hope for the future. Or so we thought."

"You thought you'd turned him around?"

Seymour nodded. "Not long after 9/11, Farid joined a group called New Beginnings. Its goal was to deprogram militants and reintegrate them into the mainstream of Islam and British public opinion. Farid was considered one of their great successes. He shaved his beard. He severed ties to his old friends. He graduated near the top of his class at King's College and landed a well-paying job with a small London ad agency. A few weeks ago, he became engaged to a woman from his old neighborhood."

"So you checked him off your list?"

"In a manner of speaking," Seymour said. "Now it appears it was all a clever deception. Farid was literally a ticking time bomb waiting to explode."

"Any idea who activated him?"

"We're poring over his telephone and computer records as we speak, along with the suicide video he left behind. It's clear his attack was connected to the bombings in Paris and Copenhagen. Whether they were coordinated by the remnants of al-Qaeda Central or a new network is now a matter of intense debate. Whatever the case, it's none of your concern. Your role in this affair is officially over."

The Jaguar crossed Cavendish Place and stopped outside the entrance of the Langham Hotel.

"I'd like my gun back."

"I'll see what I can do," Seymour said.

"How long do I have to stay here?"

"Scotland Yard would like you to remain in London for the rest of the weekend. On Monday morning, you can go back to your cottage by the sea and think of nothing other than your Titian."

"How do you know about the Titian?"

"I know everything. Everything except how to prevent a British-born Muslim from carrying out an act of mass murder in Covent Garden."

"I could have stopped him, Graham."

"Yes," Seymour said distantly. "And we would have repaid the favor by tearing you to pieces."

Gabriel stepped from the car without another word. "Your role in this affair is officially over," he murmured as he entered the lobby. He repeated it, again and again, like a mantra.

8

NEW YORK CITY

THAT SAME EVENING, THE OTHER universe inhabited by Gabriel Allon was also on edge but for decidedly different reasons. It was the fall auction season in New York, the anxious time when the art world, in all its folly and excess, convenes for two weeks of frenzied buying and selling. It was, as Nicholas Lovegrove liked to say, one of the few remaining occasions when it was still considered fashionable to be vastly rich. It was also, however, a deadly serious business. Great collections would be built, great fortunes made and lost. A single transaction could launch a brilliant career. It could also destroy one.

Lovegrove's professional reputation, like Gabriel Allon's, was by that evening firmly established. British-born and educated, he was regarded as the most sought-after art consultant in the world—a man so powerful he could move markets with an offhand remark or a wrinkle of his elegant nose. His knowledge of art was legendary, as was the size of his bank account. Lovegrove no longer had to troll for clients; they came to him, usually on bended knee and with promises of vast commissions. The secret of Lovegrove's success lay in his unfailing eye and in his discretion. Lovegrove never betrayed a confidence; Lovegrove never gossiped or engaged in double-dealing. He was the rarest of birds in the art trade—a man of his word.

His reputation notwithstanding, Lovegrove was beset by his usual case of pre-auction jitters as he hurried along Sixth Avenue. After years of falling prices and anemic sales, the art market was at last beginning to show signs of renewal. The season's first auctions had been respectable but had fallen short of expectations. Tonight's sale, the Postwar and Contemporary at Christie's, had the potential to set the art world ablaze. As usual, Lovegrove had clients at both ends of the action. Two were sellers—vendors, in the lexicon of the trade—while a third was looking to acquire Lot 12, *Ocher and Red on Red*, oil on canvas, by Mark Rothko. The client in question was unique in that Lovegrove did not know his name. He dealt only with a certain Mr. Hamdali in Paris, who in turn dealt with the client. The arrangement was unorthodox but, from Lovegrove's perspective, highly lucrative. During the past twelve months alone, the collector had acquired more than two hundred million dollars' worth of paintings. Lovegrove's commissions on those sales were in excess of twenty million dollars. If things went according to plan tonight, his net worth would rise substantially.

He rounded the corner onto West Forty-ninth Street and walked a half block to the entrance of Christie's. The soaring glass-walled lobby was a sea of diamonds, silk, ego, and collagen. Lovegrove paused briefly to kiss the perfumed cheek of a German packaging heiress before making his way to the coat check line, where he was promptly set upon by a pair of secondary dealers from the Upper East Side. He put them off with a defensive movement of his hand, then collected his bidding paddle and headed upstairs to the salesroom.

For all its intrigue and glamour, it was a surprisingly ordinary room, a cross between the United Nations General Assembly hall and the church of a television evangelist. The walls were a drab shade of gray-beige, as were the folding chairs, which were smashed tightly together to maximize the limited space. Behind the pulpitlike rostrum was a revolving display case and, next to the case, a bank of telephones staffed by a half-dozen Christie's employees. Lovegrove glanced up at the sky suites, hoping to glimpse a face or two behind the tinted glass, then turned warily toward the reporters penned like cattle in the back corner. Concealing his paddle number, he hurried past them and headed to his usual seat at the front of the room. It was the Promised Land, the place where all dealers, consultants, and collectors hoped one day to sit. It was not a spot for the faint of heart or the short of cash. Lovegrove referred to it as "the kill zone."

The auction was scheduled to begin at six. Francis Hunt, Christie's chief auctioneer, granted his fidgety audience five additional minutes to find their seats before taking his place. He had polished manners and a droll English urbanity that for some inexplicable reason still made Americans feel inferior. In his right hand was the famous "black book" that held the secrets of the universe, at least as far as this evening was concerned. Each lot in the sale had its own page containing information such as the seller's reserve, a seating chart showing the location of expected bidders, and Hunt's strategy for extracting the highest possible price. Lovegrove's name appeared on the page devoted to Lot 12, the Rothko. During a private presale viewing, Lovegrove had hinted he *might* be interested, but only if the price was right and the stars were in proper alignment. Hunt knew Lovegrove was lying, of course. Hunt knew everything.

He wished the audience a pleasant evening, then, with all the fanfare of a maître d' summoning a party of four, said, "Lot One, the Twombly." The bidding commenced immediately, moving swiftly upward in hundred-thousand-dollar increments. The auctioneer deftly managed the process with the help of two immaculately coiffed spotters who strutted and posed behind the rostrum like a pair of male models at a photo shoot. Lovegrove might have been impressed with the performance had he not known it was all carefully choreographed and rehearsed in advance. At one million five, the bidding stalled, only to be revived by a telephone bid for one million six. Five more bids followed in quick succession, at which point the bidding paused for a second time. "The bid is two point one million, with Cordelia on the telephone," Hunt intoned, eyes moving seductively from bidder to bidder. "It's not with you, madam. Nor with you, sir. Two point one, on the telephone, for the Twombly. Fair warning now. Last chance." Down came the gavel with a sharp *crack*. "Thank you," murmured Hunt as he recorded the transaction in his black book.

After the Twombly, it was the Lichtenstein, followed by the Basquiat, the Diebenkorn, the De Kooning, the Johns, the Pollock, and a parade of Warhols. Each work fetched more than the presale estimate and more than the previous lot. It was no accident; Hunt had cleverly stacked the deck to create an ascending scale of excitement. By the time Lot 12 slid onto the display case, he had the audience and the bidders exactly where he wanted them.

"On my right we have the Rothko," he announced. "Shall we start the bidding at twelve million?"

It was two million above the presale estimate, a signal that Hunt expected the work to go big. Lovegrove drew a mobile phone from the breast pocket of his Brioni suit jacket and dialed a number in Paris. Hamdali answered. He had a voice like warm tea sweetened with honey.

"My client would like to get a sense of the room before making a first bid."

"Wise move."

Lovegrove placed the phone on his lap and folded his hands. It quickly became apparent they were in for a tough fight. Bids flew at Hunt from all corners of the room and from the Christie's staff manning the telephones. Hector Candiotti, art adviser to a Belgian industrial magnate, was holding his paddle in the air like a crossing guard, a blusterous bidding technique known as steamrolling. Tony Berringer, who worked for a Russian aluminum oligarch, was bidding as though his life depended on it, which was not beyond the realm of possibility. Lovegrove waited until the price reached thirty million before picking up the phone again.

"Well?" he asked calmly.

"Not yet, Mr. Lovegrove."

This time, Lovegrove kept the phone pressed to his ear. In Paris, Hamdali was speaking to someone in Arabic. Unfortunately, it was not one of the several languages Lovegrove spoke fluently. Biding his time, he surveyed the sky suites, searching for secret bidders. In one he noticed a beautiful young woman holding a mobile phone. After a few seconds, Lovegrove noticed something else. When Hamdali was speaking, the woman was sitting silently. And when the woman was speaking, Hamdali was saying nothing. It was probably a coincidence, he thought. But then again, maybe not.

"Perhaps it's time to test the waters," suggested Lovegrove, his eyes on the woman in the skybox.

"Perhaps you're right," answered Hamdali. "One moment, please."

Hamdali murmured a few words in Arabic. A few seconds later, the woman in the skybox spoke into her mobile phone. Then, in English, Hamdali said, "The client agrees, Mr. Lovegrove. Please make your first bid."

The current bid was thirty-four million. With the arch of a single eyebrow, Lovegrove raised it by another million.

"We have thirty-five," said Hunt, in a tone that indicated a serious new predator had entered the fray. Hector Candiotti immediately countered, as did Tony Berringer. A pair of sparring telephone bidders pushed the price across the forty-million-dollar threshold. Then Jack Chambers, the real estate king, casually bid forty-one. Lovegrove wasn't terribly worried about Jack. The affair with that little tart in New Jersey had cost him dearly in the divorce. Jack wasn't liquid enough to go the distance.

"The bid is forty-one against you," Lovegrove murmured into the telephone.

"The client believes there is a great deal of posturing going on."

"It's an art auction at Christie's. Posturing is de rigueur."

"Patience, Mr. Lovegrove."

Lovegrove kept his eyes on the woman in the skybox as the bidding cracked the fifty-million-dollar threshold. Jack Chambers made a final bid at sixty; Tony Berringer and his Russian gangster did the honors at seventy. Hector Candiotti responded by waving the white flag.

"It looks like it's down to us and the Russian," Lovegrove said to the man in Paris.

"My client doesn't care for Russians."

"What would your client like to do about it?"

"What is Rothko's record at auction?"

"Seventy-two and change."

"Please bid seventy-five."

"It's too much. You'll never—"

"Place the bid, Mr. Lovegrove."

Lovegrove arched an eyebrow and raised five fingers. "The bid is seventy-five million," said Hunt. "It's not with you, sir. Nor with you. Seventy-five million, for the Rothko. Fair warning now. Last chance. All done?"

Crack.

A gasp rose in the room. Lovegrove looked up at the skybox, but the woman was gone.

9

THE LIZARD PENINSULA, CORNWALL

WITH THE APPROVAL OF SCOTLAND YARD, the Home Office, and the British prime minister himself, Gabriel and Chiara returned to Cornwall three days after the bombing in Covent Garden. *Madonna and Child with Mary Magdalene*, oil on canvas, 110 by 92 centimeters, arrived at ten the following morning. After carefully removing the painting from its protective coffin, Gabriel placed it on an antique oak easel in the living room and spent the remainder of the afternoon studying the X-rays. The ghostly images only strengthened his opinion that the painting was indeed a Titian, and a very good Titian at that.

It had been several months since Gabriel had laid hands on a painting, and he was eager to begin work right away. Rising early the following morning, he prepared a bowl of café au lait and immediately threw himself into the delicate task of relining the canvas. The first step involved adhering tissue paper over the image to avoid further paint losses during the procedure. There were a number of over-the-counter glues suitable for the task, but Gabriel always preferred to mix his own adhesive using the recipe he had learned in Venice from the master restorer Umberto Conti—pellets of rabbit-skin glue dissolved in a mixture of water, vinegar, ox bile, and molasses.

He simmered the noxious-smelling concoction on the kitchen stove until it was the consistency of syrup, and watched the morning news on the BBC while waiting for the mixture to cool. Farid Khan was now a household name in the United Kingdom. Given the precise timing of his attack, Scotland Yard and British intelligence were operating under the assumption it was linked to the bombings in Paris and Copenhagen. Still unclear was the terrorist affiliation of the bombers. Debate among the television experts was intense, with one camp proclaiming the attacks were orchestrated by al-Qaeda's old-line leadership in Pakistan and another declaring that they were clearly the work of a new network that had yet to produce a blip on the radar screens of Western intelligence. Whatever the case, European authorities were bracing for more bloodshed. MI5's Joint Terrorism Analysis Center had raised the threat level to "critical," meaning another attack was expected imminently.

Gabriel focused most intently on a report dealing with questions over Scotland Yard's conduct in the minutes before the attack. In a carefully worded statement, the commissioner of the Metropolitan Police acknowledged receiving a warning about a suspicious man in an oversized coat headed toward Covent Garden. Regrettably, said the commissioner, the tip did not rise to the level of specificity required for lethal action. He then confirmed that two SO19 officers had been dispatched to Covent Garden but said they had no choice under existing policy but to hold their fire.

As for reports of a weapon being drawn, police had questioned the man involved and determined it was not a gun but a camera. For reasons of privacy, the man's identity would not be revealed. The press appeared to accept the Met's version of events, as did the civil libertarians, who applauded the restraint shown by the police even if it had meant the loss of eighteen innocent lives.

Gabriel switched off the television as Chiara entered the kitchen. She immediately opened a window to drive out the stench of the ox bile and vinegar and berated Gabriel for fouling her favorite stainless steel saucepan. Gabriel only smiled and dipped the tip of his forefinger into the mixture. It was now cool enough to use. With Chiara peering over his shoulder, he applied the glue evenly over the yellowed varnish and adhered several rectangles of tissue paper to the surface. Titian's handiwork was now invisible and would remain so for the next several days, until the relining was complete.

Gabriel could do no more work that morning except to check on the painting periodically to make certain the glue was drying properly. He sat in the covered gazebo overlooking the sea, a notebook computer on his lap, and scoured the Internet for more information about the three bombings. He was tempted to check in with King Saul Boulevard but thought better of it. He had neglected to inform Tel Aviv of his brush with terror in Covent Garden, and to do so now would only give his former colleagues an excuse to intrude on his life. Gabriel had learned from experience it was best to treat the Office like a jilted lover. Contact had to be kept to a minimum and was best conducted in public places where a messy scene would be inappropriate.

Shortly before noon, the last remnants of a midnight gale passed over Gunwalloe Cove, leaving in its wake a clear sky of crystalline blue. After making one final check of the painting, Gabriel pulled on an anorak and a pair of hiking boots and headed out for his daily march along the cliffs. The previous afternoon he had trooped north along the Coastal Path to Praa Sands. Now he mounted the small rise behind the cottage and headed south toward Lizard Point.

It did not take long for the magic of the Cornish coast to chase away the memories of the dead and wounded in Covent Garden. Indeed, by the time Gabriel had reached the fringes of Mullion Golf Club, the last terrible image was safely concealed beneath a layer of obliterating paint. As he pressed farther south, past the rocky outcropping of the Polurrian Cliffs, he thought only of the work to be done on the Titian. Tomorrow he would carefully remove the painting from its stretcher and then adhere the weakened canvas to a swath of fresh Italian linen, pressing it firmly into place with a heavy tailoring iron. Next came the longest and most arduous phase of the restoration—removing the cracked and yellowed varnish and retouching those portions of the painting lost to time and stress. While some restorers tended to be aggressive in their retouching, Gabriel was known throughout the art world for the lightness of his touch and his uncanny ability to mimic the brushstrokes of the Old Masters. He believed it was the duty of a restorer to come and go without being seen, leaving no evidence of his presence other than a painting returned to its original glory.

By the time Gabriel reached the northern end of Kynance Cove, a line of dark clouds had obscured the sun, and the sea wind had turned markedly colder. A keen observer of Cornwall's capricious weather, he could see that the "bright interval," as British meteorologists liked to call periods of sunshine, was about to come to an abrupt end. He paused for a moment, debating where to take shelter. To the east, across a patchwork-quilt landscape, was Lizard village. Directly ahead was the point. Gabriel chose the second option. He didn't want to shorten his walk over something as trivial as a passing squall. Besides, there was a good café atop the cliffs where he could wait out the storm over a freshly baked scone and a pot of tea.

He turned up the collar of his anorak and headed along the rim of the cove as the first rain began to fall. The café appeared, veiled in mist. At the base of the cliffs, sheltering against the leeward side of the derelict boathouse, was a man in his mid-twenties with short hair and sunglasses propped on his head. A second man was loitering atop the observation point, his eye pressed to a coin-operated telescope. Gabriel knew with certainty it had been inoperative for months.

He slowed to a stop and looked toward the café just as a third man stepped onto the terrace. He wore a waterproof hat pulled close to his brow and a pair of rimless eyeglasses favored by German intellectuals and Swiss bankers. His expression was one of impatience—a busy executive who had been forced by his wife to take a holiday. He stared directly at Gabriel for a long moment before lifting his thick wrist toward his face and consulting his watch. Gabriel was tempted to turn in the opposite direction. Instead, he lowered his gaze to the footpath and walked on. Better to do it in public, he thought. It would reduce the chances of a messy scene.

10

LIZARD POINT, CORNWALL

D ID YOU REALLY HAVE TO order scones?" asked Uzi Navot resentfully.

"They're the best in Cornwall. So is the clotted cream."

Navot made no movement. Gabriel gave a perceptive smile.

"How much more weight does Bella want you to lose?"

"Five pounds. Then I get to go on maintenance," Navot added gloomily, as though it were a prison sentence. "What I wouldn't give for your metabolism. You're married to one of the world's greatest cooks, but you still have the body of a twenty-five-year-old. Me? I'm married to one of the country's foremost experts on Syria, and if I even smell a pastry, I have to let my trousers out."

"Maybe it's time you told Bella to lighten up on the dietary restrictions."

"*You* tell her," Navot said. "All those years studying the Baathists in Damascus have left a mark on her. Sometimes I feel as though I'm living in a police state."

They were seated at an isolated table near the rain-spattered windows. Gabriel was facing the interior; Navot, the sea. He was wearing a pair of corduroy trousers and a beige sweater that still smelled of the men's department at Harrods. He placed his cap on an adjacent chair and ran a hand over his cropped strawberry-blond hair. It had a bit more gray in it than Gabriel remembered, but that was understandable. Uzi Navot was now the chief of Israel's secret intelligence service. Gray hair was one of the many fringe benefits of the job.

Were Navot's brief tenure to end now, it would almost certainly be regarded as among the most successful directorships in the long and storied history of the Office. The accolades that had been bestowed upon him were the result of Operation Masterpiece, the joint Anglo-American-Israeli undertaking that had resulted in the destruction of four secret Iranian nuclear facilities. Much of the credit rightly belonged to Gabriel, though Navot preferred not to dwell on that aspect of the affair. He had been awarded the job as chief only because Gabriel had repeatedly turned it down. And the four enrichment facilities would still be spinning away if Gabriel hadn't identified and recruited the Swiss businessman who was covertly selling component parts to the Iranians.

For the moment, however, Navot's thoughts seemed focused only on the plate of scones. Unable to resist any longer, he selected one, split it with great care, and smothered it with strawberry preserves and a dollop of the clotted cream. Gabriel poured himself a cup of tea from an aluminum pot and quietly asked about the purpose of Navot's unannounced visit. He did so in fluent German, which he spoke with the Berlin accent of his mother. It was one of five languages he and Navot had in common.

"I had a number of housekeeping issues to discuss with my British counterparts. Included on the agenda was a somewhat perplexing report about one of our former agents who's now living in retirement here under MI5 protection. There was a wild rumor going around about this agent and the bombing in Covent Garden. To be honest, I was a bit dubious when I heard it. Knowing this agent well, I couldn't imagine that he would endanger his position in Britain by doing something so foolish as drawing his weapon in public."

"What should I have done, Uzi?"

"You should have called your MI5 minder and washed your hands of it."

"And if you had found yourself in a similar position?"

"If I were in Jerusalem or Tel Aviv, I wouldn't have hesitated to put the bastard down. But here . . ." Navot's voice trailed off. "I suppose I would have considered the potential consequences of my actions first."

"Eighteen people died, Uzi."

"Consider yourself lucky the death toll wasn't nineteen." Navot removed his spindly eyeglasses, something he often did before embarking on an unpleasant conversation. "I'm tempted to ask whether you actually intended to take the shot. But given your training and your past exploits, I'm afraid I know the answer. An Office agent draws his weapon in the field for one reason and one reason only. He doesn't wave it around like a gangster or make idle threats. He pulls the trigger and shoots to kill." Navot paused, then added, "Do unto others before they have a chance to do unto you. I believe those words can be found on page twelve of Shamron's little red book."

"He knows about Covent Garden?"

"You know better than to ask a question like that. Shamron knows everything. In fact, I wouldn't be surprised if he heard about your little adventure before I did. Despite my attempts to ease him into permanent retirement, he insists on staying in contact with his sources from the old days."

Gabriel added a few drops of milk to his tea and stirred it slowly. *Shamron* . . . The name was nearly synonymous with the history of Israel and its intelligence services. After fighting in the war that led to Israel's reconstitution, Ari Shamron had spent the subsequent sixty years protecting the country from a host of enemies bent on its destruction. He had penetrated the courts of kings, stolen the secrets of tyrants, and killed countless foes, sometimes with his own hands, sometimes with the hands of men such as Gabriel. Only one secret had eluded Shamron—the secret of contentment. Aged now and in dreadful health, he clung desperately to his role as the éminence grise of Israel's security establishment and still meddled in the internal affairs of the Office as though it were his private fiefdom. It was not arrogance that drove Shamron but a nagging fear that his entire life's work had been in vain. Though economically prosperous and militarily strong, Israel remained surrounded by a world that was, for the most part, hostile to its very existence. The fact that Gabriel had chosen to reside in this world was among Shamron's greatest disappointments.

"I'm surprised he didn't come here himself," Gabriel said.

"He was tempted."

"Why didn't he?"

"It's not so easy for him to travel."

"What's wrong now?"

"Everything," Navot said, shrugging his heavy shoulders. "He rarely leaves Tiberias these days. He just sits on his terrace staring out at the lake. He's driving Gilah to distraction. She's been begging me to give him something to do."

"Should I go see him?"

"He's not on his deathbed, if that's what you're implying. But you should pay a visit sometime soon. Who knows? You might actually decide that you like your country again."

"I love my country, Uzi."

"Just not enough to live there."

"You always did remind me a bit of Shamron," Gabriel said with a frown, "but now the resemblance is uncanny."

"Gilah told me the same thing not long ago."

"I didn't mean it as a compliment."

"Neither did she." Navot added another spoonful of clotted cream to his scone with exaggerated care.

"So why are you here, Uzi?"

"I want to present you with a unique opportunity."

"You sound like a salesman."

"I'm a spy," Navot said. "There's not much of a difference."

"What are you offering?"

"A chance to atone for a mistake."

"What mistake was that?"

"You should have shot Farid Khan through the back of the head before he hit his detonator switch." Navot lowered his voice and added confidingly, "That's what I would have done, if I'd been in your shoes."

"And how might I make amends for this lapse in judgment?"

"By accepting an invitation."

"From whom?"

Navot gazed silently westward.

"The Americans?" asked Gabriel.

Navot smiled. "More tea?"

The rain ceased as abruptly as it began. Gabriel left money on the table and led Navot down the steep footpath to Polpeor Cove.

The bodyguard was still leaning against the crumbled lifeboat ramp. He watched with feigned indifference as Gabriel and Navot made their way slowly across the rocky beach to the water's edge. Navot cast a distracted glance at his stainless steel wristwatch and turned up his coat collar against the gusty wind rising from the sea. Gabriel was once again struck by the uncanny resemblance to Shamron. The likeness went beyond the superficial. It was as if Shamron, by the sheer force of his indomitable will, had somehow managed to take possession of Navot, body and soul. It was not the Shamron who had been weakened by age and infirmity, thought Gabriel, but Shamron in his prime. All that was missing were the wretched Turkish cigarettes that had ravaged Shamron's health. Bella had never permitted Navot to smoke, not even for the sake of his cover.

"Who's behind the bombings, Uzi?"

"Thus far, we've been unable to make a firm attribution. The Americans, however, seem to think he's the future face of global jihadist terror—the new Bin Laden."

"Does this new Bin Laden have a name?"

"The Americans insist on sharing that information with you face-to-face. They'd like you to come to Washington, all expenses paid, of course."

"How was this invitation extended?"

"Adrian Carter called me personally."

Adrian Carter was the director of the CIA's National Clandestine Service.

"What's the dress code?"

"Black," said Navot. "Your visit to America will be entirely off the books."

Gabriel regarded Navot in silence for a moment. "You obviously want me to go, Uzi. You wouldn't be here otherwise."

"It couldn't hurt," Navot said. "At the very least, it will give us an opportunity to hear what the Americans have to say about the bombings. But there are other fringe benefits as well."

"Such as?"

"Our relationship could use a bit of retouching."

"What sort of retouching?"

"Haven't you heard? There's a new wind blowing through Washington. Change is in the air," Navot added sarcastically. "The new American president is an idealist. He believes he can repair relations between the West and Islam, and he's convinced himself that we're part of the problem."

"So the solution is to send *me*, a former assassin with the blood of several Palestinian and Islamic terrorists on his hands?"

"When spies play nicely together, it tends to spill over into the political realm, which is why the prime minister is eager for you to make the trip as well."

"The prime minister? The next thing you're going to tell me is that Shamron is involved, too."

"He is." Navot picked up a stone and hurled it into the sea. "After the Iran op, I allowed myself to think Shamron might finally fade gracefully into the background. I was wrong. He has no intention of allowing me to run the Office without his constant interference. But that's not surprising, is it, Gabriel? We both know Shamron had someone else in mind for the job. I'm fated to go down in the history of our illustrious service as the accidental chief. And you'll always be the chosen one."

"Choose someone else, Uzi. I'm retired. Remember? Send someone else to Washington."

"Adrian won't hear of it," Navot said, rubbing his shoulder. "And neither will Shamron. As for your so-called retirement, it ended the moment you decided to follow Farid Khan into Covent Garden."

Gabriel stared out at the sea and pictured the aftermath of the shot not taken: body parts and blood, Baghdad on the Thames. Navot seemed to sense what he was thinking. He pressed his advantage.

"The Americans would like you in Washington first thing in the morning. There's a Gulfstream waiting for you outside London. It was one of the planes they used for the rendition program. They've assured me the handcuffs and hypodermic needles have been removed."

"What about Chiara?"

"The invitation is for one."

"She can't stay here alone."

"Graham has agreed to send a security team from London."

"I don't trust them, Uzi. Take her back to Israel with you. She can help Gilah look after the old man for a few days until I get back."

"She might be there awhile."

Gabriel looked at Navot carefully. He clearly knew more than he was saying. He usually did.

"I just agreed to restore a picture for Julian Isherwood."

"A *Madonna and Child with Mary Magdalene*, formerly attributed to the Studio of Palma Vecchio, now tentatively attributed to Titian, pending peer review."

"Very impressive, Uzi."

"Bella's been trying to broaden my horizons."

"The painting can't stay in an empty cottage by the sea."

"Julian's agreed to take it back. As you might expect, he's rather disappointed."

"I was supposed to be paid two hundred thousand pounds for that piece."

"Don't look at me, Gabriel. The cupboard is bare. I've been forced to institute across-the-board cuts in every department. The accountants are even after me to reduce my personal expenses. My per diem is a pittance."

"Good thing you're on a diet."

Navot absently touched his midsection, as if checking to see whether it had expanded since leaving home.

"It's a long drive back to London, Uzi. Maybe you should take along some of those scones."

"Don't even think about it."

"You're afraid Bella will find out?"

"I *know* she will." Navot glared at the bodyguard leaning against the lifeboat ramp. "Those bastards tell her everything. It's like living in a police state."

11

GEORGETOWN, WASHINGTON, D.C.

T HE HOUSE STOOD IN THE 3300 BLOCK OF N STREET, one of an elegant terrace of Federal-style residences priced far beyond the reach of all but the wealthiest of Washingtonians. Gabriel climbed the curved front steps in the gray halflight of dawn and, as instructed, entered without ringing the bell. Adrian Carter waited in the foyer, dressed in wrinkled chinos, a crewneck sweater, and a tan corduroy blazer. The attire, combined with his tousled thinning hair and unfashionable mustache, gave him the air of a professor from a minor university, the sort who championed noble causes and was a constant thorn in the side of his dean. As director of the CIA's National Clandestine Service, Carter had no cause these days other than keeping the American homeland safe from another terrorist attack—though twice each month, schedule permitting, he could be found in the basement of his Episcopal church in suburban Reston preparing meals for the homeless. For Carter, the volunteer work was a meditation, a rare opportunity to thrust his hands into something other than the internecine warfare that raged constantly in the conference rooms of America's sprawling intelligence community.

He greeted Gabriel with the circumspection that comes naturally to men of the clandestine world and ushered him inside. Gabriel paused for a moment in the center hallway and looked around. Secret protocols had been made and broken in these drably furnished rooms; men had been seduced into betraying their countries for suitcases filled with American money and promises of American protection. Carter had used the property so often it was known throughout Langley as his Georgetown pied-à-terre. One Agency wit had christened it the Dar-al-Harb, Arabic for the "House of War." It was covert war, of course, for Carter knew no other way to fight.

Adrian Carter had not actively sought power. It had been foisted upon his narrow shoulders block by unwanted block. Recruited by the Agency while still an undergraduate, he had spent most of his career waging secret war against the Russians—first in Poland, where he funneled money and mimeograph machines to Solidarity; then in Moscow, where he served as station chief; and finally in Afghanistan, where he encouraged and armed the soldiers of Allah, even though he knew that one day they would rain fire and death upon him. If Afghanistan would prove to be the Evil Empire's undoing, it would provide Carter with a ticket to career advancement. He monitored the collapse of the Soviet Union not from the field but from a comfortable office at Langley, where he had recently been promoted to chief of the European Division. While his subordinates openly cheered the demise of their enemy, Carter watched the events unfold with a sense of foreboding. His beloved Agency had failed to predict Communism's collapse, a blunder that would haunt Langley for years. Worse still, in the blink of an eye, the CIA had lost its very reason for existence.

That changed on the morning of September 11, 2001. The war that would follow would be a war fought in the shadows, a place Adrian Carter knew well. While the Pentagon had struggled to come up with a military response to the horror of 9/11, it was Carter and his staff at the Counterterrorism Center who produced a bold plan to destroy al-Qaeda's Afghan sanctuary with a CIA-funded guerrilla war guided by a small force of American special operatives. And when the commanders and foot soldiers of al-Qaeda began falling into American hands, it was Carter, from his desk at Langley, who often served as their judge and jury. The black sites, the extraordinary renditions, the enhanced interrogation methods—they all bore Carter's fingerprints. He felt no remorse over his actions; he hadn't that luxury. For Adrian Carter, every morning was September 12. Never again, he vowed, would he watch Americans hurling themselves from burning skyscrapers because they could no longer bear the heat of a terrorist fire.

For ten years, Carter had managed to keep that promise. No one had done more to protect the American homeland from the much-anticipated second attack, and for his many secret sins, he had been pilloried in the press and threatened with criminal prosecution. On the advice of Agency lawyers, he had retained the services of a high-priced Washington attorney, an extravagance that had steadily drained his savings and forced his wife, Margaret, to return to teaching. Friends had urged Carter to forsake the Agency and take a lucrative position in Washington's flourishing private security industry, but he refused. His failure to prevent the attacks of 9/11 haunted him still. And the ghosts of the three thousand compelled him to keep fighting until his enemy was vanquished.

The war had taken its toll on Carter—not only on his family life, which was a shambles, but on his health as well. His face was gaunt and drawn, and Gabriel noticed a slight tremor in Carter's right hand as he joylessly filled a plate with the government-issue treats arrayed atop the sideboard in the dining room. "High blood pressure," Carter explained, as he drew coffee from a pump-action thermos. "It started on Inauguration Day, and it rises and falls in relation to the terrorist threat level. It's sad to say, but after ten years of fighting Islamic terror, I seem to have become a living, breathing National Threat Advisory."

"What level are we today?"

"Didn't you hear?" asked Carter. "We've abandoned the old color-coded system."

"What's your blood pressure telling you?"

"Red," said Carter dourly. "Bright red."

"Not according to your director of homeland security. She says there's no immediate threat."

"She doesn't always write her own lines."

"Who does?"

"The White House," said Carter. "And the president doesn't like to needlessly alarm the American people. Besides, raising the threat level would conflict with the convenient narrative making its way around the Washington chattering classes these days."

"Which narrative is that?"

"The one that says America overreacted to 9/11. The one that says al-Qaeda is no longer a threat to anyone, let alone the most powerful nation on the face of the earth. The one that says it's time to declare victory in the global war on terror and turn our attention inward." Carter frowned. "God, but I hate it when journalists use the word 'narrative.' There was a time when novelists wrote narrative and journalists were content to report facts. And the facts are quite simple. There exists in the world today an organized force that seeks to weaken or even destroy the West through acts of indiscriminate violence. This force is a part of a broader radical movement to impose *sharia* law and restore the Islamic Caliphate. And no amount of wishful thinking will make it go away."

They sat on opposite sides of the rectangular table. Carter picked at the edge of a stale croissant, his thoughts clearly elsewhere. Gabriel knew better than to rush the proceedings. In conversation, Carter could be a bit of a wanderer. Eventually, he would make his way to the point, but there would be several detours and digressions along the way, all of which would undoubtedly prove useful to Gabriel at a later date.

"In some respects," Carter continued, "I'm sympathetic to the president's desire to turn the page of history. He views the global war on terrorism as a distraction from his larger goals. You might find this difficult to believe, but I've seen him on just two occasions. He calls me Andrew."

"But at least he's given us hope."

"Hope is not an acceptable strategy when lives are at stake. Hope is what led to 9/11."

"So who's pulling the strings inside the administration?"

"James McKenna, assistant to the president for homeland security and counterterrorism, also known as the terrorism czar, which is interesting since he's issued an edict banning the word 'terrorism' from all our public pronouncements. He even discourages its use behind closed doors. And heaven forbid if we happen to place the word 'Islamic' anywhere near it. As far as James McKenna is concerned, we aren't engaged in a war against Islamic terrorists. We're engaged in an international effort against a small band of transnational extremists. These extremists, who just happen to be Muslims, are an irritant, but pose no real threat to our existence or way of life."

"Tell that to the families of those who died in Paris, Copenhagen, and London."

"That's an emotional response," Carter said sardonically. "And James McKenna doesn't tolerate emotion when it comes to talking about terrorism."

"You mean extremism," said Gabriel.

"Forgive me," Carter said. "McKenna is a political animal who fancies himself an expert on intelligence. He worked on the staff of the Senate Select Intelligence Committee in the nineties and came to Langley shortly after the Greek arrived. He lasted only a few months, but that doesn't stop him from describing himself as a veteran of the CIA. To hear McKenna tell it, he's an Agency man who has the best interests of the Agency at heart. The truth is somewhat different. He loathes the Agency and all those who toil within its walls. Most of all, he despises me."

"Why?"

"Apparently, I embarrassed him during a senior staff meeting. I don't remember the incident, but it seems McKenna has never gotten over it. Beyond that, I'm told McKenna regards me as a monster who's done irreparable harm to America's image in the world. Nothing would make him happier than to see me behind bars."

"It's good to know the U.S. intelligence community is functioning smoothly again."

"Actually, McKenna is under the impression it's working just fine now that he's running the entire show. He even managed to get himself appointed chairman of our new High-Value Detainee Interrogation Group. If a major terrorist figure is captured anywhere in the world, under any circumstances, James McKenna will be in charge of questioning him. It's a great deal of power to place in the hands of a single person, even if that person were competent. But, unfortunately, James McKenna doesn't fall into that category. He's

ambitious, he's well intentioned, but he doesn't know what he's doing. And if he isn't careful, he's going to get us all killed."

"Sounds charming," said Gabriel. "When do I get to meet
him?"

"Never."

"So why am I here, Adrian?"

"You're here because of Paris, Copenhagen, and London."

"Who carried it out?"

"A new branch of al-Qaeda," said Carter. "But I'm afraid they
had support from a person who occupies a sensitive and powerful
position in Western intelligence."

"Who?"

Carter said nothing more. His right hand was shaking.

12

GEORGETOWN, WASHINGTON, D.C.

THEY ADJOURNED TO THE REAR terrace and settled into a pair of wrought-iron chairs along the balustrade. Carter balanced a coffee cup on his knee and gazed toward the gray spires rising gracefully above Georgetown University. Paradoxically, he was speaking of a shabby district of San Diego, where, on a summer day in 1999, there arrived a young Yemeni cleric named Rashid al-Husseini. With money provided by a Saudi-based Islamic charity, the Yemeni purchased a run-down commercial property, established a mosque, and went in search of a congregation. He did most of his hunting on the campus of San Diego State University, where he acquired a devoted following among Arab students who had come to America to escape the stifling social oppression of their homelands, only to find themselves lost and adrift in the *ghurba*, the land of strangers. Rashid was uniquely qualified to serve as their guide. The only son of a former Yemeni government minister, he had been born in America, spoke colloquial American English, and was the not-so-proud owner of an American passport.

"All sorts of strays and lost souls began stumbling into Rashid's mosque, including a pair of Saudis named Khalid al-Mihdhar and Nawaf al-Hazmi." Carter glanced at Gabriel and added, "I trust you're familiar with the names."

"They were two of the muscle hijackers from American Flight 77, personally selected by none other than Osama Bin Laden himself. In January 2000, they were present at the planning meeting in Kuala Lumpur, after which the Bin Laden Unit of the CIA managed to lose track of them. Later, it was discovered that both had flown to Los Angeles and were probably still in the United States—a fact you neglected to tell the FBI."

"Much to my everlasting shame," said Carter. "But this isn't a story about al-Mihdhar and al-Hazmi."

It was a story, Carter resumed, about Rashid al-Husseini, who soon developed a reputation in the Islamic world as a magnetic preacher, a man to whom Allah had granted a beautiful and seductive tongue. His sermons became required listening, not only in San Diego but also in the Middle East, where they were distributed by audiotape. In the spring of 2001, he was offered a clerical position at an influential Islamic center outside Washington, in suburban Falls Church, Virginia. Before long, Nawaf al-Hazmi was praying there, along with a young Saudi from Taif named Hani Hanjour.

"Coincidentally," said Carter, "the mosque is located on Leesburg Pike. If you hang a left onto Columbia Pike and go a couple of miles, you run smack into the western façade of the Pentagon, which is exactly what Hani Hanjour did on the morning of 9/11. Rashid was in his office at the time. He actually heard the plane pass overhead a few seconds before impact."

It did not take long for the FBI to connect al-Hazmi and Hanjour to the Falls Church mosque, said Carter, or for the news media to beat a path to Rashid's door. What they discovered was an eloquent and enlightened young cleric, a man of moderation who condemned the attacks of 9/11 without equivocation and urged his Muslim brethren to forsake violence and terrorism in all its forms. The White House was so impressed with the charismatic imam that he was invited to join several other Muslim scholars and clerics for a private meeting with the president. The State Department thought Rashid might be the perfect sort of figure to help build a bridge between America and one and a half billion skeptical Muslims. The Agency, however, had another idea.

"We thought Rashid could help us to penetrate the camp of our new enemy," said Carter. "But before we made our approach, we had to answer a few questions. Namely, was he somehow involved in the 9/11 plot, or were his contacts with the three hijackers purely coincidental? We looked at him from every conceivable angle, starting from the assumption that he had a great deal of American blood on his hands. We looked at timetables. We looked at who was where and when. And at the end of the process, we concluded that Imam Rashid al-Husseini was clean."

"And then?"

"We dispatched an emissary to Falls Church to see whether Rashid might be willing to put his words into action. His response was positive. We picked him up the next day and took him to a secure location near the Pennsylvania border. And then the real fun began."

"You started the assessment process all over again."

Carter nodded. "But this time, we had the subject seated before us, strapped to a polygraph. We questioned him for three days, pulling apart his past and his associations, piece by piece."

"And his story held up."

"He passed with flying colors. So we placed our proposition on the table, accompanied by a great deal of money. It was a simple operation. Rashid would tour the Islamic world, preaching tolerance and moderation while at the same time supplying us with the names of other potential recruits to our cause. In addition, he was to be on the lookout for angry young men who appeared vulnerable to the siren song of the jihadis. We took him on a domestic test drive, working closely with the FBI. And then we went international."

Operating from a base in a predominately Muslim neighborhood in East London, Rashid spent the next three years crisscrossing Europe and the Middle East. He spoke at conferences, preached in mosques, and sat for interviews with fawning journalists. He denounced Bin Laden as a murderer who had violated the laws of Allah and the teachings of the Prophet. He recognized the right of Israel to exist and called for a negotiated peace with the Palestinians. He condemned Saddam Hussein as thoroughly un-Islamic, though, on the advice of his CIA handlers, he stopped short of endorsing the American invasion. His message did not always go over well with his audiences, nor were his activities confined to the physical world. With CIA assistance, Rashid built a presence on the Internet, where he attempted to compete with the jihadist propaganda of al-Qaeda. Visitors to the site were identified and tracked as they moved through cyberspace.

"The operation was regarded as one of our most successful efforts to penetrate a world that, for the most part, we had found almost entirely opaque. Rashid fed his handlers a steady stream of names, good guys and potential bad guys, and even tipped them off about some plots that were brewing. At Langley, we spent a great deal of time marveling at our cleverness. We thought it would go on forever. But it all ended rather suddenly."

The setting, fittingly enough, was Mecca. Rashid had been invited to speak at the university, a high honor for a cleric who had been cursed with an American passport. Given the fact that Mecca is closed to infidels, the CIA had no choice but to allow him to go alone. He flew from Amman to Riyadh, where he met a final time with one of his CIA handlers, then boarded an internal Saudia Airlines flight to Mecca. His speech was scheduled for eight that evening. Rashid never showed up. He had vanished without a trace.

"At first, we feared he'd been kidnapped and killed by a local branch of al-Qaeda. Unfortunately, that turned out not to be the case. Our prized possession resurfaced on the Internet a few weeks later. The eloquent, enlightened young man of moderation was gone. He'd been replaced by a raving fanatic who preached that the only way to deal with the West was to destroy it."

"He deceived you."

"Obviously."

"For how long?"

"That remains an open question," said Carter. "There are some at Langley who believe Rashid was bad from the beginning, others who theorize he was driven over the edge by the guilt of working as a spy for the infidels. Whatever the case, one thing is beyond dispute. During the time he was traveling the Islamic world on my dime, he recruited an impressive network of operatives, right under our noses. He's the ultimate talent spotter and skilled in the art of deception and misdirection. We hoped he would stick to preaching and recruiting, but that hope turned out to be misplaced. The attacks in Europe were Rashid's coming-out party. He wants to replace Osama Bin Laden as leader of the global jihadist movement. He also wants to do something Bin Laden was never able to accomplish after 9/11."

"Strike the Far Enemy in his homeland," said Gabriel. "Shed American blood on American soil."

"With a network bought and paid for by the Central Intelligence Agency," Carter added soberly. "How would you like that chiseled on your headstone? If it were ever made public that Rashid al-Husseini was once on our payroll . . ." Carter's voice trailed off. "Ashes, ashes, we all fall down."

"What do you want from me, Adrian?"

"I want you to make the bombing in Covent Garden the last attack Rashid al-Husseini ever carries out. I want you to smash his network before anyone else dies because of my folly."

"Is that all?"

"No," said Carter. "I want you to keep the entire operation secret from the president, James McKenna, and the rest of the American intelligence community."

13

GEORGETOWN, WASHINGTON, D.C.

ADRIAN CARTER WAS DOCTRINAIRE WHEN it came to matters of tradecraft, which meant he could not talk for too long within the confines of a safe house, even if it was one of his own. They descended the curved front steps and, with a single CIA security man in tow, headed westward along N Street. It was a few minutes after nine o'clock. Carter's penny loafers tapped rhythmically on the redbrick sidewalk, but Gabriel seemed to move without a sound. A Metro bus rumbled past, filled to capacity. Gabriel pictured the same bus torn in half and engulfed in flames.

"Where did he go after leaving Mecca?"

"We believe he's living under the protection of tribal elements in the Rafadh Valley of Yemen. It's a completely lawless place, without schools, paved roads, or even a reliable supply of water. In fact, the entire country is dry as a bone. Sana might be the first capital city on Earth to actually run out of water."

"But not Islamic militants," said Gabriel.

"Oh, no," Carter agreed. "Yemen is well on its way to becoming the next Afghanistan. For now, we've been content to lob the occasional Hellfire missile over the border. But it's only a matter of time before we have to put boots on the ground and drain the swamp." He glanced at Gabriel and added, "There actually are swamps in Yemen, by the way—a string of marshes along the coastline that produce malarial mosquitoes the size of buzzards. My God, what a dreadful place."

Carter walked in silence for a moment with his hands clasped behind his back and his head down. Gabriel deftly sidestepped a tree root that had risen through the sidewalk and asked how Rashid managed to communicate with his network from so remote a place.

"We haven't been able to figure that out," Carter replied. "We assume he's using local tribesmen to ferry messages to Sana or perhaps across the Gulf of Aden to Somalia, where he's forged a relationship with the al-Shabaab terror group. We're certain of one thing, though. Rashid spends no time on the phone, satellite or otherwise. He learned a great deal about American capabilities when he was on our payroll. And now that he's gone over to the other side, he's put that knowledge to good use."

"I don't suppose you also taught him how to plan and execute a synchronized series of attacks in three European countries."

"Rashid is a talent spotter and a source of inspiration," said Carter, "but he's no operational mastermind. He's clearly working with someone good. If I had to guess, the three attacks in Europe were carried out by someone who cut his teeth in—"

"Baghdad," Gabriel said, finishing Carter's thought for him.

"The MIT of terrorism," Carter added, nodding in agreement. "Its graduates are all PhDs, and they served their internships by matching wits with the Agency and the American military."

"All the more reason why *you* should deal with them."

Carter made no reply.

"Why us, Adrian?"

"Because the American counterterrorism apparatus has grown so large we can't seem to get out of our own way. At last count, we had more than eight hundred thousand people with top-secret clearances. *Eight hundred thousand*," Carter repeated incredulously, "and yet we still weren't able to prevent a single Islamic militant from planting a bomb in the heart of Times Square. Our ability to collect information is unrivaled, but we're too big and far too redundant to be effective. We *are* Americans, after all, and when confronted with a threat, we throw large amounts of money at it. Sometimes, it's better to be small and ruthless. Like you."

"We warned you about the perils of reorganizing."

"And we would have been wise to listen," said Carter. "But our unwieldy size is only part of the problem. After 9/11, the gloves came off, and we adopted a whatever-it-takes attitude when it came to dealing with the enemy. These days, we try not to mention the enemy by name, lest we offend him. At Langley, counterterrorism jobs are considered politically risky. All the best officers in the Clandestine Service are learning to speak Mandarin."

"The Chinese aren't actively plotting to kill Americans."

"But Rashid is," Carter said, "and our intelligence suggests he's planning something spectacular in the very near future. We need to break his network, and we need to do it quickly. But we can't do that if we're forced to operate under the new rules put in place by President Hope and his well-intentioned accomplice James McKenna."

"So you want us to do your dirty work for you."

"I'd do the same for you," Carter said. "And don't try to tell me that you lack the capability. The Office was the first Western-oriented intelligence service to establish an analytical unit dedicated to the global jihadist movement. You were also first to identify Osama Bin Laden as a major terrorist, and the first to have a go at killing him. If you'd succeeded, it's highly likely that 9/11 would never have happened."

They arrived at the corner of Thirty-fifth Street. The next block was closed to traffic by a barricade. On the opposite side, children from the Holy Trinity School skipped rope and tossed balls in the street, their joyous screams reverberating off the façades of the surrounding buildings. It was an idyllic scene, full of charm and life, but it made Carter visibly uneasy.

"Homeland security is a myth," he said, gazing at the children. "It's a bedtime story we tell our people to make them feel safe at night. Despite all our best efforts and all our billions spent, the United States is largely indefensible. The only way to prevent attacks on American soil is to snuff them out *before* they reach our shores. We have to rip apart their networks and kill their operatives."

"Killing Rashid al-Husseini might not be a bad idea, either."

"We'd love to," said Carter. "But that won't be possible until we can find some way into his inner circle."

Carter led Gabriel northward along Thirty-fifth Street. He removed his pipe from the pocket of his coat and began absently loading the bowl with tobacco.

"You've been fighting the terrorists longer than anyone else in the business, Gabriel—anyone but Shamron, of course. You know how to penetrate their networks, something we've never been very good at, and you know how to turn them inside out. I want you to get inside Rashid's network and destroy it. I want you to make it go away."

"Penetrating jihadist terror networks isn't the same as penetrating the PLO. They're far too clannish to accept outsiders into their midst, and their members are largely immune to earthly temptations."

"A rose is a rose is a rose. And a network is a network is a network."

"Meaning?"

"I'll grant you there are differences between jihadist and Palestinian terror networks, but the basic structure is the same. There are planners and foot soldiers, paymasters and quartermasters, couriers and safe houses. And at the points where all these pieces intersect, there is vulnerability just waiting to be exploited by someone as clever as you."

A breath of wind carried the pipe smoke into Gabriel's face. Blended exclusively for Carter by a tobacconist in New York, it smelled of burning leaves and wet dog. Gabriel waved it away and asked, "How would it work?"

"Does that mean you'll do it?"

"No," said Gabriel, "it means I want to know exactly how it would work."

"You would operate as a virtual station of the Counterterrorism Center, in much the same way the Bin Laden Unit functioned before 9/11, but with one important difference."

"The rest of the CTC won't know I'm there."

Carter nodded. "All document requests will be handled by my staff and me. And when it's time for you to go operational, I'll act as a clandestine traffic cop to make sure you don't trip over any ongoing Agency operations, and they don't trip over you."

"I would need to see everything you have. *Every*thing, Adrian."

"You'll be given access to the most sensitive intelligence available to the government of the United States, including the case files on Rashid and all the NSA intercepts. You'll also be allowed to see all the intelligence on the three attacks that's flowing to us from our sister services in Europe." Carter paused. "I would think that information alone would be tempting enough for you to accept the assignment. After all, your liaison relationships with the Europeans aren't terribly good at the moment."

Gabriel didn't respond directly. "It's too much material to review on my own. I'd need help."

"You can import as much help as you want, within reason. Given the sensitive nature of the intelligence, I'll also need someone from the Agency looking over your shoulder. Someone who knows your mischievous ways. I have a candidate in mind."

"Where is she?"

"Waiting in a café on Wisconsin Avenue."

"You're very sure of yourself, Adrian."

Carter stopped walking and checked his pipe. "Were I to stoop to raw sentimentality," he said after a moment, "I would remind you of the carnage you witnessed last Friday afternoon in Covent Garden and ask you to imagine it played out over and over again. But I won't do that, because it would be unprofessional. Instead, I will tell you that Rashid has an army of martyrs just like Farid Khan waiting to do his bidding, an army he recruited with my help. I made Rashid. He's my mistake. And I need you to destroy him before anyone else has to die."

"You might find this difficult to believe, but I actually don't have the authority to say yes to you. Uzi would have to sign off on it first."

"He already has. So has your prime minister."

"I suppose you've also had a quiet word with Graham Seymour."

Carter nodded. "For obvious reasons, Graham would like to be kept abreast of your progress. He would also like advance warning if your operation happens to wash ashore in the British Isles."

"You misled me, Adrian."

"I'm a spy," Carter said, relighting his pipe. "I lie as a matter of course. So do you. Now you just have to figure out a way to lie to Rashid. Just be careful how you go about it. He's very good, our Rashid. I have the scars to prove it."

14

GEORGETOWN, WASHINGTON, D.C.

THE CAFÉ WAS LOCATED AT the northern end of Georgetown, at the foot of Book Hill Park. Gabriel ordered a cap-
puccino from the bar and carried it through a pair of open
French doors into a small garden with vine-covered walls. Three
of the tables were in shadow; the fourth, in brilliant sunlight. A
woman sat there alone, reading a newspaper. She wore a black
running suit that clung tightly to her slender frame, and a pair of
spotless white training shoes. Her shoulder-length blond hair was
brushed straight back from her forehead and held in place by an
elastic band at the nape of her neck. Sunglasses concealed her eyes
but not her remarkable beauty. She removed the glasses as Gabriel
approached and tilted her face to be kissed. She seemed surprised
to see him.

"I was hoping it would be you," said Sarah Bancroft.

"Adrian didn't tell you I was coming?"

"He's much too old-fashioned for that," she said with a dismissive wave of her hand. She had a voice and manner of speech from another age. It was like listening to a character from a Fitzgerald novel. "He dropped me a secure e-mail last night and told me to be here at nine. I was to stay until ten-thirty. If no one appeared, I was to leave and go to work as normal. It's a good thing you came. You know how much I hate being stood up."

"I see you brought reading material," Gabriel said, glancing at the newspaper.

"You disapprove?"

"Office doctrine forbids agents to read newspapers in cafés. It's far too obvious." He paused, then added, "I thought we trained you better than that, Sarah."

"You did. But on occasion, I like to behave like a normal person. And a normal person sometimes finds it pleasurable to read a newspaper in a café on a sunny autumn morning."

"With a Glock concealed at the small of her back."

"Thanks to you, it's my constant companion."

Sarah gave a melancholy smile. The daughter of a wealthy Citibank executive, she had spent much of her childhood in Europe, where she had acquired a Continental education along with Continental languages and impeccable Continental manners. She had returned to America to attend Dartmouth, and later, after spending a year at the prestigious Courtauld Institute of Art in London, she became the youngest woman ever to earn a PhD in art history at Harvard.

But it was Sarah Bancroft's love life, not her sterling education, that led her into the world of intelligence. While finishing her dissertation, she began dating a young lawyer named Ben Callahan who had the misfortune of boarding United Airlines Flight 175 on the morning of September 11, 2001. He managed to make one telephone call before the plane plunged into the South Tower of the

World Trade Center. That call was to Sarah. With Adrian Carter's blessing, and with the help of a lost van Gogh, Gabriel inserted her into the entourage of a Saudi billionaire named Zizi al-Bakari in a daring bid to find the terrorist mastermind lurking within it. At the conclusion of the operation, she had joined the CIA and was assigned to the Counterterrorism Center. Since then, she had maintained close contact with the Office and had worked with Gabriel and his team on numerous occasions. She had even taken an Office lover, an assassin and field operative named Mikhail Abramov. Judging by the absence of a ring on her finger, the relationship was proceeding at a slower pace than she had hoped.

"We've been on-again-off-again for a while," she said, as if reading Gabriel's thoughts.

"And at the moment?"

"Off," she said. "Definitely off."

"I told you not to become involved with a man who kills for his country."

"You were right, Gabriel. You're always right."

"So what happened?"

"I'd rather not go into all the sordid details."

"He told me he was in love with you."

"He told me the same thing. Funny how that works."

"Did he hurt you?"

"I don't think I'm capable of being hurt any longer." It took a moment for Sarah to smile. She wasn't being honest; Gabriel could see that.

"Do you want me to have a word with him?"

"Heavens, no," she said. "I'm more than capable of screwing up my life completely on my own."

"He's been through a couple of difficult operations, Sarah. The last one was—"

"He told me all about it," she said. "I sometimes wish he hadn't come out of the Alps alive."

"You don't mean that."

"No," she said grudgingly, "but it felt good to say it."

"Maybe it's for the better. You should find someone who doesn't live on the other side of the world. Someone here in Washington."

"And how should I respond when they ask me where I work?"

Gabriel said nothing.

"I'm not getting any younger, you know. I just turned——"

"Thirty-seven," said Gabriel.

"Which means I'm rapidly approaching old-maid status," Sarah said, frowning. "I suppose the best I can hope for at this point is a comfortable but passionless marriage to an older man of means. If I'm lucky, he'll permit me to have a child or two, whom I'll be forced to raise on my own because he'll have no interest in them."

"Surely it's not as depressing as all that."

She shrugged and sipped her coffee. "How are things between you and Chiara?"

"Perfect," said Gabriel.

"I was afraid you were going to say that," Sarah murmured archly.

"Sarah . . ."

"Don't worry, Gabriel, I got over you a long time ago."

A pair of middle-aged women entered the garden and sat at the opposite end. Sarah leaned forward in feigned intimacy and, in French, asked Gabriel what he was doing in town. He responded by tapping the front page of her newspaper.

"Since when is our soaring national debt a problem for Israeli intelligence?" she asked playfully.

Gabriel pointed toward the front-page story about the debate raging within the American intelligence community about the provenance of the three attacks in Europe.

"How did you get dragged into it?"

"Chiara and I decided to take a stroll through Covent Garden last Friday afternoon on our way to lunch."

Sarah's expression darkened. "So the reports about an unidentified man drawing a weapon a few seconds before the attack—"

"Are true," said Gabriel. "I could have saved eighteen lives. Unfortunately, the British wouldn't hear of it."

"So who do you think was responsible?"

"You're the terrorism expert, Sarah. You tell me."

"It's possible the attacks were masterminded by the old-line al-Qaeda leadership in Pakistan," she said. "But in my opinion, we're dealing with an entirely new network."

"Led by whom?"

"Someone with the charisma of Bin Laden who could recruit his own operatives in Europe and call upon cells from other terror groups."

"Any candidates?"

"Just one," she said. "Rashid al-Husseini."

"Why Paris?"

"The ban on the facial veil."

"Copenhagen?"

"They're still seething over the cartoons."

"And London?"

"London is low-hanging fruit. London can be attacked at will."

"Not bad for a former curator at the Phillips Collection."

"I'm an art historian, Gabriel. I know how to connect dots. I can connect a few more, if you like."

"Please do."

"Your presence in Washington means the rumors are true."

"What rumors are those?"

"The ones about Rashid being on the Agency's payroll after 9/11. The ones about a good idea that went very bad. Adrian believed in Rashid and Rashid repaid that trust by building a network right under our noses. Now I suppose Adrian would like you to take care of the problem for him—off the books, of course."

"Is there any other way?"

"Not where you're concerned," she said. "What does this have to do with me?"

"Adrian needs someone to spy on me. You were the obvious candidate." Gabriel hesitated, then said, "But if you think it would be too awkward . . ."

"Because of Mikhail?"

"It's possible you'll be working together again, Sarah. I wouldn't want personal feelings to interfere with the smooth functioning of the team."

"Since when has your team ever functioned smoothly? You're Israelis. You fight with one another constantly."

"But we never allow personal feelings to influence operational decisions."

"I'm a professional," she said. "Given our history together, I shouldn't think I'd need to remind you of that."

"You don't."

"So where do we start?"

"We need to get to know Rashid a bit better."

"How are we going to do that?"

"By reading his Agency files."

"But they're filled with lies."

"That's correct," said Gabriel. "But those lies are like layers of paint on a canvas. Peel them away, and we might find ourselves staring directly at the truth."

"No one ever speaks that way at Langley."

"I know," Gabriel said. "If they did, I'd still be in Cornwall working on a Titian."

15

GEORGETOWN, WASHINGTON, D.C.

G ABRIEL AND SARAH TOOK UP residence at the house on N Street at nine the following morning. The first batch of files arrived one hour later—six stainless steel crates, all sealed with digital locks. For some unfathomable reason, Carter entrusted the combinations only to Sarah. "Rules are rules," he said, "and Agency rules state that officers of foreign intelligence services are never to be given the combinations of document receptacles." When Gabriel pointed out that he was being allowed to see some of the Agency's dirtiest laundry, Carter was unyielding. Technically speaking, the material was to remain in Sarah's possession. The taking of notes was to be kept to a minimum and photocopying was forbidden. Carter personally removed the secure fax machine and requested Gabriel's mobile phone—a request Gabriel politely declined. The phone had been issued to him by the Office and contained several features not available commercially. In fact, he had used it the previous evening to sweep the house for listening devices. He had found four. Obviously, interservice co-operation only went so far.

The initial shipment of files all focused on Rashid's time in America before 9/11 and his connections, nefarious or serendipitous, to the plot itself. Most of the material had been generated by Langley's unglamorous rival, the FBI, and had been shared during the brief period when, by presidential order, the two agencies were supposed to be cooperating. It revealed that Rashid al-Husseini popped up on the Bureau's radar within weeks of his arrival in San Diego and was the target of somewhat apathetic surveillance. There were transcripts from the court-approved wiretaps on his phones and surveillance photos shot during the brief periods when the San Diego and Washington field offices had the time and manpower to follow him. There was also a copy of the classified interagency review that officially cleared Rashid of playing any role in the 9/11 plot. It was, thought Gabriel, a profoundly naïve piece of work that chose to portray the cleric in the kindest possible light. Gabriel believed a man was the company he kept, and he had been around terror networks long enough to know an operative when he saw one. Rashid al-Husseini was almost certainly a messenger or an innkeeper. At the very least, he was a fellow traveler. And, in Gabriel's opinion, fellow travelers should rarely be taken on by intelligence services as paid agents of influence. They should be watched and, if necessary, dealt with harshly.

The next shipment contained the transcripts and recordings of Rashid's interrogation by the CIA, followed soon after by the detritus of the ill-fated operation in which he had played a starring role. The material concluded with a despairing after-action postmortem, written in the days following Rashid's defection in Mecca. The operation, it said, had been poorly conceived from the outset. Much of the blame was placed squarely at the feet of Adrian

Carter, who was faulted for lax oversight. Attached was Carter's own assessment, which was scarcely less scathing. Predicting there would be blowback, he recommended a thorough review of Rashid's contacts in the United States and Europe. Carter's director had overruled him. The Agency was stretched too thin to go chasing after shadows, the director said. Rashid was back in Yemen where he belonged. Good riddance.

"Not exactly the Agency's finest hour," Sarah declared late that evening, during a break in the proceedings. "We were fools to ever use him."

"The Agency began with the correct assumption, that Rashid was bad, but somewhere along the line it fell under his spell. It's easy to see how it happened. Rashid was very persuasive."

"Almost as persuasive as you."

"But I don't send my recruits into crowded streets to carry out acts of indiscriminate murder."

"No," said Sarah, "you send them onto secret battlefields to smite your enemies."

"It's not as biblical as all that."

"Yes, it is. Trust me, I should know." She looked wearily at the stacks of files. "We still have a mountain of material to go through, and it's only the beginning. The floodgates are about to open."

"Don't worry," Gabriel said, smiling. "Help is on the way."

———

They arrived at Dulles Airport late the following afternoon under false names and with false passports in their pockets. They were not punished for their sins; quite the opposite, a team of Agency minders whisked them through customs and then herded them into a fleet of armored Escalades for the drive into Washington. Per Adrian Carter's instructions, the Escalades departed Dulles at fifteen-minute intervals. As a result, the most storied team of operatives in the intelligence world settled into the house on N Street that evening with the neighbors being none the wiser.

Chiara arrived first, followed a moment later by an Office terrorism expert named Dina Sarid. Petite and dark-haired, Dina knew the horrors of extremist violence all too well. She had been standing on Tel Aviv's Dizengoff Street on October 19, 1994, when a Hamas suicide bomber turned the Number 5 bus into a coffin for twenty-one people. Her mother and two of her sisters were among the dead; Dina was seriously injured and still walked with a slight limp. Upon her recovery, she vowed to defeat the terrorists not with force but with her brain. A human database, she was capable of reciting the time, place, perpetrators, and casualty toll of every act of terrorism committed against Israeli and Western targets. Dina had once told Gabriel that she knew more about the terrorists than they knew about themselves. And Gabriel had believed her.

Next came a man of late middle age named Eli Lavon. Small and disheveled, with wispy gray hair and intelligent brown eyes, Lavon was regarded as the finest street surveillance artist the Office had ever produced. Blessed with a natural anonymity, he appeared to be one of life's downtrodden. In reality, he was a predator who could follow a highly trained intelligence officer or a hardened terrorist along any street in the world without arousing a flicker of interest. Lavon's ties to the Office, like Gabriel's, were now tenuous at best. He still lectured at the Academy—no Office recruit was ever sent into the field without first spending a few hours at Lavon's feet—but these days, his primary work address was Jerusalem's Hebrew University, where he taught archaeology. With but a handful of broken pottery, Eli Lavon could unlock the darkest secrets of a Bronze Age village. And given a few strands of relevant intelligence, he could do the same for a terror network.

Yaakov Rossman, a pockmarked veteran agent-runner, appeared next, followed by a pair of all-purpose field hands named Oded and Mordecai. Then came Rimona Stern, a former military intelligence officer who now dealt with issues related to Iran's disabled nuclear program. A Rubenesque woman with sandstone-colored hair, Rimona also happened to be Shamron's niece. Gabriel had known her since she was a child—indeed, his fondest memories of Rimona were of a fearless young girl on a kick scooter careening down the steep drive of her famous uncle's house. On her generous left hip was the faded scar of a wound suffered during a particularly violent spill. Gabriel had applied the field dressing; Gilah had dried Rimona's tears. Shamron had been far too distraught to offer any assistance. The only member of his family to survive the Holocaust, he could not bear to witness the suffering of loved ones.

A few minutes behind Rimona was Yossi Gavish. A tall, balding figure dressed in corduroy and tweed, Yossi was a top officer in Research, which is how the Office referred to its analytical division. Born in London, he had read classics at All Souls and spoke Hebrew with a pronounced English accent. He had also done a bit of acting—his portrayal of Iago was still recalled with great fondness by the critics in Stratford—and was a gifted cellist as well. Gabriel had yet to exploit Yossi's musical talents, but his skills as an actor had on more than one occasion proven useful in the field. There was a beachside café in St. Barts where the waitresses thought him a dream and a hotel in Geneva where the concierge had taken a private vow to shoot him on sight.

As usual, Mikhail Abramov arrived last. Lanky and fair, with a fine-boned face and eyes the color of glacial ice, he had immigrated to Israel from Russia as a teenager and joined the Sayeret Matkal, the IDF's elite special operations unit. Once described as "Gabriel without a conscience," he had personally assassinated several of the top terror masterminds from Hamas and Palestinian Islamic Jihad. Burdened with two heavy cases filled with electronic gear, he greeted Sarah with an unambiguously frigid kiss. Eli Lavon would later describe it as the frostiest embrace since Shamron, during the halcyon days of the peace process, had been forced to shake the hand of Yasser Arafat.

Known by the code name Barak, the Hebrew word for lightning, the nine men and women of Gabriel's team had many idiosyncrasies and many traditions. Among the idiosyncrasies was a ritual childlike squabble over room assignments. Among the traditions was a lavish first-night planning meal prepared by Chiara. The one that occurred at N Street was more poignant than most, in that it was never supposed to take place. Like everyone else at King Saul Boulevard, the team had expected the operation against the Iranian nuclear program to be Gabriel's last. They had been told as much by their chief in name only, Uzi Navot, who was not altogether displeased, and by Shamron, who was distraught. "I had no choice but to set him free," Shamron said after his fabled encounter with Gabriel atop the cliffs of Cornwall. "This time it's for good."

It might have been for good if Gabriel had not spotted Farid Khan walking along Wellington Street with a bomb beneath his overcoat. The men and women gathered around the dining room table understood the toll Covent Garden had taken on Gabriel. Many years earlier, in another lifetime, under another name, he had failed to prevent a bombing in Vienna that forever altered the course of his life. On that occasion, the bomb had been hidden not beneath the overcoat of a *shahid* but in the undercarriage of Gabriel's car. The victims were not strangers but loved ones—his wife, Leah, and his only son, Dani. Leah lived now in a psychiatric hospital atop Mount Herzl in Jerusalem in a prison of memory and a body destroyed by fire. She had only a vague sense that Dani was buried not far from her, on the Mount of Olives.

The members of Gabriel's team did not mention Leah and Dani that evening, nor did they dwell long on the chain of events that led Gabriel to be an unwilling witness to Farid Khan's martyrdom. Instead, they spoke of friends and family, of books they had read and movies they had seen, and of the remarkable changes currently sweeping the Arab world. In Egypt, Pharaoh had finally fallen, unleashing a wave of protest that was threatening to topple the kings and secular dictators who had ruled the region for generations. Whether the changes would bring Israel greater security or place it in greater peril was a topic of hot debate inside the Office and around the dinner table that night. Yossi, an optimist by nature, believed the Arabs, if given the opportunity to govern themselves, would have no truck with those who wished to make war with Israel. Yaakov, who had spent years running spies against hostile Arab regimes, declared Yossi dangerously delusional, as did nearly everyone else. Only Dina refused to venture an opinion, for her thoughts were focused on the crates of files waiting in the living room. She had a clock ticking in her formidable brain and believed that a minute wasted was a minute left to terrorists to plot and plan. The files held the promise of lives saved. They were sacred texts that contained secrets only she could decode.

It was approaching midnight by the time the meal finally came to an end. It was followed by the traditional spat over who would clear the dishes, who would wash, and who would dry. After recusing himself, Gabriel acquainted Dina with the files, then showed Chiara upstairs to their room. It was on the third floor, overlooking the rear garden. The red aircraft warning lights atop the spires of Georgetown University winked softly in the distance, a reminder of the city's vulnerability to aviation-based terrorism.

"I suppose there are worse places to spend a few days," Chiara said. "Where did you put Mikhail and Sarah?"

"As far apart as possible."

"What are the chances this operation might bring them back together?"

"About the same that the Arab world is suddenly going to recognize our right to exist."

"That bad?"

"I'm afraid so." Gabriel lifted Chiara's bag and placed it at the end of the bed. It sagged beneath the weight. "What have you got in here?"

"Gilah sent along a few things for you."

"Rocks?"

"Food," Chiara said. "You know how Gilah is. She always thought you were too thin."

"How is she?"

"Now that Ari isn't spending so much time around the house, she seems to be doing much better."

"Did he finally sign up for that pottery course he's always wanted to take?"

"Actually, he's back at King Saul Boulevard."

"Doing what?"

"Uzi thought he needed something to keep him occupied, so he made him your operational coordinator. He'd like you to call him first thing in the morning." Chiara kissed his cheek and smiled. "Welcome home, darling."

16

GEORGETOWN, WASHINGTON, D.C.

THERE IS A TRUISM ABOUT terror networks: putting the pieces in place is not as difficult as one might imagine. But once the mastermind pulls the trigger and carries out his first attack, the element of surprise is lost and the network exposes itself. In the earliest years of the conflict against terrorism—when Black September and Carlos the Jackal were running amok, aided by useful leftist Euro-idiots such as the Baader-Meinhof Group and the Red Brigades—intelligence officers mainly used physical surveillance, hard wiretaps, and good old-fashioned detective work to identify the members of a cell. Now, with the advent of the Internet and global satellite communications, the contours of the battlefield had been altered. The Internet had given the terrorists a powerful tool to organize, inspire, and communicate, but it had also provided intelligence services with a means of tracking their every move. Cyberspace was like a forest in winter. The terrorists could hide there for a time, hatching their plots and organizing their forces, but they could not come or go without leaving foot-prints in the snow. The challenge for the counterterrorism officer was to follow the right set of tracks, for the virtual forest was a dark and confusing place where one could wander aimlessly while innocents died.

Gabriel and his team cautiously set foot there the next morning when British intelligence, under standing agreement, shared with their American cousins the preliminary results of the inquiry into the Covent Garden bombing. Included in the material were the contents of Farid Khan's computers at home and work, a printout of every number he had dialed from his mobile phone, and a list of known Islamic extremists he had encountered while he was a member of Hizb ut-Tahrir and al-Muhajiroun. There was also a copy of the suicide tape, along with several hundred still images captured by CCTV during the final months of his life. The last photo showed him standing in Covent Garden, his arms raised above his head, a bloom of fire erupting from the explosives belt around his waist. Lying on the ground a few feet away, shielded by two men, was Gabriel. When the picture was magnified, it was possible to see the shadow of a gun in his left hand.

Carter had distributed the material to the CTC at Langley and the NSA at Fort Meade, Maryland. Then, without the knowledge of either, he delivered a third copy to the house on N Street. The next day, he dropped off a remarkably similar package from the Danish, but an entire week would elapse before he appeared with the material from Paris. "The French still haven't quite figured out that we're all in this together," Carter said. "They view the attack as a failure of their intelligence system, which means you can be sure we're getting only part of the story."

Gabriel and his team worked through the material as quickly as possible, but with the patience and attention to detail required in such an endeavor. Instinctively, Gabriel told them to approach the case as if it were an enormous canvas that had suffered extensive losses. "Don't stand off at a distance and try to see everything at once," he warned. "It will only drive you mad. Work your way in slowly from the edges. Focus on small details—a hand, an eye, the hem of a garment, a single thread running through each of the three attacks. You won't be able to see it at first, but it's there, I promise you."

With the help of the NSA and the government data miners who worked in faceless office blocks ringing the Capital Beltway, the team burrowed deep into the memory of mainframe computers and servers scattered around the world. Phone numbers begot phone numbers, e-mail accounts begot e-mail accounts, names begot names. They read a thousand instant messages in a dozen different languages. Browsing histories were scoured for intent, photographs for evidence of target casing, search histories for secret desires and forbidden passions.

Gradually, the faint outline of a terror network began to take shape. It was scattered and diffuse—here the name of a potential operative in Lyon; here the address of a possible safe flat in Malmö; here a phone number in Karachi; here a Web site of uncertain origin that offered downloadable videos of bombings and beheadings, the pornography of the jihadist world. Friendly Western intelligence services, believing they were dealing with the CIA, happily supplied material they would have normally withheld. So, too, did the secret policemen of the Islamic world. Before long, the walls of the drawing room were covered with a mind-numbing matrix of intelligence. Eli Lavon likened it to gazing upon the heavens without the aid of a star chart. It was pleasant, he said, but hardly productive when lives were at stake. Somewhere out there was an organizing principle, a guiding hand of terror. Rashid, the charismatic cleric, had built the network with his beautiful and seductive tongue, but someone else had primed it to carry out three attacks in three European cities, each at a precise moment in time. He was no amateur, this man. He was a professional terror mastermind.

Putting a name and face to this monster became Dina's obsession. Sarah, Chiara, and Eli Lavon worked tirelessly at her side while Gabriel was content to play the role of errand-runner and messenger. Twice each day, Dina supplied him with a list of questions requiring urgent answers. Sometimes, Gabriel would make his way up to the Israeli Embassy in far northwest Washington and transmit them to Shamron over the secure link. Other times, he would give them to Adrian Carter, who would then make a pilgrimage to Fort Meade to have a quiet word with the data miners. On Halloween night, as children roamed Georgetown dressed as ghosts and goblins and superheroes, Carter summoned Gabriel to a coffee shop on Thirty-fifth Street to deliver a thick packet of material.

"Where's Dina going with this?" Carter asked, prying the lid from a caffè Americano he had no intention of drinking.

"Even I'm not sure," Gabriel replied. "She has her own methodology. I just try to stay out of the way."

"She's beating us, you know. The intelligence services of the United States have two hundred analysts trying to crack this case, and they're being beaten by a single woman."

"That's because she knows exactly what will happen if we don't shut them down. And she doesn't seem to need sleep."

"Does she have a theory about who it might be?"

"She feels like she knows him."

"Personally?"

"It's always personal with Dina, Adrian. That's why she's so good at what she does."

Though Gabriel would not admit it, the case had become personal for him as well. Indeed, when he was not at the embassy or meeting with Carter, he could usually be found in "Rashidistan," which is how the team referred to the cramped library of the house on N Street. Photographs of the telegenic cleric covered the four walls. Arranged chronologically, they charted his unlikely rise from an obscure local preacher in San Diego to the leader of a jihadist terror network. His appearance had changed little during that time—the same thin beard, the same bookish eyeglasses, the same benevolent expression in his tranquil brown eyes. He did not look like a man capable of mass murder, or even like someone who could inspire it. Gabriel was not surprised; he had been tortured by men with the hands of priests and had once killed a Palestinian master terrorist who had the face of a child. Even now, more than twenty years later, Gabriel struggled to reconcile the sweetness of the man's lifeless features with the appalling amount of blood on his hands.

Rashid's greatest asset was not his banal appearance but his voice. Gabriel listened to Rashid's sermons—both in Arabic and in his colloquial American English—and to the many thoughtful interviews he gave to the press after 9/11. Mainly, he reviewed the recordings of Rashid matching wits with his CIA interrogators. Rashid was part poet, part preacher, part professor of jihad. He warned the Americans that the demographics were stacked decidedly in favor of their enemies, that the Islamic world was young, growing, and seething with a potent mix of anger and humiliation. "Unless something is done to alter the equation, my dear friends, an entire generation will be lost to the jihad." What America needed was a bridge to the Muslim world—and Rashid al-Husseini offered to play the part.

Weary of Rashid's insidious presence, the rest of the team insisted that Gabriel keep the door of the library tightly closed whenever he was listening to the recordings. But late at night, when most of the others had gone off to bed, he would disobey their order, if only to relieve the feeling of claustrophobia produced by the sound of Rashid's voice. Invariably, he would find Dina staring at the puzzle arrayed on the walls of the drawing room. "Go to sleep, Dina," he would say. And Dina would respond, "I'll sleep when you sleep."

On the first Friday of December, as snow flurries whitened the streets of Georgetown, Gabriel listened again to Rashid's final debriefing with his Agency handlers. It was the night before his defection. He seemed more excited than usual and slightly on edge. At the conclusion of the encounter, he gave his case officer the name of an Oslo-based imam who, in Rashid's opinion, was raising money for the resistance fighters in Iraq. "They're not resistance fighters, they're terrorists," the CIA man said pointedly. "Forgive me, Bill," Rashid replied, using the officer's pseudonym, "but I sometimes find it hard to remember which side I'm on."

Gabriel switched off his computer and slipped quietly into the drawing room. Dina stood silently before her matrix, rubbing at the spot on her leg that always pained her when she was fatigued.

"Go to sleep, Dina," Gabriel said.

"Not tonight," she replied.

"You've got him?"

"I think so."

"Who is it?"

"It's Malik," she said softly. "And may God have mercy on us all."

17

GEORGETOWN, WASHINGTON, D.C.

I T WAS A FEW MINUTES past two a.m., a dreadful hour, Shamron once famously said, when brilliant schemes are rarely hatched. Gabriel suggested waiting until morning, but the clock in Dina's head was ticking far too loudly for that. She personally roused the others from bed and paced the drawing room anxiously while waiting for the coffee to brew. When finally she spoke, her tone was urgent but respectful. Malik, the master of terror, had earned it.

She began her account by reminding the team of Malik's lineage—a lineage that had but one possible outcome. A descendant of the al-Zubair clan—a mixed Palestinian-Syrian family that hailed from the village of Abu Ghosh, on the western approaches to Jerusalem—he had been born in the Zarqa refugee camp in Jordan. Zarqa was a wretched place, even by the deplorable standards of the camps, and a breeding ground for Islamic extremism. An intelligent but aimless young man, Malik spent a great deal of time at the al-Falah Mosque. There he fell under the spell of an incendiary Salafist imam who guided him into the arms of the Islamic Resistance Movement, better known as Hamas. Malik joined the group's military wing, the Izzaddin al-Qassam Brigades, and studied the craft of terror with some of the deadliest practitioners in the business. A natural leader and skilled organizer, he rose quickly through the ranks and by the onset of the Second Intifada was a top Hamas terror mastermind. From the safety of the Zarqa camp, he plotted some of the deadliest attacks of the period, including a suicide bombing at a nightclub in Tel Aviv that claimed thirty-three lives.

"After that attack," Dina said, "the prime minister signed an order authorizing Malik's assassination. Malik concealed himself deep inside the Zarqa camp and plotted what would be his biggest strike yet—a bombing at the Western Wall. Fortunately, we managed to arrest the three *shahids* before they could reach their target. It's believed to be Malik's one and only failure."

By the summer of 2004, Dina continued, it was clear that the Israeli-Palestinian conflict was too small a stage for Malik. Inspired by 9/11, he slipped out of the camp and, disguised as a woman, traveled to Amman to meet with an al-Qaeda recruiter. After reciting the *bayat*, the personal oath of allegiance to Osama Bin Laden, Malik was smuggled across the border into Syria. Six weeks later, he slipped into Iraq.

"Malik was far more sophisticated than the other members of al-Qaeda in Iraq," Dina said. "He'd spent years perfecting his craft against the most formidable counterterrorism forces in the world. Not only was he an expert bomb-maker, he knew how to slip his *shahids* through even the toughest security. He was thought to have been the mastermind behind some of the insurgency's deadliest and most spectacular attacks. His crowning achievement was a one-day wave of bombings in the Shiite quarter of Baghdad that killed more than two hundred people."

Malik's final attack in Iraq was a bombing of a Shiite mosque that left fifty worshippers dead. By then, he was the target of a massive search operation being carried out by Task Force 6-26, the joint U.S. special operations and intelligence unit. Ten days after the bombing, the task force learned that Malik was hiding in a safe house ten miles north of Baghdad, along with two other senior al-Qaeda figures. That night American F-16 jets attacked the house with a pair of laser-guided bombs, but a search of the ruins produced only two sets of remains. Neither belonged to Malik al-Zubair.

"Apparently, he slipped out of the house a few minutes before the bombs fell," Dina said. "Later, he told his comrades that Allah had instructed him to leave. The incident only reaffirmed his belief that he had been chosen by God to do great things."

It was then Malik decided it was time to go international. He had developed a taste for killing Americans in Iraq and wanted to kill them in their homeland, so he traveled to Pakistan to seek funding and support from al-Qaeda's front office. Bin Laden listened carefully. Then he sent Malik packing.

"Actually," Dina added hastily, "it's believed Ayman al-Zawahiri was behind the decision to turn Malik away empty-handed. The Egyptian had several plots under way against the West and didn't want them threatened by an upstart Palestinian from Zarqa."

"So Malik went to Yemen and offered his services to Rashid instead?" asked Gabriel.

"Exactly."

"Proof," said Gabriel. "Where's the proof?"

"I'm an intelligence analyst," Dina said unapologetically. "I rarely have the luxury of absolute proof. What I'm offering you is conjecture, supported by a handful of pertinent facts."

"For example?"

"Damascus," she said. "In the autumn of 2008, the Office got a tip from an asset inside Syrian intelligence that Malik was hiding there, moving constantly among a number of safe houses owned by various members of the al-Zubair clan. At Shamron's urging, the prime minister authorized us to begin planning for Malik's long-overdue demise. Uzi was still the chief of Special Ops then. He dispatched a team of field operatives to Damascus—a team that included one Mikhail Abramov," Dina added, with a glance in his direction. "Within a few days, they had Malik under full-time surveillance."

"Go on, Dina."

"Malik wasn't so easy to follow, as Mikhail will tell you. He changed his appearance constantly—facial hair, glasses, hats, clothing, even the way he walked—but the team managed to maintain contact with him. And late on the evening of October 23, they observed Malik entering an apartment owned by a man called Kemel Arwish. Arwish liked to portray himself as a Westernized moderate who wanted to drag his people kicking and screaming into the twenty-first century. In truth, he was an Islamist who dabbled at the fringes of al-Qaeda and its affiliates. His ability to travel between the Middle East and the West without suspicion made him valuable as a courier and runner of assorted errands." Dina looked directly at Gabriel. "Since you've been spending a great deal of time familiarizing yourself with Rashid's CIA files, I trust Kemel's name and address are familiar to you."

"Rashid attended a dinner party at Kemel Arwish's apartment in 2004 when he went to Damascus on behalf of the CIA," Gabriel said. "He later told his CIA minder that he and Arwish had discussed many interesting ideas on how to tamp down the fires of jihad."

"And if you believe that one . . ."

"It could be nothing more than a coincidence, Dina."

"It could be, but I was trained to never believe in coincidences. And so were you."

"What happened to the operation against Malik?"

"He slipped through our fingers, the same way he slipped away from the Americans in Baghdad. Uzi considered putting Arwish under surveillance, but that turned out not to be necessary. Three days after Malik disappeared, the body of Kemel Arwish was found in the desert east of Damascus. He'd been granted a relatively painless death."

"Malik had him killed?"

"Maybe it was Malik, maybe it was Rashid. It doesn't much matter. Arwish was a small fish in a big pond. He'd played the role assigned to him. He'd delivered a message, and after that, he became a liability."

Gabriel appeared unconvinced. "What else have you got?"

"The design of the suicide belts worn by the *shahid*s in Paris, Copenhagen, and London," she said. "They were identical to the type of belt Malik used for his attacks during the Second Intifada, which were in turn identical to the type he used in Baghdad."

"The design didn't necessarily have to come from Malik. It could have been floating around the sewers of the jihadist underworld for years."

"There's no way Malik would have put that design up on the Internet for the world to see. The wiring, the fusing, the shaping of the charge, and the shrapnel are all his innovations. He's practically *telling* me that it's him."

Gabriel was silent. Dina raised an eyebrow and asked, "No more comments about coincidences?"

Gabriel ignored the remark. "What was his last known location?"

"There were some unconfirmed reports he was back in Zarqa, and our station chief in Turkey heard a nasty rumor he was living in grand fashion in Istanbul. The rumor turned out to be false. As far as the Office is concerned, Malik is a ghost."

"Even a ghost needs a passport."

"We believe he's carrying a Syrian passport that was personally given to him by the great reformer in Damascus. Unfortunately, we have no idea what name he's using or what he looks like. The last known photograph of Malik was taken more than twenty years ago. It's useless."

"Is there someone close to Malik that we can get to? A relative? A friend? An old comrade from his days in Hamas?"

"We tried when Malik was bombing the daylights out of us during the Second Intifada," Dina said, shaking her head. "There are no al-Zubairs left in Israel or the territories, and the ones in the camp at Zarqa are far too committed to the struggle to collaborate with us." She paused for a moment. "We might have one thing working in our favor, though."

"What's that?"

"I think his network might be running out of money."

"Says who?"

Dina pointed toward a photograph of Farid Khan, the Covent Garden bomber.

"Says him."

18

GEORGETOWN, WASHINGTON, D.C.

N THE FINAL WEEKS OF his brief but portentous life, Farid Khan, murderer of eighteen innocent souls in the land of his birth, left a series of increasingly desperate postings on an Islamic Internet message board lamenting the fact he didn't have enough money to buy a proper wedding present for his sister. Apparently, he was considering skipping the wedding to avoid embarrassment. But there was just one problem with the story, Dina pointed out. Allah had blessed the Khan family with four boys, but no girls.

"I believe he was referring to a martyrdom payment—a payment he'd been promised by Malik. That's the Hamas way. Hamas always looks after the posthumous financial needs of its *shahid*s."

"Did he ever get the money?"

"A week before the attack, he made one final posting saying that he had been granted the means to buy his sister a gift. He would be able to attend the wedding after all, thanks be to Allah."

"So Malik eventually kept his word."

"That's true, but only after his *shahid* threatened not to go ahead with the mission. The network might have enough cash on hand to fund another round of attacks, but if Rashid and Malik are going to become the next Bin Laden and Zawahiri—"

"They're going to need an infusion of working capital."

"Exactly."

Gabriel stepped forward and gazed at Dina's galaxy of names, phone numbers, and faces. Then he turned to Lavon and asked, "How much do you think it would take to create a new jihadist terror group with a truly global reach?"

"Twenty million should do it," Lavon replied. "Maybe a bit more if you want to give them first-class accommodations and travel."

"That's a lot of money, Eli."

"Terror doesn't come cheap." Lavon gave Gabriel a sidelong look. "What are you thinking?"

"I'm thinking we have two choices. We can sit here staring at our telephone and e-mail matrixes, hoping a piece of actionable intelligence falls into our lap, or . . ." Gabriel's voice trailed off.

"Or what?"

"Or we can go into the terrorism business ourselves."

"And how would we do that?"

"We give them the money, Eli. We give them the money."

There are two basic types of intelligence, Gabriel needlessly reminded his team. There is human intelligence, or "humint" in the jargon of the trade, and signals intelligence, also known as "sigint." But the ability to track the flow of money in real time through the global banking system had given spies a powerful third form of intelligence gathering sometimes referred to as "finint," or financial intelligence. For the most part, finint was highly reliable. Money didn't lie; it simply went where it was told to go. What's more, the electronic trail of intelligence left by its movements was predictive in nature. The Islamic terrorists had learned long ago how to deceive Western spy agencies with false chatter, but rarely did they invest precious financial resources in deception. Money usually went to real operatives who were engaged in real plots. Follow the money, said Gabriel, and it would illuminate the intentions of Rashid and Malik like the lights of an airport runway.

But how to go about doing it? That was the question Gabriel and his team wrestled over for the remainder of that long and sleepless night. A clever forgery? No, insisted Gabriel, the jihadist world was far too insular for that. If the team tried to create a wealthy Muslim benefactor out of whole cloth, the terrorists would plop him in front of a camera and saw off his head with a butter knife. The money would have to come from someone with unimpeachable jihadist credentials. Otherwise, the terrorists would never accept it. But where to find someone who straddled both sides of the divide? Someone who would be regarded by the jihadists as genuine and yet would still be willing to work on behalf of Israeli and American intelligence. Call the Old Man, Yaakov suggested. In all likelihood, he would have a name at the tip of his nicotine-stained fingers. And if he didn't, he would surely know where to find one.

As it turned out, Shamron did have a name, which he murmured into Gabriel's ear, via secure telephone, a few minutes after four a.m. Washington time. Shamron had been watching this person for many years. The approach would be fraught with risk for Gabriel, both personal and professional, but Shamron had in his file drawers a substantial amount of evidence to suggest it might be received in a positive manner. He took the idea to Uzi Navot, and within minutes, Navot signed off on it. And thus, with a stroke of Navot's ludicrous gold pen, the return of Gabriel Allon, the wayward son of Israeli intelligence, was made complete.

The members of the Barak team had engaged in many profound arguments over the years, yet none would ever rival the one that took place within the walls of the house on N Street that morning in December. Chiara dismissed the idea as a dangerous flight of fancy; Dina called it a waste of precious time and resources that would surely come to nothing. Even Eli Lavon, Gabriel's closest friend and ally, was glum about the prospects for success. "It will turn out to be our version of Rashid," he said. "We'll congratulate ourselves on our cleverness. Then, one day, it will blow up in our face."

Much to everyone's surprise, it was Sarah who came to Gabriel's defense. Sarah knew Shamron's candidate far better than the others, and Sarah believed in the power of redemption. "She's not her father's daughter," Sarah said. "She's different. She's trying to change things."

"That's true," said Dina, "but that doesn't mean she would ever agree to work with us."

"The worst thing she can do is say no."

"Maybe," said Lavon gloomily. "Or maybe the worst thing she can do is say *yes*."

19

VOLTA PARK, WASHINGTON, D.C.

G ABRIEL WAITED UNTIL SUNRISE BEFORE phoning Adrian Carter. Carter was already on his way to Langley, the first stop of a brutally long day. It included a morning of closed-door testimony on Capitol Hill, a midday luncheon with a delegation of visiting spies from Poland, and, lastly, a counterterrorism strategy session in the White House Situation Room, chaired by none other than James McKenna. Shortly after six that evening, exhausted and dispirited, Carter alighted from his armored Ford Escalade on Q Street and, in semidarkness, entered Volta Park. Gabriel waited on a bench near the tennis courts, coat collar up against the cold. Carter sat next to him. The armored SUV rumbled at idle in the street, discreet as a beached whale.

"Do you mind?" asked Carter, fishing his pipe and tobacco pouch from his coat pocket. "It's been a rough afternoon."

"McKenna?"

"Actually, the president decided to grace us with his presence, and I'm afraid he didn't care for what I had to say." Carter seemed to apply all his considerable powers of concentration to the task of loading his pipe. "I've had the privilege of being dressed down by four presidents during my service to this great country of ours. It's still never a pleasant experience."

"What's the problem?"

"The NSA is picking up a great deal of chatter suggesting another attack might be imminent. The president demanded to know the precise details, including the location, timing, and the weapon involved. When I couldn't answer, he became annoyed." Carter ignited his pipe, briefly illuminating his drawn features. "Twelve hours ago, I might have been willing to dismiss the chatter as insignificant. But now that I know we're up against Malik al-Zubair, I'm not so optimistic."

"When counterterrorism officers feel optimism, innocent people usually end up dead."

"Are you always so cheerful?"

"It's been a long few days."

"How sure is Dina that it's really him?"

Gabriel recited the basic elements of her case: his failed attempt to secure Bin Laden's backing, the meeting at Kemel Arwish's apartment in Amman, and the unique design of Malik's suicide belts. Carter demanded no more evidence. He had acted on far less in the past, and he had been expecting this for a long time. Malik was the type of terrorist Carter feared the most. Malik and Rashid working together was his worst nightmare come to life.

"For the record," he said, "no one inside the CTC has made any connection yet between Rashid and Malik. Dina got there first."

"She usually does."

"So what does one do with such information when one is in my position? Does one give it to the analysts toiling in the bowels of the CTC? Does one tell his director and his president?"

"One keeps it to himself, lest one blow my operation to pieces."

"What operation is that?"

Gabriel rose and led Carter across the park to a second bench overlooking the playground. Leaning close to Carter's ear, he outlined the plan while a childless swing squeaked faintly in the gentle breeze.

"This smells like Ari Shamron to me."

"With good reason."

"What do you have in mind? An anonymous donation to the Islamic charity of your choice?"

"Actually, we were thinking about something a bit more targeted in nature."

"A direct donation to Rashid's coffers?"

"Something like that."

Wind moved in the trees surrounding the playground, unleashing a downpour of leaves. Carter brushed one from his shoulder and said, "It will take too much time."

"Patience is a virtue, Adrian."

"Not in Washington. We like to do things in a hurry."

"Do you have a better idea?"

With his heavy silence, Carter made clear he didn't. "It's interesting," he conceded. "Better still, it's devious as hell. If we can actually become the primary source of funding for Rashid's network . . ."

"Then we would *own* them, Adrian."

Carter rapped his pipe against the side of the bench and slowly reloaded the bowl. "Let's not get carried away just yet. This conversation is totally moot unless you can convince a well-to-do Muslim with jihadist street cred to work with you."

"I never said it would be easy."

"But you obviously have a candidate in mind."

Gabriel glanced toward the basketball court where a member of Carter's security detail was pacing slowly.

"What's wrong?" Carter asked. "You don't trust me?"

"It's not you, Adrian. It's the eight hundred thousand other people in your intelligence community who have top-secret clearances."

"We still know how to compartmentalize information."

"Tell that to your friends and allies who allowed you to put black sites on their soil. I'm sure you promised them the program would remain secret. But it didn't. In fact, it was splashed across the front page of the *Washington Post*."

"Yes," Carter said morosely, "I seem to remember reading something about that."

"The person we have in mind comes from a country with close ties to yours. If it ever became known that this individual was working on our behalf . . ." Gabriel's voice trailed off. "Let's just say the damage would not be limited to an embarrassing newspaper story. People would die, Adrian."

"At least tell me what you're planning next."

"I need to look up a friend in New York."

"Anyone I know?"

"Only by reputation. She used to be a hotshot investigative reporter for the *Financial Journal* in London. Now she's working for CNBC."

"We have a rule against using reporters."

"But *we* don't. And as we both know, this is an Israeli operation."

"Just watch your step up there. We don't want you ending up on the evening news."

"Any other helpful advice?"

"The chatter we've been picking up might be harmless or deceptive," Carter said, rising to his feet. "But then again . . . it might not be."

He turned away without another word and headed back to his Escalade, trailed by the security man. Gabriel remained on the bench, watching the childless swing moving in the wind. After a few minutes, he left the park and walked south down the gentle slope of Thirty-fourth Street. A pair of motorcycles ridden by slender men in black helmets roared past and disappeared into the darkness. Just then, an image flashed in Gabriel's memory—a distraught raven-haired woman, kneeling over the body of her father on the Quai Saint-Pierre in Cannes. The sound of the motorcycles dissipated, along with the memory of the woman. Gabriel thrust his hands into his coat pockets and walked on, thinking of nothing at all, as the trees wept leaves of gold.

20

THE PALISADES, WASHINGTON, D.C.

T THAT SAME MOMENT, a car pulled to the curb in front of a clapboard house located in the Washington neighborhood known as the Palisades. The car, a Ford Focus, was owned by Ellis Coyle of the CIA, as was the clapboard house. A tiny structure, more cottage than home, it had pushed Coyle's finances to the breaking point. After many years overseas, he had wanted to settle down in one of the affordable suburbs of northern Virginia, but Norah had insisted on living in the District in order to be closer to her practice. Coyle's wife was a child psychologist, an odd career choice, he always thought, for a woman whose barren womb had yielded no young. Her idyllic commute, a pleasant four-block stroll along MacArthur Boulevard, stood in stark contrast with Coyle's twice-daily crossing of the Potomac River. For a while, he had tried listening to New Age music to calm his nerves but found it made him only angrier. These days, it was books on tape. He had recently completed

Martin Gilbert's masterpiece on Winston Churchill. In fact, due to repair work on Chain Bridge, it had taken him scarcely a week. Coyle had always admired Churchill's decisiveness. Lately, Coyle had been decisive, too.

He switched off the engine. He was forced to park on the street because the home for which he had paid close to a million dollars had no garage. He had hoped the cottage would serve as a beachhead in the District, a starter home that he could use to trade up for a larger property in Kent or Spring Valley or perhaps even Wesley Heights. Instead, he had watched in frustration as prices spiraled far beyond the reach of his government salary. Only the wealthiest of Washington's residents—the bloodsucking lawyers, the corrupt lobbyists, the celebrity journalists who ran down the Agency at every turn—could afford mortgages in those neighborhoods now. Even in the Palisades, the quaint wooden cottages were being torn down and replaced by mansions. Coyle's neighbor, a successful lawyer named Roger Blankman, had recently built himself an Arts and Crafts monstrosity that cast a long shadow into Coyle's formerly sunlit breakfast nook. Blankman's ill-mannered children routinely strayed onto Coyle's property, as did his army of landscapers, who were constantly making small improvements to the shape of Coyle's junipers and hedges. Coyle returned the favor by poisoning Blankman's impatiens. Coyle believed in the efficacy of covert action.

Now he sat motionless behind the wheel, staring at the light burning in his kitchen window. He could imagine the scene that would be played out next, for it changed little from night to night. Norah would be sitting at the kitchen table with her first glass of Merlot, leafing through the mail and listening to some dreadful program on public radio. She would give him a distracted kiss and remind him that Lucy, their black Labrador retriever, needed to be taken out for her nightly constitutional. The dog, like the house in the Palisades, had been Norah's idea, yet it had somehow become Coyle's task to oversee its bowel movements. Lucy usually found inspiration in Battery Kemble Park, a hillside of thick woods that was best avoided by unaccompanied women. Sometimes, when Coyle was feeling particularly rebellious, he would leave Lucy's feces in the park rather than carry it home. Coyle committed other acts of rebellion as well—acts that he kept secret from Norah and his colleagues at Langley.

One of his secrets was Renate. They had met a year earlier in the bar of a Brussels hotel. Coyle had come from Langley to attend a gathering of Western counterterrorism officials; Renate, a photographer, had come from Hamburg to take pictures of a human rights campaigner for her magazine. The two nights they spent together were the most passionate of Ellis Coyle's life. They saw each other again three months later, when Coyle invented an excuse to travel to Berlin at taxpayer expense, and again a month after that, when Renate came to Washington to shoot a gathering at the World Bank. Their lovemaking reached new levels, as did their affection for one another. Renate, who was single, pleaded with him to leave his wife. Coyle, his face streaming with tears, said he wanted nothing more. He required just one thing. It would take a bit of time, he told her, but it would not be difficult. Coyle had access to secrets—secrets that he could spin into gold. His days at Langley were numbered. So, too, were the nights he would return to Norah and their little cottage in the Palisades.

He stepped out of the car and headed inside. Norah was wearing a dowdy pleated skirt, heavy stockings, and a pair of half-moon glasses that Coyle found singularly unbecoming. He accepted her lifeless kiss and replied, "Yes, of course, dear," when she reminded him that Lucy needed to be walked. "And don't be long, Ellis," she said, frowning at the electric bill. "You know how lonely I get when you're away."

Coyle used the techniques taught to him by the Agency to smother his guilt. Stepping outside, he was treated to the sight of Blankman guiding his enormous Mercedes into the second bay of his three-car garage. Lucy growled low in her throat before pulling Coyle in the direction of MacArthur Boulevard. On the opposite side of the wide street was the entrance to the park. A brown wooden sign warned that bicycles were forbidden and that dogs had to remain leashed at all times. At the base of the sign, partially obscured by a clump of weeds, was a chalk mark. Coyle removed Lucy's leash and watched her bound freely into the park. Then he rubbed out the mark with the toe of his shoe and followed.

PART TWO

THE
INVESTMENT

21

NEW YORK CITY

A REMARKABLY ACCURATE ACCOUNT OF THE worrisome new terrorist chatter appeared the next morning in the *New York Times*. Gabriel read the story with more than passing interest on the Amtrak Acela from Washington to New York. His seatmate, a Washington political consultant, spent the entire journey shouting into her mobile phone. Every twenty minutes, a policeman in paramilitary garb strode through the carriage with a bomb-sniffing dog. It seemed the Department of Homeland Security had finally come to realize the trains of Amtrak were rolling terrorist catastrophes waiting to happen.

A prickly rain greeted Gabriel as he emerged from Penn Station. Nevertheless, he spent the next hour hiking the streets of Midtown Manhattan. At the corner of Lexington Avenue and East Sixty-third Street, he saw Chiara peering into the window of a shoe store, a mobile phone pressed to her right ear. Had she been holding it to her left, it would have meant Gabriel was under surveillance. The right meant he was clean and that it was safe to proceed to the target.

He walked across town to Fifth Avenue. Dina was perched on the stone wall bordering Central Park, a black-and-white *kaffiyeh* around her neck. A few paces farther south, Eli Lavon was buying a soft drink from a street vendor. Gabriel brushed past him without a word and headed toward the used-book stalls at the corner of East Sixtieth Street. An attractive woman stood alone at one of the trestle tables, as though killing a few minutes before an appointment. She kept her gaze downward for several seconds after Gabriel's arrival, then looked at him for a long moment without speaking. She had dark hair, olive-complected skin, and wide brown eyes. A thin smile animated her face. Not for the first time, Gabriel had the uncomfortable feeling he was being studied by a figure from a painting.

"Was it really necessary for me to take the bloody subway?" Zoe Reed asked resentfully in her posh London accent.

"We had to make certain you weren't being followed."

"I assume by your presence I'm not."

"You're clean."

"What a relief," she said archly. "In that case, you can take me to the Pierre for a drink. I've been on the air since six this morning."

"I'm afraid your face is far too well known for that. You've become quite the star since coming to America."

"I was always a star," she replied playfully. "It just doesn't count unless you're on television."

"I hear you're getting your own show."

"Prime time, actually. It's supposed to be witty news chat with an emphasis on global affairs and business. Perhaps you'd like to appear on the debut program." She lowered her voice and added conspiratorially, "We can finally tell the world how we brought down the Iranian nuclear program together. It has all the elements of a blockbuster. Boy meets girl. Boy seduces girl. Girl steals boy's secrets and gives them to the Israeli secret service."

"I don't think anyone would find it credible."

"But that's the beauty of American cable news, darling. It doesn't have to be credible. It just has to be entertaining." She brushed a drop of rain from her cheek, then asked, "To what do I owe this honor? Not another security review, I hope."

"I don't do security reviews."

"No, I don't suppose you do." She picked up a novel from the table and turned the cover toward Gabriel. "Ever read him? His character is a bit like you—moody, egotistical, but with a sensitive streak women find irresistible."

"That one's more to my taste," he said, pointing toward a battered Rembrandt monograph.

Zoe laughed. "Please let me buy it for you."

"It won't fit in my carry-on. Besides, I already own a copy."

"Of course you do." She returned the novel to its place and with feigned casualness glanced up Fifth Avenue. "I see you brought along two of your little helpers. I believe you referred to them as Max and Sally when we were at the safe house in Highgate. Not the most realistic cover names, if you ask me. Better suited to a pair of Welsh corgis than two professional spies."

"There is no safe house in Highgate, Zoe."

"Ah, yes, I remember. It was all just a bad dream." She managed a fleeting smile. "Actually it wasn't *all* bad, was it, Gabriel? In fact, it went quite smoothly until the end. But that's the way it is with affairs of the heart. They always end disastrously and someone always gets hurt. Usually, it's the girl."

She picked up the Rembrandt monograph and leafed through

the pages until she came to a painting called *Portrait of a Young Woman*. "What do you suppose she's thinking?" she asked.

"She's curious," replied Gabriel.

"About what?"

"About why a man from her recent past has reappeared without warning."

"Why has he?"

"He needs a favor."

"The last time he said that, it almost got her killed."

"It's not that kind of favor."

"What is it?"

"An idea for her new prime-time cable news program."

Zoe closed the book and returned it to the table. "She's listening. But don't try to mislead her. Remember, Gabriel, she's the one person in the world who knows when you're lying."

The rain ended as they entered the park. They drifted slowly past the Delacorte clock, then made their way to the foot of Literary Walk. For the most part, Zoe listened in studied silence, interrupting only to challenge Gabriel or to clarify a point. Her questions were posed with the intelligence and insightfulness that had made her one of the world's most respected and feared investigative reporters. Zoe Reed had made just one mistake during her celebrated career—she had fallen in love with a glamorous Swiss businessman who, unbeknownst to her, was selling restricted nuclear materials to the Islamic Republic of Iran. Zoe had atoned for her sins by agreeing to join forces with Gabriel and his allies in British and American intelligence. The result of the operation was an Iranian nuclear program in ruins.

"So you inject cash into the network," she said, "and with a bit of luck, it moves through the bloodstream until it arrives at the head."

"I couldn't have put it any better myself."

"Then what happens?"

"You cut off the head."

"What does that mean?"

"I suppose that depends entirely on the circumstances."

"Don't bullshit me, Gabriel."

"It could mean the arrest of important members of the network, Zoe. Or it could mean something more definitive."

"Definitive? What an elegant euphemism."

Gabriel paused before the statue of Shakespeare but said nothing.

"I won't be a party to a killing, Gabriel."

"Would you rather be a party to another massacre like the one in Covent Garden?"

"That's beneath even you, my love."

With a dip of his head, Gabriel conceded the point. Then he took Zoe by the elbow and led her down the walkway.

"You're forgetting one important thing," she said. "I agreed to work with you and your friends on the Iran case, but that doesn't mean I've forsaken my values. At my core, I remain a rather orthodox left-wing journalist. As such, I believe it is essential that we combat global terrorism in ways that don't compromise our basic principles."

"That sort of pithy comment sounds wonderful from the safety of a television studio, but I'm afraid it doesn't work that way in the real world." Gabriel paused, then added, "You do remember the real world, don't you, Zoe?"

"You still haven't explained what any of this has to do with me."

"We would like you to make an introduction. All you have to

do is start the conversation. Then you recede quietly into the background, never to be seen again."

"Hopefully with my head still attached." She was joking, but only a little. "Is it anyone I know?"

Gabriel waited for a pair of lovers to pass before speaking the name. Zoe stopped walking and raised an eyebrow.

"Are you serious?"

"You know better than to ask a question like that, Zoe."

"She's one of the richest women in the world."

"That's the point."

"She also happens to be notoriously press shy."

"She has good reason to be."

Zoe started walking again. "I remember the night her father was killed in Cannes," she said. "According to the press accounts, she was at his side when he was gunned down. The witnesses say she held him as he was dying. Apparently, it was bloody awful."

"So I've heard." Gabriel glanced over his shoulder and saw Eli Lavon walking a few paces behind, a Moleskine notebook under his right arm, looking like a poet in search of inspiration. "Did you ever look into it?"

"Cannes?" Zoe narrowed her eyes. "I scratched around the edges."

"And?"

"I was never able to come up with anything firm enough to take to print. The running theory in London financial circles was that he was killed as a result of some kind of internal Saudi feud. Apparently, there was a prince involved, a low-level member of the royal family who'd had several run-ins with European police and hotel staff." She looked at Gabriel. "I suppose you're going to tell me there was more to the story."

"There are things I can tell you, Zoe, and things I cannot. It's for your own protection."

"Just like last time?"

Gabriel nodded. "Just like last time."

A few paces ahead, Chiara sat alone on a bench. Zoe managed not to look at her as they passed. They walked a little farther, to the Wisteria Pergola, and huddled beneath the latticework. As the rain started up again, Gabriel explained exactly what he needed Zoe to do.

"What happens if she gets angry and decides to tell my bosses I'm working on behalf of Israeli intelligence?"

"She has far too much to lose to pull a stunt like that. Besides, who would ever believe such a wild accusation? Zoe Reed is one of the world's most respected journalists."

"There's a certain Swiss businessman who might not agree with that statement."

"He's the least of our worries."

Zoe lapsed into a thoughtful silence, which was interrupted by the pinging of her BlackBerry. She fished it from her handbag, then stared at the screen in silence, her face distraught. A few seconds later, Gabriel's own BlackBerry vibrated in his coat pocket. He managed to keep a blank expression on his face as he read it.

"Looks like it wasn't harmless chatter after all," he said. "Do you still think we should fight these monsters in ways that don't compromise your core values? Or would you like to return briefly to the real world and help us save innocent lives?"

"There's no guarantee she'll even take my call."

"She will," Gabriel said. "Everyone does."

He asked for Zoe's BlackBerry. Two minutes later, after downloading a file from a Web site claiming to offer discount travel to the Holy Land, he returned it.

"Conduct all your negotiations using this device. If there's something you need to say to us directly, just say it near the phone. We'll be listening all the time."

"Just like last time?"

Gabriel nodded. "Just like last time."

Zoe slipped the BlackBerry into her handbag and rose. Gabriel watched as she walked away, followed by Lavon and Chiara. He sat alone for several minutes, reading the first news bulletins. It appeared as though Rashid and Malik had just taken another step closer to America.

Ashes, ashes, we all fall down.

22

MADRID-PARIS

THE OLD COMPLACENCY HAD RETURNED to Madrid, but this was to be expected. It had been seven years since the deadly train bombings, and memories of that terrible morning had long since faded. Spain had responded to the massacre of its citizens by withdrawing its troops from Iraq and launching what it described as "an alliance of civilizations" with the Islamic world. Such action, said the political commentators, had succeeded in redirecting Muslim rage from Spain to America, where it rightly belonged. Submission to the wishes of al-Qaeda would protect Spain from another attack. Or so they thought.

The bomb exploded at 9:12 p.m., at the intersection of two busy streets near Puerta del Sol. It had been assembled at a rented garage in an industrial quarter south of the city and concealed in a Peugeot van. Owing to its ingenious construction, the initial force of the blast was directed leftward into a restaurant popular with Spanish governing elites. There would be no firsthand account of precisely what occurred inside, for no one lived to describe it. Had there been a survivor, he would have recounted a brief but terrible instant of airborne bodies adrift in a lethal cloud of glass, cutlery, ceramic, and blood. Then the entire building collapsed, entombing the dead and dying together beneath a mountain of shattered masonry.

The damage was greater than even the terrorist had hoped. Façades were ripped from apartment buildings for an entire block, exposing lives that, until a few seconds earlier, had been proceeding peacefully. Several nearby shops and cafés suffered damage and casualties while the small trees lining the street were shorn of their leaves or uprooted entirely. There were no visible remnants of the Peugeot van, only a large crater in the street where it once had been. For the first twenty-four hours of the investigation, the Spanish police were convinced the bomb had been detonated remotely. Later, they discovered traces of the *shahid*'s DNA sprayed amid the ruins. He was just twenty, an unemployed Moroccan carpenter from the Lavapiés district of Madrid. In his suicide video, he spoke fondly of Yaqub al-Mansur, the twelfth-century Almohad caliph known for his bloody raids into Christian lands.

It was against this dreadful backdrop that Zoe Reed of the American business news network CNBC placed her first call to the publicity department of AAB Holdings, formerly of Riyadh and Geneva, lately of the Boulevard Haussmann, in the ninth arrondissement of Paris. The time was ten past four in the afternoon, the weather in Paris predictably overcast. The inquiry received no immediate response, per standing AAB protocol.

Annually cited by *Forbes* magazine as one of the most successful and innovative investment firms in the world, the company was founded in 1979 by Abdul Aziz al-Bakari. Known to friends and detractors alike as Zizi, he was the nineteenth son of a prominent

Saudi merchant who had served as the personal banker and financial adviser to Ibn Saud, the Kingdom's founder and first absolute monarch. AAB's holdings were as extensive as they were lucrative. AAB did shipping and mining. AAB did chemicals and drugs. AAB had major stakes in American and European banks. AAB's real estate and hotel division was one of the world's largest. Zizi traveled the world on a gold-plated 747, owned a string of palaces stretching from Riyadh to the French Riviera to Aspen, and sailed the seas on a battleship-sized yacht called the *Alexandra*. His collection of Impressionist and Modern art was thought to be among the largest in private hands. For a short period, it included *Marguerite Gachet at Her Dressing Table* by Vincent van Gogh, purchased from Isherwood Fine Arts, 7–8 Mason's Yard, St. James's, London. The sale had been brokered by a young American named Sarah Bancroft, who went on to serve, briefly, as Zizi's primary art consultant.

He was the target of many rumors, particularly regarding the source of his enormous fortune. AAB's glossy prospectus claimed it had been built entirely from the modest inheritance Zizi received from his father, a claim that an authoritative American business journal, after a careful investigation, found wanting. AAB's extraordinary liquidity, it said, could be explained by only one thing: it was being used as a front for the House of Saud to quietly reinvest its petrodollars around the world. Outraged by the article, Zizi threatened to sue. Later, on the advice of his lawyers, he had a change of heart. "The best revenge is living well," he told a reporter from the *Wall Street Journal*. "And that is something I know how to do."

Perhaps, but the handful of Westerners who were granted entrée into Zizi's inner circle always sensed a certain restlessness in him. His parties were lavish affairs, yet Zizi seemed to take no pleasure in them. He neither smoked nor drank alcohol and refused to be in the presence of dogs or pork. He prayed five times a day; each winter, when the rains made the Saudi desert bloom, he retreated to an isolated encampment in the Nejd to meditate and hunt with his falcons. He claimed to be a descendant of Muhammad Abdul Wahhab, the eighteenth-century preacher whose austere, puritanical version of Islam became the official creed of Saudi Arabia. He built mosques around the world, including several in America and Western Europe, and gave generously to the Palestinians. Firms looking to do business with AAB knew better than to send a Jew to meet with Zizi. According to the rumor mill, Zizi liked Jews even less than he liked losses on his investments.

As it turned out, Zizi's charitable activities extended far beyond what was publicly known. He also gave generously to charities associated with Islamic extremism and even directly to al-Qaeda itself. Eventually, he crossed the thin but bright line separating the financiers and enablers of terrorism from the terrorists themselves. The result was an attack on the Vatican that left more than seven hundred people dead and the dome of Saint Peter's Basilica in ruins. With Sarah Bancroft's help, Gabriel hunted down the man who planned the attack—a renegade Saudi intelligence officer named Ahmed Bin Shafiq—and killed him in a hotel room in Istanbul. A week later, on the Quai Saint-Pierre in Cannes, he killed Zizi, too.

Despite his adherence to Saudi traditions, Zizi had but two wives, both of whom he had divorced, and a single child—a beautiful daughter named Nadia. She buried her father in the Wahhabi tradition, in an unmarked desert grave, and immediately consolidated her hold on his assets. She moved AAB's European headquarters from Geneva, which bored her, to Paris, where she was more comfortable. A few of the firm's more pious employees refused to work for a woman—especially one who shunned the veil and consumed alcohol—but most stayed on. Under Nadia's guiding hand, the company entered previously uncharted territories. She acquired a famous French fashion company, an Italian maker of luxury leather goods, a substantial portion of an American investment bank, and a German motion picture production company. She also made significant changes to her personal holdings. Her father's many homes and estates were quietly put up for sale, as was the *Alexandra* and his 747. Nadia now traveled on a more modest Boeing Business Jet and owned just two homes—a graceful mansion on the Avenue Foch in Paris and a lavish palace in Riyadh that she rarely saw. Despite her lack of formal business training, she had proved to be an adept and skillful manager. The total value of the assets now under AAB's control was higher than at any point in company history, and Nadia al-Bakari, at just thirty-three, was regarded as one of the richest women in the world.

AAB's media relations, such as they were, fell under the purview of Nadia's executive assistant, a well-preserved Frenchwoman of fifty named Yvette Dubois. Madame Dubois rarely bothered to acknowledge requests from reporters, especially those employed by American companies. But upon receiving a follow-up call from the famous Zoe Reed, she decided a response was in order. She allowed another day to elapse, then, for good measure, she placed the call in the middle of the night, New York time, when she assumed Ms. Reed would be sleeping. For reasons not known to Madame Dubois, that turned out not to be the case. The conversation that followed was cordial but hardly promising. Madame Dubois explained that the offer of a one-hour prime-time special, while flattering, was entirely beyond the realm of possibility. Ms. al-Bakari was traveling constantly and had several large deals pending. More to the point, Ms. al-Bakari simply didn't do the kind of interview Ms. Reed had in mind.

"Will you at least give her the request?"

"I'll give it to her," the Frenchwoman said, "but the chances are not good."

"But not zero?" Zoe asked, probing.

"Let's not play little word games, Ms. Reed. They're beneath us."

Madame Dubois's concluding remark produced an outburst of much-needed laughter at Château Treville, an eighteenth-century French manor house located north of Paris, just beyond the village of Seraincourt. Shielded from prying eyes by twelve-foot walls, it had a heated swimming pool, two clay tennis courts, thirty-two acres of manicured gardens, and fourteen ornate bedrooms. Gabriel had rented it in the name of a German high-tech firm that existed only in the imagination of an Office corporation lawyer and promptly sent the bill along to Ari Shamron at King Saul Boulevard. Under normal circumstances, Shamron would have balked at the exorbitant price tag. Instead, with no small amount of pleasure, he forwarded the bill to Langley, which had assumed responsibility for all operational expenses.

For the next several days, Gabriel and his team spent most of their time monitoring the feed from Zoe's BlackBerry, which was now functioning as a tireless little electronic spy in her pocket. They knew her precise latitude and longitude, and, when she was in motion, they knew the speed at which she was traveling. They knew when she was buying her morning coffee at Starbucks, when she was stuck in New York traffic, and when she was annoyed with her producers, which was often. By monitoring her Internet activity, they knew she was planning to remodel her Upper West Side apartment. By reading her e-mail, they knew she had many romantic suitors, including a millionaire bond trader who, despite heavy losses, somehow found the time to drop her at least two missives a day. They sensed, in spite of all her success, that Zoe was not altogether happy in America. She whispered coded greetings to them often. At night, her sleep was made restless by nightmares.

To the rest of the world, however, she projected an air of cool indomitability. And to the select few who were privileged to witness her seduction of the French publicist, she provided yet more proof that she was the greatest natural spy any of them had ever encountered. Her tradecraft was a textbook combination of sound technique matched with unyielding persistence. Zoe flattered, Zoe cajoled, and, at the end of one particularly contentious phone call, Zoe even managed a few tears. Even so, Madame Dubois proved to be more than a worthy opponent. After a week, she declared the negotiations at an impasse, only to reverse course two days later by unexpectedly sending Zoe a detailed questionnaire. Zoe completed the document in perfect French and returned it the following morning, at which point Madame Dubois adopted a posture of radio silence. At Château Treville, Gabriel's team lapsed into an uncharacteristic despair as several precious days slipped past with no further contact. Only Zoe was optimistic. She had been through many such seductions in the past and knew when the hook had been set. "I've got her, darling," she murmured to Gabriel late one night, as the BlackBerry was recharging on her bedside table. "It's only a question of when she capitulates."

Zoe's prediction proved correct, though the Frenchwoman would allow an additional twenty-four hours to elapse before announcing her conditional surrender. It came in the form of a grudging invitation. It seemed that, owing to an unexpected cancellation, Ms. al-Bakari was free for lunch in two days' time. Would Ms. Reed be willing to make the trip to Paris on such short notice? The consummate professional, Zoe waited ninety annoying minutes before returning the call and accepting.

"Let me be clear about one thing," Madame Dubois said. "This is not an interview. The luncheon will be completely off the record. If Ms. al-Bakari feels comfortable in your presence, she will consider taking the next step."

"Where shall I meet her?"

"As you might expect, Ms. al-Bakari finds it difficult to conduct business in restaurants. We've taken the liberty of booking the Louis XV Suite at the Hôtel de Crillon. She's expecting you at one-thirty. Ms. al-Bakari insists on paying. It's one of her rules."

"Does she have any others I should know about?"

"Ms. al-Bakari is sensitive about questions concerning the death of her father," Madame Dubois said. "And I wouldn't dwell on the subject of Islam and terrorism. She finds it terribly boring. *À tout à l'heure*, Ms. Reed."

23

PARIS

I N THE AFTERMATH, THE TEAM would recall the period of preparation that came next as among the most unpleasant they had ever endured. The cause was none other than Gabriel, whose brittle mood cast a pall over the rooms of Château Treville. He quibbled over the placement of observation posts, second-guessed backup plans, and even briefly considered requesting a change of venue. Under normal circumstances, the team would not have hesitated to push back, but they could sense that something about the operation had set Gabriel on edge. Dina reckoned it was Covent Garden and the terrible memories of the shot not taken, a theory that was dismissed by Eli Lavon. It was not London that weighed on Gabriel's mind, Lavon explained, but Cannes. Gabriel had violated a personal canon that night; he had killed Zizi in front of his daughter. Zizi al-Bakari, financier of mass murder, had deserved to die. But Nadia, his only child, had not been obliged to witness it.

Only Zoe Reed remained shielded from Gabriel's bout of bad

temper. She spent an unhurried final day in New York, then, at five-thirty that afternoon, boarded Air France Flight 17 bound for Paris. An experienced traveler, she carried only a small overnight bag and a briefcase containing her notebook computer and research packet, which included a file of highly classified material, along with a detailed briefing paper on strategy for the luncheon. The items were handed to Zoe shortly after takeoff by her seatmate, an operative from the Office's New York station, and were collected again shortly before landing.

Still in possession of a British passport, Zoe breezed through customs in the EU express line and took a car service into the city center. It was approaching nine when she arrived at the Crillon; after checking into her room, she changed into a tracksuit and went for a run along the footpaths of the Jardin des Tuileries. At eleven thirty, she presented herself at an exclusive salon next to the hotel for a wash and blow-dry, then returned to her room to dress for lunch. She departed her room early and was standing in the elegant lobby, hands clasped to conceal a bout of nerves, as the stately grandfather clock tolled quarter past the hour.

It was the quiet time of the year at the Crillon, the annual ceasefire between the running battle of the summer season and the celebrity-strewn ambush of the winter holidays. Monsieur Didier, the chief concierge, stood behind his barricade, gold half-moon reading glasses perched at the end of his regal nose, looking like the last man on earth anyone would ask for assistance. Herr Schmidt, the imported German day manager, stood a few feet away at reception, holding a telephone to his ear, while Isabelle, the special events coordinator, fussed with orchids in the sparkling entrance hall. Her efforts went largely unnoticed by the bored-looking Arab businessman sitting near the elevators and by the pair of lovers huddled over their café crèmes in the cold shadows of the interior courtyard. The businessman was actually an employee of AAB's generously staffed security department. The lovers were Yaakov and Chiara. The hotel staff believed them to be an agreeable couple from Montreal who had popped into Paris on short notice to comfort a friend going through a messy divorce.

As the clock struck the bottom of the hour, Isabelle drifted over to the doorway and peered expectantly into the leaden Paris afternoon. Zoe glanced into the courtyard and saw Yaakov tapping a book of matches on the tabletop. It was the prearranged signal indicating that the motorcade—two S-Class Mercedes sedans for the hired help and a Maybach 62 for Her Highness—had departed AAB's building on the Boulevard Haussmann and was en route to the hotel. At that moment, the cars were actually stuck in traffic along the narrow rue de Miromesnil. Once free of the obstruction, it took just five minutes for them to reach the entrance of the Crillon, where Isabelle, flanked by the better-looking half of the bell staff, now stood. The undercover AAB security man was no longer feigning boredom. He was now hovering at Zoe's shoulder, making little effort to conceal the fact he was armed.

Outside, six car doors opened in unison, and six men, all former members of the elite Saudi National Guard, emerged. One was familiar to Gabriel and the rest of the team: Rafiq al-Kamal, the burly former chief of Zizi al-Bakari's personal security detail, who now served in the same capacity for his daughter. It was al-Kamal who had conducted the advance sweep of the hotel earlier that morning. And it was al-Kamal who now walked a subservient step behind Nadia as she flowed from the back of her Maybach into the lobby where Zoe stood with a porcelain smile fixed upon her face and her heart beating against her breastbone.

There exist in the file rooms of King Saul Boulevard many photos of a younger version of Nadia, or, as Eli Lavon was fond of saying, Nadia before the fall. Zoe had been given access to some of the more illustrative shots during the flight from New York. They showed a petulant woman in her mid-twenties, darkly beautiful, spoiled, and superior. She was a woman who smoked cigarettes and drank alcohol behind her father's back and who, in violation of Muhammad's teachings, bared her flesh on some of the world's most glamorous beaches. Her father's death had straightened Nadia's carriage and lent a serious light to her face, yet it had robbed her of none of her beauty. She wore a radiant dress of winter white, with her dark hair hanging straight between her shoulder blades like a satin cape. Her nose was long and straight. Her eyes were wide and nearly black. Pearls lay against the caramel-colored skin of her neck. A thick gold bracelet sparkled on her slender wrist. Her scent was an intoxicating blend of jasmine, lavender, and the sun. Her hand, when it closed around Zoe's, was as cool as marble.

"It's such a pleasure to finally meet you," Nadia said in an accent that betrayed no origin other than unfathomable wealth. "I've heard so much about your work."

She smiled for the first time, a cautious effort that did not quite extend to her eyes. Zoe felt slightly claustrophobic in the enclosure of the bodyguards, but Nadia conducted herself as though she were unaware of their presence.

"I'm sorry to make you come all the way to Paris on such short notice."

"Not at all, Ms. al-Bakari."

"Nadia," she said, her smile genuine now. "I insist you call me Nadia."

Al-Kamal appeared anxious to move the party out of the lobby, as did Madame Dubois, who was rocking slightly from heel to toe. Zoe suddenly felt an unseen hand on her elbow nudging her toward the elevators. She squeezed into a cramped carriage next to

Nadia and her bodyguards and had to turn her shoulders slightly in order for the door to close. The scent of jasmine and lavender in the confined space was mildly hallucinogenic. On Nadia's breath was the faintest trace of the last cigarette she had smoked.

"Do you come to Paris often, Zoe?"

"Not as often as I used to," she answered.

"You've stayed at the Crillon before?"

"Actually, it's my first time."

"You really must allow me to pay for your room."

"I'm afraid that's not possible," Zoe said with a gracious smile.

"It's the least I can do."

"It would also be unethical."

"How so?"

"It could create the appearance that I'm accepting something of value in return for a favorable news piece. My company forbids it. Most journalistic enterprises do, at least the reputable ones."

"I didn't realize there was such a thing."

"A reputable journalistic enterprise?" Zoe offered a confiding smile. "One or two."

"Including yours?"

"Including mine," said Zoe. "In fact, I would feel much more comfortable if you would allow me to pay for lunch."

"Don't be silly. Besides," Nadia added, "I'm sure the famous Zoe Reed would never allow herself to be influenced by a nice lunch in a Paris hotel."

They passed the rest of the journey in silence. When the doors of the elevator finally rattled open, al-Kamal surveyed the vestibule before leading Zoe and Nadia briskly into the Louis XV Suite. The classical French furnishings in the sitting room had been rearranged to create the impression of an elegant private dining room. Before the tall windows overlooking the Place de la Concorde was a round table set for two. Nadia surveyed the room with approval before snuffing out the single candle burning amid the crystal and silver. Then, with a movement of her dark eyes, she invited Zoe to sit.

There ensued a somewhat farcical few moments of unfurling napkins, closing doors, furtive glances, and murmured exchanges— some in French, some in Arabic. Finally, at Nadia's insistence, the security men retreated into the corridor, accompanied by Madame Dubois, who was visibly uneasy about the prospect of leaving her boss alone with the famous reporter. The sommelier poured a few drops of Montrachet into Nadia's glass. Nadia pronounced it satisfactory, then looked at Zoe's BlackBerry, which was resting on the table like an uninvited guest. "Would you mind turning that off?" she asked, attempting to make light of the request. "One can never be too careful these days when it comes to electronic devices. You never know who might be listening."

"I understand completely," said Zoe.

Nadia returned her glass to the table and said, "I'm sure you do."

Were it not for the miniature transmitter carefully concealed in the hotel suite, those four words, at once innocent and ominous, might have been the last heard by the man of medium height and build pacing the rooms of a château north of Paris. Instead, with a few keystrokes on his notebook computer, the audio feed resumed with only a brief interruption. In the courtyard of the Crillon, the couple from Montreal departed, replaced by two women in their mid-thirties. One had sandstone-colored hair and childbearing hips; the other had dark hair and walked with a slight limp. She pretended to read a glossy Paris fashion magazine. It helped to quiet the clock ticking relentlessly in her head.

24

PARIS

S OME RECRUITMENTS ARE LIKE SEDUCTIONS, some border on extortion, and still others are like a ballet of the wounded. But even Ari Shamron, who had haunted the secret world far longer than most, would later say that he had never witnessed anything quite like the recruitment of Nadia al-Bakari. Having listened to the opening act over a secure link at King Saul Boulevard, he declared it one of the most masterful pieces of fieldwork he had ever heard. It was especially high praise given that the person doing the recruiting hailed from a profession for which Shamron had nothing but contempt.

Gabriel had instructed his recruiter to go slowly, and go slowly she did. For the first hour of the encounter, as hushed waiters entered and departed the hotel suite, Zoe questioned Nadia respectfully on the many changes she had made to AAB's investment profile and on the challenges posed by the global recession without end. Much to Gabriel's surprise, the reclusive Saudi heiress turned out to be an engaging and forthright conversationalist who seemed far wiser than her thirty-three years. Indeed, there was not a trace of tension until Zoe nonchalantly asked Nadia how often she traveled to Saudi Arabia. The question produced the first uncomfortable silence of the encounter, just as Gabriel had expected it would. Nadia regarded Zoe for a moment with her bottomless dark eyes before responding with a question of her own.

"You've been to Saudi Arabia?"

"Once," replied Zoe.

"For your work?"

"Is there any other reason for a Westerner to go to Saudi Arabia?"

"I suppose not." Nadia's expression softened. "Where did you go?"

"I spent two days in Riyadh. Then I went to the Empty Quarter to tour the new Saudi Aramco oil-drilling project at Shaybah. It was very impressive."

"Actually, you described it as 'a technological marvel that will ensure Saudi domination of the global oil market for at least another generation.'" Nadia gave a fleeting smile. "Do you really think I would agree to a meeting without first reviewing your work? After all, you do have something of a reputation."

"For what?"

"Ruthlessness," said Nadia without hesitation. "They say you have something of a puritanical streak. They say you like to destroy companies and executives who step out of line."

"I don't do that kind of work any longer. I'm on television now. We don't investigate. We just talk."

"You don't miss being a *real* journalist?"

"By that you mean a print journalist?"

"Yes."

"Occasionally," Zoe admitted, "but then I look at my bank account and I feel much better."

"Is that why you left London? For money?"

"There were other reasons."

"What kind of reasons?"

"The kind I generally don't discuss in professional settings."

"It sounds as though it had something to do with a man," Nadia said, her tone conciliatory.

"You're very perceptive."

"Yes, I am." Nadia reached for her wineglass but stopped. "I don't go to Saudi Arabia often," she said suddenly, "once every three or four months, no more. And when I do go, I don't stay for long."

"Because?"

"For the reasons you would expect." Nadia appeared to choose her next words with great care. "The laws and customs of Islam and Saudi Arabia are old and very important to our society. I've learned how to navigate the system in a way that allows me to conduct my business with a minimum of disruption."

"What about your countrywomen?"

"What about them?"

"Most aren't as lucky as you are. Women in Saudi Arabia are considered property, not people. Most spend their lives locked away indoors. They're not permitted to drive an automobile. They're not permitted to go out in public without a male escort and without first concealing themselves beneath an *abaya* and a veil. They're not permitted to travel, even inside the country, without receiving permission from their fathers or older brothers. Honor killings are permissible if a woman brings shame upon her family or engages in un-Islamic behavior, and adultery is a crime punishable by stoning. In the birthplace of Islam, women cannot even enter a mosque except in Mecca and Medina, which is odd, since the Prophet Muhammad was something of a feminist. 'Treat your women well and be kind to them,' the Prophet said, 'for they are your partners and committed helpers.' "

Nadia picked at an invisible flaw in the tablecloth. "I admire your honesty, Zoe. Most journalists trying to secure an important interview would resort to platitudes and flattery."

"I can do that, if you prefer."

"Actually, I prefer honesty. We don't have enough of that in Saudi Arabia. In fact, we avoid it at all costs." Nadia turned her gaze toward the windows. Outside, it was dark enough so that her image was reflected ghostlike in the glass. "I never realized you were so interested in the condition of Muslim women," she said softly. "There's no evidence of it in your previous work."

"How much of it did you read?"

"All of it," said Nadia. "There were many stories about corrupt businessmen but not one about the plight of Muslim women."

"I'm interested in the rights of *all* women, regardless of their faith." Zoe paused, then added provocatively, "I would think that someone in your position would be interested in them as well."

"Why would you think such a thing?"

"Because you have the power and influence to be an important role model."

"I run a large company, Zoe. I don't have the time or desire to involve myself in politics."

"You don't have any?"

"Any what?"

"Politics."

"I am a citizen of Saudi Arabia," Nadia said. "We have a king, not politics. Besides, in the Middle East, politics can be very dangerous."

"Was your father killed because of politics?" Zoe asked cautiously.

Nadia turned and gazed at Zoe. "I don't know why my father was killed. I'm not sure anyone does, other than his murderers, of course."

A heavy silence fell between them. It was broken a few seconds later by the sound of a door opening. A pair of waiters entered, bearing trays of coffee and pastries. They were followed by Rafiq al-Kamal, the chief of security, and Madame Dubois, who was tapping the face of her Cartier wristwatch as if to say the meeting had gone on long enough. Zoe feared Nadia might latch onto the signal as an excuse to take her leave. Instead, she ordered the intruders from the room with an imperious wave of her hand. She did the same for the waiter holding the tray of pastries, but accepted the coffee. She drank it black with an extraordinary amount of sugar.

"Are these the kinds of questions you propose to ask me on camera? Questions about the rights of women in Saudi Arabia? Questions about the death of my father?"

"We don't divulge the questions in advance of an interview."

"Come, come, Zoe. We both know how this works."

Zoe made a brief show of thought. "If I failed to ask you about your father, I would be brought up on charges of journalistic malpractice. It makes you a deeply compelling figure."

"What it makes me is a woman without a father." Nadia removed a packet of Virginia Slims from her handbag and ignited one with a rather ordinary-looking gold lighter.

"You were there that night in Cannes?"

"I was," said Nadia. "One minute we were all enjoying a wonderful evening in our favorite restaurant. The next I was holding my father as he lay dying in the street."

"You saw the men who killed him?"

"There were two," she said, nodding her head. "They rode motorcycles, very fast, very skillfully. At first, I thought they were just French boys having a bit of fun on a warm summer night. Then I saw the weapons. They were obviously professionals." She drew on her cigarette and exhaled a slender stream of smoke toward the ceiling. "After that, everything is a blur."

"There were reports that witnesses heard you screaming for revenge."

"I'm afraid that retribution is the Bedouin way," Nadia said sadly. "I suppose it runs in my blood."

"You admired your father," Zoe pressed.

"I did," Nadia said.

"He was an art collector."

"A voracious one."

"I understand you share your father's passion."

"My art collection is private," Nadia said, reaching for her coffee.

"Not as private as you think."

Nadia looked up sharply but said nothing.

"My sources tell me that you made an important acquisition last month. They tell me that you were the one who paid the record price for the Rothko at Christie's in New York."

"Your sources are mistaken, Zoe."

"My sources are *never* mistaken. And they've told me other things about you as well. Apparently, you're not as indifferent to the rights of women in the Islamic world as you pretend to be. You've quietly given millions of dollars to combat violence against women and millions more to promote female entrepreneurship, which you believe will have the effect of empowering Muslim women as never before. But your charitable works don't stop there. I'm told you've used your fortune to promote free and independent media in the Arab world. You've also attempted to counter the spread of dangerous Wahhabi ideology by donating to organizations that promote a more tolerant version of Islam." Zoe paused. "Taken together, your activities paint a portrait of a courageous woman who is singlehandedly trying to change the face of the modern Middle East."

Nadia managed a dismissive smile. "It's an intriguing story," she said after a moment. "It's a shame none of it is true."

"That's too bad," Zoe replied, "because there are people who would like to help you."

"What sort of people?"

"People of discretion."

"In the Middle East, people of discretion are either spies or terrorists."

"I can assure you they're not terrorists."

"So they must be spies then."

"I wasn't told their affiliation."

Nadia gave her a skeptical look. Zoe held out a card. It had no name, only the number of her BlackBerry.

"This is my private number. It is important that you proceed with caution. As you know, there are people around you who do not share your goal of changing the Islamic world for the better—including your own bodyguards."

"What is your interest in this matter, Zoe?"

"I have no interest, other than obtaining an interview with a woman I greatly admire."

Nadia hesitated. Then she accepted the card and slipped it into her handbag. At that instant, the door of the hotel suite opened again and Madame Dubois entered with Rafiq al-Kamal at her side. She was once again tapping her wristwatch. This time, Nadia rose. Looking suddenly fatigued, she extended her hand toward Zoe.

"I'm not sure I'm ready to lift the veil just yet," she said, "but I'd like some time to consider your offer. Would it be possible for you to remain in Paris for a few days?"

"It will be a terrible hardship," Zoe said jokingly, "but I'll try to manage."

Nadia released Zoe's hand and followed her security chief into the corridor. Zoe remained behind for a moment longer before returning to her room three floors below. There she powered on her BlackBerry and called her producer in New York to explain that she would be staying on in Paris to continue the negotiations. Then she placed the BlackBerry on the bedside table and sat for a long time at the end of her bed. She smelled jasmine and lavender, the scent of Nadia, and recalled the instant of their parting. Nadia's hand had been oddly cold to the touch. It was the hand of fear, thought Zoe. The hand of death.

25

SERAINCOURT, FRANCE

ZOE'S CALL TO NEW YORK sounded in the high-ceilinged rooms of Château Treville like a fanfare of trumpets. Gabriel responded by immediately dispatching a secure cable to Adrian Carter, whereupon AAB Holdings and its owner, Nadia al-Bakari, became the target of NSA surveillance. It meant that Carter now knew the name of the wealthy Muslim with unimpeachable jihadist credentials whom Gabriel wanted to fund Rashid's network. It also meant that, at any given moment, several dozen other members of the sprawling American intelligence community knew it, too. It was a risk Gabriel had no choice but to take. Israel's signals intelligence service was formidable, but its capabilities paled in comparison to those of the NSA. America's mastery of the digital world was unrivaled. It was the human factor—the ability to recruit spies and to penetrate the courts of their enemies—that eluded the Americans, and for that they had turned to the Office.

At Gabriel's request, Carter went to great lengths to conceal Nadia's name from the rest of official Washington. Despite the obvious potential implications for American-Saudi relations, he neglected to mention it to either the president or James McKenna at the weekly White House counterterrorism meeting. He also took care to safeguard the identity of the party who would be reviewing the NSA intercepts. They were sent first to Carter's personal attention at Langley and then routed to the CIA station in Paris. The deputy chief, a man who owed his career to Carter, drove them personally to the grand manor house at Seraincourt, where they were signed over to Sarah Bancroft. Of particular interest to Gabriel and the team was the telephone and e-mail account of Rafiq al-Kamal, Nadia's chief of security. Despite numerous calls placed to contacts inside the Saudi GID and Interior Ministry, al-Kamal never once mentioned the name Zoe Reed. That was not true, however, of Madame Dubois, who spent much of the next seventy-two hours burning up the lines between Paris and London, searching for dirt and gossip in Zoe's professional past. Gabriel took this as an encouraging sign. It meant that, as far as AAB was concerned, the investigative reporter from CNBC was a public-relations problem, not a security threat.

Zoe remained blissfully unaware of the intrigue swirling around her. Following Gabriel's carefully prepared script, she refrained from further contact with AAB or its employees. To help fill the empty hours, she visited museums and took long walks along the Seine, which allowed Eli Lavon and the rest of the field operatives to determine that she was free of any surveillance. As two more days slipped past with no word from Nadia, Zoe's producer in New York began to grow impatient. "I want you back in the States on Monday at the latest," he told her by telephone, "with or without the exclusive. It's simply a question of money. Nadia has barrels full of it. We're pinching every penny."

The call darkened the mood at the Seraincourt safe house, as did the speech given by the French president that afternoon to an emergency session of the National Assembly. "It is not a question of whether France will be attacked by terrorists again," the president warned, "but only a question of when and where. It is a sad fact that more lives will be lost to the fires of extremism. Regrettably, this is what it means to be a citizen of Europe in the twenty-first century."

A few minutes after the speech ended, a message arrived from the Operations Desk at King Saul Boulevard. It was just four characters in length—two letters followed by two numbers—but its meaning was unambiguous. God was cooling his heels in a Montmartre safe flat. And God wanted a word with Gabriel in private.

26

MONTMARTRE, PARIS

THE APARTMENT HOUSE STOOD ON the rue Lepic, not far from the cemetery. It was gray in color and seven floors in height, with wrought-iron balustrades and garret rooms across the top. A single leafless tree rose from the center courtyard and from the neat foyer spiraled a staircase with a well-worn runner that muffled Gabriel's footfalls as he ascended swiftly to the third floor. The door to apartment 3A hung slightly ajar; in the sitting room was an elderly man dressed in pressed khaki trousers, a white oxford cloth shirt, and a leather bomber jacket with an unrepaired tear in the left shoulder. He had settled himself at the edge of a brocade-covered wing chair with his legs slightly splayed and his large hands bunched atop the crook of his olive wood cane, like a traveler on a rail platform resigned to a long wait. Between two yellowed fingers burned the stub of a filterless cigarette. Acrid smoke swirled above his head like a private storm cloud.

"You're looking well," said Ari Shamron. "Being back in the field obviously agrees with you."

"It's not exactly how I'd planned to spend the winter."

"Then perhaps you shouldn't have followed a suicide bomber into Covent Garden."

Shamron gave a mirthless smile, then crushed out his cigarette in the ashtray on the coffee table. Six other stubs were already there, lined in a neat row, like bullets waiting to be loaded into a gun. He added the seventh and peered thoughtfully at Gabriel through the fog of smoke.

"It's good to see you, my son. I thought our meeting in Cornwall last summer was going to be our last."

"Actually, I was hoping it would be."

"Can you at least *pretend* to have some regard for my feelings?"

"No."

Shamron ignited another cigarette with his old Zippo lighter and purposely blew smoke in Gabriel's direction.

"How eloquent," said Gabriel.

"Words sometimes fail me. Fortunately, my enemies rarely do. And once again, they've managed to deliver you back into the arms of King Saul Boulevard, where you belong."

"Temporarily."

"Ah, yes," Shamron agreed with disingenuous haste. "By all means, this arrangement is purely temporary."

Gabriel went to the French doors overlooking the rue Lepic and opened one. A chill draft entered the room, bringing with it the sound of the evening traffic.

"Must you?" Shamron asked, frowning. "My doctor says I should avoid drafts."

"Mine says I should avoid secondhand smoke. Thanks to you, I have the lungs of a man who smokes forty cigarettes a day."

"At some point you're going to have to stop blaming me for everything that's gone wrong with your life."

"Why?"

"Because it's counterproductive."

"It also happens to be the truth."

"I've always found it best to avoid the truth. It invariably leads to unnecessary complications."

Gabriel closed the door, muting the sound of the traffic, and asked Shamron why he had come to Paris.

"Uzi thought you could use some extra help on the ground."

"Why didn't he tell me you were coming?"

"It must have slipped his mind."

"Does he even know you're here?"

"No."

Gabriel couldn't help but smile. "Let's try this one more time, Ari. Why are you in Paris?"

"I was worried."

"About the operation?"

"About you," Shamron said. "That's what it means to be a father. We worry about our children until the day we die."

"I'm afraid I wouldn't know anything about that."

"Forgive me, my son," Shamron said after a moment. "I should have known better. After all, that's my fault, too."

He pushed himself upright and, leaning heavily on his cane, moved into the kitchen. The components of a coffee press lay scattered across the countertop, along with an empty teakettle and an open bag of Carte Noir. Shamron made a feeble attempt to light the gas stove before raising his hands in a gesture of surrender. Gabriel nudged him toward the small café-style table and lifted the bag of coffee cautiously to his nose. It smelled like dust.

"Unless I'm mistaken," Shamron said, lowering himself into the chair, "it's the same coffee we drank the last time we were here."

"There's a market next door. Do you think you can survive alone until I get back?"

With a dismissive wave of his hand, Shamron indicated the coffee was good enough. Gabriel filled the teakettle with water and placed it on the stove to boil.

"There's still one thing I don't understand," Shamron said, watching him carefully.

"It's really not that complicated, Ari. First you pour in the coffee, then you add the water, then you push the little plunger."

"I was referring to Covent Garden. Why did you follow him? Why didn't you simply warn Graham Seymour and go back to your cottage by the sea?"

Gabriel made no response.

"Will you allow me to offer a possible explanation?"

"If you insist."

"You went after him because you knew full well the British had neither the courage nor the resolve to stop him on their own. Our European friends are in the midst of a full-blown existential crisis. I'm convinced it's one of the reasons they despise us. We have a purpose. We believe our cause is just. They believe in nothing except their thirty-five-hour workweek, their global warming, and their annual six-week vacation in the south. What boggles the mind is why you choose to live among them."

"Because once upon a time they actually believed in God, and their faith inspired them to paint like angels."

"That's true," Shamron said. "But faith in God now resides almost exclusively in the jihadis. Unfortunately, it's a faith that was born of Wahhabi intolerance and fed by Saudi money. After 9/11, the Saudis promised to put an end to the incitement that gave rise to Bin Laden and al-Qaeda. But now, just ten years later, Saudi money is once again fueling the hatred, with scarcely a word of protest from the Americans."

"They've managed to convince themselves that the Saudis are an important ally in the fight against terrorism."

"They're delusional," Shamron said. "But it's not entirely their fault. Oil isn't the only thing flowing from Saudi Arabia to the West. There's also a great deal of intelligence in the pipeline. The Saudi GID is constantly tipping off the CIA and the European services about potential plots and suspicious individuals. Occasionally, the tips contain actionable intelligence, but most of it is complete and utter crap."

"You're not *actually* suggesting," Gabriel said sardonically, "that Saudi intelligence is playing the same old double game of combating the jihadists while at the same time supporting them?"

"That's exactly what I'm suggesting. And the Americans are so economically weak at the moment they're in no position to do anything about it."

The teakettle began to hiss. Gabriel filled the press with boiling water and stood over it while waiting for the coffee to steep. He glanced at Shamron. The dour expression on his face made it abundantly clear he was still thinking about the Americans.

"Every American administration has its buzzwords. This one likes to speak in terms of *equity*. They're constantly reminding us of the *equity* they have invested across the Middle East. They have equity in Iraq, equity in Afghanistan, and equity in maintaining a stable price of oil. At the moment, we don't count for much on the American balance sheet. But if you succeed in neutralizing Rashid's network . . ."

"It might add a bit of much-needed equity to our account."

Shamron nodded grimly. "That doesn't mean, however, that we have to conduct ourselves like a wholly owned subsidiary of the CIA. In fact, the prime minister is adamant that we use this opportunity to take care of some unfinished business."

"Like Malik al-Zubair?"

Shamron nodded.

"Something tells me you knew Malik was involved in this from the beginning."

"Let's just say I had a strong suspicion that might be the case."

"So when Adrian Carter asked me to come to Washington—"

"I set aside my usual misgivings and agreed without hesitation."

"How generous of you," said Gabriel. "So why are you worried now?"

"Nadia."

"She was your idea."

"Maybe I was wrong. Maybe she's been fooling us all these years. Maybe she's more like her father than we think." He paused, then added, "Maybe we should cut her loose and find someone else."

"That person doesn't exist."

"So forge him," Shamron said. "I hear you're quite good at that."

"It's not possible, and you know it."

Gabriel carried the coffee to the table and poured out two cups. Shamron dumped sugar into his and stirred it thoughtfully for a moment.

"Even if Nadia al-Bakari agrees to work for you," Shamron

said, "you will have no means of keeping her under discipline. We have our traditional methods. *Kesef, kavod, kussit*—money, respect, sex. Nadia al-Bakari has no need for any of those things. Therefore, she cannot be controlled."

"Then I suppose we'll just have to trust each other."

"*Trust?*" Shamron asked. "I'm sorry, Gabriel, but I'm not familiar with that word." He drank some of his coffee and grimaced. "There's an old proverb that I'm particularly fond of. It says the veil that hides the future from us is woven by an angel of mercy. Unfortunately, there's no veil that can shield us from our past. It's filled with ghosts. The ghosts of loved ones. The ghosts of enemies. They're with us always. They're here with us now." His rheumy blue eyes searched the tiny kitchen for a moment before settling again on Gabriel. "Perhaps it's better to leave the past undisturbed. Better for Nadia. Better for you."

Gabriel examined Shamron carefully. "Am I mistaken, Ari, or are you actually feeling guilty about pulling me back in?"

"You made your wishes clear last summer in Cornwall. I should have respected them."

"You never did before. Why start now?"

"Because you've earned it. And the last thing you need at this stage of your life is a confrontation with the child of a man you killed in cold blood."

"I don't plan to confess my sins."

"You might not have a choice in the matter," Shamron said. "But promise me one thing, Gabriel. If you insist on using her, be certain you don't make the same mistake the Americans made with Rashid. Assume she is a mortal enemy and treat her accordingly."

"Why don't you join us? We have plenty of room at the safe house for one more."

"I'm an old man," Shamron said gloomily. "I'd just be in the way."

"So what are you going to do?"

"I'm going to sit here alone and worry. These days that seems to be my lot in life."

"Don't start worrying just yet, Ari. It's possible Nadia won't come."

"She'll come," Shamron said.

"How can you be so sure?"

"Because in her heart she knows that you are the one whispering in her ear. And she won't be able to resist the opportunity to have a look at your face."

Operational doctrine dictated that Gabriel return immediately to Château Treville, but anger obliged him to make a pilgrimage to the Champs-Élysées. He arrived shortly after midnight to find that all evidence of the bombing had been carefully erased. The shops and restaurants had been repaired. The buildings had been given new windows and a fresh coat of paint. The paving stones had been washed of the blood. There was no expression of outrage, no memorial to the dead, no plea for sanity in a world gone mad. Indeed, were it not for the pair of gendarmes standing watch over the street corner, it might have been possible to imagine that nothing disagreeable had ever occurred there. For a moment, Gabriel regretted his decision to come, but as he was leaving, a secure e-mail from the team at Seraincourt unexpectedly lifted his spirits. It said that Nadia al-Bakari, the daughter of a man whom Gabriel had killed in the Old Port of Cannes, had just been overheard canceling a trip to Saint Petersburg. Gabriel returned the

BlackBerry to his coat pocket and walked on through the lamp-light. The veil that hid his future had been torn in two. He saw a beautiful woman with raven hair crossing the forecourt of a château north of Paris. And an old man sitting alone in a Montmartre apartment, worrying himself to death.

27

PARIS

NADIA AL-BAKARI PERSONALLY TELEPHONED Zoe Reed at 10:22 a.m. the next morning to invite her to tea at her mansion on the Avenue Foch. Zoe politely declined. It seemed she already had plans.

"I'm spending the afternoon with an old friend from London. He made a pile of money in private equity and bought himself a château in the Val-d'Oise. I'm afraid he's throwing a small party in my honor."

"A birthday party?"

"How did you know?"

"My security staff conducted a discreet background check before our lunch at the Crillon. As of today you are thirty—"

"Please don't say it aloud. I'm trying to pretend it's just a bad dream."

Nadia managed to laugh. Then she asked the name of Zoe's friend from London.

"Fowler. Thomas Fowler."

"What firm is he with?"

"Thomas doesn't do firms. Thomas is militantly independent. Apparently, you met him a few years ago in the Caribbean. One of the French islands. Can't remember which. St. Barts, I think it was. Or maybe it was Antigua."

"I've never set foot on Antigua."

"So it must have been St. Barts."

There was silence.

"Did I lose you?" asked Zoe.

"No, I'm still here."

"Is something wrong?"

"Where did I meet him?"

"He said it was in a bar near one of the beaches."

"Which bar?"

"Not sure about that."

"Which beach?"

"Don't think Thomas mentioned it."

"Was Thomas alone that day?"

"Actually, he was with his wife. Lovely girl. Bit on the pushy side, but I suppose that comes with the territory."

"Which territory is that?"

"Being the wife of a billionaire like Thomas."

More silence, longer than the first.

"I'm afraid I don't remember him."

"He certainly remembers you."

"Describe him, please."

"Tallish chap. Built like a lamppost. A bit more interesting, once you get to know him. I think he did a deal a few years ago with an associate of your father."

"Do you happen to recall this associate's name?"

"Why don't you ask Thomas for yourself?"

"What are you saying, Zoe?"

On the second floor of Château Treville was a somber music room with walls covered in red silk and lavish window treatments to match. At one end of the room was a harpsichord with gilded moldings and a pastoral oil painting on the lid. At the other was an antique French Renaissance table with walnut inlay where Gabriel and Eli Lavon sat staring into a pair of computers. On one was a blinking light showing Zoe Reed's current location and altitude. On the other was a recording of the conversation she had conducted at 10:22 with Nadia al-Bakari. Ten times Gabriel and Lavon had listened to it. Ten times they could find no excuse not to proceed. It was now 11:55. Lavon frowned as Gabriel clicked the play icon one final time.

"Do you happen to recall this associate's name?"

"Why don't you ask Thomas for yourself?"

"What are you saying, Zoe?"

"I'm saying you should come to the party. I know Thomas would simply adore it, and it would give us a chance to spend some more time together."

"I'm afraid it wouldn't be appropriate."

"Why ever not?"

"Because your friend . . . forgive me, Zoe, but please tell me his name again."

"Thomas Fowler. Like the character in the Graham Greene novel."

"Who?"

"It's not important. What's important is that you come."

"I wouldn't want to be an imposition."

"You wouldn't be, for heaven's sake. Besides, it's my birthday, and I insist."

"Where exactly is your friend's home located?"

"Just north of Paris. The hotel's arranged a car for me."

"Tell the hotel to cancel it. We'll take my car instead. It will give us a chance to talk."

"Wonderful. Thomas says the dress code is château casual. But let's go light on the security, shall we? Thomas is a bit of a fanny patter, but he's otherwise quite harmless."

"I'll see you at noon, Zoe."

The call went dead. Gabriel clicked on the stop icon and then looked up to find Yossi leaning in the doorway, looking every inch the prosperous private equity mogul who was spending the weekend at his French country retreat. "For the record," he said in his lazy Oxford drawl, "I didn't appreciate the bit about a lamppost."

"I'm sure she meant it as a term of endearment."

"How would you feel if someone compared you to a lamppost?"

"Endeared."

Yossi smoothed the front of his Bond Street cashmere jacket. "Have we achieved château casual?"

"I believe we have."

"Ascot or no ascot?"

"No ascot."

"Ascot," said Lavon. "Definitely ascot."

Yossi went out. Gabriel reached for the computer mouse again, but Lavon stilled his hand.

"She knows it's us, and she's still coming. Besides," Lavon added, "it's too late to do anything about it now."

Gabriel looked at the other computer screen. The elevation reading on the icon indicated that Zoe was sinking slowly toward the lobby. This was confirmed a few seconds later when Gabriel heard the sound of the elevator doors opening, followed by the clatter of Zoe's heels as she headed across the lobby. She bade good day to Herr Schmidt, thanked Isabelle for the complimentary fruit basket that had been left in her room the previous evening, and blew a kiss to Monsieur Didier, who was at that moment attempting to secure a reservation at the Jules Verne for Chiara and Yaakov—a reservation which, regrettably, they would later be forced to cancel. Next came a burst of traffic noise as Zoe stepped outside, followed in turn by the heavy thud of a limousine door closing. The ensuing silence was coffinlike. It was broken by the pleasant voice of a woman with unimpeachable jihadist credentials.

"It's so lovely to see you again, Zoe," said Nadia al-Bakari. "I brought your friend a bottle of Latour as a château-warming gift. I hope he likes red."

"You shouldn't have."

"Don't be silly."

And with that, the icon was once again in motion, pursued by three other flashing beacons representing the surveillance teams. A moment later, they were all headed westward along the Champs-Élysées at a speed of thirty-three miles per hour. As they neared the Arc de Triomphe, Zoe offered to switch off her BlackBerry. "Don't bother," said Nadia quietly. "I trust you now, Zoe. No matter what happens, I will always consider you a friend."

28

SERAINCOURT, FRANCE

THE *BANLIEUES* OF NORTHEASTERN PARIS seemed to stretch for an eternity, but gradually the vulgar apartment blocks fell away and the first patches of green appeared. Even in winter, with the sky low and heavy, the French countryside looked as though it had been groomed for a family portrait. They roared through it in the black Maybach sedan with no escort vehicles, at least none that Zoe could see. Rafiq al-Kamal, the pumice-faced security chief, sat scowling in the front passenger seat. He wore his usual dark suit but, in deference to the informality of the occasion, no necktie. Nadia wore a rich cream-colored cashmere sweater, trim-fitting tan suede trousers, and low-heeled boots suitable for walking along wooded country lanes. To hide her nerves, she spoke without pause. About the French. About the appalling fashions that winter. About an article she had read in the *Financial Journal* that very morning regarding the deplorable financial straits of the Euro-zone economies. The heat inside the car was tropical. Zoe was perspiring beneath her clothing, but Nadia appeared slightly chilled. Her hands were curiously bloodless. Noticing Zoe's interest, she blamed it on the damp Parisian weather, of which she spoke without interruption until a road sign warned that they were approaching the village of Seraincourt.

At that instant, a motorcycle overtook them. It was a high-powered Japanese model of the sort that compelled the driver to lean forward at an uncomfortable-looking angle. He looked into Zoe's window as he passed, as though curious about the occupants of so fine an automobile, then made an obscene gesture at the driver before vanishing behind a cloud of road spray. *Hello, Mikhail*, thought Zoe. *So nice to see you again.*

She drew the BlackBerry from her handbag and dialed. The voice that answered was vaguely familiar. Of course it was, she reminded herself quickly. It belonged to her old friend Thomas Fowler from London. Thomas who made a bundle investing in God only knew what. Thomas who met Nadia a few years ago at a seaside bar in St. Barts. Thomas who was now giving Zoe directions to his showy new château—right on the rue de Vexin, left on the rue des Vallées, right on the Route des Hèdes. The gate was on the left side of the road, he said, just beyond the old vineyard. Never mind the warning sign about the dogs. It was just a bluff, for security's sake. Thomas was concerned about security. Thomas had good reason to be.

Zoe severed the connection and returned the BlackBerry to her handbag. Looking up again, she caught Rafiq al-Kamal eyeing her warily in his mirror. Nadia was gazing gloomily out her window at the passing countryside. *Smile*, thought Zoe. *We're going to a party, after all. It's important you try to smile.*

There was no formal precedent for what they were attempting to do, no established doctrine, no Office tradition upon which to draw. During the endless rehearsal sessions, Gabriel likened it to an unveiling, with Nadia as the potential buyer and Gabriel himself as the painting propped upon a display pedestal. The event would be preceded by a brief journey—a journey, he explained, that would take Nadia and the team from the present into the not-too-distant past. The nature of this trip would have to be carefully calibrated. It would have to be pleasant enough so as not to scare Nadia away, yet forceful enough to leave her no opportunity to turn back. Even Gabriel, who had devised the strategy, placed their chances of success at no better than one in three. Eli Lavon was still more pessimistic. But then Lavon, a student of biblical disasters, was a worrier by nature.

At that moment, though, the prospect of failure was the farthest thing from Lavon's thoughts. Bundled in several layers of wool, remnants of operations past, he was plodding along the grassy shoulder of the rue des Vallées, a walking stick in one hand, his head seemingly in the clouds. He paused briefly to stare at the passing Maybach limousine—to do otherwise would have been odd—but paid no attention to the little Renault hatchback that followed in the big sedan's wake like a poor relation. Behind the Renault the road was deserted, which is precisely what Lavon was hoping for. He lifted his hand to his mouth and, feigning a cough, informed Gabriel that the target was proceeding as instructed, with no surveillance other than that of the home team.

By then, the Maybach had already made the turn onto the Route des Hèdes and was sweeping past the old vineyard at flank speed. It ducked through the imposing front gate of the château, then headed up the long straight gravel drive, at the end of which stood Yossi in a pose of idleness only money could buy. He waited until the car had come to a stop before advancing slowly toward it, but froze when al-Kamal emerged in an aggressive black blur. The Saudi bodyguard stood beside the car for several seconds, his eyes flickering over the façade of the grand manor house, before finally opening the rear passenger door at a strict forty-five-degree angle. Nadia emerged slowly and in stages—a costly boot upon the gravel, a jeweled hand across the top of the door, a flash of silken hair that seemed to gather the remaining light of the afternoon.

For reasons Gabriel did not share with the others, he had decided to mark the occasion with a photograph, which resides in the file rooms of King Saul Boulevard to this day. Snapped by Chiara from a window on the second floor, it shows Nadia taking her first step across the forecourt with Zoe at her side, one hand stretched hesitantly toward Thomas Fowler, the other clutching the bottle of Latour by the neck. Her brow is already slightly furrowed, and in her eyes is the faintest flicker of recognition. It was true that she had once seen this man on the island of St. Barts, in a charming little patio bar overlooking the salt marshes of Saline. Nadia had been drinking daiquiris that day; the man, burned by the sun, had nursed a beer a few tables away. He had been accompanied by a scantily dressed woman with sandstone-colored hair and generous hips—the same woman who was now stepping from the front entrance of the house in clothing that matched Nadia's in cost and style. A woman who was now holding on to Nadia's hand as though she had no intention of ever letting go. "I'm Jenny Fowler," said Rimona Stern. "I'm so thrilled you're joining us. Please come inside before we all catch our death."

The first leg of Nadia's journey complete, they turned in unison and started toward the entrance of the house. The bodyguard briefly attempted to follow, but Nadia, in her first act of conspiracy, stilled him with a gesture of her hand and a few reassuring words of murmured Arabic. If she thought her hosts would not understand, she was mistaken; the Fowlers were both fluent Arabic speakers, as was the petite woman with dark hair waiting beneath the chandelier in the grand main foyer. Again Nadia's expression was one of distant recollection. "I'm Emma," said Dina Sarid. "I'm an old friend of the Fowlers. It's so nice to meet you."

Nadia grasped the outstretched hand, another stage of the journey complete, and allowed Dina to draw her into the vaulted great room. Standing before a row of French doors, her gaze fixed on the elaborate terraced garden, was a woman with pale blond hair and skin the color of alabaster. Hearing the sound of footsteps, the woman turned slowly and stared at Nadia for a long moment with expressionless blue eyes. She didn't bother to offer a false name. It wouldn't have been appropriate.

"Hello, Nadia," Sarah Bancroft said finally. "It's lovely to see you again."

Nadia recoiled slightly and seemed frightened for the first time. "My God," she said after a moment of hesitation. "Is it really you? I was afraid you were . . ."

"Dead?"

Nadia made no reply. Her eyes moved slowly from face to face before coming to rest on Zoe's.

"Do you know who these people are?"

"Of course."

"Do you work for them?"

"I work for CNBC in New York."

"So why are you here?"

"They need to talk to you. There was no other way."

Nadia appeared to accept the explanation, at least for the moment. Again her gaze moved around the room. This time, it settled on Sarah.

"What is this about?"

"It's about you, Nadia."

"What about me?"

"You're trying to change the Islamic world. We want to help."

"Who are you?"

"I'm Sarah Bancroft, the American girl who sold your father a painting by van Gogh. After that, he offered me a job as his personal art consultant. I went on your annual winter cruise in the Caribbean. Then I went away."

"Are you a spy?" Nadia asked, but Sarah made no reply other than to extend her hand. Nadia's journey was nearly complete. She had just one more stop to make. One last person to meet.

29

SERAINCOURT, FRANCE

SEPARATED FROM THE GRAND SALON by a pair of stately double doors was a smaller, less formal drawing room with book-lined walls and overstuffed furnishings arranged before a large stone fireplace. It was both comforting and conspiratorial, a place where kisses had been stolen, sins had been confessed, and secret alliances had been forged. Shown into the room by Sarah, Nadia had led herself on a distracted tour of the perimeter before settling at one end of a long couch. Zoe sat at the other end, as if for balance, and Sarah sat opposite, with her hands folded neatly in her lap and her gaze slightly averted. The other members of the team were scattered about in various states of repose, as if resuming the party that had been interrupted by Nadia's arrival. The one exception was Gabriel, who was standing before the unlit fire, one hand pressed to his chin, his head tilted slightly to one side. At that instant, he was trying to decide how best to answer a simple question that had been put to him by Nadia a few seconds after he had slipped into the room. Frustrated by his silence, she posed the question again now, this time with more force.

"Who are you?"

Gabriel removed the hand from his chin and used it to help with the introductions. "These are the Fowlers, Thomas and Jenny. Thomas makes money. Jenny spends it. That rather melancholy girl in the corner is Emma. She and Thomas are old friends. Actually, they were lovers once, and in her darker moments, Jenny suspects they're lovers still." He paused for a moment to place a hand on Sarah's shoulder. "And you remember this woman, of course. This is Sarah, our star. Sarah has more degrees than the rest of us put together. Despite a costly education, paid for in full by a guilty father, she was working at a down-at-heel art gallery in London a few years ago when your father came looking for a van Gogh, the one artist missing from his collection. He was so impressed by Sarah that he fired his longtime art consultant and offered her the job at several times her existing salary. The perks included an invitation to cruise the Caribbean aboard the *Alexandra*. As I recall, you were quite standoffish at first. But by the time you reached the enchanted isle of St. Barts, you and Sarah had become good friends. Confidantes, I would say."

Sarah acted as though she had heard none of it. Nadia examined her for a moment before turning back toward Gabriel.

"It was no accident that these four people all ended up on St. Barts at the same time. You see, Nadia, they are all professional intelligence officers. Thomas, Jenny, and Emma are employed by the foreign intelligence service of the State of Israel, as am I. Sarah works for the CIA. Her art expertise is quite genuine, which explains why she was selected for the operation against AAB Holdings. Your father was a secret philanthropist, just like you, Nadia. Unfortunately, his charity was directed to the opposite end of the

Islamic spectrum. He gave to the inciters, the recruiters, and directly to the terrorists themselves. When your father discovered the truth about Sarah, he handed her over to be tortured and killed. But then you already knew that, didn't you, Nadia? That's why you were so surprised to see that your friend Sarah was still very much among the living and looking none the worse for wear."

"You haven't told me your name yet."

"For the moment, my name is not important. I prefer to think of myself as a gatherer of sparks." He paused, then added, "Just like you, Nadia."

"I beg your pardon?"

"Some of our ancient rabbis believed that when God was creating the universe, He placed His divine light into special celestial containers. But it turns out Creation didn't go quite according to God's plan, and an accident occurred. The vessels were broken, and the universe became filled with sparks of divine light and shards of broken vessels. The rabbis believed the task of Creation wouldn't be complete until those sparks were gathered together. We call it Tikkun Olam, or Repair of the World. The people in this room are trying to repair the world, Nadia, and we believe that you are, too. You're trying to gather the shards of hatred that have been spread by Wahhabi preachers. You're trying to repair the damage caused by your father's support of terrorism. We applaud your efforts. And we want to help."

"How do you know all this about me?"

"Because we've been watching you for a long time."

"Why?"

"Prudence," said Gabriel. "After your father was killed in Cannes, we were afraid you would attempt to make good on your vow to avenge his death. And the last thing the world needed was another rich Saudi filling the pockets of terrorists with money. Our fears increased substantially when you quietly retained the services of a former Saudi GID officer named Faisal Qahtani to investigate the circumstances surrounding your father's death. Mr. Qahtani reported that your father had been killed by the Israeli secret service, with the blessing of the CIA and the American president. He then went on to give you chapter and verse on your father's long history of supporting the global jihadist movement." Gabriel paused. "I've always wondered which aspect of your father's life bothered you most, Nadia—that your father was a mass murderer, or that he lied to you. It can be very traumatic to learn that one has been misled by a parent."

Nadia made no response. Gabriel pressed forward.

"We know what Mr. Qahtani told you because he gave the same briefing to us for the very reasonable price of one hundred thousand American dollars, deposited into a numbered Swiss bank account." Gabriel permitted himself a brief smile. "Mr. Qahtani is a man with impeccable sources but suspect loyalties. He also has a fondness for beautiful women of the professional variety."

"Was the information accurate?"

"Which part?"

"The part about the Israeli secret service murdering my father with the blessing of the CIA and the American president."

Gabriel glanced at Zoe, who was doing an admirable job of concealing her curiosity. Now that her assignment was complete, she should have been quietly shown the door. But Gabriel had decided to allow her to remain in the room for now. His motives were purely selfish. He was acutely aware of the bond that had formed between his target and his agent of introduction. He was aware, too, that Zoe could be a powerful asset in helping to close the final deal. By her very presence, Zoe conferred legitimacy onto Gabriel's cause and nobility onto his intent.

"Murder is hardly the correct word to describe what happened to your father," he said. "But if you wouldn't mind, I would prefer to continue for a moment longer on the topic of our mutual acquaintance, the duplicitous Mr. Qahtani. He did more than simply compile a postmortem on your father's death. He also delivered a message from none other than the Saudi monarch himself. This message made it clear that certain elements of the House of Saud had known about your father's activities and had tacitly approved of them. It also made it clear that under no circumstances were you to take any retributive actions against Israeli or American targets. The House of Saud was under tremendous pressure from Washington at that time to end the Kingdom's support of extremist Islam and terrorism. The king didn't want you to cause any further complications between Riyadh and Washington."

"You were told this by Mr. Qahtani as well?"

"It was included in the original package, at no additional charge."

"Did Mr. Qahtani characterize my reaction?"

"He did," said Gabriel. "He said the warning from the House of Saud was probably needless because, in Mr. Qahtani's opinion, you had no intention of following through on your vow to avenge your father's death. What Mr. Qahtani didn't realize was that you were repulsed by what you learned about your father—so repulsed, in fact, that you became something of an extremist yourself. After consolidating your grip on AAB Holdings, you decided to use your father's fortune to undo the damage he had caused. You became a repairer of the world, a gatherer of sparks."

Nadia gave a dismissive smile. "As I said to your friend Zoe at lunch the other day, it's an interesting story, but it happens not to be true."

Gabriel sensed that her denial lacked conviction. He decided the best course of action was to ignore it completely.

"You're among friends, Nadia," he said gently. "Admirers, actually. Not only do we admire the courage of your work, but we are also in awe of the skill with which you've concealed it. In fact, it took us quite some time to figure out that you were using cleverly constructed art transactions to launder money and put it in the hands of people you were trying to help. As professionals, we salute your tradecraft. In all honesty, we couldn't have done it any better ourselves."

Nadia looked up sharply, but this time she offered no denial. Gabriel sailed on.

"As a result of your skillful dealings, you've managed to keep your work secret from Saudi intelligence and the al-Saud. It's a remarkable achievement, given the fact that you are surrounded day and night by your father's old employees and security men. At first we were puzzled by your decision to retain their services. In retrospect, the reasons are quite obvious."

"Are they?"

"You had no other choice. Your father was a wily businessman, but he didn't exactly come by his fortune honestly. The House of Zizi was bought and paid for by the House of Saud, which means the al-Saud could break you with a snap of their royal fingers."

Gabriel looked to Nadia for a reaction. Her face remained placid.

"It means you're playing a dangerous game," Gabriel continued. "You're using the monarch's money to spread ideas that could eventually threaten the monarch's grip on his throne. That makes you a subversive. A heretic. And we both know what happens to subversives and heretics who threaten the House of Saud. One way or another, they're eliminated."

"It doesn't sound as if you want to help me. In fact, it sounds as though you intend to blackmail me into doing your bidding."

"Our only interest is that your work continues. We would, however, like to give you one piece of advice."

"What sort of advice?"

"Investment advice," said Gabriel. "We think now might be a good time to make a few changes in your portfolio—changes that are more in keeping with your birthright as the one and only child of the late Zizi al-Bakari."

"My father was a financier of terrorism."

"No, Nadia, he wasn't just *any* financier of terrorism. Your father was unrivaled. Your father was Jihad Incorporated."

"Forgive me," Nadia said, "but I don't understand what you want from me."

"It's simple. We want you to follow in your father's footsteps. We want you to pick up the banner of jihad that fell from his grasp that terrible night in Cannes. We want you to avenge his death."

"You want *me* to become a terrorist?"

"Exactly."

"How would I do that?"

"By purchasing your own terrorist group. But don't worry, Nadia. You won't have to do it alone. Thomas and I are going to help you."

30

SERAINCOURT, FRANCE

THEY HAD COME TO A GOOD PLACE TO PAUSE—an oasis, thought Gabriel, who found himself suddenly bewitched by the iconography of the desert. The reason for Nadia's summons had been successfully broached. It was now time to rest for a few moments and to reflect upon the journey thus far. It was also time to deal with a bit of unpleasant business. Gabriel had a few questions that needed answering before they could continue—questions dealing with the tangled politics and ancient hatreds of the Middle East. He posed the first while crouching before the fireplace, an unlit match between his fingertips.

"How do you feel about us?" he asked, striking the match on the stonework.

"About Israelis?"

"About Jews," replied Gabriel, touching the match to the kindling. "Do you think we are children of the devil? Do you think we control the world's finances and media? Do you think we brought the Holocaust upon ourselves? Do you even believe the Holocaust happened? Do you think we use the blood of non-Jewish children to prepare our unleavened bread? Do you believe we are apes and pigs, as your Wahhabi clerics and Saudi textbooks like to portray us?"

"I didn't go to school in Saudi Arabia," said Nadia without a trace of defensiveness.

"No," said Gabriel, "you attended the most prestigious schools in Europe, just like your friend Sarah. And Sarah remembers quite clearly an incident on a beach in St. Barts when you said something quite unpleasant about a man you believed to be Jewish. She also recalls a fair amount of rough talk about Jews whenever your father and his entourage started discussing politics."

Nadia stared at Sarah with a trace of sadness, as though a confidence had been betrayed. "My father's opinions about Jews were well known," she said after a moment. "Unfortunately, I was exposed to those opinions on a daily basis, and my father's views briefly became my own." She paused and looked at Gabriel. "Have you never said something you wish you could take back? Have you never done anything for which you are deeply ashamed?"

Gabriel blew softly on the kindling but said nothing.

"I sit atop a fortune worth many billions of dollars," Nadia said. "So you'll probably not find it surprising that I don't believe Jews control the world's financial system. Nor do I believe they control the media. I do believe the Holocaust took place, that six million people perished, and that to deny its truth is an act of hate speech. I also believe the ancient blood libel to be just that, a libel, and I cringe each time I hear one of Saudi Arabia's so-called men of religion refer to Jews and Christians as apes and pigs." She paused. "Have I left anything out?"

"The devil," said Gabriel.

"I don't believe in the devil."

"And what about Israel, Nadia? Do you believe we have a right to live in peace? That we have a right to take our children to school or go to the market without fear of being blown to bits by a soldier of Allah?"

"I believe the State of Israel has a right to exist. I also believe it has a right to defend itself against those who seek to destroy it or to murder its citizens."

"And what do you think would happen if tomorrow we walked away from the West Bank and Gaza and granted the Palestinians their state? Do you think the Islamic world would ever accept us, or are we doomed to forever be regarded as an alien entity, a cancer that must be removed?"

"The latter, I'm afraid," said Nadia, "but I'm trying to help you. It might be nice if, from time to time, you didn't make things so difficult for me. Each and every day, in large ways and small, you humiliate the Palestinians and their supporters in the broader Islamic world. And when you mix humiliation with the ideology of the Wahhabis . . ."

"Bombs explode in the streets of Europe," said Gabriel. "But it takes more than just humiliation and ideology to produce terrorism on a global scale. It also takes money. The masterminds need money to inspire, money to recruit and train, and money to operate. With money, they can strike at will. Without it, they are nothing. Your father understood the power of money. So do you. That's why we went to so much trouble to speak with you, Nadia. That's why you're here."

Eli Lavon had slipped silently into the room and was watching the proceedings impassively from a perch along the windows. Nadia regarded him carefully for a moment, as if trying to place him in the cluttered drawers of her memory.

"Is he in charge?" she inquired.

"Max?" Gabriel shook his head slowly. "No, Max isn't in charge. I'm the one who's been cursed with the responsibility of command. Max is merely my guilty conscience. Max is my worried soul."

"He doesn't look worried to me."

"That's because Max is a professional. And like all professionals, Max is very good at concealing his emotions."

"Like you."

"Yes, like me."

She glanced at Lavon and asked, "What's bothering him?"

"Max thinks I've lost a step. Max is trying to prevent me from making what he thinks will be the biggest mistake of an otherwise unblemished career."

"What mistake is that?"

"You," said Gabriel. "I'm convinced you are the answer to my prayers, that we can work together in order to eliminate a grave threat to the security of the West and the Middle East. But as you can see, Max is much older than I am, and he's terribly set in his ways. He finds the idea of our partnership laughable and naïve. He believes that, as a Muslim woman from Saudi Arabia, you acquired your hatred of Jews with the milk of your mother's breast. Max is also convinced that you are, first and foremost, your father's daughter. And Max believes that, like your father, you have two faces—one you show to the West and another you show at home."

Nadia smiled for the first time. "Perhaps you should remind Max that I'm not allowed to show my face at home, at least not in public. And perhaps you should also remind Max that I risk my life every day trying to change that."

"Max is highly dubious about your philanthropic activities and the motivations behind them. Max believes they are a cover for your real agenda, which is much more in keeping with that of your late father. Max believes you are a jihadist. Simply put, Max believes you are a liar."

"Maybe *you* are the liar."

"I'm an intelligence officer, Nadia, which means I lie for a living."

"Are you lying to me now?"

"Just a little," said Gabriel contritely. "I'm afraid that crumpled little soul over there isn't really named Max."

"But he still believes I'm a liar?"

"He's hopeful that's not the case. But he needs to know that we're all on the same side before this conversation can continue."

"What side is that?"

"The side of the angels, of course."

"The same angels who murdered my father in cold blood."

"There's that word again, Nadia. Your father wasn't murdered. He was killed by enemy forces on a battlefield of his choosing. He died a martyr's death in the service of the great jihad. Unfortunately, the violent ideology he helped to propagate didn't die with him. It lives on in a crescent of sacred rage stretching from the tribal areas of Pakistan to the streets of London. And it lives on in a lethal new terror network based in the mountains of Yemen. This network has a charismatic leader, a skilled operational mastermind, and a cadre of willing *shahid*s. What it lacks is the one thing you can provide."

"Money," said Nadia.

"Money," repeated Gabriel. "The question is, are you really a woman who is singlehandedly trying to change the face of the modern Middle East, or are you actually your father's daughter?"

Nadia was silent for a moment. "I'm afraid you're going to have to decide that without my help," she said finally, "because as of this moment, this little interrogation session is officially over. If there is something you want from me, I suggest you tell me what it is. And I wouldn't wait too long. You might have questions about where I stand, but you should have none about the chief of my security detail. Rafiq al-Kamal is a true Wahhabi believer and very loyal to my father. And if I had to guess, he's starting to get a little suspicious about what's going on in here."

31

SERAINCOURT, FRANCE

THE TEAM FILED SLOWLY FROM the room—everyone but Eli Lavon, who remained at his perch near the windows, and Gabriel, who settled into the place vacated by Sarah. He gazed at Nadia for a moment in respectful silence. Then, in a somber voice borrowed from Shamron, he proceeded to tell her a story. It was the story of a charismatic Islamic cleric named Rashid al-Husseini, of a well-intentioned CIA operation gone terribly wrong, and of a lethal terror network that was starved of the operating capital it needed to achieve its ultimate goals. The briefing was remarkably complete—indeed, by the time Gabriel finally finished, the weak autumn sun had set and the room was in semidarkness. Lavon was by then a mere silhouette, indistinguishable except for the wisp of disheveled hair that surrounded his head like a halo. Nadia sat motionless at the end of the long couch, feet drawn beneath her, arms folded under her breasts. Her dark eyes stared unblinking into Gabriel's as he spoke, as though she were posing for a portrait. It was a portrait of an unveiled woman, thought Gabriel, oil on canvas, artist unknown.

From the adjacent room rose a swell of laughter. When it died away, there was music. Nadia closed her eyes and listened.

"Is that Miles Davis?" she asked.

"'Dear Old Stockholm,'" said Gabriel with a slow nod.

"I've always been very fond of Miles Davis, despite the fact that my father, as a devout Wahhabi Muslim, briefly attempted to prevent me from listening to music of any sort." She paused for a moment, still listening. "I'm also quite fond of Stockholm. Let us hope Rashid hasn't put it on his list of targets."

"A very wise man once told me that hope is not an acceptable strategy when lives are at stake."

"Perhaps not," said Nadia, "but hope is very much in vogue at the moment in Washington."

Gabriel smiled and said, "You still haven't answered my question, Nadia."

"Which question is that?"

"What was more painful? Learning that your father was a terrorist or that he had misled you?"

She stared at Gabriel with an unsettling intensity. After a moment, she removed the pack of Virginia Slims from her handbag, lit one, and then offered the pack to Gabriel. With a curt wave of his hand, he declined.

"I'm afraid your question displays a profound ignorance of Saudi culture," she said finally. "My father was highly Westernized, but he was still first and foremost a Saudi male, which meant he held my life in his hands, quite literally. Even in death, I was afraid of my father. And even in death, I never permitted myself to feel anything like disappointment in him."

"But you were hardly a typical Saudi child."

"That's true," she conceded. "My father granted me a great deal of freedom when we were in the West. But that freedom did not extend to Saudi Arabia or to our personal relationship. My father was like the al-Saud. He was the absolute monarch of our family. And I knew exactly what would happen if I ever stepped out of line."

"He threatened you?"

"Of course not. My father never spoke a cross word to me. He didn't have to. Women in Saudi Arabia know their place. From the time of their first menses, they're hidden away beneath a veil of black. And heaven help them if they ever bring dishonor upon the male who holds sway over them."

She was sitting slightly more erect now, as if mindful of her posture. The uncertain light of the fire had erased the first evidence of aging from her face. For now, she seemed the insolent, shockingly beautiful young woman whom they had first seen several years earlier floating across the paving stones of Mason's Yard. Nadia had been an afterthought during the operation against her father, an annoyance. Even Gabriel could not quite believe that the spoiled daughter of Zizi al-Bakari had been transformed into the elegant, thoughtful woman seated before him now.

"Honor is very important to the psyche of the Arab man," she continued. "Honor is everything. It was a lesson I learned quite painfully when I was just eighteen. One of my best friends was a girl named Rena. She came from a good family, not nearly as rich as ours, but prominent. Rena had a secret. She'd fallen in love with a handsome young Egyptian man she'd met in a Riyadh shopping mall. They were meeting secretly in the man's apartment. I warned Rena that she was playing a dangerous game, but she refused to stop seeing the man. Eventually, the *mutaween*, the religious police, caught her and the Egyptian together. Rena's father was so mortified he took the only course of action available to him, at least in his mind."

"An honor killing?"

Nadia nodded her head slowly. "Rena was bound in heavy chains. Then, with the rest of her family looking on, she was thrown into the swimming pool of her home. Her mother and sisters were forced to watch. They said nothing. They did nothing. They were powerless."

Nadia lapsed into silence. "When I found out what had happened," she said finally, "I was devastated. How could a father be so barbaric and primitive? How could he kill his own child? But when I asked my father those questions, he told me it was Allah's will. Rena had to be punished for her reckless behavior. It simply had to be done." She paused. "I never forgot how my father looked as he spoke those words. It was the same expression I saw on his face several years later when he was watching the collapse of the World Trade Center. It was a terrible tragedy, he said, but it was Allah's will. It simply had to be done."

"Did you ever suspect your father was involved in terrorism?"

"Of course not. I believed that terrorism was the work of the crazy jihadis like Bin Laden and Zawahiri, not a man like my father. Zizi al-Bakari was a businessman and an art collector, not a mass murderer. Or so I thought."

Her cigarette had burned down to a stub. She crushed it out and immediately lit another.

"But now, with the passage of enough time, I can see that there is a link between Rena's death and the murder of three thousand innocent people on 9/11. Each had a common ancestor—Muhammad Abdul Wahhab. Until his ideology of hatred is neutralized, there will be more terrorism and more women like Rena. Everything I do is for her. Rena is my guide, my beacon."

Nadia glanced toward the corner of the room where Lavon sat alone, veiled by darkness.

"Is Max still worried?"

"No," Gabriel said, "Max isn't worried in the least."

"What is Max thinking?"

"Max believes it would be an honor to work with you, Nadia. And so do I."

Nadia stared silently into the fire for a moment. "I have listened to your proposal," she said finally, "and I've answered as many questions as I intend to. Now you have to answer a few of mine."

"You may ask me anything you wish."

Nadia gave the faintest trace of a smile. "Maybe we should drink some of the wine I brought. I've always found that a good bottle of Latour can take the edge off even the most unpleasant conversation."

32

SERAINCOURT, FRANCE

NADIA WATCHED GABRIEL'S HANDS CAREFULLY as he uncorked the wine. He poured out two glasses, keeping one for himself and handing the other to her.

"None for Max?"

"Max doesn't drink."

"Max is an Islamic fundamentalist?"

"Max is a teetotaler."

Gabriel raised his glass a fraction of an inch in salutation. Nadia declined to reciprocate. She placed the wineglass on the table with what seemed to Gabriel to be inordinate care.

"There were a number of questions about my father's death that I was never able to answer," she said after a prolonged silence. "I need you to answer them now."

"I'm limited in what I can say."

"I would advise you to rethink that position. Otherwise—"

"What is it you wish to know, Nadia?"

"Was he targeted for assassination from the beginning?"

"Quite the opposite."

"What does that mean?"

"It means that the Americans made it abundantly clear that your father was far too important to be treated like a normal terrorist. He wasn't a member of the royal family, but he was the next best thing—a descendant of an old-line merchant family from the Nejd who claimed blood ties to none other than Muhammad Abdul Wahhab himself."

"And that made him untouchable in the eyes of the Americans?"

"'Radioactive' was the word they used."

"So what happened?"

"Sarah happened."

"They hurt her?"

"They almost killed her."

Nadia was silent for a moment. "How did you get her back?"

"We fight on a secret battlefield, but we consider ourselves soldiers, and we never leave one of our own in the hands of our enemies."

"How noble of you."

"You may not always agree with our goals and methods, Nadia, but we do try to operate by a certain code. Occasionally, our enemies do as well. But not your father. Your father played by his own rules. Zizi's rules."

"And for that he was killed on a crowded street in Cannes."

"Would you have preferred London? Or Geneva? Or Riyadh?"

"I would have preferred not to have watched my father being gunned down in cold blood."

"We would have preferred the same thing. Unfortunately, we had no other choice."

A heavy silence fell over the room. Nadia stared directly into

Gabriel's face. There was no anger in her eyes, only the faintest trace of sadness.

"You still haven't told me your name," she said finally. "That's hardly the foundation of a strong and trusting partnership."

"I believe you already know my name, Nadia."

"I do," she said after a moment. "And if the terrorists and their supporters in the House of Saud ever learn that I am working with Gabriel Allon, the very same man who killed my father, they will declare me an apostate. Then, at the first opportunity, they will slit my throat." She paused, then added, "Not your throat, Mr. Allon. Mine."

"We are well aware of the danger involved in what we are asking of you, and we will do everything within our power to ensure your safety. Each step of your journey will be as carefully planned and executed as this meeting."

"But that's not what I'm asking, Mr. Allon. I need to know whether *you* will protect me."

"You have my word," he replied without hesitation.

"The word of a man who killed my father."

"I'm afraid there's nothing I can do to change the past."

"No," she said, "only the future."

She looked at Eli Lavon, who was doing an admirable job of concealing his displeasure over what had just transpired, then gazed out the windows overlooking the terraced garden.

"We have a few more minutes of daylight," she said finally. "Why don't we take a walk, Mr. Allon? There's one more thing I need to tell you."

They set out along a gravel footpath between columns of swaying cypress pines. Nadia walked at Gabriel's right shoulder. At first, she seemed wary of getting too close, but as they moved deeper into the garden, Lavon noticed her hand resting discreetly on Gabriel's elbow. She paused once, as if compelled to do so by the gravity of her words, and a second time at the edge of the dormant fountain at the center of the garden. There she sat for several minutes, trailing her hand, childlike, across the surface of the water, as the last light retreated from the sky. After that, they were largely lost to Lavon. He saw Gabriel place his hand briefly along Nadia's cheek, then nothing more until they came walking up the footpath toward the house again with Nadia clinging to Gabriel's elbow for support.

Upon their return to the drawing room, Gabriel summoned the rest of the team, and the party resumed. At Gabriel's insistence, they spoke of anything but their shared past and their uncertain future. For now, there was no global war on terror, no new network that needed dismantling, no cause for concern whatsoever. There was only good wine, good conversation, and a group of good friends who were not really friends at all. Nadia, like Gabriel, remained largely a passive observer of the feigned bonhomie. Still posed for her portrait, her eyes moved slowly from face to face, as though they were pieces of a puzzle she was trying to assemble in her mind. Occasionally, her gaze would settle on Gabriel's hands. He made no attempt to conceal them, for there was now nothing left to hide. It was clear to Lavon and the rest of the team that Gabriel no longer harbored any doubts about Nadia's intentions. Like lovers, they had consecrated their bond with the sharing of secrets.

It was a few minutes after seven when Gabriel gave the signal that the party was at an end. Rising to her feet, Nadia seemed suddenly light-headed. She bade them all good night; then, with Zoe at her side, she headed across the darkened forecourt to her car where Rafiq al-Kamal, guardian of her father, was waiting to reclaim her. During the drive back to Paris, she once again spoke without pause, this time about her new friends, Thomas and Jenny Fowler. Gabriel monitored the conversation by way of Zoe's Black-Berry. The next morning, he watched the winking icon as it moved from the Place de la Concorde to Charles de Gaulle Airport. While waiting for her flight, Zoe phoned her producer in New York to say that, at least for now, the al-Bakari exclusive was off. Then, in a sultry whisper, she said to Gabriel, "Time to say good-bye, darling. Don't hesitate to call if you need anything else." Gabriel waited until Zoe was safely on board the aircraft before disabling the software on her phone. The light flashed three more times. Then she vanished from the screen.

33

SERAINCOURT, FRANCE

THE OPERATION BEGAN IN EARNEST at 10:15 the following morning, when Nadia al-Bakari, heiress, activist, and agent of Israeli intelligence, informed her senior staff that she intended to form a partnership with Thomas Fowler Associates, a small but highly successful private equity firm based in London. That afternoon, accompanied only by her security detail, she traveled by car to Mr. Fowler's private home north of Paris for the first round of direct negotiations. Later, she would characterize the talks as productive and intense, both of which happened to be true.

She came the next day, and the day after as well. For reasons Gabriel did not share with the others, he dispensed with much of the usual training and focused mainly on Nadia's cover story. Learning it was not difficult, for it corresponded largely to the facts. "It's *your* story," said Gabriel, "with only the slightest reordering of the salient details. It's a story of murder, vengeance, and hatred as old as the Middle East. From now on, Nadia al-Bakari is no longer part of the solution. Nadia is just like her father. She's part of the problem. She's the reason why the Arabs will never be able to escape their history."

Yossi assisted Nadia on superficial performance issues, but for the most part, she relied on Sarah for guidance. Gabriel was initially apprehensive about the renewal of their friendship, but Lavon saw their bond as an operational asset. Sarah was a timely reminder of Zizi's evil. And unlike Rena, Nadia's murdered childhood friend, Sarah had stared the monster in the eye and defeated him. She was Rena without chains, Rena resurrected.

Nadia proved to be a quick study, but Gabriel had expected nothing less. Her preparation was made easier by the fact that, having lived a double life for years, she was a natural dissembler. She also had two important advantages over other assets who had tried to penetrate the global jihadist movement: her name and her bodyguards. Her name guaranteed her instant access and credibility while her bodyguards gave her a layer of protection that most agents of penetration had to live without. As the only surviving child of a murdered Saudi billionaire, Nadia al-Bakari was one of the most heavily guarded private citizens in the world. No matter where she went, she would be surrounded by her loyal palace guard, along with a secondary ring of Office security. Getting to her would be all but impossible.

Nadia's most valuable asset, though, was her money. Gabriel was confident that she would have no shortage of suitors once she returned to the world of jihad and terror. The challenge for Gabriel and his team would be to place the money in the hands of the right one. It was Nadia herself who supplied the name of a potential candidate while walking with Gabriel and Sarah one afternoon in the garden of the château.

"He sought me out not long after my father's death and asked for a contribution to an Islamic charity. He described himself as an associate of my father. A brother."

"And the charity?"

"It was nothing more than a front for al-Qaeda. Samir Abbas is the man you're looking for. Even if he's not involved with this new network, he will know people who are."

"What does he do?"

"He's employed by TransArabian Bank at its offices in Zurich. As you probably know, TransArabian is based in Dubai and is one of the largest financial institutions in the Middle East. It's also regarded as the bank of choice for the global jihadist movement, of which Samir Abbas is a member in good standing. He manages the accounts of well-to-do Middle Eastern clients, which leaves him uniquely positioned to seek contributions for the so-called charities."

"Is any of your personal fortune under TransArabian management?"

"Not at the moment."

"Perhaps you should consider opening an account. Nothing too large. Just enough to get Samir's attention."

"How much shall I give him?"

"Can you spare a hundred million?"

"A hundred million?" She shook her head. "My father would never have given them that kind of money."

"How much then?"

"Let's make it *two* hundred million." She smiled. "That way he'll know we really mean business."

Within twelve hours of the conversation, Gabriel had a team on the ground in Zurich, and Samir Abbas, wealth-management specialist for TransArabian Bank of Dubai, was under Office surveillance. Eli Lavon remained behind at Château Treville to button up the last details of the operation, including the ticklish question of how a Paris-based Saudi businesswoman was going to fund a terror group without arousing the suspicions of the French and other European financial authorities. Through her secret funding of the Arab reform movement, Nadia had already shown them the way. All Gabriel needed was a painting and a willing accomplice. Which explained why on Christmas Eve, as the rest of France was preparing for several days of feasting and celebration, he asked Lavon to drive him to the Gare du Nord. Gabriel had a ticket for the 3:15 train to London and a catastrophic headache from lack of sleep. Lavon was more on edge than usual at this stage of an operation. Unmarried and childless, he always became depressed around the holidays.

"Are you sure you want to go through with this?"

"Take a train to London on Christmas Eve? Actually, I think I'd rather walk."

"I was talking about Nadia."

"I know, Eli."

Lavon stared out the car window at the crowds streaming toward the entrance of the train station. It was the usual lot—businessmen, students, tourists, African immigrants, and pickpockets, all watched over by heavily armed French police officers. The entire country was waiting for the next bomb to explode. So was the rest of Europe.

"Are you ever going to tell me what it was she said to you that evening in the garden?"

"No, I'm not."

Lavon had expected the answer. Even so, he couldn't conceal his disappointment.

"How long have we been working together?"

"A hundred and fifty years," said Gabriel. "And never once have I kept a shred of important information from you."

"So why now?"

"She asked me to."

"Have you told your wife?"

"I tell my wife everything, and my wife tells me nothing. It's part of the deal."

"You're a lucky man," Lavon said. "All the more reason why you shouldn't go making promises you can't keep."

"I always keep my promises, Eli."

"That's what I'm afraid of." Lavon looked at Gabriel. "Are you sure about her?"

"As sure as I am about you."

"Go," said Lavon after a moment. "I wouldn't want you to miss your train. And if you happen to see a suicide bomber in there, do me a favor and just tell a gendarme. The last thing we need right now is for you to blow up another French train station."

Gabriel handed Lavon his Beretta 9mm pistol, then climbed out of the car and headed into the ticket hall of the station. By some miracle, his train departed on time, and by five that evening he was once again walking along the pavements of St. James's. Adrian Carter would later find much symbolism in Gabriel's return to London, since it was where his journey had begun. In truth, his motives for coming back were hardly so lofty. His plan to destroy Rashid's network from the inside would entail a criminal act of fraud. And what better place to carry it out than the art world.

34

ST. JAMES'S, LONDON

G ABRIEL'S ACCOMPLICE WAS NOT YET aware of his plans—hardly surprising, since he was none other than Julian Isherwood, owner and sole proprietor of Isherwood Fine Arts, 7–8 Mason's Yard. Among the many hundreds of paintings controlled by Isherwood's gallery was *Madonna and Child with Mary Magdalene*, formerly attributed to the Venetian master Palma Vecchio, now tentatively attributed to none other than the great and mighty Titian himself. For the moment, however, the painting remained locked away in Isherwood's underground storage room, its image hidden by a protective layer of tissue paper. Isherwood had come to loathe the painting almost as much as the man who had defaced it. Indeed, in Isherwood's troubled mind, the glorious swath of canvas had come to symbolize all that was wrong with his life.

As far as Isherwood was concerned, it had been an autumn to forget. He had sold just one picture—a minor Italian devotional piece to a minor collector from Houston—and had acquired nothing more than a chronic barking cough that could empty a room quicker than a bomb threat. Word on the street was that he was in the throes of yet another late-life crisis, his seventh or eighth, depending on whether one counted the prolonged Blue Period he endured after being dumped by the girl who worked the coffee machine at the Costa in Piccadilly. Jeremy Crabbe, the tweedy director of the Old Master department at Bonhams, thought a surprise party might lift Isherwood's sagging spirits, an idea that Oliver Dimbleby, Isherwood's tubby nemesis from Bury Street, dismissed as the dumbest he'd heard all year. "Given Julie's precarious health at the moment," said Oliver, "a surprise party might kill him." He suggested fixing Isherwood up with a talented tart instead, but then that was Oliver's solution to every problem, personal or professional.

On the afternoon of Gabriel's return to London, Isherwood closed his gallery early and, having nothing better to do, headed over to Duke Street through a pelting rain to have a drink at Green's. Aided by Roddy Hutchinson, universally regarded as the most unscrupulous dealer in all of St. James's, Isherwood quickly consumed a bottle of white Burgundy, followed by a dose of brandy for his health. Shortly after six, he teetered into the street again to find a taxi, but when one finally approached, he was overcome by a retching coughing fit that left him incapable of lifting his arm. "Bloody hell!" snapped Isherwood as the car swept past, soaking his trousers. "Bloody, bloody, bloody *hell*!"

His outburst brought on another round of staccato barking. When finally it subsided, he noticed a figure leaning against the brickwork of the passageway leading to Mason's Yard. He wore a Barbour raincoat and a flat cap pulled low over his brow. The right foot was crossed over the left, and the eyes were sweeping back and forth along the street. He gazed at Isherwood for a moment with a mixture of bemusement and pity. Then, without word or sound, he turned and started across the cobbles of the old yard. Against all better judgment, Isherwood followed after him, hacking his lungs out like a consumption patient on the way to the sanatorium.

***

"Let me see if I understand this correctly," said Isherwood. "First you cover my Titian in rabbit-skin glue and tissue paper. Then you deposit it in my storage room and disappear to parts unknown. Now you reappear unannounced, looking, as usual, like something the cat dragged in, and tell me that you need the aforementioned Titian for one of your little extracurricular projects. Have I left anything out?"

"In order for this scheme to work, Julian, I'll need you to deceive the art world and to conduct yourself in a way that some of your colleagues might consider unethical."

"Just another day at the office, petal," said Isherwood with a shrug. "But what's in it for *moi*?"

"If it works, there will be no more attacks like the one in Covent Garden."

"Until the next jihadi loon comes along. Then we'll be back at square one again, won't we? Heaven knows I'm no expert, but it seems to me the terrorism game is a bit like the art trade. It has its peaks and valleys, its good seasons and bad, but it never goes away."

In the upper exhibition room of Isherwood's gallery, the overhead lamps glowed with the softness of votive candles. Rain pattered on the skylight and dripped from the hem of Isherwood's sodden overcoat, which he had yet to remove. Isherwood frowned at the puddle on his parquet floor and then looked at the wounded painting propped upon the baize-covered pedestal.

"Do you know how much that thing is worth?"

"In a fair auction, ten million in the shade. But in the auction I have in mind . . ."

"Naughty boy," said Isherwood. "Naughty, naughty boy."

"Have you mentioned it to anyone, Julian?"

"The painting?" Isherwood shook his head. "Not a peep."

"You're sure about that? No moment of indiscretion at the bar at Green's? No pillow talk with that preposterously young woman from the Tate?"

"Her name's Penelope," Isherwood said.

"Does she know about the picture, Julian?"

"'Course not. That's not the way it works when one has a coup, petal. One doesn't brag about such things. One keeps it very quiet until the moment is just right. Then one announces it to the world with all the usual fanfare. One also expects to be compensated for one's cleverness. But under your scenario, I'll be expected to actually take a loss—for the good of God's children, of course."

"Your loss will be temporary."

"How temporary?"

"The CIA is handling all operational expenses."

"That's not a line one hears every day in an art gallery."

"One way or another, Julian, you'll be compensated."

"Of course I will," Isherwood said with mock confidence. "This reminds me of the time my Penelope told me her husband wouldn't be home for another hour. I'm rather too old to be leaping over garden walls."

"Still seeing her?"

"Penelope? Left me," Isherwood said, shaking his head. "They all leave me eventually. But not you, petal. And not this damn cough. I'm starting to think of it as an old friend."

"Have you seen a doctor?"

"Couldn't get an appointment. The National Health Service is so bad these days, I'm thinking about becoming a Christian Scientist."

"I thought you were a hypochondriac."

"Orthodox, actually." Isherwood picked at the tissue paper in the upper-right portion of the canvas.

"Every flake of paint you dislodge I have to put back."

"Sorry," said Isherwood, slipping his hand into his coat pocket. "There's precedent for it, you know. A couple of years ago, Christie's sold a painting attributed to the School of Titian for the paltry sum of eight thousand quid. But the painting wasn't a School of Titian. It was a *Titian* Titian. As you might imagine, the owners weren't terribly pleased. They accused Christie's of malpractice. The lawyers got involved. There were ugly stories in the press. Bad feelings all round."

"Perhaps we should give Christie's a chance to redeem itself."

"They might actually like that. There's just one problem."

"Just one?"

"We've already missed the big Old Master sales."

"That's true," Gabriel acknowledged, "but you're forgetting about the special Venetian School auction planned for the first week of February. A newly discovered Titian might be just the thing to gin up a bit of extra excitement."

"Naughty boy. Naughty, naughty boy."

"Guilty as charged."

"Considering my past connection to certain unsavory elements of this operation, it might be wise to put some distance between the gallery and the final sale. That means we'll need to enlist the services of another dealer. Given the circumstances, he'll have to be greedy, sneaky, cunning, and a first-class shit."

"I know what you're thinking," said Gabriel, "but are you sure he can handle it?"

"He's perfect," Isherwood said. "All you need now is a Titian that actually looks like one."

"I think I can manage that."

"Where do you intend to work?"

Gabriel looked around the room and said, "This will do quite nicely."

"Is there anything else you require?"

Gabriel handed him a list. Isherwood slipped on his reading glasses and frowned. "One bolt of Italian linen, one professional-grade iron, one pair of magnifying visors, one liter of acetone, one liter of methyl proxitol, one liter of mineral spirits, one dozen Winsor & Newton Series 7 brushes, one pair of standing halogen work lamps, one copy of *La Bohème* by Giacomo Puccini . . ." He glared at Gabriel over his glasses. "Do you know how much this is going to cost me?"

But Gabriel seemed not to hear. He was standing before the canvas, one hand resting against his chin, his head tilted meditatively to one side.

* * *

Gabriel believed the craft of restoration was a bit like making love. It was best done slowly and with painstaking attention to detail, with occasional breaks for rest and refreshment. But in a pinch, if the craftsman and his subject matter were adequately acquainted, a restoration could be done at extraordinary speed, with more or less the same result.

Of the subsequent ten days Gabriel would later be able to recall very little, for they were a near-sleepless blur of linen, solvent, medium, and pigment, set to the music of Puccini and lit by the harsh white glare of his halogen work lamps. His initial fears about the condition of the canvas thankfully proved overblown. Indeed, once he had completed the relining and removed the yellowed varnish, he found Titian's original work to be largely intact except for a chain of bare spots across the body of the Virgin and four lines of abrasion where the canvas had sloughed against the old stretcher. Having restored several Titians in the past, he was able to repair the painting almost as swiftly as the master himself had been able to paint it. His palette was Titian's palette, as were his brushstrokes. Only the conditions of his studio were different. Titian had no doubt worked with a team of gifted apprentices and journeymen while Gabriel had no assistant other than Julian Isherwood, which meant he had no help at all.

He wore no wristwatch so that he would have only the vaguest idea of time, and when he slept, which was seldom, he did so on a camp bed in the corner of the room, beneath a luminous landscape by Claude. He drank coffee by the bucket from Costa and subsisted largely on butter cookies and tea biscuits that Isherwood smuggled into the gallery from Fortnum & Mason. Having no time to waste on shaving, he allowed his beard to grow. Much to his dismay it came in even grayer than the last time. Isherwood said the beard made it look as though Titian himself were standing before the canvas. Given Gabriel's uncanny skill with a brush, it wasn't far from the truth.

On his final evening in London, Gabriel stopped at Thames House, the riverfront headquarters of MI5, where, as promised, he informed Graham Seymour that the operation had in fact washed ashore in the British Isles. Seymour's mood was foul and his thoughts clearly elsewhere. The son of the future king had decided to marry in late spring, and it was up to Seymour and his colleagues at the Metropolitan Police Service to see that nothing spoiled the occasion. Listening to Seymour bemoan his plight, Gabriel couldn't help but think of the words Sarah had spoken in the garden of the café in Georgetown. London is low-hanging fruit. London can be attacked at will.

As if to illustrate the point, Gabriel emerged from Thames House to find the Jubilee Line of the Underground had been shut down at the height of the evening rush due to a suspicious package. He headed back to Mason's Yard on foot and, with Isherwood peering over his shoulder, applied a coat of varnish to the newly restored Titian. The next morning, he instructed Nadia to deposit two hundred million dollars with TransArabian Bank. Then he climbed into a taxi and headed for Heathrow Airport.

35

ZURICH

FEW COUNTRIES HAD PLAYED A more prominent role in the life and career of Gabriel Allon than the Swiss Confederation. He spoke three of its four languages fluently and knew its mountains and valleys like the clefts and curves of his wife's body. He had killed in Switzerland, kidnapped in Switzerland, and exposed some of its most repulsive secrets. One year earlier, in a café at the base of the glacier at Les Diablerets, he had taken a solemn vow never to set foot in the country again. It was funny how things never seemed to go according to plan.

Behind the wheel of a rented Audi, he glided past the dour banks and storefronts of the Bahnhofstrasse, then turned onto the busy road running along the western shore of Lake Zurich. The safe house was located two miles south of the city center. It was a modern structure, with far too many windows for Gabriel's comfort, and a small T-shaped dock that had been sugared by a recent snow. Entering, he heard a female voice singing softly in Italian. He smiled. Chiara always sang to herself when she was alone.

He left his bag in the foyer and followed the sound into the living room, which had been converted into a makeshift field command post. Chiara was staring at a computer screen while at the same time peeling the skin from an orange. Her lips, when kissed by Gabriel, were very warm, as though she were suffering from a fever. He kissed them for a long time.

"I'm Chiara Allon," she murmured, stroking the bristly gray hair on his cheeks. "And who might you be?"

"I'm not sure any longer."

"They say aging can cause memory problems," she said, still kissing him. "You should try fish oil. I hear it helps."

"I'd rather have a bite of that orange instead."

"I'm sure you would. It's been a long time."

"A very long time."

She broke the fruit into segments and placed one in Gabriel's mouth.

"Where's the rest of the team?" he asked.

"They're watching an employee of TransArabian Bank who also happens to have ties to the global jihadist movement."

"So you're all alone?"

"Not anymore."

Gabriel loosened the buttons of Chiara's blouse. Her nipples firmed instantly to his touch. She gave him another piece of the fruit.

"Maybe we shouldn't do this in front of a computer," she said. "You never know who might be watching."

"How much time do we have?"

"As much as you need."

She took his hand and led him upstairs. "Slowly," she said, as he lowered her onto the bed. "Slowly."

———

The room was in semidarkness by the time Gabriel fell away exhausted from Chiara's body. They lay for a long time together in silence, close but not quite touching. From outside came the distant rumble of a passing boat, followed a moment later by the lapping of wavelets against the dock. Chiara rolled onto one elbow and traced her finger along the ridgeline of Gabriel's nose.

"How long are you planning to keep it?"

"Since I require it to breathe, I intend to keep it for as long as possible."

"I was talking about your beard, darling."

"I hate it, but something tells me I might need it before this operation is through."

"Maybe you should keep it after the operation, too. I think it makes you look . . ." Her voice trailed off.

"Don't say it, Chiara."

"I was going to say distinguished."

"That's like calling a woman elegant."

"What's wrong with that?"

"You'll understand when people start saying you look elegant."

"It won't be so bad."

"It will never happen, Chiara. You're beautiful and you'll always be beautiful. And if I keep this beard after the operation, people will start to mistake you for my daughter."

"Now you're being unreasonable."

"It *is* biologically possible."

"What is?"

"For you to be my daughter."

"I've never actually thought about it that way."

"Don't," he said.

She laughed quietly and then said nothing more.

"What are you thinking about now?" Gabriel asked.

"What might have happened if you hadn't noticed that boy with the bomb under his jacket walking along Wellington Street. We would have been sitting down to lunch when the bomb exploded. It would have been a tragedy, of course, but our lives would have gone on as normal, just like everyone else's."

"Maybe this *is* normal for us, Chiara."

"Normal couples don't make love in safe houses."

"Actually, I've always enjoyed making love to you in safe houses."

"I fell in love with you in a safe house."

"Which one?"

"Rome," she said. "That little flat off the Via Veneto where I took you after the Polizia di Stato tried to kill you in that dreadful *pensione* near the train station."

"The Abruzzi," Gabriel said heavily. "What a pit."

"But the safe flat was lovely."

"You barely knew me."

"I knew you very well, actually."

"You made me fettuccini with mushrooms."

"I only make my fettuccini with mushrooms for people I love."

"Make me some now."

"You have some work to do first."

Chiara flipped a switch on the wall above the bed. A tiny halogen reading lamp burned laserlike into Gabriel's eye.

"Must you?" he asked, squinting.

"Sit up."

She took a file folder from the bedside table and handed it to him. Gabriel lifted the cover and for the first time saw the face of Samir Abbas. It was angular, bespectacled, and lightly bearded, with thoughtful brown eyes and a deeply receded hairline. At the time the photo was snapped, he had been walking along a street in a residential section of Zurich. He was wearing a gray suit, the uniform of a Swiss banker, and a silver necktie. His briefcase looked expensive, as did his shoes. His overcoat was unbuttoned and his hands were gloveless. He was talking on a mobile phone. Judging by the shape of his mouth, it appeared to Gabriel he was speaking German.

"Here's the man who's going to help you buy a terror group," Chiara said. "Samir Abbas, born in Amman in 1967, educated at the London School of Economics, and hired by TransArabian Bank in 1998."

"Where does he live?"

"Up in Hottingen, near the university. If the weather is good, he walks to work, for the sake of his waistline. If it's bad, he takes the streetcar from Römerhof down to the financial district."

"Which one?"

"The Number Eight, of course. What else would he take?"

Chiara smiled. Her knowledge of European public transit, like Gabriel's, was encyclopedic.

"Where's his flat?"

"At Carmenstrasse Four. It's a small postwar building with a stucco exterior, six flats in all."

"Wife?"

"Take a look at the next picture."

It showed a woman walking along the same street. She was wearing Western clothing except for a *hijab* that framed a childlike face. Holding her left hand was a boy of perhaps four. Holding her right was a girl who looked to be eight or nine.

"Her name is Johara, which means 'jewel' in Arabic. She works part-time as a teacher at an Islamic community center on the west side of the city. The older child attends classes there. The boy is in the day-care facility. Both children speak fluent Swiss German, but Johara is much more comfortable in Arabic."

"Does Samir go to a mosque?"

"He prays in the apartment. The children like American cartoons, much to their father's dismay. No music allowed, though. Music is strictly forbidden."

"Does she know about Samir's charitable endeavors?"

"Since they use the same computer, it would be hard to miss."

"Where is it?"

"In the living room. We popped it the day after we arrived. It's giving us fairly decent audio and visual coverage. We're also reading his e-mail and monitoring his browsing. Your friend Samir enjoys his jihadi porn."

"What about his mobile?"

"That took a bit of doing, but we got that, too." Chiara pointed to the photograph of Samir. "He carries it in the right pocket of his overcoat. We got it on the streetcar while he was on his way to work."

"We?"

"Yaakov handled the bump, Oded picked his pocket, and Mordecai did the technical stuff. He popped it while Samir was reading the newspaper. The whole thing took two minutes."

"Why didn't anyone tell me about this?"

"We didn't want to bother you."

"Is there anything else you neglected to tell me?"

"Just one thing," Chiara said.

"What's that?"

"We're being watched."

"By the Swiss?"

"No, not the Swiss."

"Who then?"

"Three guesses. First two don't count."

Gabriel snatched up his secure BlackBerry and started typing.

36

LAKE ZURICH

I T TOOK THE BETTER PART of forty-eight hours for Adrian Carter to find his way to Zurich. He met Gabriel in the late afternoon on the prow of a ferry bound for the suburb of Rapperswil. He wore a tan mackintosh coat and carried a copy of the *Neue Zürcher Zeitung* beneath his arm. The newsprint was wet with snow.

"I'm surprised you're not wearing your Agency credentials," Gabriel said.

"I took precautions coming here."

"How did you travel?"

"Economy plus," Carter said resentfully.

"Did you tell the Swiss you were coming?"

"Surely you jest."

"Where are you staying?"

"I'm not."

Gabriel looked over his shoulder toward the skyline of Zurich, which was barely visible behind a cloak of low clouds and falling snow. The entire scene was devoid of color—a gray city by a gray lake. It suited Gabriel's mood.

"When were you planning to tell me, Adrian?"

"Tell you what?"

Gabriel handed Carter an unmarked letter-sized envelope. Inside were eight surveillance photographs of eight different CIA field operatives.

"How long did it take you to spot them?" Carter asked, flipping morosely through the pictures.

"Do you really want me to answer that question?"

"I suppose not." Carter closed the envelope. "My best field personnel are currently deployed elsewhere. I had to use what was available. A couple of them are fresh off the Farm, as we like to say."

The Farm was the CIA's training facility at Camp Peary, Virginia.

"You sent probationers to watch us? If I wasn't so angry, I'd be insulted."

"Try not to take it personally."

"This little stunt of yours could have blown us all sky-high. The Swiss aren't stupid, Adrian. In fact, they're quite good. They watch. They listen, too. And they get extremely annoyed when spies operate on their soil without signing the guestbook on the way in. Even experienced field agents have gotten into trouble here, ours included. And what does Langley do? It sends eight fresh-faced kids who haven't been to Europe since their junior year abroad. Do you know one of them actually bumped into Yaakov a couple of days ago because he was looking down at a *Streetwise Zurich* map? That's one for the books, Adrian."

"You've made your point."

"Not yet," Gabriel said. "I want them out of here. Tonight."

"I'm afraid that's not possible."

"Why?"

"Because higher authority has taken an intense interest in your operation. And higher authority has decided it requires an American operational component."

"Tell higher authority it already has an American operational component. Her name is Sarah Bancroft."

"A single analyst from the CTC doesn't count."

"That single analyst could run circles around any of the eight dolts you sent here to keep watch over us."

Carter stared at the lake but said nothing.

"What's going on, Adrian?"

"It's not what. It's who." Carter returned the envelope to Gabriel. "How much will it cost me to get you to burn those damn pictures?"

"Start talking."

37

LAKE ZURICH

T HERE WAS A SMALL CAFÉ on the upper deck of the passenger cabin. Carter drank muddy coffee. Gabriel had tea.
Between them they shared a rubbery egg sandwich and a
bag of stale potato chips. Carter kept the receipt for his expenses.

"I asked you to keep her name closely held," Gabriel said.

"I tried to."

"What happened?"

"Someone tipped off the White House. I was brought into
the Oval Office for a bit of enhanced interrogation. McKenna
and the president worked me over together, bad cop, bad cop.
Stress positions, sleep deprivation, denial of food and drink—
all the techniques we're now forbidden to use against the enemy.
It didn't take long for them to break me. Suffice it to say the
president now knows my name. He also knows the name of the
Muslim woman with impeccable jihadist credentials you're in bed
with—operationally speaking, of course."

"And?"

"He's not happy about it."

"Really?"

"He's fearful that U.S.-Saudi relations will suffer grave damage if the operation ever crashes and burns. As a result, he's no longer willing to allow Langley to be a mere passenger."

"He wants you flying the plane?"

"Not just that," Carter said. "He wants us maintaining the plane, fueling the plane, stocking the plane's galleys, and loading the luggage into the plane's cargo hold."

"Total control? Is that what you're saying?"

"That's what I'm saying."

"It makes no sense, Adrian."

"Which part?"

"All of it, frankly. If we're running the show, the president has complete deniability with the Saudis if something goes wrong. But if Langley is in charge, any chance of deniability goes right out the White House window. It's as if he's trying to block a blow with his chin."

"You know, Gabriel, I never looked at it in those terms." Carter picked up the last potato chip. "Do you mind?"

"Enjoy."

Carter popped the chip in his mouth and spent a long moment thoughtfully brushing the salt from his fingertips. "You have a right to be angry," he said finally. "If I were you, I'd be angry, too."

"Why?"

"Because I sailed into town with a cheap story thinking I could slip it past you, and you deserve better. The truth is that the president and his faithful if ignorant servant James A. McKenna aren't concerned that the al-Bakari operation is going to fail. In fact, they're afraid it's going to succeed."

"Try again, Adrian. It's been a long few days."

"It seems the president is head over heels in love."

"Who's the lucky girl?"

"Nadia," murmured Carter into his crumpled paper napkin. "He's crazy about her. He loves her story. He loves her courage. More important, he loves the operation you've built around her. It's exactly the kind of thing he's been looking for. It's clean. It's smart. It's forward-leaning. It's built for the long haul. It also happens to dovetail nicely with the president's view of the world. A partnership between Islam and the West to defeat the forces of extremism. Brainpower over brute force. He wants Rashid's network taken down and tied up with a bow before the next election, and he doesn't want to share credit."

"So he wants to go it alone? No partners?"

"Not entirely," Carter said. "He wants us to bring in the French, the British, the Germans, and the Spaniards, since they were the ones attacked."

"What about the partridge in a pear tree?"

"He works for a private security firm now. Doing quite nicely, from what I hear."

"Need-to-know," Gabriel said. "It isn't an advertising slogan, Adrian. It's a sacred creed. It keeps operations from being blown. It keeps assets alive."

"Your concerns have been duly noted."

"And dismissed."

Carter said nothing.

"Where does that leave me and the rest of my team?"

"Your team will quietly withdraw from the field and be replaced by Agency personnel. You will stay on in an advisory capacity until the show is up and running."

"And after that?"

"You'll be eased out of the production."

"I have news for you, Adrian. The show is already up and running. In fact, the star of the show is making her debut here in Zurich tomorrow afternoon."

"We're going to have to postpone that until the new management team is in place."

Gabriel saw the lights of Rapperswil glowing faintly along the shoreline. "You're forgetting one thing," he said after a moment. "The star of the show is a diva. She's very demanding. And she won't work with just anyone."

"You're saying she'll work for you, the man who killed her father, but not us?"

"That's what I'm saying."

"I'd like to test that proposition for myself."

"Be my guest. If you wish to speak to Nadia, she can be reached at her office on the Boulevard Haussmann, in the ninth arrondissement of Paris."

"Actually, we were hoping that you might work with us on the transition."

"Hope is not an acceptable strategy when lives are at stake." Gabriel held up the envelope of snapshots. "Besides, if I were advising Nadia, I'd tell her to stay as far away from you and your Farm-fresh field operatives as possible."

"We're grown-ups, you and I. We've been through the wars together. We've saved lives. We've done the dirty jobs that no one else wanted to do or had the guts to do. But at this moment in time, I am resenting the hell out of you."

"I'm glad I'm not alone."

"Do you really think this is something I *want* to do? He's the president, Gabriel. I can either follow his orders or quit. And I have no intention of quitting."

"Then please tell the president that I wish him nothing but the best," Gabriel said. "But at some point, you should remind him that Nadia is only the first step toward breaking Rashid's network. In the end, it won't be clean or smart or forward-leaning. I just hope the president doesn't fall out of love when it comes time to make the tough decisions."

The ferry shuddered as it nudged against the side of the dock. Gabriel stood abruptly. Carter gathered up the empty cups and wrappers and swept the crumbs onto the floor with the back of his hand.

"I need to know your intentions."

"I intend to return to my command post and tell my team that we're going home."

"Is that final?"

"I never make threats."

"Then do me one favor."

"What's that?"

"Drive slowly."

They left the ferry a few seconds apart and made their way along the slick jetty to a little car park at the edge of the terminal. Carter climbed into the passenger seat of a Mercedes and headed for the German border; Gabriel slipped behind the wheel of his Audi and sped over the Seedamm, toward the opposite side of the lake. Despite Carter's admonition, he drove very fast. As a result, he was pulling up to the safe house when Carter called him back with the outlines of the new operational accord. Its parameters were simple and unambiguous. Gabriel and his team would be allowed to retain their ascendency in the field so long as the operation did not touch the sacred soil of Saudi Arabia. On this point, said Carter, there

was no room for further negotiation. The president would not permit Israeli intelligence to make mischief in the land of Mecca and
Medina. Saudi was the game-changer. Saudi was the third rail. If
the operation crossed the Saudi border, said Carter, all bets were
off. Gabriel killed the connection and sat alone in the darkness,
debating what to do. Ten minutes later, he called Carter back and
reluctantly accepted the terms. Then he headed into the safe house
and told his team they were playing on borrowed time.

38

PARIS

ROM THE MANY FLOORS OF her mansion on the Avenue Foch, Nadia al-Bakari had carved for herself a comfortable pied-à-terre. It contained an office, a sitting room, her bedroom suite, and a private art gallery hung with twelve of her most cherished paintings. Scattered throughout the apartment were many photographs of her father. In none was he smiling, preferring instead to display the *juhayman*, the traditional "angry face" of the Arabian Bedouin. The one exception was an unposed photo snapped by Nadia aboard the *Alexandra* on the final day of his life. His expression was vaguely melancholy, as if he were somehow aware of the fate that awaited him later that night in the Old Port of Cannes.

Framed in silver, the photograph stood on Nadia's bedside table. Next to it was a Thomas Tompion clock, purchased at auction for the sum of two and a half million dollars and given to Nadia on the occasion of her twenty-fifth birthday. Lately, it had been running several minutes fast, which Nadia found eerily appropriate. She had been gazing at its stately features on and off since waking with a start at three a.m. Craving caffeine, she could feel the onset of a pounding headache. Nevertheless, she remained motionless in her large bed. During the final session of her training, Gabriel reminded her to avoid any changes to her daily schedule—a schedule that several dozen members of her household and personal staff could recite from memory. Without fail, she rose each morning at seven sharp, not a moment sooner or later. Her breakfast tray was to be left on the credenza in her office. Unless otherwise specified, it was to contain a thermos flask of *café filtre*, a pitcher of steamed milk, a glass of freshly squeezed orange juice, and two six-inch slices of *tartine* with butter and strawberry preserves on the side. Her newspapers were to be placed on the right side of her desk— the *Wall Street Journal* on top, followed by the *International Herald Tribune*, the *Financial Journal*, and *Le Monde*—along with her leather-bound itinerary for the day. The television was to be tuned to the BBC, with the volume muted and the remote within easy reach.

It was now half past six. Thinking of anything but the throbbing in her head, she closed her eyes and willed herself into a gauzy half sleep, which was disturbed thirty minutes later by the butterfly knock of her longtime housekeeper, Esmeralda. As was her custom, Nadia remained in bed until Esmeralda had departed. Then she pulled on a dressing gown and, under the watchful gaze of her father, padded barefoot into her office.

The smell of freshly brewed coffee greeted her. She poured a cup, added milk and three spoonfuls of sugar, and sat down at her desk. On the television screen were images of mayhem in Islamabad, the aftermath of yet another powerful al-Qaeda car bombing that had killed more than a hundred people, nearly all of them

Muslims. Nadia left the volume on mute and lifted the leather cover of her itinerary. It was strikingly benign. After two hours of private time, she was scheduled to depart her residence and fly to Zurich. There, in a conference room at the Dolder Grand Hotel, she and her closest aides would meet with executives from a Zug-based optical firm owned in large part by AAB Holdings. Immediately afterward, she would conduct a second meeting, without aides present. The topic was listed as "private," which was always the case when Nadia's personal finances were involved.

She closed the leather folder and, as was her custom, spent the next hour reading the newspapers over coffee and toast. Shortly after eight, she logged on to her computer to check the status of the Asian markets, then spent several minutes switching among the various cable news networks. Her tour ended with Al Jazeera, which had moved on from the carnage in Islamabad to report an Israeli military strike in the Gaza Strip that had killed two top Hamas terror planners. Describing the strike as "a crime against humanity," the Turkish prime minister called on the United Nations to punish Israel with economic sanctions—a call rejected, in the next segment, by an important Saudi cleric. "The time for diplomacy has ended," he told the fawning Al Jazeera questioner. "It is now time for *all* Muslims to join the armed struggle against the Zionist interlopers. And may God punish those who dare to collaborate with the enemies of Islam."

Switching off the television, Nadia returned to her bedroom and changed into exercise clothing. She had never cared for physical activity, and since turning thirty she cared for it even less. She dutifully elevated her heart rate and strained her limbs each morning because it was something that, as a modern businesswoman who lived mainly in the West, she was expected to do. Still suffering from a mild headache, she shortened her already-brief daily routine. After a leisurely stroll atop the conveyor belt of her treadmill, she stretched for several minutes on a rubber yoga mat. Then she lay on her back very still, with her ankles pressed together and her arms extended from her sides. As always, the pose created a sensation of weightlessness. On that morning, however, it also produced a shockingly clear revelation of her future. She lay there for several moments, her pose unchanged, and debated whether to go through with the trip to Zurich. One phone call is all it would take, she thought. One phone call and the burden would be lifted. It was a call she could not bring herself to make. She believed she had been put on earth, in this time and place, for a reason. She believed the same was true for the man who had killed her father, and she did not want to disappoint him.

Nadia stood and, fighting off a wave of dizziness, returned to her bedroom. After bathing and perfuming her body, she entered her dressing room and selected her clothing, forsaking the light colors that she preferred for more somber shades of gray and black. Her hair she arranged piously. Her face, as she glided past Rafiq al-Kamal into the back of her limousine thirty minutes later, was set in the *juhayman* of the Bedouin. The transformation was nearly complete. She was a wealthy Saudi woman plotting to avenge the murder of her father.

The car slipped through the front gate of the mansion and turned into the street. As it headed along the Bois de Boulogne, Nadia noticed the man she knew as Max walking a few paces behind a woman who may or may not have been Sarah. Just then, a motorcycle appeared briefly next to her window, ridden by a slender, helmeted figure in a black leather jacket. Something about him made Nadia feel a sudden painful stab of memory. It was probably nothing, she told herself as the bike vanished into a side street. Just a touch of last-minute nerves. Just her mind playing tricks.

At the behest of the al-Saud, Nadia had been compelled to keep more than just her father's old security detail. The basic structure of the company remained the same, as did most of the senior personnel. Daoud Hamza, a Stanford-educated Lebanese, still ran the day-to-day operations. Manfred Wehrli, a granite-calm Swiss moneyman, still managed the finances. And the legal team known as Abdul & Abdul still kept things reasonably above board. Accompanied by twenty additional aides, footmen, factotums, and assorted hangers-on, they were all gathered in the VIP lounge of Le Bourget Airport by the time Nadia arrived. At the stroke of ten, they filed onto AAB's Boeing Business Jet, and by 10:15 they were Zurich bound. They spent the hour-long flight crunching numbers around the conference table and upon arrival at Kloten Airport piled into a convoy of Mercedes sedans. It bore them at considerable speed up the wooded slopes of the Zürichberg to the graceful entrance of the Dolder Grand Hotel, where management escorted them to a conference room with an Alpine-sounding name and a view of the lake that was worth the outrageous price of admission. The delegation from the Swiss optical firm had already arrived and was partaking freely of the lavish buffet. The AAB team sat down and began opening their briefcases and laptops. AAB personnel never ate during meetings. Zizi's rules.

The meeting had been scheduled to last two hours. It ran thirty minutes over and concluded with a pledge by Nadia to invest an additional twenty million francs in the Swiss company to help it upgrade its factories and product line. After a few benedictory remarks, the Swiss delegation departed. Crossing the elegant lobby, they passed a thin, lightly bearded Arab in his early forties sitting alone with his briefcase at his side. Five minutes later, a phone call summoned him to the conference room the Swiss had just vacated. Waiting there alone was a beautiful woman of unimpeachable jihadist credentials.

"May God's blessings be upon you," she said in Arabic.

"And upon you as well," Samir Abbas responded in the same language. "I trust your meeting with the Swiss went well."

"Earthly matters," said Nadia with a dismissive wave of her hand.

"God has been very generous to you," Abbas said. "I've put together some proposals on how I think your money should be invested."

"I don't need investment advice from you, Mr. Abbas. I do quite well on my own."

"Then how might I be of service, Miss al-Bakari?"

"You may begin by having a seat. And then you can switch off your BlackBerry. One can never be too careful these days when it comes to electronic devices. You never know who might be listening."

"I understand completely."

She managed to smile. "I'm sure you do."

39

ZURICH

THEY SAT ON OPPOSITE SIDES of the conference table, with no refreshment other than bottles of Swiss mineral water, which neither of them touched. Between them lay two smart phones, screens dark, SIM cards removed. Having averted his gaze from Nadia's unveiled face, Samir Abbas appeared to be studying the chandelier above his head. Concealed amid the lights and crystal was a miniature short-range transmitter installed earlier that morning by Mordecai and Oded. They were now monitoring its signal from a room on the fourth floor, all charges paid in full by the National Clandestine Service of the Central Intelligence Agency. Gabriel was listening at the safe house on the opposite shore of the lake via a secure microwave link. His lips were moving slightly, as if he were trying to feed Nadia her next line.

"I would like to begin by offering you my sincerest apology," she said.

Abbas appeared momentarily perplexed. "You've recently

deposited two hundred million dollars in the financial institution for which I work, Miss al-Bakari. I cannot imagine why you would apologize."

"Because not long after my father's death, you asked me to make a donation to one of the Islamic charities with which you are associated. I turned you away—rather brusquely, if I remember correctly."

"I was wrong to have approached you at so sensitive a time."

"I know you only had my best interests at heart. *Zakat* is extremely important to our faith. In fact, my father believed the giving of alms to be the most important of the Five Pillars of Islam."

"Your father was generous to a fault. I could always count on him when we were in need."

"He always spoke very highly of you, Mr. Abbas."

"And of you as well, Miss al-Bakari. Your father loved you dearly. I cannot imagine the pain of your loss. Take peace in the knowledge that your father is with God in Paradise."

"*Inshallah*," she said wistfully, "but I'm afraid I've not had a single day of peace since his murder. And my pain has been compounded by the fact that his killers have never been punished for their crime."

"You have a right to your anger. We all do. Your father's murder was an insult to all Muslims."

"But what to do with this anger?"

"Are you asking me for advice, Miss al-Bakari?"

"Of the spiritual variety," she said. "I know you are a man of great faith."

"Like your father," he said.

"Like my father," she repeated softly.

Abbas looked directly into her eyes briefly before averting his gaze once more. "The Koran is more than a recitation of Allah's word," he said. "It is also a legal document that governs every aspect of our lives. And it is quite clear about what is to be done in the case of murder. It is known as *al-quisas*. As the surviving next of kin, you have three options. You may simply forgive the guilty party out of the goodness of your heart. You may accept a payment of blood money. Or you may do to the killer the same as he did to the victim, without killing anyone except the guilty party."

"The men who killed my father were professional assassins. They were sent by others."

"Then it is the men who dispatched the assassins who are ultimately responsible for your father's death."

"And if I cannot find it in my heart to forgive them?"

"Then, by the laws of Allah, you are entitled to kill them. Without killing anyone else," he added hastily.

"A difficult proposition, wouldn't you agree, Mr. Abbas?"

The banker made no response other than to gaze directly into Nadia's face for the first time without the slightest trace of Islamist decorum.

"Is something wrong?" asked Nadia.

"I know who killed your father, Miss al-Bakari. And I know why he was killed."

"Then you also know that it is not possible for me to punish them under the laws of Islam." She paused, then added, "Not without help."

Abbas picked up Nadia's disabled BlackBerry and examined it in silence.

"You have nothing to be nervous about," she said quietly.

"Why would I be nervous? I manage accounts for high-net-worth individuals for TransArabian Bank. In my spare time, I solicit funds for legitimate charities to help ease the suffering of Muslims around the world."

"Which is why I asked to see you."

"You wish to make a contribution?"

"A substantial one."

"To whom?"

"To the sort of men who can deliver to me the justice I am owed."

Abbas returned Nadia's BlackBerry to the table but said nothing. Nadia held his gaze for an uncomfortably long moment.

"We reside in the West, you and I, but we are children of the desert. My family came from the Nejd, yours from the Hejaz. We can say a great deal with very few words."

"My father used to speak to me only with his eyes," Abbas said wistfully.

"Mine, too," said Nadia.

Abbas removed the cap from his bottle of mineral water and poured some slowly into a glass, as though it were the last water on the face of the earth. "The charities with which I am associated are entirely legitimate," he said finally. "The money is used to build roads, schools, hospitals, and the like. Occasionally, some of it finds its way into the hands of a group based in the northwest tribal areas of Pakistan. I'm sure this group would be very grateful for any assistance. As you know, they lost their primary patron recently."

"I'm not interested in the group based in the tribal areas of Pakistan," Nadia said. "They're no longer effective. Their time has passed."

"Tell that to the people of Paris, Copenhagen, London, and Madrid."

"It is my understanding that the group based in the tribal areas of Pakistan had nothing to do with those attacks."

Abbas looked up sharply. "Who told you such a thing?"

"A man on my security staff who maintains close contact with the Saudi GID."

Nadia was surprised at how easily the lie rose to her lips. Abbas screwed the cap back onto the bottle and appeared to consider her response carefully.

"One hears rumors about the Yemeni preacher," he said finally. "The one who carries an American passport and speaks like one as well. One also hears rumors that he's expanding his operations. His charitable operations, of course," Abbas added.

"Do you know how to make contact with his organization?"

"If you are serious about trying to help them, I believe I can make an introduction."

"The sooner the better," she said.

"These are not the type of men who like to be told what to do, Miss al-Bakari, especially by women."

"I'm not just any woman. I am the daughter of Abdul Aziz al-Bakari, and I have been waiting for a very long time."

"So have they—hundreds of years, in fact. They are men of great patience. And you must be patient, too."

———

The meeting unwound in the same precise manner with which it had been planned and executed. Abbas returned to his office, Nadia to her airplane, Oded and Mordecai to the safe house on the western shore of the lake. Gabriel didn't bother to acknowledge their arrival. He was hunched over the computer in the living room, headphones over his ears, resignation on his face. He clicked pause, then rewind, then play.

"These are not the type of men who like to be told what to do, Miss al-Bakari, especially by women."

"*I'm not just any woman. I am the daughter of Abdul Aziz al-Bakari, and I have been waiting for a very long time.*"

"*So have they—hundreds of years, in fact. They are men of great patience. And you must be patient, too.*"

"*I have one request, Mr. Abbas. Because of what happened to my father, it is essential that I know who I will be meeting with and that I will be safe.*"

"*You needn't worry, Miss al-Bakari. The person I have in mind poses absolutely no threat to your security.*"

"*Who is it?*"

"*His name is Marwan Bin Tayyib. He's the dean of the department of theology at the University of Mecca and a very holy man.*"

Gabriel clicked pause, then rewind, then play.

"*His name is Marwan Bin Tayyib. He's the dean of the department of theology at the University of Mecca and a very holy man.*"

Gabriel pressed stop. Then, reluctantly, he forwarded the name to Adrian Carter at Langley. Carter's response arrived five minutes later. It was a reservation for the morning flight back to Washington. Economy plus, of course. Carter's revenge.

40

LANGLEY, VIRGINIA

W ELL DONE," SAID CARTER. "A bravura performance. A work of art. Truly."

He was standing outside the elevators on the
seventh-floor executive suite, smiling with all the sincerity of
the artificial plants that flourished in the permanent gloom of his
office. It was the kind of consoling smile worn by executives at
sacking time, thought Gabriel. The only thing missing from the
picture was the gold watch, the modest severance package, and the
complimentary dinner for two at Morton's steak house. "Come,"
said Carter, patting Gabriel's shoulder, something he never did. "I
have something to show you."

After descending into a subterranean level of the building, they
hiked for what seemed like a mile along gray-and-white corridors.
Their destination was a windowed observation deck overlooking
a cavernous open space that had the atmosphere of a Wall Street
trading floor. On each of the four walls flickered video display

panels the size of billboards. Beneath them, two hundred computer screens illuminated two hundred faces. Precisely what they were doing Gabriel did not know. Truth be told, he was no longer certain he was still at Langley or even in the Commonwealth of Virginia.

"We decided it was time to bring everyone under one roof," explained Carter.

"Everyone?" asked Gabriel.

"This is your operation," Carter said.

"This is all for *one* operation?"

"We're Americans," said Carter with a trace of contrition. "We only do big."

"Does it have its own zip code?"

"Actually, it doesn't even have a name yet. For now, we're calling it Rashidistan in your honor. Let me give you the nickel tour."

"Under the circumstances, I believe I'm owed at least ten cents' worth."

"Are we going to have another pissing match over turf?"

"Only if it's necessary."

Carter led Gabriel down a tight spiral staircase onto the floor of the op center. The stale air smelled of freshly laid carpeting and overheated electrical circuitry. A young woman with spiky black hair brushed past without a word and sat at one of the many worktables at the center of the room. Gabriel looked up at one of the video screens and saw several famous Washington pundits chatting in the warm glow of a television studio. The audio was muted.

"Are they plotting a terrorist attack?"

"Not that I'm aware of."

"So why are we watching them?" asked Gabriel, looking around the room with a combination of wonder and despair. "Who *are* all these people?"

Even Carter, the nominal leader of the operation, appeared to deliberate for a moment before responding. "Most come from inside the Agency," he said finally, "but we've also got NSA, FBI, DOJ, and Treasury, along with several dozen green-badgers."

"Are they some sort of endangered species?"

"Quite the opposite," said Carter. "The people you see wearing green credentials are all private contractors. Even I'm not sure how many we have working at Langley these days. But I do know one thing. Most of them make far more than I do."

"Doing what?"

"A few of them are former counterterrorism types who've tripled their salaries by going to work for private firms. In many cases, they do the exact same jobs and hold the exact same clearances. But now they're paid by ACME Security Solutions or some other private entity instead of the Agency."

"And the rest?"

"Data miners," said Carter, "and thanks to that meeting in Zurich yesterday, they've hit the mother lode." He pointed toward one of the worktables. "That group over there is handling Samir Abbas, our friend from TransArabian Bank. They're tearing him limb from limb, e-mail from e-mail, phone call from phone call, financial transaction from financial transaction. They've managed to assemble a data trail that predates 9/11. As far as we're concerned, Samir alone has been worth the price of admission to this operation. It's remarkable he's managed to escape our notice all these years. He's the real thing. And so is his friend at the University of Mecca."

The girl with spiky black hair handed Carter a file. Then he led Gabriel into a soundproof conference room. A single window looked onto the floor of the op center. "Here's your boy," Carter said, handing Gabriel an eight-by-ten photograph. "The Saudi dilemma incarnate."

Gabriel looked down at the photograph and saw Sheikh Marwan Bin Tayyib staring unsmilingly back at him. The Saudi cleric wore the long unkempt beard of a Salafi Muslim and the expression of a man who did not care to have his photograph taken. His red-and-white *ghutra* hung from his head in a way that revealed the white *taqiyah* skullcap beneath it. Unlike most Saudi men, he did not secure his headdress with the black circular cord known as an *agal*. It was a display of piety that told the world he cared little about his appearance.

"How much do you know about him?" Gabriel asked.

"He comes from the Wahhabi heartland north of Riyadh. In fact, there's a mud hut in his hometown where Wahhab himself is said to have stayed once. The men of his town have always regarded themselves as keepers of the true faith, the purest of the pure. Even now, foreigners aren't welcome. If one happens to come to town, the locals hide their faces and walk the other way."

"Does Bin Tayyib have ties to al-Qaeda?"

"They're tenuous," said Carter, "but undeniable. He was a key figure in the awakening of Islamic fervor that swept the Kingdom after the takeover of the Grand Mosque in 1979. In his doctoral thesis, he argued that secularism was a Western-inspired plot to destroy Islam and ultimately Saudi Arabia. It became required reading among certain radical members of the House of Saud, including our old friend Prince Nabil, the Saudi interior minister who to this day refuses to admit that nineteen of the 9/11 hijackers were citizens of his country. Nabil was so impressed by Bin Tayyib's thesis he personally recommended him for the influential post at the University of Mecca."

Gabriel handed the photograph back to Carter, who looked at it disdainfully before returning it to the file.

"This isn't the first time Bin Tayyib's name has been connected to Rashid's network," he said. "Despite his radical past, Bin Tayyib serves as an adviser to Saudi Arabia's much-vaunted terrorist rehabilitation program. At least twenty-five Saudis have returned to the battlefield after graduating from the program. Four are believed to be in Yemen with Rashid."

"Any other connections?"

"Guess who was the last person to be seen in Rashid's presence on the night he crossed back over to the other side."

"Bin Tayyib?"

Carter nodded. "It was Bin Tayyib who issued the invitation for Rashid to speak at the University of Mecca. And it was Bin Tayyib who served as his escort on the night of his defection."

"Did you ever raise this with your friends in Riyadh?"

"We tried."

"And?"

"It went nowhere," Carter admitted. "As you know, the relationship between the House of Saud and the members of the clerical establishment is complicated, to say the least. The al-Saud can't rule without the support of the *ulema*. And if they were to move against an influential theologian like Bin Tayyib at our behest . . ."

"The jihadists might take offense."

Nodding his head, Carter delved back into the file folder and produced two sheets of paper—transcripts of NSA intercepts.

"Our friend from TransArabian Bank made two interesting phone calls from his office this morning—one to Riyadh and a second to Jeddah. In the first call, he says he's doing business with Nadia al-Bakari. In the second, he says he has a friend who wants to discuss spiritual matters with Sheikh Bin Tayyib. Separately, the two calls appear entirely innocent. But put them together . . ."

"And it leaves no doubt that Nadia al-Bakari, a woman of unimpeachable jihadist credentials, would like to have a word with the sheikh in private."

"To discuss spiritual matters, of course." Carter returned the transcripts to the file. "The question is," he said, closing the cover, "do we let her go?"

"Why wouldn't we?"

"Because it would violate all our standing agreements with the Saudi government and its security services. The Hadith clearly states that there shall not be two religions in Arabia. And the al-Saud have made it clear they won't tolerate two intelligence services, either."

"When are you going to realize they are the problem rather than the solution?"

"The day we no longer need their oil to power our cars and our economy," Carter said. "We've arrested and killed hundreds of Saudi citizens since 9/11, but not inside Saudi Arabia itself. The country is off limits to infidels like us. If Nadia goes to see Sheikh Bin Tayyib, she has to go alone, without backup."

"Can we bring the mountain to Muhammad?"

"If you're asking whether Bin Tayyib can travel outside Saudi Arabia for a meeting with Nadia, the answer is no. He's on too many watch lists for that. No European country in its right mind would let him in. If Bin Tayyib bites, we have no choice but to send Nadia up the mountain by herself. And if the al-Saud find out she's there on our behalf, heads will roll."

"Maybe you should have thought of that before you created an entire separate government agency to handle this," Gabriel said, pointing at the op center beyond the window. "But that's your problem now, Adrian. Under the terms of our most recent operational accord, this is the point where I hand over the keys and fade quietly into the background."

"I'm wondering whether you might accept a few amendments," said Carter cautiously.

"I'm listening."

"Before I became the leader of the world's largest counterterrorism force, I actually recruited and ran spies. And if there's one thing a spy hates, it's change. You found Nadia. You recruited her. It makes sense for you to continue running her."

"You want me to serve as her case officer?"

"I suppose I do."

"Under your supervision, of course."

"The White House is adamant that the Agency assume overall control of the operation. I'm afraid my hands are tied."

"It's not like you to hide behind higher authority, Adrian."

Carter made no reply. Gabriel appeared to give the matter serious thought, but in reality his mind was already made up. He tilted his head toward the soundproof glass and asked, "Do you have any room out there for me?"

Carter smiled. "I've already made an ID badge so you can get into the building unescorted," he said. "It's green, of course."

"Green is the color of our enemy."

"Islam isn't the enemy, Gabriel."

"Oh, yes, I forgot."

Carter stood and escorted Gabriel to a small gray cubicle in the far corner of the op center. It contained a desk, a chair, an internal-line telephone, a computer, a document safe, a burn bag, and a coffee cup with the CIA emblem on the side. The girl with spiky black hair brought him a stack of files and then returned wordlessly to her pod. As Gabriel opened the first file, he looked up and saw Carter admiring the view of Rashidistan from the observation platform. He looked pleased with himself. He had a right to. The operation was his now. Gabriel was just another private contractor, a man in a gray box with a green badge around his neck.

41

RIYADH, SAUDI ARABIA

THE BOEING BUSINESS JET OWNED and operated by AAB Holdings entered the airspace of the Kingdom of Saudi Arabia at precisely 5:18 p.m. As was customary, its British pilot immediately informed the passengers and crew of this development so that any females on board could begin exchanging their Western clothing for appropriate Islamic dress.

Ten of the women on board the plane did so at once. The eleventh, Nadia al-Bakari, remained in her usual seat, working through a thick stack of paperwork, until the first lights of Riyadh appeared like bits of amber scattered across the desert floor. A century earlier, the Saudi capital had been little more than a mud-walled desert outpost, all but unknown to the Western world, a speck on the map somewhere between the slopes of the Sarawat Mountains and the shores of the Persian Gulf. Oil had transformed Riyadh into a modern metropolis of palaces, skyscrapers, and shopping malls. Yet in many respects the trappings of petrowealth were a mirage.

For all the billions the al-Saud had spent trying to modernize their sleepy desert empire, they had squandered billions more on their yachts, their whores, and their vacation homes in Marbella. Worse still, they had done little to prepare the country for the day the last well ran dry. Ten million foreign workers toiled in the oil fields and the palaces, yet hundreds of thousands of young Saudi men could find no work. Oil aside, the country's biggest exports were dates and Korans. And bearded fanatics, thought Nadia grimly, as she watched the lights of Riyadh grow brighter. When it came to producing Islamic extremists, Saudi Arabia was a market leader.

Nadia lifted her gaze from the window and glanced around the interior of the aircraft. The forward seating compartment was arranged in the manner of a *majlis*, with comfortable chairs along the fuselage and rich Oriental rugs spread across the floor. The seats were occupied by AAB's all-male senior staff—Daoud Hamza, the legal team of Abdul & Abdul, and, of course, Rafiq al-Kamal. He was staring at Nadia with a look of transparent disapproval, as if silently trying to remind her it was time to change her clothing. They were about to touch down in the land of invisible women, which meant Rafiq would become more than just Nadia's bodyguard. He would also serve as her male chaperone and by law would be obligated to accompany her everywhere she went in public. In a few minutes' time, Nadia al-Bakari, one of the world's richest women, would have the rights of a camel. Fewer, she thought resentfully, for even a camel was permitted to show its face in public.

Without a word, she rose to her feet and made her way toward the back of the aircraft to her elegantly appointed private quarters. Opening the closet, she saw her Saudi uniform hanging limply from the rod: a simple white *thobe*, an embroidered black *abaya* cloak, and a black *niqab* facial veil. Just once, she thought, she would like to walk the streets of her country in loose-fitting white clothing rather than inside a constricting black cocoon. It wasn't possible, of course; even wealth on the scale of the al-Bakaris offered no protection against the fanatical *mutaween* religious police. Besides, this was hardly the moment to test Saudi Arabia's social and religious norms. She had come to her homeland to meet privately with Sheikh Marwan Bin Tayyib, the dean of the department of theology at the University of Mecca. Surely the esteemed religious scholar would find it odd if, on the eve of that meeting, Nadia was arrested by the bearded ones for failing to wear proper Islamic attire.

Reluctantly, she shed her pale Oscar de la Renta pantsuit and with clerical slowness robed herself in black. With the *niqab* now hiding the face God had given her, she stood before the mirror and examined her appearance. Only her eyes were visible, along with a tempting trace of flesh around her ankles. All other visual proof of her existence had been erased. In fact, her return to the forward passenger cabin provoked scarcely a glance from her male colleagues. Only Daoud Hamza, a Lebanese by birth, bothered to acknowledge her presence. The others, all Saudis, kept their eyes conspicuously averted. The illness had returned, she thought, the illness that was Saudi Arabia. It didn't matter that Nadia was their employer. Allah had made her a woman, and upon arrival in the land of the Prophet, she would assume her proper place.

Their landing at King Khalid International Airport coincided with the evening prayer. Forbidden to pray with the men, Nadia had no choice but to wait patiently while they completed this most important pillar of Islam. Then, surrounded by several veiled women, she headed awkwardly down the passenger stairs, struggling not to trip over the hem of her *abaya*. A frigid wind was ripping over the tarmac, bringing with it a thick brown cloud of Nejdi dust. Leaning into the wind for balance, Nadia followed her male colleagues toward the general aviation terminal. There they went their separate ways, for the terminal, like every other public space in Saudi Arabia, was segregated by gender. Despite the AAB luggage tags, their bags were carefully searched for pornography, liquor, or any other hint of Western decadence.

Emerging from the opposite side of the building, she climbed into the back of a waiting Mercedes limousine with Rafiq al-Kamal for the twenty-two-mile drive into Riyadh. The dust storm had reduced visibility to only a few meters. Occasionally, the headlamps of an approaching car bobbed toward them like the running lights of a small ship, but for the most part, they seemed entirely alone. Nadia wanted desperately to remove her *niqab* but knew better. The *mutaween* were always on the lookout for unveiled women riding in automobiles—especially rich Westernized women returning home from Europe.

After fifteen minutes, the skyline of Riyadh finally pricked the brown-black gloom. They sped past Ibn Saud Islamic University and navigated a series of traffic circles to the King Fahd Road, the main thoroughfare of Riyadh's thriving new al-Olaya financial district. Directly ahead rose the silver Kingdom Center tower, looking like a misplaced modern attaché case waiting to be reclaimed by its errant owner. In its shadow was the glittering new Makkah Mall, which had reopened after the evening prayer and was now under assault by hordes of eager shoppers. Baton-wielding *mutaween* moved among the crowds in pairs, looking for evidence of inappropriate conduct or relationships. Nadia thought of Rena, and for the first time since her summons to the house in Seraincourt, she felt a stab of genuine fear.

It receded a moment later when the car turned onto Musa Bin Nusiar Street and headed into al-Shumaysi, a district of walled palaces populated by al-Saud princes and other Saudi elite. The al-Bakari compound lay at the western edge of the district on a street patrolled constantly by police and troops. An ornate blend of East and West, the palace was surrounded by three acres of reflecting pools, fountains, lawns, and palm groves. Its towering white walls were designed to keep even the most determined enemy at bay but were no match for the dust, which was billowing across the forecourt as the limousine slipped through the security gate.

Standing at attention in the portico were the ten members of the permanent household staff, Asians all. Emerging from the back of her Mercedes, Nadia would have liked to greet them warmly. Instead, playing the role of a distant Saudi heiress, she walked past without a word and started up the sweeping central staircase. By the time she reached the first landing, she had torn the *niqab* from her face. Then, in the privacy of her rooms, she removed her clothing and stood naked before a full-length mirror, until a wave of dizziness drove her to her knees. When it passed, she washed the dust of the Nejd from her hair and lay on the floor with her ankles together and her arms extended, waiting for the familiar feeling of weightlessness to carry her away. It was nearly over, she thought. A few months, perhaps only a few weeks. Then it would be done.

It was just half past eleven a.m. at Langley, but in Rashidistan the atmosphere was one of permanent evening. Adrian Carter sat at the command desk, a secure phone in one hand, a single sheet of white paper in the other. The phone was connected to James Mc-Kenna at the White House. The sheet of paper was a printout of the latest cable from the CIA's Riyadh Station. It stated that NAB, the Agency's not-so-cryptic cipher for Nadia al-Bakari, had arrived home safely and appeared to be under no surveillance—jihadist, Saudi, or anything in between. Carter read the cable with a look of profound relief on his face before dealing it across the desk to Gabriel, whose face remained expressionless. They said nothing more to each other. They didn't need to. Their affliction was shared. They had an agent in hostile territory, and neither one of them would have a moment's peace until she was back on her plane again, heading out of Saudi airspace.

At noon Washington time, Carter returned to his office on the seventh floor while Gabriel headed to the house on N Street for some much-needed sleep. He woke at midnight and by one a.m. was back in Rashidistan, with his green badge around his neck and Adrian Carter sitting tensely at his side. The next cable from Riyadh arrived fifteen minutes later. It said NAB had departed her walled compound in al-Shumaysi and was now en route to her offices on al-Olaya Street. There she remained until one in the afternoon, when she was driven to the Four Seasons Hotel for a luncheon with Saudi investors, all of whom happened to be men. Upon departure from the hotel, her car turned right onto King Fahd Street—curious, since her office was in the opposite direction. She was last seen ten minutes later, heading north on Highway 65. The CIA team made no attempt to follow. NAB was now entirely on her own.

42

NEJD, SAUDI ARABIA

T HE WIND BLEW ITSELF OUT at midday, and by late afternoon, peace had once more been imposed upon the Nejd. It would be a temporary peace, as most were in the harsh plateau, for in the distant west, black storm clouds were creeping over the passes of the Sarawat Mountains like a Hejazi raiding party. It had been two weeks since the first rains, and the desert floor was aglow with the first hesitant growth of grass and wildflowers. Within a few weeks, the land would be as green as a Berkshire meadow. Then the blast furnace would reignite and from the sky not a drop of rain would fall—not until the next winter when, Allah willing, the storms would once again come rolling down the slopes of the Sarawat.

To the people of the Nejd, the rain was one of the few welcome things to come from the west. They regarded nearly everything else, including their so-called countrymen from the Hejaz, with contempt and scorn. It was their faith that made them hostile to outside influences, a faith that had been given to them three centuries earlier by an austere reformist preacher named Muhammad Abdul Wahhab. In 1744, he formed an alliance with a Nejdi tribe called the al-Saud, thus creating the union of political and religious power that would eventually lead to the creation of the modern state of Saudi Arabia. It had been an uneasy alliance, and from time to time, the al-Saud had felt compelled to put the bearded zealots of the Nejd in their place, sometimes with the help of infidels. In 1930, the al-Saud had used British machine guns to massacre the holy warriors of the Ikhwan in the town of Sabillah. And after 9/11, the al-Saud had joined forces with the hated Americans to beat back the modern-day version of the Ikhwan known as al-Qaeda. Yet through it all, the marriage between the followers of Wahhab and the House of Saud had endured. They were dependent on one another for their very survival. In the unforgiving landscape of the Nejd, one could not ask for much more.

Despite the extremes of climate, the newly laid surface of Highway 65 was smooth and black, like the rivers of crude that flowed beneath it. Running in a northwesterly direction, it followed the path of the ancient caravan route linking Riyadh with the oasis town of Hail. A few miles south of Hail, near the town of Buraydah, Nadia instructed her driver to turn onto a smaller two-lane road running westward into the desert. Rafiq al-Kamal was by now visibly uneasy. Nadia had told him nothing of her plans to travel to the Nejd until the moment of their departure from the Four Seasons, and even then her explanations had been opaque. She said she was having dinner at the family camp of Sheikh Marwan Bin Tayyib, an important member of the *ulema*. After the dinner—which would be strictly segregated by gender, of course—she would meet privately with the sheikh to discuss matters related to *zakat*. It would not be necessary for her to take along a chaperone to the meeting since the cleric was a good and learned man known for his extreme piety. Nor were there any concerns about safety. Al-Kamal had accepted her edicts, but clearly they did not please him.

It was now a few minutes past five, and the light was slowly seeping from the endless sky. They sped through groves of date, lemon, and orange trees, slowing only once to allow a leathered old shepherd to drive his goats across the road. Al-Kamal appeared to relax with each passing mile. A native of the region, he pointed out some of its more important landmarks as they flashed past his window. And in Unayzah, a starkly religious town known for the purity of its Islam, he asked Nadia to make a small detour so he could see the modest home where, as a child, he had lived with one of his father's four wives.

"I never knew you came from here," Nadia said.

"So does Sheikh Bin Tayyib," he said, nodding. "I knew him when he was a boy. We attended the same school and prayed in the same mosque. Marwan was quite a firebrand back then. He got into trouble for throwing a rock through the window of a video shop. He thought it was un-Islamic."

"What about you?"

"I didn't mind the shop. There wasn't much else to do in Unayzah but watch videos and go to the mosque."

"It's my understanding the sheikh has moderated his views since then."

"The Muslims of Unayzah don't know the meaning of the word 'moderation,'" al-Kamal said. "If Marwan has changed in any way since then, it is for public consumption only. Marwan is an Islamist through and through. And he has very little use for the al-Saud, despite the fact that they pay him well. I'd watch your step around him."

"I'll keep that in mind."

"Maybe I should attend the meeting with you."

"I'll be fine, Rafiq."

Al-Kamal fell silent as they left Unayzah and plunged once more into the desert. Directly before them, across a sea of boulders and stones, rose a barren escarpment of rock, its edges carved and scored by millions of years of wind and sand. The sheikh's camp lay to the north of the outcropping along the edge of a deep *wadi*. Nadia could feel heavy stones thudding against the undercarriage of the car as they drove along a pitted unpaved track.

"I wish you'd told me where we were going," al-Kamal said, clutching the armrest for support. "We could have taken one of the Range Rovers."

"I didn't think it would be this bad."

"It's a desert camp. How did you think we were going to get there?"

Nadia laughed in spite of herself. "I hope my father isn't watching this."

"Actually, I hope he is." Al-Kamal looked at her for a long moment without speaking. "I never left your father's side, Nadia, even when he was discussing highly sensitive business with men like Sheikh Bin Tayyib. He trusted me with his life. Unfortunately, I couldn't protect him that night in Cannes, but I would have gladly stepped in front of those bullets. And I would do the same for you. Do you understand what I'm saying to you?"

"I think I do, Rafiq."

"Good," he said. "If God wills it, this meeting tonight will be a success. But next time, tell me first so I can make proper arrangements. It's better that way. No surprises."

"Zizi's rules?" she asked.

"Zizi's rules," he replied, nodding his head. "Zizi's rules are like the teachings of the Prophet, peace be upon him. Follow them carefully and God will grant you a long and happy life. Ignore them . . ." He shrugged his heavy shoulders. "That's when bad things happen."

They came upon a cluster of cars parked haphazardly along the edge of the *wadi*: Range Rovers, Mercedes, Toyotas, and a few battered pickup trucks. Adjacent to the parking area, aglow with internal lighting, stood two large communal tents. A dozen smaller tents were scattered across the desert floor, each fitted with a generator and a satellite dish. Nadia smiled beneath the cover of her *niqab*. The Saudis loved to return to the desert each winter to reconnect with their Bedouin heritage, but their devotion to the old ways only went so far.

"The sheikh is obviously doing quite well for himself."

"You should see his villa in Mecca," al-Kamal said. "This is all bought and paid for by the government. As far as the al-Saud are concerned, it's money well spent. They take care of the *ulema*, and the *ulema* takes care of them."

"Why this spot?" asked Nadia, looking around.

"Long before there was such a thing as Saudi Arabia, members of the sheikh's clan used to bring their animals here in the winter. The Bin Tayyibs have been camping here for centuries."

"The next thing you're going to tell me is that you came here when you were a boy."

Al-Kamal gave a rare smile. "I did."

The security man gestured to the driver to park in a spot isolated from the other cars. After helping Nadia out of the backseat, he paused to look at a Toyota Camry. But for the thin coating of fine powdery dust, it looked as though it had just rolled onto the dock at Dhahran.

"Your dream car?" asked Nadia sardonically.

"It's the model they give to graduates of the terrorist rehabilitation program. They give them a car, a down payment on a house, and a nice girl to marry—all the trappings of a normal life so they stay tethered to this world rather than the world of jihad. They buy the loyalty of the *ulema*, and they buy the loyalty of the jihadis. It's the way of the desert. It's the al-Saud way."

Al-Kamal instructed the driver to stay with the car and then led Nadia toward the two communal tents. Within a few seconds a young man appeared to welcome them. He wore a calf-length *thobe* in the style of the Salaf and a *taqiyah* skullcap with no headdress. His beard was long but sparse, and his eyes were unusually gentle for a Saudi man. After offering them the traditional greeting of peace, he introduced himself as Ali and said he was a *talib*, or student, of Sheikh Bin Tayyib. He looked to be about thirty.

"The meal is just getting started. Your bodyguard is free to join us, if he wishes. The women are over there," he added, gesturing toward the tent on the left. "There are several members of the sheikh's family here tonight. I'm sure you'll be made to feel very welcome."

Nadia exchanged a final brief glance with al-Kamal before setting off toward the tent. Two veiled women appeared and, greeting her warmly in Nedji Arabic, drew her through the opening. Inside were twenty more women just like them. They were seated on thick Oriental rugs, around heaping platters of lamb, chicken, eggplant, rice, and flat bread. Some wore the *niqab* like Nadia, but most were fully veiled. In the enclosed space of the tent, their energetic chatter sounded like the clicking of cicadas. It fell silent for a few seconds while Nadia was introduced by one of the women who had greeted her. Apparently, they had been waiting for Nadia's arrival to begin eating, for one of the women loudly exclaimed, *"Alhamdu lillah!"*—Thanks be to God! Then the women set upon the platters as if they had not eaten in many days and would not see food again for a very long time.

Still standing, Nadia searched the shapeless veiled forms for a moment before settling herself between two women in their twenties. One was named Adara, the other Safia. Adara came from Buraydah and was the sheikh's niece. Her brother had gone to Iraq to fight the Americans and had vanished without a trace. Safia turned out to be the wife of Ali, the *talib*. "I was named for the Muslim woman who killed a Jewish spy in the time of the Prophet," she said proudly before adding the obligatory "peace be upon him." Rafiq al-Kamal had been right about the Toyota Camry; it had been given to Ali after his graduation from the terrorist rehabilitation program. Safia had been given to him as well, along with a respectable dowry. They were expecting their first child in four months' time. *"Inshallah*, it will be a boy," she said.

"If it is the will of God," repeated Nadia with a serenity that did not match her thoughts.

Nadia served herself a small portion of chicken and rice and looked around at the other women. A few had removed their *niqab*s, but most were attempting to eat with their faces covered, including Adara and Safia. Nadia did the same, all the while listening to the constant hum of chatter around her. It was frightfully banal: family gossip, the newest shopping center in Riyadh, the accomplishments of their children. Only their sons, of course, for their female offspring were symbols of reproductive failure. This was how they spent their lives, locked away in separate rooms, in separate tents, in the company of women just like themselves. They attended no theater productions, because there was not one playhouse in the entire country. They went to no discotheques, because music and dancing were both strictly *haram*. They read nothing but the Koran—which they studied separately from men—and heavily censored magazines promoting clothing they were not allowed to wear in public. Occasionally, they would grant one another physical pleasure, the dirty little secret of Saudi Arabia, but for the most part they led lives of crushing, depressing boredom. And when it was over they would be buried in the Wahhabi tradition, in a grave with no marker, beneath the blistering sands of the Nejd.

Despite it all, Nadia couldn't help but feel strangely comforted by the warm embrace of her people and her faith. That was the one thing Westerners would never understand about Islam: it was all-encompassing. It woke you in the morning with the call to prayer and covered you like an *abaya* as you moved through the rest of your day. It was in every word, every thought, and every deed of a pious Muslim. And it was here, in this communal gathering of veiled women, in the heart of the Nejd.

It was then she felt the first terrible pang of guilt. It swept up on her with the suddenness of a sandstorm and without the courtesy of a warning. By throwing in her lot with the Israelis and the Americans, she was effectively renouncing her faith as a Muslim. She was a heretic, an apostate, and the punishment for apostasy was death. It was a death these veiled, bored women gathered around her would no doubt condone. They had no choice; if they dared to rise to her defense, they would suffer the same fate.

The guilt quickly passed and was replaced by fear. To steel herself, she thought of Rena, her guide, her beacon. And she thought how appropriate it was that her act of betrayal should occur here, in the sacred land of the Nejd, in the comforting embrace of veiled women. And if she had any misgivings about the path she had chosen, it was too late. Because through the opening in the tent she could see Ali, the bearded *talib*, coming across the desert in his short Salafi *thobe*. It was time to have a quiet word with the sheikh. After that, Allah willing, the rains would come, and it would be done.

43

NEJD, SAUDI ARABIA

S HE FOLLOWED THE *TALIB* INTO the desert, along the rim of the *wadi*. There was no proper footpath, only a swath of beaten earth, the remnants of an ancient camel track that had been carved into the desert floor long before anyone in the Nejd had ever heard of a preacher called Wahhab or even a trader from Mecca called Muhammad. The *talib* carried no torch, for no torch was needed. Their way was lit by the hard white stars shining in the vast sky and by the *hilal* moon floating above a distant spire of rock, like a crescent atop the world's tallest minaret. Nadia carried her high heels in one hand and with the other lifted the hem of her black *abaya*. The air had turned bitterly cold, but the earth felt warm against her feet. The *talib* was walking a few paces ahead. His *thobe* appeared luminescent in the moon glow. He was reciting verses of the Koran softly to himself, but to Nadia he spoke not a word.

They came upon a tent with no satellite dish or generator. Two men crouched outside the entrance, their young, bearded faces lit by the faint glow of a small fire. The *talib* offered them a greeting of peace, then pulled open the flap of the tent and gestured for Nadia to enter. Sheikh Marwan Bin Tayyib, dean of the department of theology at the University of Mecca, sat cross-legged on a simple Oriental carpet, reading the Koran by the light of a gas lantern. Closing the book, he regarded Nadia through his small round spectacles for a long moment before inviting her to sit. She lowered herself slowly to the carpet, careful not to expose her flesh, and arranged herself piously next to the Koran.

"The veil becomes you," Bin Tayyib said admiringly, "but you may remove it, if you wish."

"I prefer to keep it on."

"I never realized you were so devout. Your reputation is that of a liberated woman."

The sheikh clearly did not mean it as a compliment. He intended to test her, but then she had expected nothing less. Neither had Gabriel. *Hide only us*, he had said. *Adhere to the truth when possible. Lie as a last resort.* It was the way of the Office. The way of the professional spy.

"Liberated from what?" Nadia asked, deliberately provoking him.

"From the *sharia*," said the sheikh. "I'm told you never wear the veil in the West."

"It is impractical."

"It is my understanding that more and more of our women are choosing to remain veiled when they travel. I'm told that many Saudi women cover their faces when they are having tea at Harrods."

"They don't run large investment companies. And most of them drink more than just tea when they're in the West."

"I hear you are one of them."

Adhere to the truth when possible. . . .

"I confess that I am fond of wine."

"It is *haram*," he said in a scolding tone.

"Blame it on my father. He permitted me to drink when I was in the West."

"He was lenient with you?"

"No," she said, shaking her head, "he wasn't lenient. He spoiled me terribly. But he also gave me his great faith."

"Faith in what?"

"Faith in Allah and His Prophet Muhammad, peace be upon him."

"If my memory is correct, your father regarded himself as a descendant of Wahhab himself."

"Unlike the al-Asheikh family, we are not direct descendants. We come from a distant branch."

"Distant or not, his blood flows through you."

"So it is said."

"But you have chosen not to marry and have children. Is this, too, a matter of practicality?"

Nadia hesitated.

Lie as a last resort. . . .

"I came of age in the wake of my father's murder," she said. "My grief makes it impossible for me to even contemplate the idea of marriage."

"And now your grief has led you to us."

"Not grief," Nadia said. "Anger."

"Here in the Nejd, it is sometimes difficult to tell the two apart." The sheikh gave her a sympathetic smile, his first. "But you should know that you are not alone. There are hundreds of Saudis just like you—good Muslims whose loved ones were killed by the Americans or are rotting to this day in the cages of Guantánamo Bay. And many have come to the brothers in search of revenge."

"None of them watched their father being murdered in cold blood."

"You believe this makes you special?"

"No," Nadia said, "I believe it is my money that makes me special."

"Very special," the sheikh said. "It's been five years since your father was martyred, has it not?"

Nadia nodded.

"That is a long time, Miss al-Bakari."

"In the Nejd, it is the blink of an eye."

"We expected you sooner. We even sent our brother Samir to make contact with you. But you rejected his entreaties."

"It wasn't possible for me to help you at the time."

"Why not?"

"I was being watched."

"By whom?"

"By everyone," she said, "including the al-Saud."

"They warned you against taking any action to avenge your father's death?"

"In no uncertain terms."

"They said there would be financial consequences?"

"They didn't go into specifics, except to say the consequences would be grave."

"And you believed them?"

"Why wouldn't I?"

"Because they are liars." Bin Tayyib allowed his words to hang in the air for a moment. "How do I know that you are not a spy sent here by the al-Saud to entrap me?"

"How do I know that *you* are not the spy, Sheikh Bin Tayyib? After all, you are the one who's on the al-Saud payroll."

"So are you, Miss al-Bakari. At least that's the rumor."

Nadia gave the sheikh a withering look. She could only imagine how she must have appeared to him—two coal-black eyes glaring over a black *niqab*. Perhaps there was value to the veil after all.

"Try to see it from our point of view, Miss al-Bakari," Bin Tayyib continued. "In the five years since your father's martyrdom, you have said nothing about him in public. You seem to spend as little time in Saudi Arabia as possible. You smoke, you drink, you shun the veil—except, of course, when you are trying to impress me with your piety—and you throw away hundreds of millions of dollars on infidel art."

Obviously, the sheikh's test was not yet over. Nadia remembered the last words Gabriel had spoken to her at Château Treville. *You're Zizi's daughter. Never let them forget it.*

"Perhaps you're right, Sheikh Bin Tayyib. Perhaps I should have cloaked myself in a *burqa* and declared my intention to avenge my father's death on television. Surely that would have been the wiser course of action."

The sheikh gave a conciliatory smile. "I've heard all about your wicked tongue," he said.

"I have my father's tongue. And the last time I heard his voice, he was bleeding to death in my arms."

"And now you want vengeance."

"I want justice—God's justice."

"And what of the al-Saud?"

"They seem to have lost interest in me."

"I'm not surprised," Bin Tayyib said. "Even the House of Saud isn't sure whether it's going to survive the turmoil sweeping the

Arab world. They need friends wherever they can find them, even if they happen to wear the short *thobes* and unkempt beards of the Salaf."

Nadia couldn't believe what she was hearing. If the sheikh was speaking the truth, the rulers of Saudi Arabia had renewed the Faustian bargain, the deal with the devil that had led to 9/11 and countless other deaths after that. The al-Saud had no choice, she thought. They were like a man holding a tiger by the ears. If they kept their grip on the beast, they might survive a little longer. But if they released it, they would be devoured in an instant.

"Do the Americans know about this?" she asked.

"The so-called special relationship between the Americans and the House of Saud is a thing of the past," Bin Tayyib said. "As you know, Miss al-Bakari, Saudi Arabia is forming new alliances and finding new customers for its oil. The Chinese don't care about things like human rights and democracy. They pay their bills on time, and they don't poke their noses into things that are none of their business."

"Things like jihad?" she asked.

The sheikh nodded. "The Prophet Muhammad, peace be upon him, taught us there were Five Pillars of Islam. We believe there is a sixth. Jihad is not a choice. It is an obligation. The al-Saud understand this. Once again, they are willing to look the other way, provided the brothers don't make trouble inside the Kingdom. That was Bin Laden's biggest mistake."

"Bin Laden is dead," said Nadia, "and so is his group. I'm interested in the one who can make bombs go off in the cities of Europe."

"Then you are interested in the Yemeni."

"Do you know him?"

"I've met him."

"Do you have the ability to speak to him?"

"That is a dangerous question. And even if I could speak to him, I certainly wouldn't bother to tell him about a rich Saudi woman who's looking for vengeance. You have to believe in what you are doing."

"I am the daughter of Abdul Aziz al-Bakari and a descendant of Muhammad Abdul Wahhab. I certainly *believe* in what I am doing. And I am after far more than just vengeance."

"What *are* you after?"

Nadia hesitated. The next words were not her own. They had been dictated to her by the man who had killed her father.

"I wish only to resume the work of Abdul Aziz al-Bakari," she said gravely. "I will place the money in the hands of the Yemeni to do with as he pleases. And perhaps, if God wills it, bombs will one day explode in the streets of Washington and Tel Aviv."

"I suspect he would be most grateful," the sheikh said carefully. "But I am certain he will be unable to offer any sort of guarantees."

"I'm not looking for any guarantees. Only a pledge that he will use the money wisely and carefully."

"You are proposing a one-time payment?"

"No, Sheikh Bin Tayyib, I am proposing a long-term relationship. He will attack them. And I will pay for it."

"How much money are you willing to provide?"

"As much as he needs."

The sheikh smiled.

"Al-hamdu lillah."

Nadia remained in the tent of the sheikh for another hour. Then she followed the *talib* along the edge of the *wadi* to her car. The skies poured with rain during the drive back to Riyadh, and it was still raining late the following morning when Nadia and her entourage boarded their plane for the flight back to Europe. Once clear of Saudi airspace, she removed her *niqab* and *abaya* and changed into a pale Chanel suit. Then she telephoned Thomas Fowler at his estate north of Paris to say that her meetings in Saudi Arabia had gone better than expected. Fowler immediately placed a call to a little-known venture capital firm in northern Virginia—a call that was automatically routed to Gabriel's desk in Rashidistan. Gabriel spent the next week carefully monitoring the financial and legal maneuverings of one Samir Abbas of the TransArabian Bank in Zurich. Then, after dining poorly with Carter at a seafood restaurant in McLean, he headed back to London. Carter let him take an Agency Gulfstream. No handcuffs. No hypodermic needles. No hard feelings.

44

ST. JAMES'S, LONDON

O N THE DAY AFTER GABRIEL'S return to London, the venerable Christie's auction house announced a surprise addition to its upcoming sale of Venetian Old Masters: *Madonna and Child with Mary Magdalene*, oil on canvas, 110 by 92 centimeters, previously attributed to the workshop of Palma Vecchio, now firmly attributed to none other than the great Titian himself. By midday, the phones inside Christie's were ringing off the hook, and by day's end, no fewer than forty important museums and collectors had dipped their oars into the water. That evening, the atmosphere in the bar at Green's Restaurant was electric, though Julian Isherwood was notably not among those present. "Saw him getting into a cab in Duke Street," Jeremy Crabbe muttered into his gin and bitters. "Looked positively dreadful, poor sod. Said he was planning to spend a quiet evening alone with his cough."

It is rare that a painting by an artist like Titian resurfaces, and when one does, it is usually accompanied by a good story. Such was certainly the case with *Madonna and Child with Mary Magdalene*, though whether it was tragedy, comedy, or morality tale depended entirely on who was doing the telling. Christie's released an abridged version for the sake of the painting's official provenance, but in the little West London village of St. James's, it was immediately written off as well-sanitized hogwash. Eventually, there came to exist an *unofficial* version of the story that unfolded roughly along the following lines.

It seemed that at some point the previous August, an unidentified Norfolk nobleman of great title but shrinking resources reluctantly decided to part with a portion of his art collection. This nobleman made contact with a London art dealer, also unidentified, and asked whether he might be willing to accept the assignment. This London art dealer was busy at the time—truth be told, he was sunning himself in the Costa del Sol—and it was late September before he was able to make his way to the nobleman's estate. The dealer found the collection lackluster, to put it mildly, though he did agree to take several paintings off the nobleman's hands, including a very dirty work attributed to some hack in the workshop of Palma Vecchio. The amount of money that changed hands was never disclosed. It was said to be quite small.

For reasons not made clear, the dealer allowed the paintings to languish in his storage rooms before commissioning a hasty cleaning of the aforementioned Palma Vecchio. The identity of the restorer was never revealed, though all agreed he gave a rather good account of himself in a remarkably short period of time. Indeed, the painting was in such fine shape that it managed to catch the wandering eye of one Oliver Dimbleby, the noted Old Master dealer from Bury Street. Oliver acquired it in a trade—the other paintings involved were never disclosed—and promptly hung it in his gallery, viewable by appointment only.

It would not remain there long, however. In fact, just forty-eight hours later, it was purchased by something called Onyx Innovative Capital, a limited liability investment firm registered in the Swiss city of Lucerne. Oliver didn't deal directly with OIC, but rather with an agreeable bloke named Samir Abbas of the TransArabian Bank. After thrashing out the final details over tea at the Dorchester Hotel, Abbas presented Oliver with a check for twenty-two thousand pounds. Oliver quickly deposited the money into his account at Lloyds Bank, thus consecrating the sale, and began the messy process of securing the necessary export license.

It was at this point that the affair took a disastrous turn, at least from Oliver's point of view. Because on a dismal afternoon in late January there came to Oliver's gallery a rumpled figure dressed in many layers of clothing, who, with a single offhand question, sent the apples rolling across the proverbial floor. Oliver would never reveal the identity of the man, except to say he was learned in the field of Italian Renaissance art, particularly the Venetian School. As for the question posed by this man, Oliver was willing to repeat it verbatim. In fact, for the price of a good glass of Sancerre, he would act out the entire scene. For Oliver loved nothing more than to tell stories on himself, especially when they were less than flattering, which was almost always the case.

"I say, Oliver, old chap, but is that Titian spoken for?"

"Not a Titian, my good man."

"Sure about that?"

"Positive as I can be."

"Who is it, then?"

"Palma."

"Really? Rather good for a Palma. Workshop or the man him-self?"

"Workshop, love. Workshop."

It was then the rumpled figure leaned precariously forward to have a closer look—a lean that Oliver re-created nightly at Green's to uproarious laughter.

"Sold, is it?" asked the rumpled figure, tugging at his earlobe.

"Just last week," said Oliver.

"As a Palma?"

"Workshop, love. Workshop."

"How much?"

"My good man!"

"If I were you, I'd find some way to wriggle out of it."

"Whatever for?"

"Look at the draftsmanship. Look at the brushwork. You just let a Titian slip through your fingers. Shame on you, Oliver. Hang your head. Confess your sins."

Oliver did neither, but within minutes he was on the phone to an old chum at the British Museum who had forgotten more about Titian than most art historians would ever know. The chum hurried over to St. James's in a deluge and stood before the canvas looking like the only survivor of a shipwreck.

"Oliver! How could you?"

"Is it that obvious?"

"I'd stake my reputation on it."

"At least you have one. Mine will be in the loo if this gets out."

"You do have *one* option."

"What's that?"

"Call Mr. Abbas. Tell him the check bounced."

And don't think the idea didn't cross Oliver's devious little mind. In fact, he spent the better part of the next forty-eight hours trying to find some legally and morally acceptable loophole that he might use to extricate himself from the deal. Finding none—at least not one that would allow him to sleep at night—he called Mr. Abbas to inform him that Onyx Innovative Capital was actually the proud owner of a newly discovered Titian. Oliver offered to take the painting to market, hoping to at least salvage a healthy commission out of the debacle, but Abbas called back the very next day to say OIC was going in a different direction. "Tried to let me down easy," Oliver said wistfully. "Pleasure doing business with you, Mr. Dimbleby. Lunch next time you're in Zurich, Mr. Dimbleby. And by the way, Mr. Dimbleby, the lads from Christie's will be stopping by in an hour."

They appeared with the suddenness of professional kidnappers and carried the painting over to King Street, where it was examined by a parade of Titian experts from around the globe. Each rendered the same verdict, and, miraculously, not one violated the draconian confidentiality agreement that Christie's had made them sign for their fee. Even the normally loquacious Oliver managed to keep quiet until after Christie's unveiled its prize. But then Oliver had reason to hold his tongue. Oliver was the goat who let a Titian slip through his hooves.

But even Oliver seemed to find a bit of pleasure in the frenzy that followed the announcement. And why ever not? It really had been a dreadful winter till that point, with the government austerity and the blizzards and the bombings. Oliver was only happy he was able to lighten the mood, even if it meant playing the fool for drinks at Green's. Besides, he knew the role well. He had played it many times before, to great acclaim.

On the night of the auction, he gave what would be his final performance to a standing-room-only crowd. At its conclusion, he made three curtain calls, then joined the throng heading over to Christie's for the big show. Management had been kind enough to reserve a second-row seat for him, directly in front of the auctioneer's rostrum. Seated to his left was his friend and competitor, Roddy Hutchinson, and to Roddy's left was Julian Isherwood. The seat to Oliver's right was unoccupied. A moment later, it was filled by none other than Nicholas Lovegrove, art adviser to the vastly rich. Lovegrove had just flown in from New York. Private, of course. Lovegrove didn't do commercial anymore.

"Why the long face, Ollie?"

"Thoughts of what might have been."

"Sorry about the Titian."

"Win some, lose some. How's biz, Nicky?"

"Can't complain."

"Didn't realize you dabbled in Old Masters."

"Actually, they terrify me. Look at this place. It's like being in a bloody church—all angels and saints and martyrdom and crucifixion."

"So what brings you to town?"

"A client who wants to venture into new territory."

"Client have a name?"

"Client wishes to remain anonymous—*very* anonymous."

"Know the feeling. Your client planning to venture into new territory by acquiring a Titian?"

"You'll know soon enough, Ollie."

"Hope your client has deep pockets."

"I only do deep pockets."

"Word on the street is that it's going to go big."

"Pre-show hype."

"I'm sure you're right, Nicky. You're always right."

Lovegrove didn't bother to dispute this. Instead, he drew a mobile phone from the breast pocket of his blazer and scrolled through the contacts. Oliver being Oliver, he snuck a quick peek at the screen after Lovegrove placed the call. *Now isn't that interesting*, he thought. *Isn't that interesting indeed.*

45

ST. JAMES'S, LONDON

T HE PAINTING ENTERED THE ROOM at the midway point, like a pretty girl arriving at a party fashionably late. It had been a rather dull party until that moment, and the pretty girl did much to brighten the room. Oliver Dimbleby sat up a bit straighter in his folding chair. Julian Isherwood fussed with the knot of his necktie and winked at one of the women on the telephone dais.

"Lot Twenty-seven, the Titian," purred Simon Mendenhall, Christie's slinky chief auctioneer. Simon was the only man in London with a suntan. It was beginning to smudge the collar of his custom-made shirt. "Shall we begin at two million?"

Terry O'Connor, the last Irish tycoon with any money, did the honors. Within thirty seconds, the bid in the room stood at six and a half million pounds. Oliver Dimbleby leaned to his right and murmured, "Still think it was hype, Nicky?"

"We're still in the first turn," Lovegrove whispered, "and I hear there's a strong headwind on the backstretch."

"I'd recheck the forecast if I were you, Nicky."

The bidding stalled at seven. Oliver, with a scratch of his nose, nudged it to seven and a half.

"Bastard," muttered Lovegrove.

"Anytime, Nicky."

Oliver's bid reignited the frenzy. Terry O'Connor steamrolled his way through several consecutive bids, but the other contenders refused to back down. The Irishman finally lowered his paddle at twelve, at which point Isherwood accidentally entered the fray when Mendenhall mistook a discreet cough for a bid of twelve and a half million pounds. It was no matter; a few seconds later a telephone bidder stunned the room by offering fifteen million. Lovegrove pulled out his phone and dialed.

"Where do we stand?" asked Mr. Hamdali.

Lovegrove gave him the lay of the land. In the time it had taken him to place the call, the telephone bid had already been eclipsed. It was back in the room with Terry O'Connor at sixteen.

"Mr. O'Connor fancies himself a pugilist, does he not?"

"Welterweight champ at university."

"Let's hit him with a stiff uppercut, shall we?"

"How stiff?"

"Enough to know we mean business."

Lovegrove caught Mendenhall's eye and raised two fingers.

"I have twenty million in the room. It's not with you, madam. Nor with you, sir. And it's not with Lisa on the telephone. It's in the room, with Mr. Lovegrove, at twenty million pounds. Do I have twenty million five?"

He did. It was with Julian Isherwood. Terry O'Connor immediately took it to twenty-one. The telephone bidder countered at twenty-two. A second entered at twenty-four, followed soon after by a third at twenty-five. Mendenhall was twisting and turning like a flamenco dancer. The bidding had taken on the quality of a fight to the death, which was exactly what he wanted. Lovegrove lifted his phone to his ear and said, "Something doesn't smell right to me."

"Bid again, Mr. Lovegrove."

"But—"

"Please bid again."

Lovegrove did as he was instructed.

"The bid is now twenty-six million, in the room, with Mr. Lovegrove. Will someone give me twenty-seven?"

Lisa waved her hand from the telephone desk.

"I have twenty-eight on the telephone. Now it's twenty-nine at the back of the room. Now thirty. Now it's at thirty-one with Mr. O'Connor in the room. Thirty-two now. Thirty-three. No, I won't take thirty-three and half, because I'm looking for thirty-four. And it looks as though I may have it with Mr. Isherwood. Do I? Yes, I do. It's in the room, thirty-four million, with Mr. Isherwood."

"Bid again," said Hamdali.

"I would advise against it."

"Bid again, Mr. Lovegrove, or my client will find an adviser who will."

Lovegrove signaled thirty-five. In the space of a few seconds, the telephone bidders ran it past forty.

"Bid again, Mr. Lovegrove."

"I would—"

"Bid."

Mendenhall acknowledged Lovegrove's bid of forty-two million pounds.

"Now it's forty-three with Lisa on the telephone. Now it's forty-four with Samantha. And forty-five with Cynthia."

And then came the lull Lovegrove was looking for. He glanced at Terry O'Connor and saw the fight had gone out of him. To Hamdali he said, "How badly does your client want this painting?"

"Badly enough to bid forty-six."

Lovegrove did so.

"The bid is now forty-six, in the room, with Mr. Lovegrove," said Mendenhall. "Will anyone give me forty-seven?"

On the telephone desk, Cynthia began waving her hand as though she were trying to signal a rescue helicopter.

"It's with Cynthia, on the phone, at forty-seven million pounds."

No other telephone bidders followed suit.

"Shall we end this?" asked Lovegrove.

"Let's," said Hamdali.

"How much?"

"My client likes round numbers."

Lovegrove arched an eyebrow and raised five fingers.

"The bid is fifty million pounds," said Mendenhall. "It's not with you, sir. Nor with Cynthia on the telephone. Fifty million, in the room, for the Titian. Fair warning now. Last chance. All done?"

Not quite. For there was the sharp crack of Mendenhall's gavel, and the elated gasp of the crowd, and a final excited exchange with Mr. Hamdali that Lovegrove couldn't quite hear because Oliver Dimbleby was shouting something into his other ear, which he couldn't quite hear, either. And then there were the disingenuous handshakes with the losers, and the obligatory flirtation with the press over the identity of the buyer, and the long walk upstairs to

Christie's business offices, where the final paperwork was buttoned up with an air of funereal solemnity. It was approaching ten o'clock by the time Lovegrove signed his name to the last document. He emerged from Christie's portentous doorway to find Oliver and the boys milling about in King Street. They were heading over to Nobu for a spicy tuna roll and a look-see at the latest Russian talent. "Join us, Nicky," bellowed Oliver. "Revel in the company of your English brethren. You've been spending too much time in America. You're no bloody fun any longer."

Lovegrove was tempted but knew the outing was likely to end badly, so he saw them into a caravan of taxis and headed back to his hotel on foot. Walking along Duke Street, he saw a man emerge from Mason's Yard and climb into a waiting car. The man was of medium height and build; the car was a sleek Jaguar sedan that reeked of British officialdom. So did the handsome silver-haired figure already seated in the back. Neither cast so much as a glance in Lovegrove's direction as he walked past, but he had the uncomfortable impression they were sharing a private joke at his expense.

He felt the same way about the auction—the auction in which he had just played a starring role. Someone had been had tonight; Lovegrove was sure of it. And he feared it was his client. It was no skin off Lovegrove's back. He had earned several million pounds just for raising his finger in the air a few times. Not a bad way to make a living, he thought, smiling to himself. Perhaps he should have accepted Oliver's invitation to the post-auction bash. No, he thought, rounding the corner into Piccadilly, it was probably better he'd begged off. Things would end badly. They usually did whenever Oliver was involved.

46

LANGLEY, VIRGINIA

THREE BUSINESS DAYS LATER, THE venerable Christie's auction house, King Street, St. James's, deposited the sum of fifty million pounds—less commissions, taxes, and numerous transactional fees—into the Zurich branch of Trans-Arabian Bank. Christie's received confirmation of the transfer at 2:18 p.m. London time, as did the two hundred men and women gathered in the subterranean op center known as Rashidistan. There arose in the room a loud cheer that echoed throughout the chambers of the American intelligence community and even inside the White House itself. The celebration did not last long, however, for there was a great deal of work to be done. After many weeks of toil and worry, Gabriel's operation had finally borne fruit. Now the harvest would commence. And after the harvest, God willing, would come the feast.

The money spent a restful day in Zurich before moving on to TransArabian's headquarters in Dubai. Not all of it, though. At the direction of Samir Abbas, who had power of attorney, two million pounds were wired into a small private bank on Zurich's Talstrasse. Additionally, Abbas authorized large donations to a number of Islamic groups and charities—including the World Islamic Fund for Justice, the Free Palestine Initiative, the Centers for Islamic Studies, the Islamic Society of Western Europe, the Islamic World League, and the Institute for Judeo-Islamic Reconciliation, Gabriel's personal favorite. Abbas also allotted himself a generous consulting fee, which, curiously, he drew in cash. He gave a portion of the money to the imam of his mosque to do with as he pleased. The rest he concealed in the pantry of his Zurich apartment, an act that was captured by the camera of his compromised computer and projected live onto the giant screens of Rashidistan.

Owing to TransArabian's long-suspected links to the global jihadist movement, Langley and the NSA were already well acquainted with its ledger books, as were the terror-finance specialists at Treasury and the FBI. As a result, Gabriel and the staff in Rashidistan were able to monitor the money almost in real time as it flowed through a series of fronts, shells, and dummy corporations—all of which had been hastily created in lax jurisdictions in the days following Nadia's meeting with Sheikh Bin Tayyib in the Nejd. The speed with which the money moved from account to account demonstrated that Rashid's network possessed a level of sophistication that belied its size and relative youth. It also revealed—much to Langley's alarm—that the network had already expanded far beyond the Middle East and Western Europe.

The evidence of Rashid's global reach was overwhelming. There was the three hundred thousand dollars that appeared suddenly in the account of a trucking firm in Ciudad del Este, Paraguay. And the five hundred thousand dollars paid to a commercial construction company in Caracas. And the eight hundred thousand dollars funneled to an Internet consulting firm based in Montreal—a firm owned by an Algerian previously linked to al-Qaeda in the Islamic Maghreb. The largest single payment—two million dollars—went to QTC Logistics, a freight forwarding and customs brokerage firm based in the judicially porous Gulf emirate of Sharjah. Within hours of the money's arrival, the Rashidistan team was monitoring QTC's phones and poring over its records dating back three years. The same was true of the Internet firm in Montreal, though the physical surveillance of the Algerian was delegated to the Canadian Security and Intelligence Service. Gabriel argued strenuously against bringing the Canadians into the investigation but was overruled by Adrian Carter and his newfound ally at the White House, James A. McKenna. It was just one of many battles, large and small, that Gabriel would lose as the operation slipped further and further from his grasp.

As the intelligence streamed into the op center, the staff produced an updated network matrix that dwarfed the one assembled by Dina and Gabriel's team following the first attacks. McKenna dropped by every few days just to marvel at it, as did members of the various congressional committees involved in intelligence and homeland security. And on a snowy afternoon in late February, Gabriel spotted the president himself standing on the upper observation deck with the CIA director and Adrian Carter standing proudly at his side. The president was clearly pleased by what he saw. It was clean. It was smart. It was forward-leaning. A partnership between Islam and the West to defeat the forces of extremism. Brainpower over brute force.

The operation had been Gabriel's creation, Gabriel's work of art, yet it had so far failed to provide any firm leads regarding the whereabouts of the network's operational mastermind or its inspirational leader. Which is why it came as a surprise to Gabriel when he started hearing rumors about pending arrests. He confronted Adrian Carter the next day in the center's soundproof conference room. Carter spent a moment rearranging the contents of a file before finally confirming the rumors were true. Gabriel tapped the green badge hanging around his neck and asked, "Does this allow me to offer an opinion?"

"I'm afraid it does."

"You're about to make a mistake, Adrian."

"It wouldn't be my first."

"My team and I went to a great deal of time and effort to put this operation in place. And now you're going to blow it sky-high by pulling a few operatives off the street."

"I'm afraid you've mistaken me for someone else," Carter said impassively.

"Who's that?"

"Someone who has the power to rule by executive fiat. I'm the deputy director for operations of the Central Intelligence Agency. I have superiors in this building. I have ambitious counterparts from other agencies with competing interests. I have a director of national intelligence, congressional committees, and James A. McKenna. And, last but not least, I have a president."

"We're spies, Adrian. We don't make arrests. We save lives. You have to be patient, just like your enemies. If you continue to let the money flow, you'll be able to stay one step ahead of them for *years*. You'll watch them. You'll listen to them. You'll let them waste valuable time and effort plotting and planning attacks that will never take place. And you'll make arrests only as a last resort— and only if they're necessary to prevent a bomb from exploding or a plane from falling out of the sky."

"The White House disagrees," said Carter.

"So this is political?"

"I'd rather not speculate on the motives behind it."

"What about Malik?"

"Malik is a rumor. Malik is a hunch on Dina's part."

Gabriel studied Carter skeptically. "You don't believe that, Adrian. After all, you were the one who said the European bombings were planned by someone who cut his teeth in Baghdad."

"And I stand by that. But the goal of this operation was never to find one man. It was to dismantle a terror network. Thanks to your work, we believe we have enough evidence to take down at least sixty operatives in a dozen countries. When was the last time anyone arrested sixty of the bad guys? It's an amazing accomplishment. It's *your* accomplishment."

"Let's just hope they're the right sixty operatives. Otherwise, it might not stop the next attack. In fact, it might push Rashid and Malik to accelerate their planning."

Carter unwound a paper clip, the last in all of Langley, but said nothing.

"Have you considered what this is going to mean for Nadia's security?"

"It's possible Rashid might find the timing of the arrests suspicious," Carter admitted. "That's why we plan to protect her with a series of well-placed leaks to the press."

"What kind of leaks?"

"The kind that portray the arrests as the culmination of a multiyear investigation that began while Rashid was still in America. We believe it will sow discord inside his inner circle and leave the network paralyzed."

"Do we?"

"That is our hope," said Carter without a trace of irony in his voice.

"Why wasn't I consulted about any of this?" asked Gabriel.

Carter held up his paper clip, which was now perfectly straight. "I thought that's what we were doing now."

The conversation was their last for several days. Carter kept to the seventh floor while Gabriel spent most of his time overseeing the withdrawal of his troops from the field. By the end of February, the Agency had assumed total responsibility for the physical and electronic surveillance of Nadia al-Bakari and Samir Abbas. Of Gabriel's original operation nothing remained but a pair of empty safe houses—one in a small village north of Paris, another on the shores of Lake Zurich. Ari Shamron decided to stick Château Treville in his back pocket but ordered the Zurich house shut down. Chiara handled the paperwork herself before flying to Washington to be with Gabriel. They settled into an Office flat on Tunlaw Road, across the street from the Russian Embassy. Carter put a pair of watchers on them, just to be on the safe side.

With Chiara in Washington, Gabriel sharply curtailed the amount of time he spent in Rashidistan. He would arrive at Langley in time for the morning senior staff meeting, then spend a few hours peering over the shoulders of the analysts and the data miners before returning to Georgetown to meet Chiara for lunch. Afterward, if the skies were clear, they would do a bit of shopping or stroll the pleasant streets discussing their future. At times, it seemed they were merely resuming the conversation that had been interrupted by the bombing in Covent Garden. Chiara even raised the subject of working at Isherwood's gallery. "Think about it," she said when Gabriel objected. "That's all I'm saying, darling. Just think about it."

For the moment, though, Gabriel could think only of Nadia's security. With Carter's approval, he reviewed the Agency's plans for Nadia's long-term protection and even had a hand in drafting the material that would be leaked to the American press. Mainly, he waged a tireless campaign from within Rashidistan to prevent the arrests from happening, telling anyone who would listen that the Agency, by bowing to political pressure, was about to make a catastrophic blunder. Carter stopped attending meetings where Gabriel was present. There was no point. The White House had ordered Carter to bring down the hammer. He was now in constant contact with friends and allies in a dozen countries, coordinating what was to be the single biggest haul of jihadist militants and operatives since the fall of Afghanistan.

On a Friday morning in late March, Gabriel pulled him aside long enough to say that he was planning to leave Washington to return to England. Carter suggested Gabriel stay a little longer. Otherwise, he was going to miss the big show.

"When does it start?" asked Gabriel gloomily.

Carter looked at his watch and smiled.

Within hours the dominoes began to fall. They toppled so quickly, and on such a wide scale, that the press struggled to keep pace with the unfolding story.

The first arrests took place in the United States, where FBI SWAT teams executed a series of simultaneous raids in four cities. There was the cell of Egyptians in Newark that was planning to derail a New York–bound Amtrak train. And the cell of Somalis in Minneapolis that was plotting chemical attacks against several downtown office buildings. And the cell of Pakistanis in Denver that was in the final stages of a plot to murder hundreds of people with a series of attacks on crowded sporting facilities. Most alarming, however, was Falls Church, Virginia, where a six-member cell was in the final stages of a plan to attack the new U.S. Capitol

Visitor Center. On one of the suspect's computers, the FBI found casing photos of tourists and schoolchildren waiting to be admitted. Another suspect had recently rented an isolated warehouse to begin preparing the peroxide-based bombs. The money had come from the Algerian in Montreal, who was arrested at the same time, along with eight other Canadian residents.

In Europe, the haul was even larger. In Paris, the terrorists were plotting to attack the Eiffel Tower and the Musée d'Orsay. In London, they had targeted the Millennium Wheel and Parliament Square. And in Berlin, they were preparing a Mumbai-style assault on visitors to the Holocaust memorial near the Brandenburg Gate. Copenhagen and Madrid, victimized by the first round of attacks, yielded additional cells. So did Stockholm, Malmö, Oslo, and Rome. Across the Continent, bank accounts were frozen and businesses were shut down. All thanks to Nadia's money.

One by one, prime ministers, presidents, and chancellors appeared before the press to proclaim that disaster had been averted. The American president spoke last. Resolute, he described the threat as the most serious since 9/11 and hinted that more arrests were coming. When asked to describe how the cells had been uncovered, he deferred to his counterterrorism adviser, James McKenna, who refused to answer. He went to great pains, however, to point out that the breakthrough had been achieved without resorting to tactics used by the previous administration. "The threat has evolved," declared McKenna, "and so have we."

The following morning, the *New York Times* and the *Washington Post* carried lengthy articles describing a multi-agency intelligence and law enforcement triumph nearly a decade in the making. In addition, both papers ran editorials lauding the president's "twenty-first century vision for the struggle against global extremism," and by that evening, on the cable talk shows, members of the opposing political party looked disheartened. The president had done more than eliminate a dangerous terror network, said one noteworthy strategist. He had just guaranteed himself another four years in office. The race for 2012 was over. It was time to start thinking about 2016.

47

THE PALISADES, WASHINGTON, D.C.

THAT SAME EVENING, THE CIA director summoned the staff to the Bubble, Langley's futuristic auditorium, for a pep rally. Ellis Coyle chose not to attend. Such events, he knew, were as predictable as his nights at home with Norah. There would be the usual drivel about pride restored and an Agency on the mend, an Agency that had finally found its place in a world without the Soviet Union. Coyle had heard the same speech from seven previous directors, all of whom had left the CIA weaker and more dysfunctional than they had found it. Drained of talent, weakened by the reorganization of the American intelligence community, the Agency was a smoldering ruin. Even Coyle, a professional dissembler, could not sit in the Bubble and pretend that the arrest of sixty suspected terrorists heralded a brighter future—especially since he knew the truth about how the breakthrough had been achieved.

There was a four-car pileup on Canal Road. As a result, Coyle was able to listen to the end of *Atlas Shrugged* during the drive home. He arrived in the Palisades to find Roger Blankman's house ablaze with a Gatsbyesque light and dozens of luxury cars lining the narrow street. "He's having another party," said Norah as she accepted Coyle's loveless kiss. "It's a fund-raiser of some sort."

"I suppose that's why we weren't invited."

"Don't be petty, Ellis. It doesn't suit you."

She added an inch of Merlot to her glass as Lucy entered the kitchen, leash in mouth. Coyle attached it dutifully to her collar and together they walked to Battery Kemble Park. Near the base of the wooden sign, at a precise forty-five-degree angle falling left to right, was a chalk mark. It meant there was a package waiting for Coyle at drop site number three. Coyle rubbed out the mark with the toe of his shoe and entered.

It was dark in the trees, but Coyle had no need of a flashlight; he knew the footpath the way a blind man knows the streets around his home. From MacArthur Boulevard, it ran flat for only a few paces before rising sharply up the slope of the hill. At the top of the park was a clearing where the hundred-pound guns of the old battery had once stood. To the right was a narrow tributary spanned by a wooden footbridge. Drop site number three was just beyond the bridge beneath a fallen oak tree. It was difficult to access, especially for a man of early middle age with chronic back problems, but not for Lucy. She knew each of the drop sites by the sound of its spoken number, and could clean them out in a matter of seconds. What's more, unless the Bureau had discovered some way to speak to dogs, she could never be called to testify. Lucy was a perfect field agent, thought Coyle: smart, capable, fearless, and utterly loyal.

Coyle paused for a moment to listen for the sound of footfalls or voices. Hearing nothing, he gave Lucy the command to empty drop site three. She darted into the woods, her black coat rendering her all but invisible, and splashed into the streambed. A moment later, she came scrambling up the embankment with a stick in her mouth and dropped it obediently at Coyle's feet.

It was about a foot in length and approximately two inches in diameter. Coyle took hold of each end and gave a sharp twist. It came apart easily, revealing a hidden compartment. Inside the compartment was a small slip of paper. Coyle removed it, then reassembled the stick and gave it to Lucy to return to the drop site. In all likelihood, Coyle's handler would collect it before dawn. He wasn't the smartest intelligence officer Coyle had ever encountered, but he was thorough in a plodding sort of way, and he never made Coyle wait for his money. That was hardly surprising. The officer's service faced many threats, both internal and external, but a shortage of money was not one of them.

Coyle read the message by the glow of his mobile phone and then dropped the slip of paper into a plastic Safeway bag. It was the same bag he used five minutes later to collect Lucy's nightly offering. Tightly knotted, it swung like a pendulum, beating warmly against Coyle's wrist, as he strode down the footpath toward home. It wouldn't be long now, he thought. A few more secrets, a few more trips into the park with Lucy at his side. He wondered whether he would really have the nerve to leave. Then he thought of Norah's dowdy eyeglasses, and his neighbor's enormous house, and the book about Winston Churchill he had listened to while stuck in traffic. Coyle had always admired Churchill's decisiveness. In the end, Coyle would be decisive, too.

Across the river at Langley, the party continued for much of the next week. They celebrated their hard work. They celebrated the superiority of their technology. They celebrated the fact that they had finally managed to outwit their enemy. Mainly, though, they celebrated Adrian Carter. The operation, they said, would surely be regarded as one of Carter's finest. The black marks had been erased; the sins had been forgiven. Never mind that Rashid and Malik were still out there somewhere. For now, they were terrorists without a network, and it was all Carter's doing.

Rashidistan remained open for business, but its ranks were thinned by a wave of hasty reassignments. What had begun as a highly secretive intelligence-gathering endeavor was now a matter largely for policemen and prosecutors. The team no longer tracked the flow of money through a terror network. Instead, it engaged in heated debates with lawyers from the Justice Department over what evidence was admissible and what should never see the light of day. None of the lawyers bothered to ask the opinion of Gabriel Allon, the legendary but wayward son of Israeli intelligence, because none knew he was there.

With the operation winding down, Gabriel devoted most of his time and energy to leaving it. At the request of King Saul Boulevard, he conducted a series of exit briefings and negotiated a permanent system of sharing the intelligence harvest, knowing full well the Americans would never live up to the terms. The accord was signed with great fanfare in a sparsely attended ceremony in the director's office, after which Gabriel proceeded to the Office of Personnel to hand in his green credentials. What should have taken five minutes consumed more than an hour as he was forced to sign countless written promises, none of which he had any intention of keeping. When Personnel's lust for ink had finally been satisfied, a uniformed guard escorted Gabriel down to the lobby. He remained there for a few minutes to watch a new star being carved into the CIA's Memorial Wall, then headed into the first violent thunderstorm of Washington's all-too-brief spring.

By the time Gabriel reached Georgetown, the rain had ended and the sun was again shining brightly. He met Chiara for lunch at a quaint outdoor café near American University, then walked her back to Tunlaw Road to pack for the flight home. Arriving at the apartment building, they found an armored black Escalade waiting outside the entrance, its tailpipe gently smoking. A hand beckoned. It belonged to Adrian Carter.

"Is there a problem?" asked Gabriel.

"I suppose that depends entirely on how you look at it."

"Can you get to the point, Adrian? We have a plane to catch."

"Actually, I've taken the liberty of canceling your reservations."

"How thoughtful of you."

"Get in."

PART THREE

THE
EMPTY
QUARTER

48

THE PLAINS, VIRGINIA

T HE HOUSE STOOD ON THE highest point of the land, shaded by a coppice of oak and elm. It had a tarnished copper roof and a handsome double-decker porch overlooking a green pasture. The neighbors had been led to believe that the owner was a wealthy Washington lobbyist named Hewitt. There was no Washington lobbyist named Hewitt, at least not one associated with the charming forty-acre gentleman's farm located two miles east of The Plains on Country Road 601. The name had been chosen randomly by the computers of the Central Intelligence Agency, which owned and operated the farm through a front company. The Agency also owned the John Deere tractor, the Ford pickup truck, the Bush Hog rotary cutter, and a pair of bay horses. One was named Colby; the other was called Helms. According to Agency wits, they were subjected, like all CIA employees, to annual polygraphs to make certain they hadn't switched sides, whatever side that might be.

The following afternoon, both horses were nibbling on the new grass in the lower pasture as the Escalade bearing Gabriel and Chiara came churning up the long gravel drive. A CIA security man admitted them into the house, then, after relieving them of their coats and mobile devices, pointed them toward the great room. Entering, they saw Uzi Navot peering longingly at the buffet and Ari Shamron attempting to coax a cup of coffee from the pump-action thermos. Seated near the dormant fireplace, dressed for a long weekend in the English countryside, was Graham Seymour. Adrian Carter sat next to him, frowning at something James McKenna was whispering urgently in his ear.

The men gathered in the room represented a secret brotherhood of sorts. Since the attacks of 9/11, they had worked together on numerous joint operations, most of which the public knew nothing about. They had fought for one another, killed for one another, and in some cases bled for one another. Despite the occasional disagreement, their bond had managed to transcend time and the fickle whims of their political masters. They saw their mission in stark terms—they were, to borrow a phrase from their enemy, the "Shura Council" of the civilized world. They took on the unpleasant chores no one else was willing to perform and worried about the consequences later, especially when lives were at stake. James McKenna was not a member of the council, nor would he ever be. He was a political animal, which meant by definition he was part of the problem. His presence promised to be a complicating factor, especially if he planned to spend the entire time whispering in Carter's ear.

McKenna was clearly most comfortable when seated at a rectangular table, so at his suggestion, they moved into the formal dining room. It was obvious why Carter did not like him;

McKenna was everything Carter was not. He was young. He was fit. He looked good behind a podium. He was also supremely sure of himself, regardless of whether that certainty was warranted or supported by the facts. McKenna had no blood on his hands and no professional sins in his past. He had never confronted his enemy over the barrel of a gun or questioned him in an interrogation room. He didn't even speak any of his enemy's languages. Yet he had read many briefing books about him and had spoken with great sensitivity about him in many meetings. His main contribution to the literature of counterterrorism was a piece he had once written for *Foreign Affairs* magazine in which he argued the United States could absorb another terrorist attack and emerge stronger for it. The piece had captured the attention of a charismatic senator, and when the senator became president, he placed much of the responsibility for the country's safety in the hands of a political hack who had once spent a week at Langley getting coffee for the director.

There ensued an awkward moment over who would sit at the head of the table, Carter or McKenna. In the unwritten rules of the brotherhood, chairmanship of meetings was determined by geography, but there were no bylaws about what to do when confronted by a political interloper. Eventually, McKenna surrendered the head of the table to Carter and settled in next to Graham Seymour, who seemed to threaten him less than the quartet of Israelis. Carter placed his pipe and his tobacco pouch on the table for later deployment, then lifted the lid of a secure notebook computer. Stored on its hard drive was a copy of an NSA intercept. It was a phone call, placed at 10:36 a.m. Central European Time the previous day, between the Zurich branch of TransArabian Bank and the Paris offices of AAB Holdings. The parties to the call had been

Samir Abbas, a banker with uncomfortably close ties to questionable Islamic charities, and his new client, Nadia al-Bakari. They had spoken for two minutes and twelve seconds, in formal Arabic. Carter distributed copies of an NSA translation. Then he pulled up the audio file on the computer and clicked play.

The first voice on the recording belonged to Nadia's executive secretary, who asked Abbas to hold while she transferred the call. Nadia picked up exactly six seconds later. After the obligatory Islamic expression of peace, Abbas said he had just spoken to "an associate of the Yemeni." It seemed the Yemeni's enterprise had suffered a string of recent setbacks and was in desperate need of additional financing. The associate wished to appeal to Nadia personally and was willing to discuss future plans, including several pending deals in America. This associate, whom Abbas described as "extremely close" to the Yemeni, had suggested Dubai as a meeting site. Apparently, he was a frequent visitor to the fabulously rich emirate and even kept a modest apartment in the Jumeirah Beach district. Needless to say, the associate of the Yemeni was well aware of Miss al-Bakari's security concerns and would be willing to meet her in a place where she would feel both safe and comfortable.

"Where?"

"The Burj Al Arab."

"When?"

"A week from Thursday."

"I'm supposed to be in Istanbul that day on business."

"The associate's schedule is very busy. It will be his one and only chance to meet with you for the foreseeable future."

"When does he need an answer?"

"I'm afraid he needs it now."

"What time would he like to see me?"

"Nine in the evening."

"My bodyguards won't permit any changes."

"The associate assures me there won't be any."

"Then please tell him I'll be at the Burj next Thursday evening at nine p.m. And tell him not to be late. Because I never invest money with people who are late for meetings."

"I assure you he won't be late."

"Will there be anyone else in attendance?"

"Just me—unless, of course, you would rather go alone."

"Actually, I would prefer it if you came."

"Then I would be honored to be at your side. I'll be waiting in the lobby. You have my mobile number."

"I'll see you next Thursday, Inshallah.*"*

"Inshallah, *Miss al-Bakari.*"

Carter clicked pause.

"The next recording is a call that was placed to Samir's home just six hours earlier. He was sleeping soundly at the time and wasn't pleased when the phone rang. His mood changed when he heard the voice at the other end. The gentleman never bothered to identify himself. He placed the call from Jeddah, Saudi Arabia, using a cell phone that had no history and no longer seems to be operative. There's some dropout and a great deal of background noise. Here's a sample."

Carter clicked play.

"Tell her we need more money. Tell her we're willing to discuss future plans. Make it clear that we're sending someone important."

Pause.

"So who exactly is the close associate of the Yemeni who wishes to meet with Nadia?" Carter asked rhetorically. "This phone call appears to provide the answer. It took a bit of work because of the poor quality, but NSA was able to manipulate the recording and conduct voice-match analysis. They ran it through every database we have, including databases of radio and cell phone communications collected in Iraq during the height of the insurgency. One hour ago, they came up with a match. Anyone care to venture a guess as to the identity of the man Samir Abbas was speaking to?"

"I'm tempted to say it was Malik al-Zubair," Gabriel said, "but that's not possible. You see, Adrian, Malik is a rumor. Malik is a hunch on Dina's part."

"No, he's not," Carter conceded. "Dina was right. Malik is for real. He was in Jeddah two days ago. And he may or may not be coming to the Burj Al Arab hotel in Dubai next Thursday evening to have a word with his new patron, Nadia al-Bakari. The question is, what do we do about it?"

Carter rapped his pipe against the rim of his ashtray. The Shura Council was now in session.

49

THE PLAINS, VIRGINIA

I T WAS AN AMERICAN OPERATION, which meant it was an American decision to make. McKenna clearly had no intention of offering the first opinion, lest the ground shift suddenly beneath his feet, so he adroitly deferred to Carter, who began, in typical Carter fashion, with a detour. It was to a place called Forward Operating Base Chapman, a CIA post in remote eastern Afghanistan, where, in December 2009, a CIA asset named Humam Khalil Abu-Mulal al-Balawi came calling to deliver a report to his handlers. A Jordanian physician with links to the jihadist movement, Dr. Balawi had been providing the CIA with critical information used to target al-Qaeda militants in Pakistan. His true mission, however, was to penetrate the CIA and Jordanian intelligence—a mission that came to a disastrous conclusion that day when he detonated a bomb hidden beneath his coat, killing seven CIA officers. It was among the worst single attacks against the Agency in its history, and certainly the worst during Adrian Carter's long career as director of operations.

It demonstrated that al-Qaeda was willing to expend extraordinary time and effort to exact revenge against the intelligence services that pursued it. And it proved that when spies ignore the basic rules of tradecraft, officers could end up dead.

"Are you suggesting that Nadia al-Bakari is in league with al-Qaeda?" asked McKenna.

"I'm suggesting nothing of the sort. In fact, it is my opinion that when the secret history of the global war on terror is finally written, Nadia will be regarded as one of the most valuable assets who ever worked on the side of the West. Which is why I would hate to lose her because we got greedy and sent her into a situation we shouldn't have."

"Malik isn't inviting her to South Waziristan," McKenna said. "He's asking to meet with her in one of the most famous hotels in the world."

"Actually," Carter replied, "we don't know whether it's going to be Malik al-Zubair or Nobody al-Nobody. But that's beside the point."

"What *is* the point?"

"It violates tradecraft. You remember tradecraft, don't you, Jim? Rule one says we control as many environmental factors as possible. We choose the time. We choose the place. We pick out the furniture. We order the drinks. And, if possible, we serve the drinks. And we sure as hell don't let someone like Nadia al-Bakari get within a country mile of a man like Malik."

"But sometimes we play the hand we're dealt," McKenna countered. "Isn't that what you told the president the day after we lost those seven CIA officers?"

Gabriel noticed a rare flash of anger in Carter's eyes, but when he spoke again, his voice was as calm and underpowered as ever. "My father was an Episcopal minister, Jim. I don't play cards."

"Then what are you recommending?"

"This operation has worked better than any of us ever dared to hope," Carter said. "Maybe we shouldn't push our luck with a risky pass play late in the fourth quarter."

Shamron appeared annoyed. He considered the use of American sports metaphors to be inappropriate for a business as vital as espionage. In Shamron's opinion, intelligence officers did not blow fourth-quarter leads, or strike out, or fumble the ball. There was only success or failure—and the price of failure in a neighborhood like the Middle East was usually blood.

"Call it a day?" Shamron asked. "Is that what you're saying, Adrian?"

"Why not? The president got his victory, and so did the Agency. Better still, everybody lives to fight another day." Carter brushed the palms of his hands together twice and said, *"Halas."*

McKenna seemed perplexed. Gabriel explained the reference to him.

"*Halas* is the Arabic word for 'finished.' But Adrian knows all too well that this war will never be finished. It's a forever war. And he's afraid it will be a good deal bloodier if he allows a skilled mastermind like Malik to slip through his fingers."

"No one wants Malik's head on a pike more than I do," Carter agreed. "He deserves it for the mayhem he caused in Iraq, and his removal from the face of the earth will make us all safer. Suicide bombers are a dime a dozen. But masterminds—true terror masterminds—are extremely hard to replace. Eliminate the masterminds like Malik, and you're left with a bunch of jihadist wannabes trying to figure out how to mix their peroxide bombs in their mother's basement."

"So why not let Nadia make the meeting?" asked McKenna. "Why not let her listen to what Malik has to say about his future plans?"

"Because I've got that funny feeling at the back of my neck."

"But they trust her. Why wouldn't they? She's Zizi's daughter. She's a descendant of Wahhab himself, for God's sake."

"I'll grant you they trusted her *once*," Carter replied, "but it's an open question whether they trust her now that their network has been rolled up."

"You're jumping at shadows," McKenna said. "But I suppose that's to be expected. After all, you've been at this a very long time. For the last ten years, you've been reading their e-mail and listening to their phone conversations, looking for hidden meaning. But sometimes there is none. Sometimes a wedding is just a wedding. And sometimes a meeting in a hotel is just a meeting in a hotel. Besides, if we can't get a heavily guarded businesswoman like Nadia al-Bakari in and out of the Burj Al Arab safely, then maybe we're in the wrong business."

Carter was silent for a moment. "Any chance we can keep this professional, Jim?"

"I thought we were."

"Should I assume you're speaking for the White House?"

"No," said McKenna. "You should assume I'm speaking for the president."

"Since you're so in tune with the president's thinking, why don't you tell us all what the president wants."

"He wants what all presidents want. He wants a second term. Otherwise, the inmates will be running the asylum again, and all the progress we've made in the war against terrorism will be wiped away."

"You mean *extremism*," said Carter, correcting him. "But what about the meeting in Dubai?"

"Both the president and I would like her to attend—with the good guys looking over her shoulder, of course. Listen to what he has to say. Take his picture. Get his fingerprints. Record his voice. Determine whether he's Malik or some other heavyweight member of the network."

"And what do we tell our friends in the Emirati security services?"

"Our friends in the Emirates have been less-than-reliable allies on a number of issues ranging from terrorism to money laundering to the illicit arms trade. Besides, in my experience, one never quite knows just whom one is speaking to in the Emirates. He might be a committed opponent of the jihadists, or he might be a second cousin once removed."

"So we say nothing?" Carter asked.

"Nothing," McKenna replied.

"And if we determine it's Malik?"

"Then the president would like him taken out of circulation."

"What does that mean?"

"Use your imagination, Adrian."

"I did that after 9/11, Jim, and you said publicly that I should be put in jail for it. So if you wouldn't mind, I'd like to know *exactly* what the president is asking me to do."

It was Shamron, not McKenna, who answered.

"He's not asking *you* to do anything, Adrian." Shamron looked at McKenna and asked, "Isn't that correct?"

"I was told to watch my step around you."

"I was told the same thing."

McKenna seemed pleased by this. "The president is unwilling to authorize an American covert action in a quasi-friendly Arab country at a sensitive time like this," he said. "He feels it could embarrass the regime and thus leave it vulnerable to the forces of change sweeping the Middle East."

"But Israelis running amok in Dubai is another matter entirely."

"It does happen to dovetail nicely with the facts."

"What facts are those?"

"Malik has a great deal of Israeli blood on his hands, which means you have every reason to want him dead."

"Well played, Mr. McKenna," Shamron said. "But what do we get in return?"

"The gratitude of the most important and transformative American president in a generation."

"Equity?" asked Shamron.

McKenna smiled and said, "Equity."

50

THE PLAINS, VIRGINIA

I T WAS AT THIS POINT in the proceedings that James A. McKenna, special assistant to the president for homeland security and counterterrorism, thankfully chose to take his leave. Carter summoned his secret brethren to the sitting room and asked whether anyone could recall where Khalid Sheikh Mohammed, mastermind of the 9/11 plot, had been hiding the night of his capture. They all did, of course, but it was Chiara who answered.

"He was in a house in Rawalpindi, just down the road from the headquarters of the Pakistani military."

"Of all places," Carter said, shaking his head. "And do you happen to remember how we got him?"

"You sent in an informant to confirm it was really him. After laying eyes on the target, the informant slipped into the bathroom and sent you a text message."

"And a few hours later, the man who planned the worst terror attack in history was in handcuffs, looking shockingly like the guy who works on my wife's Volvo. I took a great deal of grief for the things we did to KSM and the places we put him, but that picture of him being led away was worth it all. And all it took was a guy with a cell phone. Simple as that."

"If we agree to do this," Gabriel said, "you may rest assured Nadia won't be running to the toilet to send any text messages."

"*If* you agree to do it?" Carter inclined his head toward Shamron and Navot, who were seated next to each other on the couch, with their arms folded and their faces set in the same inscrutable mask. "They're very good at hiding their thoughts," Carter said, "but I can tell you exactly what's running through their devious little minds. They want Malik in the worst way—maybe even more than the president and McKenna. And there's no way they're going to pass up a chance of getting him. So let's skip the playing-hard-to-get portion of tonight's performance and get down to the planning."

Gabriel looked to his superiors for guidance. Navot was rubbing at the spot on the bridge of his nose where his fashionable eyeglasses pinched him. Shamron had yet to move. He was staring past Gabriel toward Chiara, as if offering her a chance to intervene. She didn't take it.

"For the record," Gabriel said, "we're not going to Dubai to capture anyone. If it's Malik, he won't leave there alive."

"I'm quite certain I didn't hear McKenna mention anything about an arrest."

"Just so we're clear."

"We are," said Carter. "Think of yourself as a Hellfire missile, but without the collateral damage and innocent deaths."

"Hellfire missiles don't need passports, hotel rooms, and airline tickets. They also don't have a problem operating in Arab countries. We do." Gabriel paused. "You *do* realize that Dubai is an Arab country, don't you, Adrian?"

"I think I may have read something about that."

Gabriel hesitated. They were now about to enter sensitive territory dealing with capabilities and operational tendencies. Intelligence agencies guard these secrets jealously and expose them to allies only under duress. For the Office, it was akin to heresy. With a nod, Gabriel delegated the task to Uzi Navot, who slipped on his eyeglasses again and stared at Carter for a long moment without speaking.

"We live in a complex world, Adrian," he said finally, "so sometimes it helps to simplify things. As far as we are concerned, there are two types of countries—places where we can operate with impunity and places where we can't. We call the first category *base* countries."

"Like the United States," Carter acknowledged with a smile.

"And the United Kingdom," Navot added with a glance toward the deputy director of MI5. "Despite your best efforts, we come and go as needed and do pretty much as we please. If we get into trouble, we have a network of safe houses and bolt-holes that were put in place by the man seated at my side. In the event of a disaster, God forbid, our agents can take sanctuary in an embassy or ask for help from a friendly secret policeman like Graham."

Shamron gave Navot a murderous look. Navot carried on as though he hadn't noticed.

"We refer to the second category as *target* countries. These are hostile lands. No embassies. No safe houses. The secret policemen aren't friendly. In fact, were they to get their hands on us, they would torture us, shoot us, hang us on television for their people to see, or put us in jail for a very long time."

"What do you need?" asked Carter.

"Passports," said Gabriel, taking over for Navot. "The kind that allow us to enter Dubai without an advance visa."

"What flavor?"

"American, British, Canadian, Australian."

"Why Canadian and Aussie?" asked Graham Seymour.

"Because we're going to need a large team, and I need to spread them out geographically."

"Why not use your own false passports?"

This time it was Shamron who answered. "Because they require a great deal of time, effort, and scheming to produce. And we would prefer not to waste them on an operation that we're carrying out for the sake of American *equity*."

Carter couldn't help but smile at the slight directed toward James McKenna. "We'll get you all the passports you need," he said.

"And credit cards to go with them," added Gabriel. "Not the prepaid kind. I want real credit cards from real banks."

Carter nodded his head, as did Graham Seymour.

"What else?" Carter asked.

"Dubai's geography presents us with challenges," Navot said. "As far as we're concerned, there's only one way in and out."

"The airport," said Carter.

"That's right," Gabriel replied. "But we can't be held hostage by commercial flights. We need our own airplane, American registry, clean provenance."

"I'll get you a G5."

"A Gulfstream isn't big enough."

"What do you want?"

Gabriel told him. Carter stared at the ceiling, as if calculating the impact of the request on his operational budgets.

"Next I suppose you'll tell me you want an American crew, too."

"I do," Gabriel said. "I also need weapons."

"Make and model?"

Gabriel recited them. Carter nodded. "I'll bring them in through the embassy. Does that cover everything?"

"Everything but the star of the show," said Gabriel.

"Judging by the sound of her voice on that intercept, you're not going to have any difficulty convincing her to do it."

"I'm glad you feel that way," Gabriel said, "because she deserves to know that the full faith and credit of the American government are behind her." Gabriel paused, then added, "And so do we."

"I've promised you passports, money, guns, and a Boeing Business Jet with an American crew. What other gesture of American support would you like?"

"I'd like a word with your boss."

"The director?"

Gabriel shook his head. Carter went to the secure phone and dialed.

It was approaching ten p.m. when the Escalade entered the White House grounds through the Fifteenth Street gate. A uniformed Secret Service agent gave Carter's credentials a cursory glance, then instructed the driver to pull forward for a quick sniff from Oscar, the omnivorous Alsatian that had tried to take a chunk out of Gabriel's leg during his last visit. The beast found nothing disagreeable about Carter's official vehicle other than the right-front tire, against which he urinated forcefully before returning to his crate.

The inspection complete, the SUV maneuvered its way through a labyrinth of reinforced concrete and steel to the parking lot located along East Executive Drive. Carter and Chiara remained inside the vehicle while Gabriel set out alone up the gentle slope of the drive toward the Executive Mansion. Waiting beneath the awning of the Diplomatic Entrance was a tall, trim figure dressed in a dark suit and an open-neck white shirt. The greeting was cordial but restrained—a brief handshake, followed by a languid gesture of the arm that suggested a stroll around the most heavily guarded eighteen acres on earth. Gabriel gave a terse nod, and when the president of the United States turned to his right, toward the old magnolia tree that had never quite recovered from being struck by an airplane, Gabriel followed.

Carter watched the two men intently as they headed down the drive—one crisp and precise in his movements, the other graceful and loose limbed. As they were nearing the walkway leading to the Oval Office, they paused suddenly and turned in unison to face one another. Even from a distance, and even in the darkness, Carter could see that the exchange was not altogether pleasant.

Their dispute apparently resolved, they set off again, past the putting green and the small playground that had been erected for the president's young children, and disappeared from view. The agent-runner in Carter compelled him to mark the time on his secure Motorola cell phone, which he did a second time when Gabriel and the president reappeared. The president's hands were now in the pockets of his trousers, and he was bent forward slightly at the waist, as if leaning into a stiff headwind. Gabriel appeared to be doing most of the talking. He was stabbing at the air with his finger, as if trying to reinforce a particularly important point.

Their circuit of the South Lawn complete, the two men arrived back at the Diplomatic Entrance, where they had one final exchange. Gabriel appeared resolute at the end of it, as did the president. He placed a hand on Gabriel's shoulder, then, with a final nod of his head, entered the White House. Gabriel stood there for a moment, entirely alone. Then he turned and headed back down the drive to the Escalade. Carter said nothing until they had navigated their way through the security labyrinth and were back on Fifteenth Street.

"How was he?"

"He definitely knows your name," Gabriel said. "And he admires you a great deal."

"Perhaps he could say something to his terrorism czar."

"I'm working on that."

"Anything else I need to know?"

"Our conversation was private, Adrian, and it will remain so."

Carter smiled. "Good man."

51

THE CITY, LONDON

T HE VENTURE CAPITAL FIRM OF Rogers & Cressey occupied the ninth floor of a glass-and-steel affront to architecture located on Cannon Street, not far from Saint Paul's Cathedral. Within London financial circles, R&C had a well-deserved reputation for stealth and low cunning. Therefore, it came as no surprise that the acquisition of Thomas Fowler Associates was conducted with a discretion bordering on state secrecy. There was a brief press release no one noticed and a curiously out-of-focus publicity picture that appeared only on R&C's tedious Web site. The picture had been posed by a man who was highly skilled in the visual arts and snapped by a photographer who did most of his work in surveillance vans and darkened windows.

As expected, Thomas Fowler and his team of associates, of which there were twelve, hit the ground running. They moved into a corner suite of offices on a Tuesday morning and by that evening were busy assembling the pieces of their first deal as part of the R&C family. It was a complex deal, with many variables, much risk, and a host of competing interests. But when stripped to its barest form, it involved a patch of vacant waterfront property in Dubai and a billionaire Saudi investor named Nadia al-Bakari.

Fowler and his team were well acquainted with Miss al-Bakari, having conducted a series of secret meetings with her at a château north of Paris. They exchanged e-mails with the heiress on Wednesday, and by Thursday morning, her private plane was touching down at London's Stansted Airport. R&C provided the ground transportation with clandestine assistance from MI5. The fee for the two armored Bentleys raised eyebrows among the accountants at Thames House, which was watching its bottom line like every other department in Her Majesty's cash-strapped government. Any misgivings were assuaged when Graham Seymour sent the bills along to Langley for immediate payment. Langley mumbled something about shared sacrifice and a special relationship. Then it paid the bill through one of its seemingly bottomless accounts, and the matter was never raised in polite company again.

It is not unusual to see Bentley limousines in Cannon Street, though a few heads did turn at the sight of Nadia al-Bakari emerging from one into a crowd of dark-suited security men. They guided her into the lobby of R&C's unpardonable building, where a young man with a face like a parson stood waiting to receive her. If he offered a name, no one happened to catch it. In truth, he was Nigel Whitcombe, a young MI5 officer who had cut his operational teeth working with Gabriel against a Russian arms dealer named Ivan Kharkov.

Whitcombe led Nadia and her bodyguards into a waiting elevator and with the press of a button sent it upward to the ninth floor. Waiting in the foyer were R&C's senior partners, including the newest addition to the team, Thomas Fowler, who was known in some circles as Yossi Gavish. He was wearing a gray chalk-stripe suit by Anthony Sinclair of Savile Row and a smile that promised lavish profits. He greeted Nadia as though she were an old friend; then, with Whitcombe trailing, he led her to R&C's regal conference room. Whitcombe invited her bodyguards to have a seat in the corridor, which they did without objection. Then he followed Yossi and Nadia into the conference room and closed the doors with a reassuring *thump*.

The blinds were tightly drawn, the lighting tastefully subdued. There was a polished mahogany table around which sat the members of Gabriel's team, who were polished as well. Even Gabriel was dressed for the occasion. He was seated in the power position of the table along the windows, with Adrian Carter and Graham Seymour to one side and Ari Shamron and Uzi Navot on the other. Shamron watched Nadia carefully as she lowered herself into a chair next to Sarah, who was almost unrecognizable in a dark wig and glasses.

Still playing the role of Thomas Fowler, Yossi made a round of animated but pseudonymous introductions. It was a mere formality; the room was soundproof and electronically impenetrable. As a result, Gabriel had no misgivings about playing an NSA intercept over the sound system. It had been recorded five days earlier, at 10:36 a.m. Central European Time. The first voice belonged to Samir Abbas of TransArabian Bank.

"The associate's schedule is very busy. It will be his one and only chance to meet with you for the foreseeable future."

"When does he need an answer?"

"I'm afraid he needs it now."

"What time would he like to see me?"

"Nine in the evening."

"My bodyguards won't permit any changes."

"The associate assures me there won't be any."

"Then please tell him I'll be at the Burj next Thursday evening at nine p.m. And tell him not to be late. Because I never invest money with people who are late for meetings."

Gabriel pressed the stop button on the remote control and looked at Nadia. "I would like to begin this meeting by thanking you. By saying yes to Samir, you bought us some much-needed time to contemplate our next move. We were all impressed, Nadia. You handled yourself amazingly well for an amateur."

"I've been living in two different worlds for a long time, Mr. Allon. I'm not an amateur." Her gaze traveled around the table before settling on Shamron. "I see your numbers have grown since the last time we were together."

"I'm afraid this is just the traveling ensemble."

"There are others elsewhere?"

"A multitude," said Gabriel. "And at this moment, many of them are fretting over a single question."

"What's that?"

"Whether we should allow you to go to Dubai or whether we should call Samir back and tell him you're too busy to make the trip."

"Why would we tell him that?"

"I'll answer that question in a moment," Gabriel said. "But first I want you to listen to another recording."

He reached for the remote and pressed play.

52

THE CITY, LONDON

WHAT'S HIS NAME?"

"I'm not going to tell you."

"Why not?"

"Because it doesn't matter. And knowing it would only place you in danger later."

"You do think of everything."

"We try, but sometimes even we make mistakes."

She asked to hear the recording again. Gabriel pressed play.

"He sounds Jordanian to me," Nadia said, listening intently.

"He *is* Jordanian." Gabriel paused the recording. "He's also one of the most brutal terrorists any of us have ever encountered. We've suspected for some time he was involved with Rashid's network. Now we're sure of it."

"How?"

"The same way you know he's a Jordanian."

"The sound of his voice?"

Gabriel nodded. "Unfortunately, we know it too well. We heard it when he was dispatching *shahid*s to bomb the cafés and buses of Tel Aviv and Jerusalem. And our American friends heard it on the airwaves of the Sunni Triangle when he was helping to bring chaos to Iraq. But it's been a long time since we've heard from him—so long, in fact, that some members of our fraternity actually deluded themselves into believing he was dead. Unfortunately, this call proves he's very much alive."

Nadia seemed to have run out of questions for now. She looked at Carter and Graham Seymour and frowned.

"I see you've brought along your partners."

"We felt it was time for you to get acquainted."

"Who are they?"

"The dignified gentleman with gray hair is Graham. He's British."

"Obviously." Her gaze shifted to Carter. "And him?"

"That's Adrian."

"American?"

"I'm afraid so."

Her gaze swept across Gabriel and settled once again on Shamron.

"Where did you find this one?"

"In the deepest well of time."

"Does he have a name?"

"He prefers to be called Herr Heller."

"What does Herr Heller do?"

"Mostly, he steals secrets. Sometimes, he thinks of innovative ways to neutralize terrorist groups. It's because of Herr Heller that you're here now. It was his idea to ask you to penetrate Rashid's network."

"Does he think I should attend the meeting in Dubai next week?"

"It is an opportunity he finds hard to resist. But he has concerns about the authenticity of the invitation. And he would never allow you to go into a situation where he could not guarantee your safety."

"I've stayed at the Burj Al Arab many times. It never struck me as a particularly dangerous place. Unless it's filled with Brits," she added with a glance at Graham Seymour. "Your countrymen tend to let their hair down a bit too much when they're in Dubai."

"So I've heard."

She looked at Gabriel again and said, "I read in the newspapers that the terrorists suffered a major setback last week. The American president sounded very pleased."

"He had a right to."

"I assume my money had something to do with it."

"Your money had *every*thing to do with it."

"So you've dealt Rashid's network a serious blow."

Gabriel nodded slowly.

"But not a permanent blow?"

"Nothing about this business is permanent, Nadia."

"Do you have enough information to locate Rashid?"

"Not at the moment."

"What about the man whose name you won't tell me?"

Gabriel shook his head. "We don't know what name he's using, what kind of passport he's carrying, or even what he looks like."

"But you *do* know that he would like to see me next Thursday evening in Dubai." Nadia drew a cigarette from her handbag and ignited it. "It seems to me the choice is obvious, Mr. Allon. Having destroyed the network, you must now cut off the head. Otherwise, you'll all be back here in a year or two, trying to figure out how to break a *new* network."

Gabriel stared directly at Shamron without speaking. Finally, with an almost imperceptible nod of his head, Shamron nudged him forward.

"We lie for a living," Gabriel said, looking at Nadia again, "but we consider ourselves men of our word. To that end, we made a promise to you, and we would like to keep it."

"What promise was that?"

"We asked you to help us by funneling money into a terrorist network. But we never said anything about asking you to identify a murderer face-to-face."

"The situation has changed."

"But our commitment to you hasn't."

She blew a slender stream of smoke toward the ceiling and smiled. "Your concern for my safety is admirable, but it is entirely unwarranted. As you know, I am one of the most heavily protected private citizens in the world. While I'm on the ground in Dubai, I will be surrounded at all times by a very large team of security guards. They will search any room I enter and pat down anyone who comes into my presence. I'm the perfect person for an assignment like this because no harm can come to me."

Gabriel shot another glance in Shamron's direction. Once again, Shamron responded with a nod.

"It's not just your physical safety that concerns us," Gabriel said. "We also have to take into account your emotional and psychological well-being. There are some assets who think nothing of giving up someone from their own community for money or spite or respect or a dozen other reasons I could name. And there are others who find it a deeply traumatic experience that affects them profoundly for years afterward."

"I don't consider jihadist terrorists to be members of my community or my faith, just as they surely don't consider me to be members of theirs. Besides, haven't you already used my money to identify and arrest more than sixty suspected terrorists?" She paused, then added, "Forgive me, Mr. Allon, but it seems to me that you are making a distinction without a difference."

Gabriel leaned forward, closing the gap between himself and his agent. He wanted no misunderstandings, no ambiguity, and absolutely nothing lost in translation.

"Do you understand what will happen to this man if he turns out to be the one we're looking for?"

"I shouldn't think you would need to ask a question like that."

"Can you live with a memory like that?"

"I already do." She managed a smile. "Besides, as you know, Mr. Allon, nothing lasts forever."

Gabriel leaned back in his chair and spent a moment contemplating his hands. This time he didn't bother looking to Shamron for guidance. The decision was his and his alone.

"We need time to prepare you."

Nadia drew a leather portfolio from her handbag and looked at her schedule. "I'm in Moscow tomorrow, Prague the next day, and Stockholm the day after that."

"How's your weekend look?"

"I was planning to go to Casablanca for a bit of sun."

"We might need you to cancel that trip."

"I'll think about it," she said stubbornly. "But I do happen to be free for the rest of the afternoon."

Gabriel accepted a file folder from Uzi Navot. Inside was the last known photograph of Malik al-Zubair, along with several computer-generated photo illustrations. Gabriel laid them out in a row on the table.

"This is the man who may or may not be coming to see you next Thursday night at the Burj Al Arab hotel in Dubai," he said, pointing to the old photograph. His hand moved to the photo il-lustrations. "Here he is with twenty extra pounds. Here he is with a beard. Here he is without a beard. With a mustache. With a prayer scar. Without a prayer scar. With eyeglasses. With short hair. Long hair. Gray hair. No hair at all . . ."

53

THE CITY, LONDON

T HE *FINANCIAL JOURNAL* OF LONDON had lost much of its luster since being acquired by the Russian oligarch Viktor Orlov, yet it caused a commotion in the City the next morning when it reported that the mercenary house of Rogers & Cressey was assembling the pieces of a major project in Dubai. The story gained additional momentum when Zoe Reed of CNBC reported that the venture was being bankrolled in part by AAB Holdings, the Saudi investment firm controlled by the reclusive heiress Nadia al-Bakari. Reached for comment in Paris, AAB's underworked spokeswoman Yvette Dubois issued a text-book non-denial denial, but in London that evening, the lights burned late in R&C's Cannon Street offices. Veteran observers of the firm weren't surprised. R&C, they said, always did its best work in the dark.

Had they been privy to R&C's soundproof conference rooms and secure phone lines, they would have heard a language quite unlike any spoken elsewhere in the business world. Its etymology could be traced to a massacre at the Munich Olympic Games in September 1972 and to a secret operation of vengeance that followed. The world had changed much since then, but the principles enshrined in the series of assassinations remained inviolable. *Aleph, Bet, Ayin, Qoph*: four letters of the Hebrew alphabet. Four operational rules that were as timeless and durable as the man who had written them.

Within certain sections of R&C's offices, he was known as Herr Heller. But once he entered the rooms reserved for Gabriel and his team, he was referred to as Ari, or the Old Man, or the *Memuneh*, the Hebrew word meaning "the one in charge." Owing to a scrap of paper bearing Uzi Navot's signature, Shamron was in fact the nominal commander of the operation, but for practical reasons, he ceded responsibility for the planning and execution to Gabriel and his able deputy, Eli Lavon. It was not a difficult concession for Shamron to make. Gabriel and Lavon shared Shamron's methodology along with his basic instincts and deepest fears. To hear them speak was to hear the voice of the *Memuneh*. And to watch them meticulously plan the demise of a monster like Malik was to see Shamron in the prime of his life.

For many reasons, the operation would be among the most difficult Gabriel and his team had ever carried out. The hostile nature of the environment was only one obstacle. They did not know for certain the target would be there, or, if he did appear, whether they would be presented with an opportunity to kill him that did not risk exposure. Like Adrian Carter, Gabriel did not approve of games of chance. Therefore, on the first day of the planning, he drew a line in the sand that was not to be crossed. They were to leave the suicide missions to their enemies. If their prey could not be taken down without risk to the hunting party, they were to tag him and wait for another opportunity. And under no circumstances would they take a shot at *any*one unless they were certain beyond a reasonable doubt that the man they were aiming at was Malik al-Zubair.

They worked around the clock to eliminate as many other variables as possible. Housekeeping, the Office division responsible for safe accommodations, secured three apartments in Dubai, while Transport prepositioned a half-dozen cars and motorcycles at various points around the city-state. King Saul Boulevard also managed to create a reasonable bolt-hole. Its name was the *Neptune*, a Liberian-registered cargo vessel that in reality was a floating radar and eavesdropping station operated by AMAN, Israel's military intelligence service. On board was a team of Sayeret Matkal commandos capable of rapid seaborne deployment. Securing the vessel for the operation had cost Navot dearly, and he made it clear that it was to be used only as a last resort. Nor were the Americans or the British ever to know of its existence, since the *Neptune* spent much of its time soaking up Anglo-American signals traffic flying through the airwaves of the Persian Gulf.

But the team's primary source of anxiety during those days of hasty preparation revolved around the safety of their asset, Nadia al-Bakari. Once again, Gabriel laid down unmovable markers. The time Nadia spent on the ground in Dubai would be brief and highly choreographed. She would be surrounded at all times by two rings of security—one ring consisting of her own bodyguards and a second provided by the Office. After the meeting at the Burj Al Arab, she would return immediately to the airport and board her plane. At that point, the clandestine Office security ring would melt away, and Nadia would once again be entrusted to the sole care of her own detail.

Their preparation time with her was limited, as they had known it would be. After agreeing to cancel her trip to Morocco, she returned to London on Saturday to attend an intimate dinner party at the Fowlers' Mayfair town house at which no food was actually consumed. On Sunday, she was in Milan for an important fashion show, but she managed to find her way back to Cannon Street on Monday for a final briefing. At the conclusion, they gave her a Prada handbag, a Chanel suit, and a Harry Winston wristwatch. The handbag contained a well-hidden transmitter capable of broadcasting securely to a range of five kilometers. A backup transmitter was sewn into the lining of the Chanel suit, along with two miniature GPS tracking beacons. A third tracking beacon was hidden inside the Harry Winston watch. It was the same watch that Nadia's father had given to Sarah five years earlier as an inducement to come to work for him. A jeweler employed by Identity had buffed out the original inscription and replaced it with *To the future, Thomas.* Nadia's eyes glistened as she read it. Leaving, she embraced Gabriel in a way that made Shamron visibly uncomfortable.

"Is there something you'd like to tell me about our girl?" he asked Gabriel as they stood in the window watching Nadia climb into her car.

"She's one of the most remarkable women I've ever met. And if any harm comes to her, I'll never forgive myself."

"Now tell me something I *don't* know," Shamron said.

"She knows who killed her father. And she forgives him."

The team assumed that their enemies were watching and their friends were listening, and so they conducted themselves accordingly. For the most part, they remained barricaded inside the Cannon Street offices of Rogers & Cressey, with all outside errands handled by British personnel who had no direct connection to the operation. Shamron spent most of his time in an Office flat on

Bayswater Road that was known to MI5. Gabriel dropped by once a day to walk with him on the footpaths of Kensington Gardens. On their last day in London, the British followed them. So did the Americans.

"I've always preferred to do my killing alone," Shamron said, looking glumly at the watchers trailing them along the edge of the Long Water. "I'm surprised your friend the president didn't insist on going to the U.N. for a resolution."

"I managed to talk him out of it."

"What *did* you talk about with him?"

"Adrian Carter," said Gabriel. "I told the president that we would take care of Malik only if the Justice Department dropped its investigation into Adrian's handling of the war on terror."

"He agreed?"

"It was somewhat veiled," said Gabriel, "but unmistakable. He also agreed to my second demand."

"Which was?"

"That he fire James McKenna before he gets us all killed."

"We always assumed the president and McKenna were insepa-rable."

"In Washington, no two people are ever inseparable."

Shamron was beginning to tire. They walked to the Italian Gardens and sat on a bench overlooking a fountain. Shamron did a poor job of concealing his irritation. Waterworks, like all other forms of human amusement, bored him.

"You should know that your efforts have already earned us valu-able political capital with the Americans," he said. "Last night, the secretary of state quietly agreed to all our conditions for resuming the peace process with the Palestinians. She also hinted that the president might be willing to pay a visit to Jerusalem in the near future. We assume it will take place *before* the next election."

"Don't underestimate him."

"I never have," Shamron said, "but I'm not sure I envy him. The great Arab Awakening has occurred on his watch, and his actions will help to determine whether the Middle East tips toward people like Nadia al-Bakari or the jihadists like Rashid al-Husseini." Shamron paused. "I'll admit even I don't know how it's going to turn out. I only know that killing a man like Malik will make it easier for the forces of progress and decency to prevail."

"Are you saying the entire future of the Middle East depends on the outcome of my operation?"

"That would be hyperbolic on my part," Shamron said. "And I've always tried to avoid hyperbole at all costs."

"Except when it suits your purposes."

Shamron gave a trace of a smile and lit one of his Turkish cigarettes. "Have you given any thought to who's going to enforce the sentence that's been imposed on Malik?"

"In all likelihood, that decision will be made by Malik himself."

"Which is just one of many things about this operation that I don't care for." Shamron smoked in silence for a moment. "I know you've always preferred the finality of a firearm, but in this case, the needle is a far better option. A noisy kill will only make it harder for you and your team to escape. Hit him with a healthy dose of suxamethonium chloride. He'll feel a pinprick. Then he'll have trouble breathing as the paralysis sets in. Within a few minutes, he'll be dead. And you'll be boarding a private plane at the airport."

"Suxamethonium has one thing in common with a bullet," Gabriel said. "It stays in the body long after the victim is dead. Eventually, the medical examiners in Dubai will find it, and the police will be able to piece together exactly what happened."

"It's the price we pay for operating in modern hotels. Just do your best to shield that face of yours from the cameras. If your picture ends up in the newspaper again, it will complicate your return to civilian life." Shamron observed Gabriel in silence for a moment. "That *is* what you wish to do, is it not?"

Gabriel made no reply. Shamron dropped his cigarette to the ground and crushed it out with his heel.

"You can't fault me for trying," Shamron said.

"I would have been disappointed if you hadn't."

"I actually permitted myself to hope your answer might be different this time."

"Why?"

"Because you're allowing your wife to go to Dubai."

"I didn't have a choice. She insisted."

"You tell the president of the United States to fire one of his closest aides but you acquiesce to an ultimatum from your wife?" Shamron shook his head and said, "Maybe I should have chosen *her* to be the next chief of the Office."

"Make Bella Navot her deputy."

"Bella?" Shamron smiled. "The Arab world would tremble."

They parted, ten minutes later, at Lancaster Gate. Shamron returned to the Office safe flat while Gabriel headed to Heathrow Airport. By the time he arrived, he was Roland Devereaux, formerly of Grenoble, France, lately of Quebec City, Canada. He had the passport of a man who traveled too much and a demeanor to match. After sailing through check-in and passport control, he made his way under covert MI5 escort to the first-class passenger lounge of British Airways. There he found a quiet place far from the in-flight alcoholics and watched the news on television. Bored by an ill-informed discussion of the current terror threat, he opened his businessman's notebook and from memory sketched a beautiful young woman with raven hair. It was a portrait of an unveiled woman, thought Gabriel. A portrait of a spy.

He tore the sketch into small pieces the instant his flight was being called and dropped them into three different rubbish bins as he walked to his gate. After settling into his seat, he made one final check of his e-mail. He had several; all were false but one. It was from a nameless woman who said she had loved him always. Switching off the BlackBerry, he felt a stab of uncharacteristic panic. Then he closed his eyes and ran through the operation one last time.

54

DUBAI

T HE LEAVES OF THE PALM JUMEIRAH, the world's larg- est man-made island, lay flat upon the torpid waters of the Gulf, sinking slowly beneath the weight of unsold luxury villas. In the monstrous pink hotel rising at the apex of the island, a gentle rain fell onto the marble floor of the sprawling lobby. Like nearly everything else in Dubai, the rain was artificial. In this case, however, it was unintended; the ceiling had sprung yet another leak. Rather than repair it, management had opted for a small yellow sign warning patrons, of which there were few, to watch their step.

Farther up the coastline, in the financial quarter, there was more evidence of the misfortune that had befallen the city-state. Construction cranes, once the very symbols of Dubai's economic miracle, loomed motionless over half-finished office blocks and condominium towers. The luxury shopping malls were all but empty, and there were rumors of unemployed European expats

sleeping in the sand dunes of the desert. Many had fled the emirate rather than face the prospect of a stay in its infamous debtors'
prison. At one point, an estimated three thousand abandoned cars
had jammed the airport parking lot. Taped to some of the wind-
shields were hastily scrawled notes of apology to creditors. A used
car in Dubai had almost no value. Traffic jams, once a major problem, were virtually unheard of.

The Ruler still gazed down upon his fiefdom from countless
billboards, but these days his expression seemed a bit dour. His
plan to turn a sleepy fishing port into a center of global trade, finance, and tourism had been crushed by a mountain of debt. The
Dubai dream had turned out to be unsustainable. What's more, it
had also produced an ecological disaster in the making. The residents of Dubai had the largest carbon footprint in the world. They
consumed more water than anyone else on the planet, all of which
came from energy-consuming desalinization plants, and burned
untold amounts of electricity refrigerating their homes, offices,
swimming pools, and artificial ski slopes. Only the foreign laborers did without air-conditioning. They toiled beneath the merciless sun—in some cases, for up to sixteen hours a day—and lived
in squalid fly-infested bunkhouses without so much as a fan to cool
them. So wretched was their existence that hundreds chose suicide
each year, a fact denied by the Ruler and his business associates.

For the eighty thousand charmed citizens of Dubai, life could
not have been much better. The government paid for their health
care, housing, and education, and guaranteed their employment
for life—provided, of course, they refrained from criticizing the
Ruler. Their grandparents had subsisted on camel's milk and dates;
now an army of foreign workers powered their economy and saw
to their every whim and need. The men floated imperiously about
the city in pristine white *kandouras* and *ghutras*. Few expatriates

ever spoke to an Emirati. When they did, the exchange was rarely pleasant.

There was a strict hierarchy inside the foreign community as well. The Brits and other well-to-do expatriates sequestered themselves in the smart districts of Satwa and Jumeirah while the proletariat of the developing world lived mainly on the other side of Dubai Creek, in the old quarter known as Deira. To wander its streets and squares was to walk through many different countries—here a province of India, here a village in Pakistan, here a corner of Tehran or Moscow. Each community had imported a little something from home. From Russia had come crime and women, both of which could be found in abundance at the Odessa, a discotheque and bar located not far from the Gold Souk. Gabriel sat alone at a darkened banquette near the back, a glass of vodka at his elbow. At the next table, a red-faced Brit was fondling an underfed waif from the Russian hinterland. None of the girls bothered Gabriel. He had the look of a man who had come only to watch.

That was not true, however, of the lanky blond-haired Russian who entered the Odessa with a flourish a few minutes after midnight. He sauntered over to the bar to pat a couple of the more shapely backsides before making his way to the table where Gabriel sat. One of the girls immediately tried to join them, but the lanky Russian waved her away with a long, pale hand. When the waitress finally came, he ordered vodka for himself and another for his friend.

"Drink something," said Mikhail. "Otherwise, no one will think you're really a Russian."

"I don't want to be a Russian."

"Neither do I. That's why I moved to Israel."

"Was I followed from my hotel?"

Mikhail shook his head.

Gabriel poured his drink between the seat cushions of the banquette and said, "Let's get out of here."

Mikhail spoke only Russian as they walked to the apartment house near the Corniche. It was a typical Gulf-style building, a four-level blockhouse with a few covered parking spaces on the ground level. The stairwell smelled of chickpeas and cumin, as did the flat on the top floor. It had a two-burner stove in the kitchen and a pullout couch in the sitting room. Powdery desert sand covered every surface. "The neighbors are from Bangladesh," Mikhail said. "There are at least twelve of them in there. They sleep in shifts. Someone needs to tell the world the way these people are really treated here."

"Let it be someone other than you, Mikhail."

"Me? I'm just an enterprising young man from Moscow trying to make his fortune in the city of gold."

"Looks like you came at the wrong time."

"No kidding," said Mikhail. "A few years ago, this place was swimming in money. The Russian mafia used the real estate industry to launder their fortunes. They'd buy apartments and villas and then sell them a week later. These days, even the girls at the Odessa are struggling to make ends meet."

"I'm sure they'll manage somehow."

Mikhail removed a suitcase from the only closet and popped the latches. Inside were eight pistols—four Berettas and four Glocks. Each had matching suppressors.

"The Berettas are nines," Mikhail said. "The Glocks are forty-fives. Man-stoppers. They make big holes and a lot of noise, even with the suppressors. This weapon, however, makes no noise at all."

He removed a zippered cosmetics bag. Inside were hypodermic needles and several vials labeled INSULIN. Gabriel took two needles and two bottles of the drug and slipped them into his coat pocket.

"How about a gun?" asked Mikhail.

"They're frowned upon at the Burj Al Arab."

Mikhail handed over a Beretta, along with a spare magazine filled with rounds. Gabriel slipped them into the waistband of his trousers and asked, "What kind of cars did Transport get for us?"

"BMWs and Toyota Land Cruisers, the new ship of the desert. If we decide that the associate of the Yemeni is Malik, we shouldn't have any trouble tailing him once he leaves the hotel. This isn't Cairo or Gaza. The roads are all very straight and wide. If he heads for one of the other emirates, we can follow him. But if he makes a run for Saudi, we'll have to hit him before he gets to the border. That could get messy."

"I'd like to avoid a desert shoot-out, if at all possible."

"So would I. Who knows? With a bit of luck, he'll decide to spend the night at his apartment in Jumeirah Beach. We'll give him a bit of medicine to help him sleep and then . . ." Mikhail's voice trailed off. "So how's life at the Burj?"

"Just what you'd expect from the world's only seven-star hotel."

"I hope you're enjoying yourself," Mikhail said resentfully.

"If you'd listened to me, you'd be living in America now with Sarah."

"Doing what?"

Gabriel was silent for a moment. "It's not too late, Mikhail," he said finally. "For some reason, she's still in love with you. Even a fool like you should be able to see that."

"It's just not going to work out for us."

"Why?" Gabriel looked around the filthy little apartment. "Because you want to live like this?"

"You're one to talk." Mikhail closed the suitcase and returned it to the closet. "Did she ask you to say something?"

"She'd kill me if she knew."

"What *did* she tell you?"

"That you behaved rather badly." Gabriel paused, then added, "Something you swore you wouldn't do."

"I didn't mistreat her, Gabriel. I just——"

"Went through hell in Switzerland."

Mikhail made no response.

"Do yourself a favor when this is over," Gabriel said. "Find an excuse to go to America. Spend some time with her. If there's anyone in the world who understands what you've been through, it's Sarah Bancroft. Don't let her slip away. She's special."

Mikhail smiled sadly, the way the young always smile at foolish old men. "Go back to your hotel," he said. "Try to sleep. And make sure you hide those vials somewhere the maids won't find them. There's a huge black market for stolen medicine. I wouldn't want there to be a tragic accident."

"Any other advice?"

"Take a taxi back to the Burj. They drive worse than we do. Only the poor and the suicidal walk in Dubai."

Contrary to Mikhail's advice, Gabriel made his way on foot through the teeming alleyways of Deira to the embankment of Dubai Creek. Not far from the main souk was an *abra* station. It was Dubai's version of Venice's *traghetto*, a small ferry that shuttled passengers from one side of the creek to the other. During the crossing, Gabriel fell into conversation with a weary-looking man from the border regions of Pakistan. The man had come to Dubai to escape the Taliban and al-Qaeda and was hoping to earn enough money to send for his wife and four children. So far, he had only been able to find odd jobs that left him barely able to support himself, let alone a family of six.

As they were getting off the ferry, Gabriel slipped five hundred dirhams into the pocket of the man's baggy trousers. Then he stopped at an all-night kiosk to pick up a copy of the *Khaleej Times*, Dubai's English-language newspaper. On the front page was a story about the upcoming visit by Nadia al-Bakari, chairwoman of AAB Holdings. Gabriel slipped the newspaper beneath his arm and walked a short distance before flagging down a passing taxi. Mikhail was right, he thought, climbing into the safety of the backseat. Only the poor and suicidal walked in Dubai.

55

DUBAI INTERNATIONAL AIRPORT

H IS ROYAL HIGHNESS, THE MINISTER OF FINANCE, stood at the edge of the sunlit tarmac, resplendent in his gold-and-crystal-trimmed robes. To his right stood ten identically attired junior ministers, and to their right loitered a flock of bored-looking reporters. The ministers and the reporters were about to engage in a time-honored ritual in the Sunni Arab kingdoms of the Gulf: the airport arrival. In a world with no tradition of independent reporting, airport comings and goings were regarded as the pinnacle of journalism. See the dignitary land. See the dignitary fly away after productive talks characterized by mutual respect. Truth was rarely spoken at these events, and the hamstrung press never dared to report it. Today's ceremony would be something of a milestone, for in a few minutes' time, even the princes would be deceived.

The first aircraft appeared shortly after noon, a flash of silver-white above a cloud of pinkish dust from the Empty Quarter of

Saudi Arabia. On board was an English tycoon named Thomas Fowler who was not an Englishman at all and, in truth, hadn't a penny to his name. Descending the passenger stairs, he was trailed by a wife who was not really his wife and by three female aides who knew much more about Islamic terrorism than business and finance. One worked for the Central Intelligence Agency while the other two were employed by the secret intelligence service of the State of Israel. The team of bodyguards protecting the party also worked for Israeli intelligence, though their passports identified them as citizens of Australia and New Zealand.

The English tycoon advanced on the minister with his hand extended like a bayonet. The minister's own emerged indolently from his robes, as did those of his ten junior ministers. The requisite greetings complete, the Englishman was escorted to the press to make a brief statement. He spoke without aid of notes but with great authority and passion. Dubai's recession was over, he declared. It was now time to resume the march toward the future. The Arab world was changing by the minute. And only Dubai—progressive, tolerant, and stable Dubai—could show it the way.

The final portion of the statement did not provoke the response from the press it deserved because it was largely drowned out by the arrival of a second aircraft—a Boeing Business Jet bearing the logo of AAB Holdings of Riyadh and Paris. The party that was soon spilling from its forward cabin door dwarfed that of the English tycoon. First came the law firm of Abdul & Abdul. Then Herr Wehrli, the Swiss moneyman. Then Daoud Hamza. Then Hamza's daughter Rahimah, who had come for the party. After Rahimah came a pair of security men, followed by Mansur, the chief of AAB's busy travel department, and Hassan, the chief of IT and communications.

Finally, after a delay of several seconds, Nadia al-Bakari

stepped through the doorway with her security chief, Rafiq al-Kamal, trailing a step behind. She wore an unadorned black *abaya* that flowed from her body like an evening gown and a silky black headscarf that revealed all of her face and much of her lustrous hair. This time, it was the minister who advanced. He assumed his greeting was private, which was not the case. It was captured by Nadia's compromised BlackBerry and by the transmitter concealed in her stylish Prada handbag, and broadcast securely to the forty-second floor of the Burj Al Arab hotel, where Gabriel and Eli Lavon sat tensely before their computers.

The welcome ceremony complete, the minister gestured disdainfully toward the reporters, but the notoriously reclusive heiress declined and headed directly for her limousine. At which point the minister suggested she ride with him instead. After consulting briefly with Rafiq al-Kamal, Nadia climbed into the back of the minister's official car—a moment that was broadcast to the entire country, thirty minutes later, on Dubai TV. Gabriel dispatched a secure e-mail to Adrian Carter at Rashidistan, informing him that NAB was safely on the ground. But this time she was not alone. NAB was at the side of the minister of finance. And NAB was the lead of the midday news.

The property in question wasn't much to look at—a few uninviting acres of salt flats and sand located just up the beach from the Palm Jumeirah. An Italian company had broken ground on a rather conventional resort a few years back but had been forced to pull up stakes when the financing went the way of water in the desert. AAB Holdings and its British partner, the predatory investment firm of Rogers & Cressey, wished to resuscitate the project, though their plans were anything but conventional. The high-rise hotel would surpass the Burj Al Arab in luxury, the fitness centers and tennis facilities would be among the finest in the world, and the swimming pools would be both architectural and environmental wonders. Top chefs would operate the restaurants while internationally renowned stylists would run the hair salons. The condominium units would start at the equivalent of three million dollars. The shopping arcade would make the Mall of the Emirates seem positively downmarket.

The impact on Dubai's reeling economy promised to be immense. According to AAB's own projections, the development would pump more than a hundred million dollars into Dubai's economy on an annual basis. In the short term, it would send an unambiguous signal to the rest of the global financial community that the emirate was once again open for business. Which was why the minister appeared to be hanging on Nadia's every word as she toured the site, blueprints in hand, a construction hard hat on her head. The image was carefully crafted on her part. No longer could the Muslim world oppress more than half its population simply because of gender. Only when the Arabs treated women as equals could they regain their former glory.

After leaving the site, the delegations headed to the minister's ornate offices to discuss a package of incentives that Dubai was proposing to help close the deal. At the conclusion of the meeting, Nadia was driven to the palace for a private word with the Ruler, after which she embarked on what was described as the private portion of her schedule. It included tea with members of the Dubai Women's Business Forum, a visit to an Islamic school for girls, and a tour of the migrant workers camp at Sonapur. Moved to tears by the terrible conditions, she broke her long public silence, calling on government and business to impose minimum standards for pay and treatment of migrant workers. She also pledged twenty million dollars of her own money to help construct a new camp at Sonapur, complete with air-conditioned bunkhouses, running water, and basic recreational facilities. Neither Dubai TV nor the *Khaleej Times* dared to publicize the remarks. The minister had warned them not to.

It was approaching six in the evening when Nadia left the camp and started back to Dubai city. Darkness had fallen by the time her motorcade reached the Jumeirah Beach district, and the famous dhow-shaped wings of the Burj Al Arab were lit the color of magenta. The general manager and his senior staff were waiting outside the entrance as Nadia emerged from the back of her car, the hem of her *abaya* soiled by the grime of Sonapur. Weary from a day of travel and meetings that had begun at dawn in Paris, she gave them a perfunctory greeting before heading directly to her usual suite on the forty-second floor. Two members of her security detail were already stationed outside the door. Rafiq al-Kamal gave the rooms a cursory inspection before allowing Nadia to enter.

"My last meeting of the day will run from nine until ten or so," she said, tossing the Prada handbag onto a divan in the sitting room. "Tell Mansur to book an eleven o'clock departure slot. And please ask Rahimah to be on time for once in her life. Otherwise, she can fly back to Paris on Air France."

"Perhaps I should tell her to be at the airport no later than eleven-thirty."

"It's tempting," Nadia said, smiling, "but I don't think her father would appreciate that."

Al-Kamal seemed reluctant to leave.

"Is something wrong?" she asked.

He hesitated. "At the camp today . . ."

"What is it, Rafiq?"

"No one ever lifts a finger for those poor wretches. It's about time someone spoke up. I'm glad it was you." He paused, then added, "And I was proud to be at your side."

She smiled. "Nine o'clock," she said. "Don't be late."

"Zizi's rules," he said.

She nodded. "Zizi's rules."

Alone, Nadia stripped off the *abaya* and headscarf and changed into the Chanel suit. She covered a portion of her hair with a matching scarf and slipped on the Harry Winston wristwatch. Then she checked her appearance in the mirror. *Adhere to the truth when possible. Lie as a last resort.* The truth was staring back at her in the glass. The lie was in the next room. She opened the communicating door to the adjoining suite and knocked twice. The door swung back instantly, revealing a woman who may or may not have been Sarah Bancroft. She placed a finger to her lips and drew Nadia silently inside.

56

BURJ AL ARAB HOTEL, DUBAI

T HE SUITE WAS REGISTERED UNDER the name Thomas
Fowler. Thus the jungle of complimentary flowers, the platters of complimentary Arabian sweets, and the unopened
bottle of complimentary Dom Pérignon sweating in a bucket of
melted ice. The recipient of this largess was pacing the garish sitting
room, working over the final details of a land and development deal
he had no intention of actually making. Every few seconds, a member of his staff would pose a question or rattle off a few encouraging numbers—all for the benefit of the Ruler's hidden microphones.
None of the staff bothered to acknowledge Nadia's presence, nor did
they seem to think it odd when Sarah immediately led her into the
bathroom. In the vanity area was a tentlike structure made of an
opaque silver material. Sarah relieved Nadia of her BlackBerry before opening the flap. Gabriel was already seated inside. He gestured
for Nadia to sit in the empty chair.

"A tent in the bathroom," said Nadia, smiling. "How Bedouin of you."

"You're not the only people who come from the desert."

She looked around the interior, clearly intrigued. "What is it?"

"We call it the *chuppah*. It allows us to speak freely in rooms we know are bugged."

"May I have it when we're done?"

He smiled. "I'm afraid not."

She touched the fabric. It had a metallic quality.

"Isn't the *chuppah* used in Jewish wedding ceremonies?"

"We take our vows beneath the *chuppah*. They're very important to us."

"So is this our wedding ceremony?" she asked, still stroking the fabric.

"I'm already spoken for. Besides, I gave you a solemn vow in a manor house outside Paris."

She placed her hand in her lap. "Your script for today was a work of art," she said. "I only hope I did it justice."

"You were magnificent, Nadia, but that was a rather expensive ad lib at Sonapur."

"Twenty million dollars for a new camp? It was the least I could do for them."

"Shall I ask the CIA to pick up the tab?"

"My treat," she said.

Gabriel examined Nadia's Chanel suit. "It fits you well."

"Better than the ones I have custom made."

"We're tailors by trade, highly specialized tailors. That suit can do everything except walk into a meeting with a monster who has a great deal of blood on his hands. For that, we need you." He paused, then said, "Last chance, Nadia."

"To back out?"

"We wouldn't think of it like that. And none of us would think any less of you."

"I don't break commitments, Mr. Allon—not anymore. Besides, we both know that there isn't time for second thoughts now." She looked at the Harry Winston watch. "In fact, I'm expecting a call from my banker any minute. So if you have any final words of advice . . ."

"Just remember who you are, Nadia. You're the daughter of Zizi al-Bakari, a descendant of Wahhab. No one tells you where to go, or what to do. And no one ever changes the plan. If they try to change the plan, you tell them the meeting is off. Then you call Mansur and tell him to move up the departure slot. Are we clear?"

She nodded.

"We assume the meeting will take place in a suite rather than in a public part of the hotel. It is critical that you make Samir say the room number before you leave the lobby. Insist on it. And if he tries to mumble it, repeat it loudly enough for us to hear. Understood?"

She nodded again.

"We'll try to send someone up in the elevator with you, but he'll have to get off on a separate floor. After that, you'll be beyond our reach, and Rafiq will be your only protection. Under no circumstances are you to enter the room without him. This is another red line. If they try to talk you into it, leave immediately. If everything goes smoothly, go inside and start the meeting. This isn't a social gathering or a political discussion. This is a business transaction. You listen to what he has to say, you tell him what he wants to hear, and then you leave for the airport. Your plane is your lifeboat. And your eleven o'clock departure slot is your excuse to keep things moving. At ten o'clock you're—"

"Out the door," she said.

Gabriel nodded. "Remember your BlackBerry etiquette. Offer to switch yours off as a show of your good intentions. Ask them to power off their devices and remove SIM cards. If they refuse or say it isn't necessary, don't draw any lines in the sand. It's not important."

"Where are the bugs?"

"What bugs?"

"Let's not play games, Mr. Allon."

He tapped the side of the Prada bag and nodded toward the front of the Chanel suit. "It's possible they'll ask you to leave the bag in another room. If they do, agree without hesitation. There's no way they'll ever find what's hidden in there."

"And if they ask me to remove my clothing?"

"They're holy warriors. They wouldn't dare."

"You'd be surprised." Nadia looked down at her bustline.

"Don't bother looking for the microphones. You'll never find them. We could have concealed a camera in the suit as well, but for your safety, we chose not to."

"So you won't be able to see what's going on in the room?"

"Once you switch off the BlackBerry, we'll be blind. That means you'll be the only one to know what he looks like. If it's safe—and *only* if it's safe—call me after the meeting and tell me something about his appearance. Just a few details. Then hang up and head to the airport. We'll follow you for as long as we can."

"And after that?"

"You go home to Paris and forget we ever existed."

"Somehow I don't think that's going to be possible."

"It won't be as difficult as you think." He took hold of her hand. "It's been an honor to work with you, Nadia. Don't take this the wrong way, but I hope we never see each other again after tonight."

"I will not wish such a thing." She looked at her watch, the

watch her father had given to Sarah, and noticed it was three minutes past nine. "He's late," she said. "The Arab disease."

"We set it fast intentionally to keep you moving."

"What time is it really?" she asked, but before Gabriel could
answer, the BlackBerry started to ring. It was nine o'clock sharp.
It was time for Nadia to go.

57

LANGLEY, VIRGINIA

I T WAS A CURIOSITY OF Ari Shamron's long and storied career that he had spent almost no time at Langley, a feat he
considered one of his greatest accomplishments. Therefore, he
was predictably appalled to learn that Uzi Navot had agreed to
establish his command post at Langley's glittering Rashidistan op
center. For Shamron, it was an admission of weakness to accept
the American invitation, a cardinal sin in the world of espionage,
but Navot saw it in more pragmatic terms. The Americans were
not the enemy—at least not tonight—and they had technological
capabilities that were far too valuable to refuse merely out of
professional pride.

In a minor concession to Shamron, Rashidistan was cleared of
the nonessential and uninitiated, leaving only a skeleton crew of
the battle-hardened and unrepentant. At 9 p.m. Dubai time, most
were hovering anxiously around the pod in the center of the room,
where Shamron, Navot, and Adrian Carter sat staring at the lat-

est secure transmission from the Burj Al Arab team. It stated that Nadia al-Bakari was heading to the lobby, with her trusted chief of security Rafiq al-Kamal at her side. The three spymasters knew the message had already been eclipsed by events on the ground, because they were listening to Nadia and al-Kamal striding across the Burj's soaring 590-foot atrium. The source of the audio was her compromised BlackBerry, which was tucked inside her compromised Prada handbag.

At 9:04 local time, the device captured a brief conversation between Nadia and her banker, Samir Abbas. Because it was conducted in rapid colloquial Arabic, Carter did not understand it. That was not true, however, for Navot and Shamron.

"Well?" asked Carter.

"She's going upstairs to meet with someone," Navot said. "Whether it's Malik al-Zubair or Nobody al-Nobody remains to be seen."

"Were you able to understand the room number?"

Navot nodded his head.

"Shall we send it to Gabriel?"

"That won't be necessary."

"He heard it?"

"Clear as a bell."

The elevator doors slid open without a sound. Nadia allowed Abbas and al-Kamal to step into the corridor first, before following closely after them. Curiously, she felt nothing like fear, only resolution. It was oddly similar to the sense of determination she had carried into her first important business meeting after solidifying her control of AAB Holdings. There had been many members of her father's team quietly hoping for her to fail—and a few who'd actually conspired against her—but Nadia had managed to surprise them all. When it came to matters of business, she had proven to be her father's equal. Now she would have to be his equal in a part of his life never written about in the pages of *Forbes* and the *Wall Street Journal*. Just a few minutes, she reminded herself. That's all it would take. A few minutes in one of the safest hotels in the world, and a monster with the blood of thousands on his hands would receive the justice he deserved.

Abbas stopped at Room 1437 and knocked with the same softness with which Esmeralda tapped on Nadia's door each morning in Paris. Quite unexpectedly, she thought of the Thomas Tompion clock on her bedside table and of the many unsmiling photographs of her father framed in silver. As she waited for the door to open, she resolved to finally send the clock out for repair. She also vowed to dispose of the photographs. After tonight, she thought, the pretense would come to an end. Her time on earth was limited, and she had no wish to spend her final days beneath the *juhayman* of a murderer.

When Abbas knocked a second time, the door retreated halfway, revealing a broad-shouldered man dressed in the white *kandoura* and *ghutra* of a native Emirati. He wore tinted eyeglasses rimmed in gold and a neatly trimmed beard with patches of gray around the chin. In the center of his flat forehead was a pronounced *ʒebiba* prayer scar that looked as though it had been recently irritated. He looked nothing at all like any of the photo illustrations Nadia had been shown in London.

The robed figure opened the door a few inches wider and with a movement of his eyes invited Nadia to enter. He permitted Rafiq al-Kamal to follow, but instructed Abbas to return to the lobby. The robed figure had the accent of a man from Upper Egypt. Behind him stood two more men in pristine white robes and headdresses. They, too, were wearing gold-rimmed eyeglasses and trimmed beards flecked with gray. When the door closed, the Egyptian raised his hand to his ear and said softly, "Your mobile phone, please."

Nadia drew the BlackBerry from her handbag and surrendered it. The Egyptian immediately handed the device to one of his clones, who disabled it with a swiftness that suggested a facility with technology.

"Now yours," said Nadia in a clear voice. She nodded toward the other two men and added, "Theirs, too."

The broad-shouldered Egyptian was clearly unaccustomed to being addressed by women in anything but a subservient manner. He looked toward his two colleagues and with a nod instructed them to disable their mobile devices. They did so without protest.

"Are we finished?" asked Nadia.

"Your bodyguard's phone," he said. "And your bag."

"What about my bag?"

"We would feel more comfortable if you left it here by the door. I assure you that your valuables will be safe."

Nadia let the bag slip from her shoulder in a way that suggested her patience was at an end. "We don't have all night, my brothers. If you would like to petition me for another donation, I suggest we get on with it."

"Forgive us, Miss al-Bakari, but our enemies have enormous technical resources. Surely a woman in your position knows what can happen when people get careless."

Nadia looked at al-Kamal, who responded by handing over his phone.

"I'm told that you wish to have your bodyguard present during the meeting," the Egyptian said.

"No," Nadia said, "I *insist* on it."

"You trust this man?" he replied, glancing at al-Kamal.

"With my life."

"Very well," he said. "This way, please."

She followed the three robed men into the sitting room of the suite, where two more men in Emirati dress waited in the half-light. One was seated on a couch watching an account of the latest bombing in Pakistan on Al Jazeera. The other was admiring the view of the skyscrapers along Sheikh Zayed Road. He rotated slowly around, like a statue atop a plinth, and appraised Nadia thoughtfully through tinted glasses rimmed in gold. He did not speak. Neither did Nadia. In fact, at that instant, she was not at all certain she was capable of speech.

"Is something wrong, Miss al-Bakari?" he asked in Jordanian Arabic.

"You just happen to look a great deal like a man who used to work for my father," she replied without hesitation.

He was silent for a long moment. Finally, he glanced at the television screen and said, "You just missed yourself on the evening news. You've had quite a busy day today. My compliments, Miss al-Bakari. Your father would have played it the same way. I hear he was always very skillful in the way he mixed legitimate business with *zakat*."

"He taught me well."

"Do you really intend to build it?"

"The resort?" She gave an ambivalent shrug. "The last thing Dubai needs right now is another hotel."

"Especially one that serves alcohol and allows drunken foreigners to parade around the beach half-naked."

Nadia made no response other than to look at the other men in the room.

"It's just a security precaution on my part, Miss al-Bakari. The walls have eyes as well as ears."

"It's remarkably effective," she said, looking directly into his face. "You haven't told me your name."

"You may call me Mr. Darwish."

"My time is limited, Mr. Darwish."

"One hour, according to my colleagues."

"Fifty minutes, actually," Nadia said, glancing at her watch.

"Our enterprise has suffered a severe setback."

"So I've read."

"We need additional financing to rebuild."

"I gave you several million pounds."

"I'm afraid that nearly all of it has been frozen or seized. If we are to rebuild our organization, particularly in the West, we will need an infusion of new capital."

"Why should I reward your incompetence?"

"I can assure you, Miss al-Bakari, that we've learned from our mistakes."

"What sorts of changes are you planning to make?"

"Better security, coupled with an aggressive plan to take the fight directly to our competitors."

"An expansion?" she asked.

"If you are not growing, Miss al-Bakari, you are dying."

"I'm listening, Mr. Darwish."

With Nadia's BlackBerry disabled and her handbag lying on the floor of the entrance hall, audio coverage of the meeting under way in Room 1437 was being supplied, quite literally, by the clothes on her back. Though the transmitter woven into the seams had an extremely short range, it was more than enough to securely broadcast a clear signal to the forty-second floor of the same building. There, behind a door that was double-locked and barricaded by furniture, Gabriel and Eli Lavon waited for their computers to supply the real name of the man who had just introduced himself as Mr. Darwish.

The voice-identification software had declared the first few seconds of the meeting inadequate for comparison. That changed when Mr. Darwish started talking about money. Now the software was rapidly comparing a sample of his voice to previous intercepts. Gabriel was confident of the conclusion the computers were about to make. In fact, he was all but certain of it. The murderer had already signed his name, not with his voice but with the four numbers. They were the numbers of the room where the meeting was taking place. Gabriel had no need to add them, subtract them, multiply them, or rearrange their order in any way. He only had to convert the numbers from a twenty-four-hour clock to a twelve-hour clock: 1437 hours was 2:37 p.m., the time at which Farid Khan had detonated his bomb in Covent Garden.

Five minutes after Nadia's entry into the suite, the computer handed down its verdict. Gabriel raised his secure radio to his lips and instructed his team to begin preparing to carry out the sentence. It was Malik, he said. And may God have mercy on them all.

58

BURJ AL ARAB HOTEL, DUBAI

THE LANKY RUSSIAN PRESENTED HIMSELF at reception thirty seconds later. He had a fine-boned, bloodless face and eyes the color of glacial ice. His American passport identified him as Anthony Colvin, as did his American Express card. He drummed his fingers on the countertop while waiting for the pretty Filipina to find his reservation. He was holding a mobile phone to his ear as though his life depended on it.

"Here we are," sang the Filipina. "We have you in a one-bedroom deluxe suite on the twenty-ninth floor, for three nights. Is that correct, Mr. Colvin?"

"If you wouldn't mind," he said, lowering the mobile phone, "I'm looking for something on the fourteenth floor."

"The twenty-ninth is considered more desirable."

"My wife and I spent our honeymoon on the fourteenth. We'd like to stay there again. For sentimental reasons," he added. "Surely you understand."

She didn't. The Filipina worked twelve-hour shifts and shared a one-room apartment in Deira with eight other girls. Her love life consisted of fending off drunken gropers and rapists who assumed, wrongly, that she moonlighted in Dubai's thriving sex trade. She clicked a few keys on her computer terminal and gave a plastic smile.

"Actually," she said, "we do have a number of rooms available on the fourteenth floor. Do you recall the room where you and your wife stayed on your honeymoon?"

"I believe it was 1437," he said.

She appeared crestfallen. "Unfortunately, that room is currently occupied, Mr. Colvin. However, the suite next to it is available, as is the one directly across the hall."

"I'll take the one across the hall, please."

"It's a bit more expensive."

"No problem," said the Russian.

"I'll need to see your wife's passport."

"She's joining me tomorrow."

"Please ask her to stop by when she arrives."

"First thing," he assured her.

"Do you require assistance with your luggage?"

"I can manage, thanks."

She gave him a pair of electronic room keys and pointed him toward the appropriate elevator. As promised, his room was directly across the hall from 1437. Entering, he immediately switched on the Do Not Disturb light and double-locked the door. Then he opened his suitcase. Inside were a few articles of clothing that stank of chickpeas and cumin. There was also a Beretta 9mm, a Glock .45, two hypodermic needles, two vials of suxamethonium chloride, a notebook computer, and an adjustable high-resolution snake camera. He mounted the camera to the bottom of the door and connected its wiring to the computer. After adjusting the angle of the view, he filled the hypodermic needles with suxamethonium chloride and the guns with bullets. Then he settled in before the computer and waited.

For the next forty-five minutes, he was treated to a view of the Burj Al Arab not seen on its Web site or in its glossy brochures. Frantic room service waiters. Weary chambermaids. An Ethiopian nanny holding the hand of a hysterical child. An Australian businessman walking arm in arm with a Ukrainian prostitute. Finally, at ten sharp, he saw a beautiful Arab woman stepping from Room 1437 with a vigilant bodyguard at her back. When the woman and bodyguard were gone, a broad-shouldered man leaned out the doorway and looked both ways along the corridor. White *kandoura* and *ghutra*. Tinted eyeglasses rimmed in gold. A neatly trimmed beard with flecks of gray around the chin. The Russian picked up the Glock, the man-stopper, and quietly chambered a round.

59

BURJ AL ARAB HOTEL, DUBAI

THE DETAILS OF NADIA AL-BAKARI'S departure from the Burj Al Arab were handled not by Gabriel and his team but by Mansur, the chief of AAB's travel department. There were no belongings for her to collect, because Mansur had seen to them personally. Nor were there any bills to pay, because they had already been forwarded to AAB headquarters in Paris. All Nadia had to do was make her way to the Burj's circular drive, where her car waited just outside the front entrance. After climbing into the backseat, she asked her driver and Rafiq al-Kamal to give her a moment of privacy. Alone, she dialed a number that had been stored in the memory of her BlackBerry. Gabriel answered immediately in Arabic.

"Tell me what he looked like."

"White *kandoura*. White *ghutra*. Tinted eyeglasses with gold rims. A neatly trimmed beard with a bit of gray."

"You did well, Nadia. Go to the airport. Go home."

"Wait!" she snapped. "There's something else I need to tell you."

———————

Though Nadia did not know it, Gabriel was seated in the lobby, looking like a man who had come to Dubai for work rather than pleasure, which was indeed the case. On the table before him was a notebook computer. Attached to his ear was a hands-free mobile phone that doubled as a secure radio. He used it to alert his far-flung team that the operation had just hit its first snag.

———————

Nadia tapped her BlackBerry on the window and signaled that she was ready to leave. A few seconds later, as they were speeding over the causeway separating the Burj from the mainland, Rafiq al-Kamal asked, "Is there anything I need to know?"

"That meeting never happened."

"What meeting?" asked the bodyguard.

Nadia managed a smile. "Tell Mansur we're on our way to the airport. Tell him to move up our departure slot if he can. I'd like to get back to Paris at a reasonable hour."

Al-Kamal pulled out his phone and dialed.

———————

"Maybe Allah really is on his side after all," said Adrian Carter. He was staring in disbelief at Gabriel's latest transmission from Dubai. It said that Malik al-Zubair, master of terror, was about to walk out of the Burj Al Arab surrounded by four carbon copies.

"I'm afraid God has very little to do with this," said Navot. "Malik has been matching wits against the best intelligence services in the world for years. He knows how the game is played."

Navot looked at Shamron, who was twirling his old Zippo lighter nervously between his fingers.

Two turns to the right, two turns to the left.

"We have four vehicles outside that hotel," Navot said. "Under our operating rules, that's enough to follow *one* car—two at most. If five similarly dressed men get into five different cars . . ." His voice trailed off. "We might want to start thinking about getting them out of there, boss."

"We've gone to a great deal of effort to put a team on the ground in Dubai tonight, Uzi. The least we can do is let them stick around long enough to try to have a look at Malik's face." He glanced at the row of clocks glowing along one of Rashidistan's walls and asked, "What is the status of Nadia's airplane?"

"Fueled and ready for takeoff. The rest of her staff is boarding now."

"And where is the star of the show at this moment?"

"Heading northeast on Sheikh Zayed Road at forty-six miles per hour."

"May I see her?"

Carter snatched up a phone. A few seconds later, a winking red light appeared on one of the wall monitors, moving northeast across the grid of Dubai city. Shamron twirled his lighter anxiously as he watched its steady progress.

Two turns to the right, two turns to the left . . .

The first Range Rover eased into the drive of the Burj Al Arab two minutes after Nadia's departure. A second appeared soon after, followed by a Mercedes GL and a pair of Denalis. Gabriel keyed into his secure radio, but Mikhail was on the air first.

"They're leaving the room," he said.

Gabriel didn't have to ask how many. The answer was outside in the drive. Five SUVs for five men. Gabriel had to establish which of the five was Malik before any of the men set foot outside the hotel. And there was only one way to do it. He gave the order.

"There are five of them and one of me," Mikhail replied.

"The longer you talk, the greater the chances we'll lose him."

Mikhail keyed out without another word. Gabriel glanced down at his laptop to check Nadia's location.

She was halfway to the airport.

———————

Mikhail secured the room and stepped into the corridor. The Glock was now at the small of his back with the suppressor screwed into place. The loaded syringe was in the outside pocket of his coat. He glanced to his right and saw the five men in white *kandouras* and *ghutras* stepping around a corner into the elevator vestibule. He walked normally for a few seconds but quickened his pace after hearing the chime indicating that a carriage had arrived. By the time he reached the vestibule, the five men had entered the elevator and the gleaming gold doors were beginning to close. He shouldered his way inside, mumbling an apology, and stood at the front of the carriage as the doors closed for a second time. In the reflection, he could see five matching men. Five matching beards flecked with gray. Five pairs of matching eyeglasses rimmed in gold. Five prayer scars that looked recently irritated. There was just one difference. Four of the men were staring directly at Mikhail. The fifth seemed to be looking down at his shoes.

Malik . . .

———————

Twenty-two floors above, Samir Abbas, fund-raiser for the global jihadist movement, was catching up on a bit of legitimate work for TransArabian Bank when he heard a knock at the door. He had been expecting it; the Egyptian had said he would send someone when the meeting with Nadia was over. As it turned out, he sent not one man but two. They were dressed like Emiratis, but their accents betrayed them as Jordanians. Abbas admitted them without hesitation.

"The meeting went well?" he asked.

"Very well," said the older of the two men. "Miss al-Bakari has agreed to make another donation to our cause. We have a few details we need to discuss with you."

Abbas turned to lead them into the seating area. Only when he felt the garrote biting into his neck did he realize his mistake. Unable to draw a breath or utter a sound, Abbas clawed desperately at the thin metal wire carving into his skin. The lack of oxygen quickly sapped his strength, and he was able to offer only token resistance as the men pushed him facedown to the floor. It was then Abbas felt something else carving into his neck, and he realized they intended to take his head. It was the punishment for infidels and apostates and the enemies of jihad. Samir Abbas was none of those things. He was a believer, a secret soldier in the army of Allah. But in a moment, for reasons he did not understand, he would be a *shahid*.

Mercifully, Abbas began to lose consciousness. He thought of the money he had hidden in the pantry of his flat in Zurich, and he hoped that Johara or the children might one day find it. Then he forced himself to go still and to submit to the will of God.

The knife made a few more vicious strokes. Abbas saw a burst of brilliant white light and assumed it was the light of Paradise. Then the light was extinguished and there was nothing at all.

60

BURJ AL ARAB HOTEL, DUBAI

THE ELEVATOR STOPPED TWICE BEFORE reaching the lobby. A sunburned British woman boarded on the eleventh floor, a Chinese businessman on the seventh. The new arrivals forced Mikhail to retreat deeper into the carriage. He was now standing so close to Malik he could smell the coffee on his breath. The Glock was pressed reassuringly against Mikhail's spine, but it was the syringe in his coat pocket that occupied his thoughts. He was tempted to shove the needle into Malik's thigh. Instead, he stared at the ceiling, or at his watch, or at the numbers flashing on the display panel—anywhere but at the face of the murderer standing next to him. When the doors finally opened a third time, he followed the British woman and the Chinese businessman toward the bar.

"He's the second one from the left," he said into his phone.

"Are you sure?"

"Sure enough to hit him right now if you tell me to."

"Not here."

"Don't let him leave. Do it now while we have a chance."

Gabriel went off the air. Mikhail entered the bar, counted slowly to ten, and walked out.

Gabriel was packing up his laptop and conducting a false telephone conversation in rapid French as Malik and his four comrades came floating through the lobby in their white robes. Outside, they engaged in a swirl of handshakes and formal kisses before making their way separately toward the SUVs. Despite the final element of physical deception, Gabriel had no problem tracking Malik as he climbed into the back of one of the Denalis. When the five cars were gone, a pair of Toyota Land Cruisers took their place. Mikhail managed to look vaguely bored as he slipped past the valet and climbed into the front passenger seat of the first. Gabriel entered the second. "Put on your seat belt," Chiara said as she accelerated away. "These people drive like maniacs."

The news that Malik was under Office surveillance reached Rashidistan at 10:12 p.m. Dubai time. It provoked a brief outburst of emotion among the skeleton crew, but not among the three spymasters gathered around the pod in the center of the room. Shamron seemed particularly aggrieved as he watched the winking red light making its way along Sheikh Zayed Road.

"It occurs to me that we haven't heard from our friend Samir Abbas in some time," he said, eyes still on the wall monitor. "Would it be possible to call his mobile phone from a number he would recognize?"

"Anyone in particular?" asked Carter.

"Make it his wife," Shamron said. "Samir always struck me as the family type."

"You just referred to him in the past tense."

"Did I?" Shamron asked absently.

Carter looked at one of the techs and said, "Make it happen."

The residents of Dubai are not only among the richest people in the world, but they are also statistically some of its worst drivers. A collision—be it with another car, pedestrian, or object—occurs every two minutes in the emirate, resulting in three fatalities a day on average. The typical driver thinks nothing of slashing across multiple lanes of heavy traffic or tailgating at a hundred miles per hour while talking on his cell phone. As a result, few people took notice of the high-speed chase that occurred shortly after ten p.m. on the road to Jebel Ali. It was just another night at the races.

The road had four lanes in each direction with a grassy median down the center and traffic signals that most locals dismissed as unwanted advice. Gabriel clung to the armrest as Chiara ably maneuvered the big Land Cruiser through the herd of other vehicles just like it. Because it was a Thursday evening, the beginning of the weekend in the Islamic world, the traffic was heavier than on a typical night. Enormous sport-utility vehicles were the norm rather than the exception. Most were driven by bearded men wearing white *kandouras* and *ghutras*.

The five cars of Malik's motorcade were engaged in something like a rolling shell game. They weaved, they swerved, they flashed their high beams for slower traffic to give way—all perfectly appropriate conduct on the anarchic roads of Dubai. Chiara and the three other drivers of the chase team did their best to maintain contact. It was a perilous business. Despite the lawlessness of the roads, the Emirati police didn't look kindly upon foreigners who got into accidents. Malik knew this, of course. Gabriel wondered what else Malik knew. He was beginning to worry that the elaborate security measures were more than simply precautions, that Malik, as usual, was one step ahead of his enemies.

They were approaching the port of Jebel Ali. They shot past the glittering Ibn Battuta theme park and shopping mall, then a desalinization plant: Dubai in a snapshot. Gabriel scarcely noticed the landmarks. He was watching the carefully choreographed maneuver occurring on the road directly ahead. Four of the SUVs were now side by side across the four lanes of traffic. They had reduced their speed and were engaged in a blocking tactic. The fifth, the Denali in which Malik was riding, was accelerating rapidly.

"He's getting away, Chiara. You have to get past them."

"Where?"

"Find a way."

Chiara swerved hard to the left. Then to the right. Each time an SUV blocked the way.

"Force your way between them."

"Gabriel!"

"Do it!"

She tried. There was no way through.

They were nearing the end of the Jebel Ali Free Zone. Beyond it lay the expanse of desert separating Dubai from the emirate of Abu Dhabi. Gabriel could no longer see Malik's Denali; it was but a distant star in a galaxy of other taillights. Directly ahead, a stoplight switched from green to amber. The four SUVs slowed instantly, surely a first in Dubai, and came to a stop. As car horns began to sound, one of the Malik replicas stepped out and stared at Gabriel for a long moment before dragging his thumb knifelike across his own throat. Gabriel took a quick radio roll call of the team and determined all were safe and accounted for. Then he dialed Nadia's BlackBerry. There was no answer.

61

DUBAI

T HE BOEING BUSINESS JET OWNED and operated by AAB Holdings departed Dubai International Airport at 10:40 that evening. All available evidence suggested that Nadia al-Bakari, the company's chairwoman, was not on board at the time.

Her BlackBerry had gone off the air at 10:14 p.m., as her car was crossing Dubai Creek, and was no longer emitting a signal of any kind. In the moments preceding the break, she had been chatting amiably with Rafiq al-Kamal. The last audio captured by the device was a muffled thumping that could have been anything from a death struggle to the sound of Nadia tapping her forefinger on the screen, something she often did while riding in cars. The transmitters hidden in her handbag and clothing were, at the moment of the disruption, far beyond the range of the listening posts inside the Burj Al Arab and therefore provided no clues as to what had transpired.

Only the GPS beacons remained functional. Eventually, they ceased moving at an empty lot along the Dubai-Hatta Road, not far from the polo club. Gabriel found the Chanel suit at 10:53 p.m. and the watch a few minutes later. He carried the items over to the Land Cruiser and examined them in the light of the dash. The fabric of the suit was torn in several places and there were blood-stains on the collar. The crystal of the watch was smashed, though the inscription on the back remained clearly legible. *To the future, Thomas.*

He told Chiara to start back to the hotel, then sent a message to Langley on his BlackBerry. The reply came two minutes later. Gabriel swore softly as he read it.

"What does it say?"

"They want us to leave for the airport immediately."

"What about Nadia?"

"There is no Nadia," Gabriel said, slipping the BlackBerry into his coat pocket. "Not as far as Langley and Shamron are concerned. Not anymore."

"So we leave her behind?" asked Chiara angrily, her eyes on the road. "Is that what they want us to do? Use her money and her name and then throw her to the wolves? Do you know what they're going to do to her?"

"They're going to kill her," Gabriel said. "And she won't be given the courtesy of a decent death. That's not the way they conduct their business."

"Maybe she's already dead," Chiara said. "Maybe that's what Malik's friend was trying to tell you."

"She might be," Gabriel conceded, "but I doubt it. They wouldn't have bothered to remove her clothing and her jewelry if they intended to kill her quickly. It suggests they wanted to have a word with her in private, which is understandable. After all, they lost their network because of her."

Gabriel's BlackBerry chimed a second time. It was Langley again, asking for confirmation he had received the message to abort. Gabriel ignored it and stared sullenly out the window at the lights of the financial district.

"Is there anything we can do for her?" asked Chiara.

"I suppose that depends entirely on Malik."

"Malik is a monster. And you can be sure he knows you're here in Dubai."

"Even monsters can be reasoned with."

"Not jihadists. They're beyond reason." She drove in silence for a moment with one hand on the wheel and the other clutching the fabric of Nadia's bloodstained suit. "I know you made her a promise," she said finally, "but you made a promise to me, too."

"Should I let her die, Chiara?"

"God, no!"

"What do you want me to do?"

"Why do I have to make this decision?"

"Because you're the only one who can."

Chiara was wrenching at the fabric of Nadia's suit, tears streaming down her cheeks. Gabriel asked whether she wanted him to drive. She seemed not to hear him.

———

Gabriel's message flashed across the screens of Rashidistan thirty seconds later. Shamron stared at it in consternation. Then he lit a cigarette in violation of Langley's draconian no-smoking policy and said, "Now might be a good time to put some birds in the air and boots on the ground." Carter and Navot responded by reaching simultaneously for their phones. Within a few minutes, the birds were taking off from a secret CIA installation in Bahrain, and the boots were headed silently across the black waters of the Gulf toward the beach at Jebel Ali.

By the time Gabriel and Chiara returned to the hotel, the rest of the team was already engaged in a hasty but methodical evacuation. It had commenced upon receipt of Shamron's order and was being conducted under the auspices of one Thomas Fowler, newly minted partner in the venture capital firm of Rogers & Cressey. The hotel's management had been led to believe the sudden checkout was the result of a health emergency suffered by one of Mr. Fowler's employees. The fixed-base operator at Dubai International Airport had been told the same story. It was preparing Mr. Fowler's private aircraft for a two a.m. departure. The crew had been told to anticipate no delays.

Despite the urgency of the situation, the team managed to maintain strict operational discipline inside the hotel. In rooms they assumed to be bugged, they referred to one another by false names and spoke mainly of business and finance. Only their stricken expressions betrayed the anguish they were all feeling, and only when they were beneath the protective shroud of the *chuppah* did they dare to speak the truth. Shielded from the Ruler's listening devices, Gabriel conducted a tense call with Shamron and Navot at Rashidistan. He also spoke face-to-face with the members of his team. Most of the encounters were businesslike; a few were confrontational. Chiara came to him last. Alone, she reminded him of the afternoon they had made love in the safe house by Lake Zurich, when her body had burned as if from fever. Then she kissed his lips one final time before collecting her luggage and heading to the lobby.

Shamron had always believed careers were defined less by the successes achieved than the calamities survived. "Any fool can take a victory lap," he once famously remarked during a lecture at the Academy, "but only a truly great officer can maintain his composure and his cover when his heart is breaking." If that were indeed the case, Shamron would have witnessed the very definition of greatness that night as Gabriel's fabled team filed out of the Burj Al Arab and set off for the airport. Only Chiara appeared distraught, in part because her heart truly was breaking, but also because she had volunteered to play the role of the seriously ill employee. Management wished her well as they helped her into the back of a hotel limousine. Mr. Fowler tipped the valets lavishly before climbing in after her.

They followed the same route Nadia had taken earlier that evening but arrived at the airport without incident. After a cursory check of their passports, they chose to board the aircraft immediately rather than wait in the luxuriously appointed VIP lounge. A cancellation allowed them to depart earlier than expected, and by one thirty, they were rising over the blackness of the Empty Quarter.

Two members of the team were not on board. Mikhail was headed toward an isolated beach west of Jebel Ali; Gabriel, to the old quarter of Dubai known as Deira. After leaving his Toyota Land Cruiser along the Corniche, he walked to the shabby little apartment house near the Gold Souk and climbed the staircase that stank of chickpeas and cumin. Alone in the apartment, he sat at the peeling kitchen table, staring at the screen of his BlackBerry. To help pass the time, he replayed the operation in his mind. Somewhere along the line, there had been a leak or an act of betrayal. He was going to find the person responsible. And then he was going to kill him.

───────

It was another twenty minutes before Mikhail heard the crackle of a voice in his earpiece. It spoke a word or two, no more. Even so, he recognized it. He had heard it many times before—in the hellholes of Gaza, in the hills of southern Lebanon, in the alleyways of Jericho and Nablus and Hebron. He flashed his headlights twice, briefly illuminating the chalky white beach, and drummed his fingers anxiously on the steering wheel as a blacked-out Zodiac bobbed ashore. Four men slipped out, each carrying nylon gear bags. They looked like Arabs. They moved like Arabs. They even wore cologne that made them smell like Arabs. But they were not Arabs. They were members of the elite Sayeret Matkal. And one of them, Yoav Savir, was Mikhail's former commanding officer.

"Long time no see," Yoav said as he climbed into the front passenger seat. "What happened?"

"We lost someone very important."

"What's his name?"

"Her," said Mikhail. "Her name is Nadia."

"Who's got her?"

"Malik."

"Which Malik?"

"The only Malik that matters."

"Shit."

───────

The lights of the giant Shaybah oil-drilling facility glowed like neon green embers on the wall monitors of Rashidistan. The image was being transmitted live by an unmanned Predator drone, now under the control of a crew at Langley. At Carter's direction, the aircraft banked eastward, over the string of oases along the Saudi-Emirates border, then followed the main highway back toward Dubai city, its night-vision and thermal-imaging cameras searching the desert floor for any sign of life where ordinarily there was none. As the Predator approached the port of Jebel Ali, its cameras settled briefly on a small Zodiac heading back out to sea, a single figure aglow in the stern. No one in Rashidistan paid much attention to the image because they were monitoring a conversation on Gabriel's BlackBerry. The computers recognized the number of the caller. They also recognized his voice. It was Malik al-Zubair. The only Malik that mattered.

62

DEIRA, DUBAI

'M SURPRISED YOU ANSWERED. PERHAPS it's true what they say about you."

"What's that, Malik?"

"That you are courageous. That you are a man of your word. Personally, I remain skeptical. I've never met a Jew who was not a coward and a liar."

"I never realized Zarqa had such a large Jewish community."

"Thankfully, there are no Jews in Zarqa, only victims of the Jews."

"Where is she, Malik?"

"Who?"

"Nadia," said Gabriel. "What have you done with her?"

"Why would you assume we have her?"

"Because there's only one place where you could have gotten this telephone number."

"Clever Jew."

"Let her go."

"You're not in a position to make demands at the moment."

"I'm not demanding anything," Gabriel said calmly. "I'm asking you to let her go."

"As a humanitarian gesture?"

"Call it whatever you like. Just do the decent thing."

"You murdered her father in front of her and you're asking *me* to do the decent thing?"

"What do you want, Malik?"

"We demand that you release all the brothers who were arrested by the Americans and their allies after your little deception. In addition, we demand that you free the brothers being held illegally at Guantánamo Bay."

"No Palestinian prisoners? You disappoint me."

"I wouldn't want to interfere with the ongoing negotiations between you and the brothers of Hamas."

"Ask for something reasonable, Malik—something I can actually give you."

"We never negotiate with terrorists. Release our brothers, and we will release your spy with no further harm."

"What have you done to her?"

"I can assure you it was nothing compared to the pain suffered by our brothers each and every day in the torture chambers of Cairo and Amman and Riyadh."

"Haven't you been reading the papers, Malik? The Arab world is changing. Pharaoh is gone. The House of Saud is cracking. The little Hashemite king of Jordan is frightened for his life. The decent people of the Arab world have achieved in a matter of months what al-Qaeda and its ilk couldn't accomplish with years of senseless slaughter. Your time has passed, Malik. The Arab world doesn't want you. Let her go."

"I'm afraid I can't do that, Allon." He paused for a moment, as if pondering a way out of the impasse he had created. "But there is one other possibility."

Gabriel listened to Malik's instructions. So did Shamron, Navot, and Adrian Carter.

"What happens if we don't accept?" Gabriel asked.

"Then she will suffer the traditional punishment for apostasy. But don't worry. You'll be able to watch her death on the Internet. The Yemeni plans to use it as a recruiting device to replace all the operatives we lost because of her."

"I need proof she's still alive."

"I'm afraid you'll just have to trust me," Malik said. And then the line went dead.

Gabriel's BlackBerry rang a few seconds later. It was Adrian Carter.

"He's definitely still in the Emirates."

"Where?"

"NSA hasn't been able to triangulate it yet, but they think he might be out in the western desert, near the Liwa oasis. We have a bird over the area now and two more headed that way."

Gabriel removed a small device from an internal pouch of his overnight bag. It was about the size of an average antibiotic tablet. On one side was a miniature metallic switch. He flipped it, then asked, "Can you see the signal?"

"Got it," said Carter.

Gabriel swallowed the device. "Can you still see it?"

"Got it."

"The Fish Souk, ten minutes."

"Got it."

Gabriel was still wearing the business attire of his cover identity. He briefly considered changing into something more appropriate for a night in the desert, but realized that wouldn't be necessary. His captors would surely do that for him. He placed his wristwatch in his bag along with his BlackBerry, wallet, passport, weapon, and a few meaningless scraps of pocket litter. He was no longer in possession of syringes or suxamethonium chloride, only Advil and anti-diarrhea medicine. He took enough Advil to temporarily dull the pain of any injuries he might suffer in the next few hours and enough of the anti-diarrhea medicine to turn his bowels to concrete for a month. Then he locked the bag in the closet and headed downstairs to the street.

Six minutes remained for Gabriel to make the short walk to the Fish Souk. It was located near the mouth of Dubai Creek along the Corniche. Despite the late hour, there were groups of young men taking the night air along the waterfront—Pakistanis, Bangladeshis, Filipinos, and four Arabs who were not Arabs at all. Gabriel stood next to a streetlamp to make himself clearly visible, and within a few seconds, a Denali SUV stopped directly in front of him. Behind the wheel was one of the Malik clones. Another was seated in the back. So was Rafiq al-Kamal, Nadia al-Bakari's former chief of security.

It was al-Kamal who gestured for Gabriel to climb in and al-Kamal, thirty seconds later, who delivered the first blow—an elbow to Gabriel's chest that nearly stopped his heart. Then they forced him to the floor and pummeled him until there was no strength left in their arms. The harvest was over, thought Gabriel, as he slipped into unconsciousness. Now it was time for the feast.

63

THE EMPTY QUARTER, SAUDI ARABIA

T HE MAPS REFER TO IT ominously as the Rub' al-Khali—literally, the Quarter of Emptiness. The Bedouin, however, know it by another name. They call it the Sands. Covering an area the size of France, Belgium, and the Netherlands, it stretches from Oman and the Emirates, across Saudi Arabia, and into portions of Yemen. Dunes the size of mountains roam the desert floor in the relentless wind. Some stand alone. Others link themselves into chains that meander for hundreds of miles. In summer the temperature routinely exceeds one hundred forty degrees, cooling to a hundred degrees at night. There is almost no rain, little in the way of plant or animal life, and few people other than the Bedouin and the bandits and the terrorists from al-Qaeda who move freely across the borders. Time matters little in the Sands. Even now, it is measured in the length of the walk to the next well.

Like most Saudis, Nadia al-Bakari had never set foot in the Empty Quarter. That changed three hours after her abduction, though Nadia was unaware of it. Having been injected with the general anesthetic ketamine, she believed herself to be wandering lost through the gilded rooms of her youth. Her father appeared to her briefly; he wore the traditional robes of a Bedouin and the angry face known as the *juhayman*. His body had been pierced by bullets. He made her touch his wounds, then chided her for conspiring with the very men who had inflicted them. She would have to be punished, he said, just as Rena had been punished for bringing dishonor upon her family. It was the will of God. There was nothing to be done.

It was at the instant her father condemned her to death that Nadia felt herself beginning to float upward through the layers of consciousness. It was a slow rise, like a diver ascending from a great depth. When she finally reached the surface, she forced her eyes open and drew an enormous breath. Then she took stock of her surroundings. She was lying on her side on a rug that smelled of male body odor and camel. Bound at the wrists, she was cloaked in a thin garment of sheer white cotton. It was aglow with moonlight, as was the Salafi-style *thobe* of the man watching over her. He wore a *taqiyah* skullcap with no headdress and carried an automatic weapon with a banana-shaped magazine. Even so, his eyes were unusually gentle for an Arab man. Then Nadia realized she had seen them before. They were the eyes of Ali, the *talib* of Sheikh Marwan Bin Tayyib.

"Where am I?" she asked.

He answered truthfully. It was not a good sign.

"How's Safia?"

"She's well," the *talib* said, smiling in spite of the situation.

"How long now until the baby comes?"

"Three months," he said.

"*Inshallah*, it will be a boy."

"Actually, the doctors say we will have a girl."

"You don't sound displeased."

"I'm not."

"Have you chosen a name?"

"We're going to call her Hanan."

In Arabic, it meant "mercy." Perhaps there was hope after all.

The *talib* began to recite verses of the Koran softly to himself. Nadia rolled onto her back and gazed up at the stars. They seemed close enough to touch. There was only the sound of the Koran and a distant hum of some sort. For a moment, she assumed it was another hallucination caused by the drugs—or perhaps, she thought, by the abnormality in her brain. Then she closed her eyes, silencing the voice of the *talib*, and listened intently. It was no hallucination, she concluded. It was an aircraft of some sort. And it was getting closer.

––––––––––––

A single narrow road links the Emirati oasis town of Liwa with the Shaybah oil facility on the other side of the border in Saudi Arabia. Nadia had passed through the checkpoint as the sleeping, veiled wife of one of her captors. Gabriel was made to suffer the same indignity, though, unlike Nadia, he was fully aware of what was happening.

Beneath his veil, he wore the blue coveralls of a Dubai laborer. They had been given to him in a produce warehouse in al-Khaznah, a desert town in the Emirate of Abu Dhabi, after he had been stripped of his own clothing and searched for beacons and listening devices. He had also been given a second beating, with Rafiq al-Kamal doing most of the heavy lifting. Gabriel supposed the Saudi had a right to be cross with him. After all, Gabriel had killed his old boss and then recruited the boss's daughter as an agent. Al-Kamal's involvement in Nadia's abduction puzzled Gabriel. At whose behest, he wondered, was the Saudi here? The terrorists? Or the al-Saud?

For now, it didn't matter. What mattered was keeping Nadia alive. It would require one last lie. One last deception. He conceived the lie on the road to Shaybah while wearing the blue coveralls of a laborer and the black veil of a woman. Then he told it to himself again and again, until he believed every word of it to be true.

On the giant plasma screens of Langley, Gabriel was but a smudge of winking green light making its way across the Empty Quarter. A cluster of five more lights blinked near the oasis town of Liwa. They represented the positions of Mikhail Abramov and the Sayeret Matkal team.

"There's no way they're going to get through that border checkpoint," said Carter.

"So they'll go around it," said Shamron.

"There's a fence along the entire border."

"Fences mean nothing to the Sayeret."

"How are they going to get a Land Cruiser over it?"

"They have *two* Land Cruisers," said Shamron, "but I'm afraid neither one is going over that fence."

"What are you saying?"

"We wait until Gabriel stops moving."

"And then?"

"They walk."

"In the Empty Quarter?" Carter asked incredulously.

"That's what they're trained to do."

"What happens if they run into a Saudi military patrol?"

"Then I suppose we'll have to say Kaddish for the patrol," said Shamron. "Because if they bump into Mikhail Abramov and Yoav Savir, they will cease to exist."

There was an all-night gas station and market in Liwa that catered to foreign laborers and truck drivers. The Indian behind the counter looked as though he hadn't slept in a month. Yoav, the Arab who was not an Arab, bought enough food and water for a small army, along with a few cheap *ghutra*s and some loose-fitting cotton clothing favored by Pakistanis and Bangladeshis. He told the Indian that he and his friends planned to spend a day or two in the dunes communing with God and nature. The night manager told him about a particularly inspiring formation north of Liwa, along the Saudi border. "But be careful," he said. "The area is full of smugglers and al-Qaeda. Very dangerous." Yoav thanked the Indian for the warning. Then he paid the bill without haggling and headed outside to the Land Cruisers.

They started northward as the Indian had suggested, but once clear of the town, made an abrupt turn to the south. The dunes were the color of rose and as high as the Judean Hills. They drove for an hour, keeping always to the hard sand flats, before coming to a stop near the Saudi border fence. With dawn fast approaching, they covered the Land Cruisers in camouflage netting and changed into the clothing they had bought in Liwa. Yoav and the other Sayeret men looked like Arabs, but Mikhail looked like a Western explorer who had come in search of the lost city of Arabia. His expedition commenced thirty minutes later, when the green smudge of light that was Gabriel Allon finally stopped moving at a point forty miles due west of the team's position. They loaded their packs with as much weaponry and water as they could carry. Then they scaled the Saudi border fence and started walking.

64

THE EMPTY QUARTER, SAUDI ARABIA

THE TENT HAD BEEN ERECTED in the cleft of an enormous horseshoe-shaped dune. It was made of black goat hair in the tradition of the Bedouin and surrounded by several sun-bleached pickup trucks and jeeps. A few feet from the entrance, four veiled women with henna tattoos on their hands brewed coffee with cardamom seeds around a small fire. None seemed to notice the beaten man in blue coveralls who stumbled from the back of a Denali SUV, shivering in the cold morning air.

The cleft of the dune was still in darkness, but light glowed faintly above its ridgeline and the stars were in full retreat. Prodded by al-Kamal, Gabriel started unsteadily toward the tent. His head throbbed but his thoughts remained clear. They were focused on a lie. He would pay it out slowly, morsel by morsel, like cakes sweetened with honey. He would make himself irresistible to them. He would buy time for Mikhail and the Sayeret team to home in on the signal emanating from the device in his bowels. He pushed the beacon from his thoughts. There was no beacon, he reminded himself. There was only Nadia al-Bakari, a woman of impeccable jihadist credentials whom Gabriel had blackmailed into doing his bidding.

Malik was now standing in the opening of the tent. He had traded his gleaming white *kandoura* for a gray *thobe*. His feet were bare, though his head was wrapped in a red-checkered *ghutra*. He regarded Gabriel menacingly, as though debating where to place the first blow, then stepped to one side. Al-Kamal responded by shoving Gabriel forcefully between the shoulder blades, propelling him headlong into the tent.

The undignified nature of his arrival seemed to bring enormous pleasure to the men gathered inside. Eight in all, they were seated in a semicircle, drinking the cardamom-scented coffee from thimble-sized cups. A few wore the traditional curved *jambia* daggers of Yemeni men, but one was peering into the screen of a notebook computer. His face was familiar to Gabriel, as was the sound of his voice when finally he spoke. It was the voice of a man to whom Allah had granted a beautiful and seductive tongue. It was the voice of Rashid.

To the thermal-imaging cameras of the Predator drone circling overhead, the gathering in the goat-hair Bedouin tent appeared as eleven amoeba-like orbs of light. Nearby there were several other human heat sources as well. There were four figures seated around a small fire. There was a ring of security posts scattered amid the dunes. And there were two figures about a thousand yards from the tent's southern flank—one lying supine on the desert floor, the other seated cross-legged. As dawn slowly broke, Shamron asked Carter whether it might be possible to have a look at the two figures through a normal lens. Another five minutes would elapse until there was sufficient light, but when the image appeared on the screens of Langley, it was remarkably clear. It showed a raven-haired woman in white being guarded by a bearded man holding what appeared to be an AK-47. A short distance away, on the other side of a large dune, a cylindrical hole had been dug in the desert floor. Next to the hole was a pile of stones.

When the staff at Rashidistan regained its composure, Carter said, "There's no way Mikhail and the Sayeret team can get there in time. And even if they do, they're going to be spotted."

"Yes, Adrian," Shamron said, "I realize that."

"Let me call Prince Nabil at the Interior Ministry."

"Why would you waste time doing that?"

"Maybe he can do something to prevent them from being killed."

"Maybe," said Shamron. "Or maybe this is all Nabil's doing."

"You think Nabil sold her out to Rashid and Malik?"

"As far as Nabil is concerned, she's a heretic and a dissident. What better way to get rid of her than hand her over to the bearded ones to be executed?"

Carter swore softly. Shamron looked at the image from the desert.

"I take it the Predators are fully armed?" he asked.

"Hellfire missiles," replied Carter.

"Have you ever fired one into Saudi Arabia?"

"Not a chance."

"I assume you would need clearance from the president before doing so."

"You assume correctly."

"Then please call him now, Adrian."

65

THE EMPTY QUARTER, SAUDI ARABIA

R ASHID BEGAN WITH A LECTURE. He was part poet, part preacher, part professor of jihad. He warned that Israel would soon go the way of Pharaoh's regime in Egypt. He predicted *sharia* was coming to Europe whether Europe wanted it or not. He declared that the American century was finally over, *al-hamdu lillah*. It was one of the few Arabic expressions he used. The rest was delivered in his impeccable colloquial English. It was like being tutored in the principles of the Salaf by a kid from Best Buy.

He spoke not to Gabriel but to a digital camera mounted atop a tripod. Occasionally, he wagged a long finger for emphasis or pointed it toward his famous captive, who was seated a few feet away, squinting slightly in the glare of two standing lamps. Gabriel could only imagine how the heat blooms must have appeared to the Predator drones overhead. He felt as though he were sitting in the jihadi version of a television studio, with Rashid playing the role of confrontational host. Malik, master of terror, was pacing slowly behind the cameras. That was the nature of their relationship, thought Gabriel. Rashid was the on-camera talent. Malik was the dogged producer who saw to the messy details. Rashid inspired. Malik maimed and murdered, all in the name of Allah.

When Rashid finally concluded his opening monologue, he turned to the main portion of this morning's program: the interview. He began by asking Gabriel to state his name and place of residence. When Gabriel answered, "Roland Devereaux, Quebec City, Canada," Rashid showed a flash of anger. There was a petulance to it that Gabriel might have found amusing if he were not surrounded by men with curved *jambia* daggers. Rashid's ideas were monstrous, but in person he was oddly unthreatening. That's what Malik was for.

"Your *real* name," Rashid snapped. "Tell me the name you were given at your birth."

"You know my real name."

"Why won't you say it now?" asked Rashid. "Are you ashamed of it?"

"No," said Gabriel, "I just don't use it often."

"Say it now."

Gabriel did.

"Where were you born?"

"In the Valley of Jezreel, in the State of Israel."

"And where were your parents born?"

"Germany."

Rashid clearly saw this as proof of a great historical crime. "Your parents were survivors of the so-called Holocaust?" he asked.

"No, they were survivors of the *actual* Holocaust."

"Are you employed by the intelligence service of the State of Israel?"

"Sometimes."

"Are you an assassin?"

"I have killed in the line of duty."

"You consider yourself a soldier?"

"Yes."

"You have killed many Palestinians?"

"Yes, many."

"Are you proud of your work?"

"No," Gabriel said.

"Then why do you do it?"

"Because of people like you."

"Our cause is just."

"Your cause is grotesque."

Rashid seemed suddenly rattled. His exclusive was not going as planned. He guided it back onto firmer ground.

"Where were you on the evening of August 24, 2006?"

"I was in Cannes," Gabriel said without hesitation.

"In France?"

"Yes, in France."

"And what were you doing there?"

"I was supervising an operation."

"What was the nature of this operation?"

"It was a targeted killing."

"And who was the target?"

"Abdul Aziz al-Bakari."

"Who ordered his assassination?"

"I don't know."

Rashid clearly did not believe him but appeared unwilling to waste valuable airtime on ancient history. "Did you take part in his actual killing?" he asked.

"Yes."

"Did you see Nadia al-Bakari that night?"

"Yes, I did."

"When did you see her next?"

"In December."

"Where?"

"At a château north of Paris."

"What transpired next?"

What transpired, said Gabriel, was an elaborate operation to blackmail one of the richest women in the world into doing the bidding of Israeli and American intelligence. Through an informant, the CIA had learned that Rashid's nascent network was desperately in need of financial assistance. The Agency wanted to provide the money to the network and then track it as it moved through the various cells and business fronts. There was only one problem. The money had to come from someone the terrorists trusted. The CIA asked Israeli intelligence whether it had any ideas. Israeli intelligence did. Her name was Nadia al-Bakari. An emissary of Israeli intelligence visited Miss al-Bakari in Paris under false pretenses and made it clear that AAB Holdings would be destroyed if she didn't agree to cooperate.

"How was the company to be harmed?" asked Rashid.

"Through a campaign of well-orchestrated leaks to our friends in the media."

"Jewish friends, of course."

"Yes, of course."

"What would have been the nature of these leaks?"

"That AAB Holdings was a jihadist enterprise, the way it had been under her father."

"Go on."

Gabriel complied. For the camera, he adopted an expression of reticence. It was a lie, like the other lies that flowed from his swollen lips. He spun them slowly and in great detail. Rashid appeared to hang on every word.

"Your account is interesting," Rashid said, "but I'm afraid it contradicts what we've already been told by Miss al-Bakari. She says she willingly helped you."

"She was instructed to say that."

"You threatened her?"

"Constantly."

"Where did the money come from for the operation?"

"It was Nadia's."

"You forced her to use her own money?"

"That's correct."

"Why didn't you use government money?"

"Budgets are tight."

"You couldn't find a wealthy Jewish donor to fund the project?"

"It was too sensitive."

Rashid looked contemptuously at the camera, then at Gabriel. "Miss al-Bakari visited Dubai yesterday," he said after a moment. "What was the purpose of the visit?"

"I believe she was there to conclude a major land and development deal."

"The real purpose, Allon."

"We sent her there to identify a senior operative in your network."

"He was to be arrested?"

"No," said Gabriel, "he was to be killed."

The cleric smiled. His guest had just made an important admission, one Rashid could use to generate headlines around the world.

"It strikes me that this episode is typical of the entire so-called war on terror. You cannot defeat us, Allon. And each time you try, you only make us stronger."

"You're not getting stronger," Gabriel countered. "In fact, you're dying. The Arab world is changing. Your time has passed."

Rashid's smile evaporated. He spoke with the tone of a stern teacher frustrated with a dull pupil. "Surely, Allon, a man such as yourself is not so naïve as to think this great Arab Awakening is going to produce Western-style democracy in the Middle East. The revolt might have started with the students and the secularists, but the brothers will have the last word. We are the future. Regrettably, it is a future you will not be around to see. But before you leave this earth, I am obligated to ask you a final question. Do you wish to submit to the will of Islam and become a Muslim?"

"Only if it prevents you from killing Nadia."

"Unfortunately, that's not possible. Her crime is far worse than yours."

"Then I'll remain a Jew."

"So be it."

Rashid rose to his feet. Malik switched off the camera.

The Empty Quarter was ablaze with light by the time the first figures emerged from the tent. There were ten in all—five in white, five in black. They climbed quickly into the caravan of jeeps and pickup trucks and circled the encampment at high speed collecting the security men. A moment later, they were streaking southeast across the Sands toward Yemen.

"How much do you want to bet that one of those bastards is Rashid?" Adrian Carter asked helplessly.

"All the more reason you should take the shot," said Navot.

"The White House won't allow it. Not on Saudi soil. And not without knowing exactly who's down there."

"They're terrorists and friends of terrorists," Shamron said. "Take the shot."

"And what if one of them is Gabriel?"

"I'm afraid that's not possible," said Shamron.

"How can you be so certain?"

Shamron pointed wordlessly toward one of the screens.

"Are you sure it's him?" asked Carter.

"I'd recognize that walk anywhere."

66

THE EMPTY QUARTER, SAUDI ARABIA

T HE *TALIB* WALKED ALONG THE base of a vast star-shaped dune. He carried his automatic weapon in one hand and with the other led Nadia by the binding at her wrists. As they rounded the dune, she saw the hole that had been dug in the desert floor. Next to it was a pyramid of stones. In the razor-sharp sun, they looked as white as exposed bone. Nadia tried to be brave, as she imagined Rena had been brave in the final moments before her death. Then she felt the desert begin to spin, and she collapsed.

"It won't be as bad as you think," the *talib* said, pulling her gently to her feet. "The first few will cause great pain. Then, *inshallah*, you will lose consciousness and you won't feel a thing."

"Please," said Nadia, "you must find some way to spare me this."

"It is the will of God," said the *talib*. "There is nothing to be done."

"It is not the will of God, Ali. It is the will of evil men."

"Walk," was all he said. "You have to walk."

"Would you do this to Safia?"

"Walk."

"Would you, Ali?"

"If she violated the laws of God, I would have no choice."

"And what about Hanan? Would you stone your own child?"

This time, the *talib* said nothing. After a few paces, he began to recite verses of the Koran softly to himself, but to Nadia he spoke not another word.

On the other side of the mountainous dune, Gabriel padded barefoot across the sand with Malik at his side. Four other men surrounded them. Three had been with Malik in Dubai; the fourth was Rafiq al-Kamal. The bodyguard had been assigned the task of carrying the knife that would be used for Gabriel's execution and the video camera that would record it. Malik and the others carried automatic weapons. They were old Soviet-issue AK-47s, the kind you could buy for a few riyals even in the most remote villages of Yemen. As Gabriel worked his wrists carefully against the silver duct tape, he tried to calculate the odds of getting his hands on one of the weapons. They were not good, he thought, but death by gunfire was surely better than death by beheading. If he were to die in the Empty Quarter on this morning, he planned to die on his own terms. And, if possible, he was going to take Malik al-Zubair with him.

Emerging from the shadow of the dune, Gabriel saw Nadia for the first time since she had walked past him in the lobby of the Burj Al Arab. Cloaked in her death shroud, she appeared paralyzed by fear. So did the sparsely bearded young jihadi who was guarding her. Malik walked over and shoved the boy out of the way. Then he seized Nadia's dark hair and pulled her toward Gabriel. "Look at what you've done," he shouted over her screams. "This is what happens when you seduce our people into renouncing their faith."

"She never renounced her faith, Malik. Let her go."

"She worked for you against us. She has to be punished. And for your sins, you shall cast the first stone."

"I won't do it." Gabriel looked searchingly toward the sky. One last deception. One last lie. "And neither will you, Malik."

Malik smiled. It was genuine.

"This isn't Pakistan or Yemen, Allon. This is Saudi Arabia. And the Americans would never fire a Hellfire missile against the territory of their great ally, the House of Saud. Besides, no one knows where you are. You are completely alone."

"Are you sure about that, Malik?"

Clearly, he wasn't. Still clutching a handful of Nadia's hair, he tilted his face to the sky. So did the others, including al-Kamal. He was standing about three feet to Gabriel's left, holding the knife and the camera.

"Listen carefully," Gabriel said. "Can you hear it? It's circling just overhead. It's watching with its cameras. Let her go, Malik. Otherwise, we're all going to die in a flash of fire. You'll go to your God; Nadia and I will go to ours."

"There is no God but God, Allon. There is only Allah."

"I hope you're right, Malik, because you're about to see His face. Do you want to be a martyr? Or do you prefer to leave the martyrdom to others?"

Malik flung Nadia aside and swung the Kalashnikov wildly toward Gabriel's head. Gabriel easily sidestepped the blow and delivered a vicious knee to Malik's groin that sent him sprawling to the sand. Then Gabriel pivoted with his arms extended and his hands formed like the blade of an ax. The blade connected squarely with Rafiq al-Kamal's neck, crushing his larynx. Gabriel looked at Nadia and at the pile of bone white stones. Then he flailed his arms like a madman against the sky and screamed, "Take the shot! Take the shot! It's Malik, damn it! Take the shot!"

Adrian Carter hung up the phone with the White House and buried his face in his hands. Uzi Navot watched for a few seconds longer, then closed his eyes. Only Shamron refused to look away. It was his fault, all of it. The least he could do was see it through to the end.

Malik had risen to one knee and was groping blindly about for his fallen Kalashnikov. Gabriel was still raging at the merciless sky. He heard the metallic *clack-clack* of the rifle's cocking handle and saw the barrel rise. Then, from the corner of one eye, he glimpsed the ghostlike flash of Nadia's sparkling white death shroud as she came hurtling toward him. As she passed before the gun, two crimson flowers bloomed violently in the center of her chest, though her face appeared oddly serene as she collapsed onto Gabriel. Malik tore her away and pointed the Kalashnikov downward at Gabriel's face, but before he could pull the trigger again, the side of his head exploded in a flash of pink. Several more gunshots followed until only the young jihadi remained standing. He peered down at Gabriel, his face eclipsing the sun, then looked mournfully at Nadia.

"It was God's will that she die today," he said, "but at least she did not suffer."

"No," said Gabriel, "she did not suffer."

"Are you hit?" asked the boy.

"One round," said Gabriel.

"Will they come for you?"

"Eventually."

"Can you hold out until they arrive?"

"I think so."

"I have to leave you here alone. I have a wife. I have a child on the way."

"Boy or girl?" asked Gabriel, his strength beginning to ebb.

"Girl."

"Have you chosen a name?"

"Hanan."

"Be kind to her," said Gabriel. "Treat her always with respect."

The boy stepped away; the sun beat upon Gabriel's face. He heard an engine turning over, then glimpsed a cloud of dust moving across the sea of sand. After that, there was only the empty silence of the desert. He waved his arms one final time toward the sky to tell them he was still alive. Then he closed Nadia's eyes and wept against her breast as her body turned slowly to stone.

PART FOUR

THE
AWAKENING

67

PARIS-LANGLEY-RIYADH

MORE THAN TWENTY-FOUR HOURS WOULD elapse before AAB Holdings finally revealed to the world that its chairwoman and chief executive, Nadia al-Bakari, was missing and presumed kidnapped. According to a company statement, she had been traveling by limousine at the time of her disappearance, en route from Dubai's famed Burj Al Arab hotel to the airport. Two calls had been placed from the car, both from the phone of her longtime security chief. During the first, he had instructed the head of AAB's travel department to move up the departure of the company's aircraft by fifteen minutes, from 11:00 p.m. to 10:45. Seven minutes later, he had phoned again to say Miss al-Bakari was feeling ill and would return to the hotel to spend the night. It was her wish, he said, that the rest of the staff return to Paris as planned. Needless to say, Emirati authorities now regarded the second call as highly suspect, though they had yet to determine whether the security man was part of a conspiracy or merely another victim. The bodyguard was missing, as was the driver of the car.

As expected, the news sent shockwaves through already jittery global financial markets. Share prices tumbled in Europe, where AAB's portfolio was vast, and trading on Wall Street opened sharply lower. Hardest hit, though, was Dubai, Inc. Having spent untold billions portraying itself as an oasis of stability in a turbulent region, the emirate now appeared to be a place where even heavily guarded billionaires were not safe. The Ruler took to the airwaves to declare his city-state secure and open for business, but investors weren't so sure. They pummeled Dubai-based firms and sovereign wealth funds with a merciless wave of selling that left the city of gold teetering once more on the brink of insolvency.

When an additional twenty-four hours passed with no word on Nadia's fate, the press was left with no option but to speculate wildly on what might have transpired. One theory held that she was murdered by a Russian criminal gang who had lost millions investing in AAB Holdings. Another posited that she had offended powerful interests in Dubai with her call for better treatment of the emirate's migrant laborers. Still another suggested the kidnapping was but a ruse, that Nadia al-Bakari, one of the world's richest women, had simply gone into hiding for reasons no one could imagine.

Regrettably, it was this final theory that gained the most traction in certain quarters of the press, and before long, there was a rash of Nadia sightings at glamorous locations around the globe. The last had her living on a remote island in the Baltic Sea with the son of Sweden's wealthiest man.

That report appeared on the same day the Kingdom of Saudi Arabia finally announced that her body had been found in the Empty Quarter. The bodies of several men had been found with her, according to the Saudis, including that of her security chief. All had been killed by gunfire, as had Miss al-Bakari. As of yet, Saudi authorities had no suspects.

In keeping with past utterances by the Saudi regime, the statement told only part of the story. It did not say, for example, that Saudi intelligence was already acutely aware of the circumstances surrounding Miss al-Bakari's murder. Nor did it mention that a Saudi military patrol had recovered her body within a few hours of her death, along with the only survivor of the incident. Seriously wounded, this survivor was now the subject of intense, if secret, backchannel negotiations between the Central Intelligence Agency and friendly elements of the House of Saud. Thus far, the talks had produced no breakthroughs. In fact, as far as the government of Saudi Arabia was concerned, the man in question did not exist. They promised to mount a search for him, but held out little in the way of hope. The Empty Quarter, they said, did not treat intruders kindly. *Inshallah*, they would find his corpse, but only if the Bedouin did not get to him first.

The miniature GPS tracking beacon lodged in Gabriel's body told an entirely different story. It was the story of a man who, having been found alive in the Empty Quarter, had been flown by helicopter to Riyadh and deposited at the sprawling compound run by the Mabahith, the secret police division of the Interior Ministry. A week into his stay, it appeared as though he were taken out for a slow drive across Riyadh to the desert east of the city. For several anxious hours, the staff at Rashidistan feared the worst, that he had been executed and buried in the Wahhabi tradition, in a grave with no marker. Eventually, the Agency's analysts were able to confirm, with palpable relief, that his new location was in fact Riyadh's main sewage treatment plant. It meant that Gabriel had finally passed the beacon from his intestinal tract. It also meant that he was now off the grid and entirely beyond Langley's reach.

The bullet had broken two of Gabriel's ribs and damaged his right lung. The Saudis waited until he was sufficiently recovered before commencing their interrogation. It was conducted by a tall, angular man with a face like a falcon. His olive-drab uniform was starched and pressed, but contained little in the way of insignia. He called himself Khalid. He'd gone to school in England and had the diction of a BBC newsreader.

He began by asking for Gabriel's name and a brief description of how he had ended up in the Empty Quarter clinging to the corpse of a Saudi woman. Gabriel gave his name as Roland Devereaux of Quebec City. He claimed that he had been kidnapped by Islamic extremists while on business in Dubai, that he had been beaten unconscious and driven into the desert to be killed. There had been an argument among the terrorists that led to an exchange of gunfire. He didn't know the nature of the argument because he spoke no Arabic.

"None at all?"

"I can order coffee."

"How do you like it?"

"Medium sweet."

"What was the nature of your business in Dubai?"

"I work for a freight-forwarding firm."

"And the woman who died in your arms?"

"I'd never seen her before."

"Did you ever learn her name?"

Gabriel shook his head, then asked whether his embassy knew where he was.

"Which embassy is that?" asked the Saudi.

"The Canadian Embassy, of course."

"Oh, yes," Khalid said, smiling. "What was I thinking?"

"Have you contacted them?"

"We're working on it."

The officer jotted a few words in his notebook and departed. Gabriel was handcuffed and returned to his cell. After that, no one spoke to him for many days.

When next Gabriel was taken to the interrogation room, he arrived to find a stack of file folders piled ominously on the table. Khalid the falcon was smoking, something he had refrained from during their first encounter. This time, he posed no questions. Instead, he launched into a monologue not unlike the one Gabriel had endured at the feet of Rashid al-Husseini. In this case, however, the subject was not the inevitable triumph of Salafist Islam but the long and controversial career of an Israeli intelligence officer named Gabriel Allon. Khalid's account was remarkably accurate. Particular attention was paid to Gabriel's role in the killing of Abdul Aziz al-Bakari and to his subsequent use of Zizi's daughter as a means of penetrating the terror network of Rashid al-Husseini and Malik al-Zubair.

"It was Nadia who died in your arms in the Empty Quarter," the Saudi said. "Malik was there, too. We'd like you to tell us how it all happened."

"I'm afraid I don't know what you're talking about."

"Your video confession is all over the Internet and television, Allon. If you don't cooperate with us, we'll have no choice but to put you on trial and publicly execute you."

"How sporting of you."

"I'm afraid the wheels of Saudi justice do not grind slowly."

"If I were you, I'd tell His Highness to rethink the part about a public execution. It might cost him his oil fields."

"The oil fields belong to the people of Saudi Arabia."

"Oh, yes," said Gabriel. "What was I thinking?"

For the next several nights, Gabriel's cell echoed with the screams of men being tortured. Unable to sleep, he developed an infection that required a round of intravenous antibiotics. Several more pounds melted from his slight frame. He grew so thin that when he was delivered for his next interrogation session, even the falcon appeared concerned.

"Perhaps you and I can come to an accommodation," he suggested.

"What sort of accommodation?"

"You will answer my questions and, in time, I will see that you are returned to your loved ones with your head still attached."

"Why should I trust you?"

"Because as of this moment, my dear one, I'm the only friend you have."

There is a truism about interrogations. Sooner or later, everyone talks. Not only terrorists, but professional intelligence officers as well. But it is *how* they talk, and what they say, that determines whether they will be capable of looking their colleagues in the eye if they are released. Gabriel understood this. So did the falcon.

Together they spent the next week engaged in a delicate ballet of mutual deception. Khalid posed many carefully worded questions to which Gabriel responded with many half-truths and outright lies. The operations he betrayed did not exist. Nor did the paid assets, the safe houses, or the methods of secure communication; it had all been invented in the copious amounts of time Gabriel spent locked in his cell. There were some things he claimed not to know and others he refused to divulge. For example, when Khalid asked for the names of all undercover case officers based in Europe, Gabriel said nothing. He also refused to answer when asked for the names of the officers who had worked with him against Rashid and Malik. Gabriel's intransigence did not anger the falcon. In fact, he seemed to respect Gabriel more for it.

"Why not give me a few false names I can take to my superiors?" asked Khalid.

"Because your superiors know me well enough to realize I would never betray my closest friends," said Gabriel. "They would never believe the names were real."

There is another truism about interrogations. They sometimes reveal more about the man asking the questions than the one answering them. Gabriel had come to believe that Khalid was a true professional rather than a true believer. He was not an altogether unreasonable man. He had a conscience. He could be bargained with. Slowly, gradually, they were able to forge something like a bond. It was a bond of lies, the only kind possible in the secret world.

"Your son was killed that night in Vienna?" Khalid asked suddenly one afternoon. Or perhaps it was already late at night; Gabriel had only a vague grasp of time.

"My son has nothing to do with this."

"Your son has everything to do with this," Khalid said knowingly. "Your son is the reason you followed that *shahid* into Covent Garden. He's also the reason you allowed Shamron and the Americans to lure you back into the game."

"You have good sources," said Gabriel.

Khalid accepted the compliment with a smile. "But there's one thing I still don't understand," he said. "How were you able to convince Nadia to work with you?"

"I'm a professional, like you."

"Why didn't you ask for our help?"

"Would you have given it?"

"Of course not."

The Saudi flipped through the pages of his notebook, frowning slightly, as if trying to decide where to take the questioning next. Gabriel, a skilled interrogator in his own right, knew the performance was all for his benefit. Finally, almost as an afterthought, the Saudi asked, "Is it true she was ill?"

The question managed to take Gabriel by surprise. He found no reason to answer with anything but the truth. "Yes," he said after a moment, "she didn't have long to live."

"We'd heard rumors to that effect for some time," the Saudi replied, "but we were never sure."

"She kept it a secret from everyone, including her staff. Even her closest friends knew nothing."

"But *you* knew?"

"She took me into her confidence because of the operation."

"And the nature of this illness?" the Saudi asked, his pencil hovering over his notebook as if Nadia's illness were but a small detail that needed clearing up for the official record.

"She suffered from a disorder called arteriovenous malformation," Gabriel replied evenly. "It's an abnormal connection between the veins and arteries in the brain. Her doctors had told her she couldn't be treated. She knew it was only a matter of time before she suffered a devastating hemorrhagic stroke. It was possible she could have died at any moment."

"So she committed suicide in the desert by stepping in front of a bullet meant for you?"

"No," said Gabriel. "She sacrificed herself." He paused, then added, "For all of us."

Khalid looked down at his file again. "Unfortunately, she's become a martyr to our more progressive women. Questions are being raised about her philanthropic activities. Apparently, she was something of a reformer."

"Is that why you had her killed?"

Khalid's face remained expressionless. "Miss al-Bakari was killed by Rashid and Malik."

"That's true," said Gabriel, "but someone told them she was working for us."

"Perhaps they had a source close to your operation."

"Or perhaps you did," Gabriel responded. "Perhaps Rashid and Malik were just pawns, a convenient means of eliminating a grave danger to the House of Saud."

"That is mere conjecture on your part."

"True," said Gabriel, "but it's supported by history. Whenever the al-Saud feel threatened, they turn to the bearded ones."

"The bearded ones, as you call them, are more of a threat to us than they are to you."

"Then why are you still supporting them? It's been ten years since 9/11. Ten *years*," Gabriel repeated, "and Saudi Arabia is still a cash machine for terrorists and Sunni extremist groups. There's only one possible explanation. The deal with the devil has been renewed. The House of Saud is willing to turn a blind eye to Islamic terror as long as the sacred rage is directed outward, away from the oil fields."

"We're not as blind as you think."

"I funneled tens of millions of dollars into a Sunni terrorist group in a deal struck on Saudi soil."

"Which is why you now find yourself here."

"Then I assume Sheikh Bin Tayyib is in custody somewhere in the building as well?"

Khalid smiled uncomfortably but made no response. He posed a few more questions, none of any significance, then the session was concluded. Afterward, he took the unusual step of walking Gabriel back to his cell. He lingered for a moment in the corridor before unlocking the door. "I'm told the American president has taken an intense personal interest in your case," he said. "If I had to guess, I'd say your stay with us is almost over."

"When am I leaving?"

"Midnight."

"What time is it now?"

The falcon smiled. "Five past."

———————

A fresh suit of clothing had been laid upon the bed in Gabriel's cell. Khalid gave him a moment of privacy to dress. Then he escorted Gabriel up several flights of stairs to an internal courtyard. An SUV idled in the moonlight. It was large and American, as were the four men standing around it. "I left two things for you in the breast pocket of the suit," Khalid said quietly as they crossed the courtyard. "One is the bullet that passed through Nadia and struck you. The other is a note for Adrian Carter. Think of it as a small parting gift to help you remember your stay with us."

"What is it?"

"Some information he might find helpful. I'd appreciate it if you kept my name out of it."

"Is it any good?"

"The information? I suppose you'll just have to trust me."

"I'm afraid I'm not familiar with that word."

"Didn't you learn anything from her?" Khalid nodded toward the SUV. "I'd get in quickly, if I were you. His Highness has been known to change his mind."

Gabriel shook the Saudi's hand before surrendering himself to the Americans. They drove at high speed to a military air base north of Riyadh and hustled him onto a waiting Gulfstream. There was an Agency doctor on board; he spent much of the flight pumping fluid into Gabriel's emaciated body and fretting over the condition of the wound in his side. Finally, he permitted Gabriel to sleep. Tormented by dreams of Nadia's death, he woke with a start as the plane bumped onto the runway at London City Airport. When the cabin door opened, he saw Chiara and Shamron waiting on the tarmac. He suspected they were the only two people on earth who looked worse than he did.

68

THE LIZARD PENINSULA, CORNWALL

S HAMRON SETTLED INTO THE SPARE bedroom. He gave every indication his stay was permanent. The nightmare in the Empty Quarter, he told Chiara, had given him one last mission.

He appointed himself Gabriel's personal bodyguard, physician, and grief counselor. He offered advice that was not solicited and suffered his patient's depression and mood swings in stoic silence. Rarely did he allow Gabriel to stray out of his sight. He stalked him through the rooms of the cottage, walked with him along the sand beach in the cove, and even followed him when he went into the village to do the marketing. Gabriel told the shopkeepers that Shamron was his uncle from Milan. In public, he spoke to Shamron only in Italian, of which Shamron understood not a word.

Within days of Gabriel's return to Cornwall, the weather turned rainy, which suited all their moods. Chiara cooked elaborate meals and watched with relief as Gabriel regained some of the weight he had lost in the Saudi prison. His emotional state, however, remained unchanged. He slept little and seemed incapable of talking about what had happened in the desert. Uzi Navot dispatched a doctor to examine him. "Guilt," said the doctor after spending an hour alone with Gabriel. "Enormous, unfathomable, unremitting guilt. He promised to protect her, but in the end, he let her down. He doesn't like to fail women."

"What can we do?" Chiara asked.

"Give him time and space," the doctor said. "And don't ask too much of him for a while."

"I'm not sure having Ari around is helping matters."

"Good luck trying to dislodge him," the doctor said. "Gabriel will eventually recover, but I'm not so sure about the Old Man. Let him stay as long as he wants. He'll know when it's time to leave."

A daily routine eluded Gabriel. Unable to sleep at night, he slept in daylight, when his conscience allowed it. He moped, he stared at the rain and the sea, he walked in the cove. Sometimes, he sat on the veranda and worked with charcoal on paper. The sketches he produced were all of the operation. Many were of Nadia. Alarmed, Chiara secretly photographed the sketches and e-mailed the pictures to the doctor for analysis. "He's his own best therapist," said the doctor reassuringly. "Let him work it out on his own."

Nadia was with them always. They made no effort to keep her at bay; even if they had tried, events in the Middle East would have made it impossible. From Morocco to the Emirates, the Arab world was aflame with a new wave of popular unrest. This time, even the old Sunni monarchies appeared vulnerable. Emboldened by Nadia's brutal murder, Arab women poured into the streets by the thousands. Nadia was their martyr and patron saint. They chanted her name and carried signs bearing her photograph. In a macabre twisting of her message and beliefs, some said they wanted to emulate her by dying as martyrs, too.

The keepers of the old order tried to tarnish Nadia's reputation by branding her an Israeli spy and provocateur. Because of Gabriel's confession, which played ceaselessly on the Internet and the pan-Arab news networks, the charges against Nadia were widely dismissed. Her cultish following grew even larger when Zoe Reed of CNBC devoted an entire edition of her prime-time program to Nadia's posthumous impact on the Arab Awakening. During the broadcast, Zoe revealed that she had conducted several private meetings with Nadia during which the Saudi heiress acknowledged secretly funneling tens of millions of dollars to reform-minded organizations across the Arab and Islamic world. The program also accused the intelligence services of Saudi Arabia of complicity in her death—an accusation that brought a swift denunciation from the House of Saud, along with the usual threats about withholding oil from the West. This time, no one paid much attention. Like every other regime in the region, the al-Saud were now hanging on for dear life.

By then, it was June and the Americans were clamoring for a post-operational debriefing. Chiara imposed strict limitations on the amount of time the inquisitors would be allowed to spend with their subject—two hours in the morning, two hours in the late afternoon, three days in all. Posing as tourists, they stayed at a dreadful little bed-and-breakfast in Helston that Gabriel had chosen personally. The sessions were held at the dining room table. Shamron remained at Gabriel's side throughout, like a defense attorney at a deposition. There was no recording.

Chiara feared the debriefings would reopen wounds that were just then beginning to heal. Instead, they proved to be precisely the sort of therapy Gabriel so desperately required. The strictures of professionalism imposed a cold and emotionless tone on the proceedings. The debriefers posed their questions with the dryness of policemen investigating a minor traffic mishap, and Gabriel responded in kind. Only when the debriefers asked him to describe the moment of Nadia's death did his voice catch with emotion. When Shamron asked for a change of subject, the debriefers produced a photo of a young Saudi who had recently graduated from the terrorist rehabilitation program and placed it carefully on the table.

"Do you recognize him?"

"Yes," said Gabriel. "He's the one who killed Malik and the others."

"His name is Ali al-Masri," said one of the Americans.

"Where is he?"

"Living quietly in Jeddah. He's fallen out of the orbit of Sheikh Bin Tayyib and seems to have left the jihadist movement for good. His wife just gave birth to a little girl."

"Hanan," said Gabriel. "The child's name is Hanan."

The session was their last. That evening, Chiara lifted her ban on television during dinner so they could watch the Arab world unraveling. The regimes in Syria and Jordan were teetering, and there were reports the Saudis had ordered the National Guard to fire on protesters in Riyadh and Jeddah, killing dozens. Prince Nabil, the powerful Saudi interior minister, blamed the unrest on the Shiite regime in Iran and on followers of Nadia al-Bakari. His comments had the unintended effect of raising her profile among the demonstrators to new heights.

The following morning, Nadia became a posthumous hero to the art world as well when the Museum of Modern Art in New York announced that it had been entrusted with her entire collection. In return for the works, estimated to be worth at least five billion dollars, MoMA had agreed to allow Nadia's estate to appoint the first curator. As she strode to the podium to meet the New York press for the first time, the denizens of the art world breathed an enormous sigh of relief. They did not know much about Sarah Bancroft, but at least she was one of them.

She called Chiara the next day. She had heard from Adrian Carter that Gabriel's recovery wasn't going well and had an idea she thought might help. It was a job offer. A commission. Chiara accepted it without bothering to consult with Gabriel. She asked only for the dimensions and a deadline. The dimensions were large. The deadline was tight. Two months was all he would have. Chiara wasn't worried; her husband had relined and restored a Titian in a matter of days. Two months was an eternity. He began work the following morning by adhering a bolt of white canvas to a stretcher he made himself. Then he placed Chiara at one end of the couch and manipulated her limbs like those of a wooden sketch model until they conformed to the image in his memory. He spent a week working out the composition on paper. Satisfied, he began to paint.

The days of midsummer were very long. The portrait gave them purpose. Gabriel worked for several hours in the morning, took a break at midday for a meal and a walk in the cove, then worked again in the evening until the sun dropped into the sea. Much to his dismay, Shamron watched over him constantly. Chiara watched, too, but from a distance. Just as she had hoped, the work proved to be Gabriel's salvation. There were some people who dealt with grief by talking to therapists, she thought, and others who felt compelled to write about it. But for Gabriel, the healing balm of oil on canvas had always been best, just as it had been for his mother before him. Standing before the easel, he had total control. Missteps could be corrected with a few strokes of the brush, or hidden beneath a layer of obliterating paint. No one bled. No one died. No one sought vengeance. There was only beauty and truth as he saw it.

He worked without an underdrawing and with a palette influenced by the colors he had seen in the Empty Quarter. Blending the meticulous draftsmanship of the Old Masters with the freedom of the Impressionists, he created a mood that was both classical and contemporary. He hung pearls around her neck and adorned her hands with diamonds and gold. A clock face shone moonlike over her shoulder. Orchids lay at her bare feet. For several days, he struggled with the background. In the end, he chose to depict her rising out of Caravaggesque darkness. Or was she actually sinking into the darkness? That would be determined by the uprising raging on the streets of the Arab world.

Despite the intensity of the work, Gabriel's appearance improved dramatically. He gained weight. He slept more. The pain of his injuries receded. With time, he felt strong enough to return to the cliff tops. Each day, he roamed a little farther, leaving Shamron no choice but to watch from a distance. His mood darkened as Gabriel slipped slowly from his grasp. He knew it was time to leave; he just didn't know how to go about it. Chiara quietly tried to arrange a crisis of some sort that would require him to return to King Saul Boulevard. Failing, she had no choice but to enlist the help of Gilah, who sounded as if she were thoroughly enjoying Shamron's prolonged absence. Reluctantly, she decreed that her husband could remain in Cornwall only until the painting was finished. Then he would have to come home.

And so it was with a sense of foreboding that Shamron watched

Nadia al-Bakari come slowly to life on the canvas. As the painting neared completion, Gabriel worked harder than ever. Yet at the same time, he appeared reluctant to finish. Beset by a rare case of indecision, he made countless minor additions and subtractions. Shamron privately relished Gabriel's apparent inability to let go of the painting. Every day Gabriel delayed completion was another day Shamron would have with him.

Eventually, the revisions stopped and Gabriel began the process of making peace with his work. Not just Nadia—all of it. Shamron saw the shadow of death lift gradually from Gabriel's face. And on a clear morning in late August, he entered Gabriel's makeshift studio to find him looking remarkably like the gifted young man he had plucked from the Bezalel Academy of Arts and Design in Jerusalem in the terrible autumn of 1972. Only Gabriel's hair was different. Then it had been almost as black as Nadia's. Now it was stained with gray at the temples—smudges of ash on the prince of fire.

He was standing before the canvas with one hand pressed to his chin and his head tilted slightly to one side. Nadia glowed under the intense white light of the halogen work lamps. It was a portrait of an unveiled woman. A portrait of a martyr. A portrait of a spy.

Shamron watched Gabriel for several minutes without speaking. Finally, he asked, "Is it finished, my son?"

"Yes, Abba," replied Gabriel after a moment, "I think it is."

The shippers came the next morning. By the time Gabriel returned from his walk along the cliffs, Shamron had gone. It was better that way, he told Chiara before leaving. The last thing Gabriel needed now was another messy scene.

69

NEW YORK CITY

I T WAS SARAH BANCROFT'S IDEA to hold the gala opening of the Nadia al-Bakari wing on the anniversary of 9/11. The head of New York's Joint Terrorism Task Force suggested it might be wiser, given the current level of Middle East unrest, if she chose a less symbolic date, but Sarah held firm. The event would be held the evening of September 11. And if the task force couldn't find a way to secure it, Sarah knew people who could.

The demonstrators arrived for the party early, jamming West Fifty-third Street by the thousands. Most were feminists and human rights activists who supported Nadia's goals of sweeping change in the Middle East, but a few wild-eyed jihadis from Brooklyn and New Jersey showed up to denounce her as a heretic. None seemed to notice Gabriel and Chiara as they stepped from the back of an Escalade and slipped into the museum. A security guard escorted them upstairs to MoMA's business offices, where they found Sarah struggling with the zipper of her evening gown.

Everywhere there were stacks of MoMA's official monograph for the collection. Gabriel's portrait of Nadia was on the cover.

"You pushed us to the limit," Sarah said, kissing his cheek. "We almost had to go with a backup cover."

"I had a bit of difficulty making a few final decisions." Gabriel looked around the large office. "Not bad for a former curator from the Phillips Collection. I hope your colleagues never find out about the little sabbatical you took after leaving Isherwood Fine Arts in London."

"They're under the impression I spent several years engaged in a private course of study in Europe. The hole in my provenance seems to have only added to my allure."

"Something tells me your love life will be much improved." He glanced at her dress. "Especially after tonight."

"It's Givenchy. It was scandalously expensive."

"It's beautiful," said Chiara, helping Sarah with the zipper, "and so are you."

"It's funny how different the world looks when you're not sitting in a dark room at Langley tracking the movements of terrorists."

"Just don't forget they're out there," Gabriel said. "Or that some of them know your name."

"I suspect I'm the most carefully watched museum curator in the world."

"Who's handling it?"

"The Agency," said Sarah, "with help from the joint task force. I'm afraid they're rather annoyed with me at the moment. So is Adrian. He's trying to find some way of keeping me on the payroll."

"How is he?"

"Much better now that James McKenna has left the White House."

"Did he land on his feet?"

"According to the rumor mill, he's going to the Institute of Peace."

"I'm sure he'll be very happy there." Gabriel picked up a copy of the monograph and examined the cover.

"Would you like to see the real thing before the crowd arrives?"

He looked at Chiara. "Go," she said, "I'll wait here."

Sarah led him downstairs to the entrance of the al-Bakari wing. The caterers were laying out tables of canapés and opening the first bottles of champagne. Gabriel walked over to Nadia's portrait and read the biographical plaque mounted next to it. The description of the circumstances surrounding her death was far from accurate. Her father was described only in passing.

"It's not too late," said Sarah.

"For what?"

"To sign your name to the painting."

"I considered it."

"And?"

"I'm not ready to be a normal person. Not yet."

"I'm not sure I'm ready, either. But at some point . . ." Her voice trailed off. "Come," she said, leading him through a passageway, "you have to see the rest to believe it. Our old friend Zizi had remarkable taste for a terrorist."

They walked alone through rooms hung with paintings, Sarah in her evening gown, Gabriel in his black tie. In another time, they might have been playacting in one of Gabriel's operations. But not now. With Nadia's help, Gabriel had returned Sarah to the world where he had found her, at least for the moment.

"There's more," she was saying, gesturing toward a wall hung with Monet, Renoir, Degas, and Sisley. "Much more. We can only display about a quarter of what Nadia gave us. We're already making arrangements to lend portions of the collection to museums around the world. I think Nadia would have liked that."

They entered a room hung with paintings by Egon Schiele. Sarah walked over to a portrait of a young man who looked vaguely like Mikhail. "I told you not to say anything to him," she said, glancing over her shoulder at Gabriel. "You really shouldn't have."

"I'm not sure I know what you're talking about."

"You're one of the most gifted deceivers I've ever met, but you've never been able to lie to the people you care about. Especially women."

"Why didn't you invite him tonight?"

"And how would I have introduced him?" asked Sarah. "I'd like you to meet my friend, Mikhail Abramov. Mikhail is an assassin for the Israeli secret service. He helped to kill the man who once owned these paintings. We did a few ops together. It was fun while it lasted." She gave another glance in Gabriel's direction. "Do you see my point?"

"There are ways to get around things like that, Sarah, but only if you're willing to make the effort."

"I'm still willing."

"Does he know that?"

"He knows." She turned away from the canvas and touched the side of Gabriel's face. "Why do I have this terrible feeling I'm never going to see you again?"

"Send me a picture to clean every once in a while."

"I can't afford you."

She looked at her watch. It was the one Nadia had been wearing at the time of her abduction. It was still set three minutes fast.

"I need to practice my speech once before the guests arrive," she said. "Would you care to make a few remarks this evening?"

"I'd rather go back to my cell in Riyadh."

"I still don't know exactly what I'm going to say about her."

"Tell the truth," said Gabriel. "Just not all of it."

At the stroke of seven, the art world, in all its folly and excess, came spilling into the Nadia al-Bakari Wing of the Museum of Modern Art. Gabriel and Chiara remained at the cocktail reception for only a few minutes before retreating to a parapet above the atrium to listen to the speeches. Sarah addressed the crowd last. Somehow, she managed to walk the fine line between truth and fiction. Her speech was part eulogy, part call to action. Nadia had given the world more than just her art, said Sarah. She had given her life. Her body was now buried in an unmarked grave in the Nejd, but this exhibit would be her memorial. As the art world roared its approval, Gabriel's BlackBerry vibrated in the breast pocket of his jacket. He slipped into a quiet corner to take the call, then returned to Chiara's side.

"Who was it?" she asked.

"Adrian."

"What does he want?"

"He'd like us to come down to Langley."

"When?"

"Now."

70

LANGLEY, VIRGINIA

RASHID HAD BEEN CARTER'S FOLLY, Carter's bright idea gone terribly wrong. Gabriel had cleaned up the worst of the mess. Khalid the falcon, with his parting gift, had given Carter the means to sweep up the rest.

The gift had been a young Saudi jihadi named Yusuf. Langley and the NSA had been tracking his phone for several months. Yusuf was now one of Rashid's most trusted couriers. Rashid gave Yusuf coded messages; Yusuf delivered the messages to the faithful. He was expecting a phone call that evening from a man in Germany. Yusuf believed the man was the leader of a new cell in Hamburg. But there was no new cell in Hamburg. Carter and the team at Rashidistan had invented it.

"He's sitting in the front passenger seat of that Daihatsu," Carter explained, nodding toward one of the giant display screens in the Rashidistan op center. "At the moment, they're traveling on a remote road in the Rafadh Valley of Yemen. They picked up two men about an hour ago. We believe one of them is Rashid. In ten minutes, our phantom cell leader from Hamburg is going to call Yusuf. We've asked him to keep Yusuf talking for as long as possible. If we get lucky, Rashid will say something while the call is hot. As you know, Rashid is a bit on the loquacious side. He used to drive his Agency handlers crazy. He never shuts his damn mouth."

"Who makes the decision whether to take the shot?" Gabriel asked.

"NSA will tell me if they can pick up any other voices in the background and whether they can make a positive match. If the computers say he's there, we hit him. If there's even a sliver of doubt, we hold our fire. Remember, the last thing we want to do is kill Yusuf before he can lead us to the prize."

"I want to listen," Gabriel said.

"That's why you're here."

Gabriel slipped on a set of headphones. Ten minutes crawled past. Then the agent in Hamburg dialed. Two men began conversing in Arabic. In his mind, Gabriel set them aside. They were unimportant now. They were but a doorway to the man with a beautiful and seductive tongue. *Talk to me*, thought Gabriel. *Tell me something important, even if it's only another lie.*

Yusuf and the ersatz Hamburg cell leader were still speaking, but the conversation was clearly starting to wind down. Thus far, there had been no sound in the background other than the rattle of the SUV over the pitted Yemeni road. Finally, Gabriel heard what he had been waiting for. It was an offhand remark, nothing more. He didn't bother to mentally translate it; he was listening only to the tone and timbre of the voice. He knew it well. It was the voice that had condemned him to death in the Empty Quarter.

Do you wish to submit to the will of Islam and become a Muslim?

Gabriel turned to Adrian Carter. He was speaking tensely into the phone connected to the NSA. Gabriel was tempted to ask what they were waiting for, but he knew the answer. They were waiting for the computers to tell them what he already knew, that the voice in the background was Rashid's. He watched the SUV careening along the road in Yemen and listened as the two jihadis, one real, the other a clever forgery, concluded their call. Carter slammed down the phone in a flash of uncharacteristic anger. "Sorry to bring you all the way down here for nothing," he said. "Maybe next time."

"There's not going to be a next time, Adrian."

"Why not?"

"Because it ends here, right now."

Carter hesitated. "If I order the Predator to fire," he said, "four people will die, including Yusuf."

"They're four terrorists," said Gabriel. "And one of them is Rashid al-Husseini."

"Are you sure?" Carter asked one last time.

"Take the shot, Adrian."

Carter reached for the phone connected to the Predator control room, but Gabriel stopped him.

"What's wrong?" asked Carter.

"Nothing," said Gabriel. "Just wait a minute."

He was staring at the clock. Thirty seconds later, he nodded his head and said, "Now." Carter relayed the order, and the Daihatsu disappeared in a flash of brilliant white. A few members of the Rashidistan team began to applaud, but Carter sat with his hands over his face, saying nothing at all.

"I've done this a hundred times," he said finally, "and each time I still feel like I'm going to be sick."

"He deserved to die—for Nadia, if nothing else."

"So why do I feel this way?"

"Because, in the end, it's never clean or smart or forward-leaning, even when you take the shot from a room on the other side of the world."

"Why did you make me wait?"

"Look at the time in Yemen."

It was 10:03 a.m., the moment United Airlines Flight 93 plunged into a field in Shanksville, Pennsylvania, instead of its likely target, the dome of the U.S. Capitol. Carter said nothing more. His right hand was shaking.

After that, there was just one last issue still to be resolved. In the end, it came down to a simple business transaction: five million dollars for a name. It was provided by Faisal Qahtani, Shamron's old source from the Saudi GID. Fittingly enough, the five million dollars were deposited into the Zurich branch of TransArabian Bank.

They put the target under surveillance and spent weeks debating what to do. From his lakeside throne in Tiberias, Shamron decreed that only biblical justice would suffice. But Uzi Navot, in a sign of his rising influence, managed to overrule him. Gabriel had nearly given up his life in a quest for American equity, and under no circumstances would Navot squander it on an ill-advised covert operation in the heart of the American capital. Besides, he said, giving the Americans the name of a traitor would add still more value to King Saul Boulevard's side of the ledger.

Navot waited until his next official visit to Washington to whisper the name to Adrian Carter. In return, he made only one request. Carter readily agreed. It was, he said, the least they could do.

The Bureau took over the surveillance and started tearing through phone records, credit card bills, and computer hard drives. Before long, they had more than enough to proceed to the next stage. They sent a plane to Cornwall. Then they put a chalk mark at the base of the brown wooden sign along MacArthur Boulevard and waited.

The chalk mark was in the shape of a cross. It intrigued Ellis Coyle, because it was the first time it had been used. It meant Coyle's handler wished to conduct a crash face-to-face meeting. It was risky—any direct contact between source and case officer was inherently dangerous—but it was also a rare opportunity.

Coyle rubbed out the mark with the toe of his shoe and entered the park with Lucy at his heels. The leash was still attached to the dog's collar. Coyle didn't dare remove it. A bitter old dowager from Spring Valley had confronted him recently about his failure to collect Lucy's droppings. There had been threats of community sanction, perhaps even a word with the authorities. The last thing Coyle needed now was an encounter with the police, not when he was just a few weeks from retirement. He promised to end his rebellious ways and began secretly plotting the demise of the dowager's hateful little pug.

It was a few minutes past nine, and the clearing at the top of the trail was in darkness. Coyle glanced toward the picnic tables and saw the dark silhouette of a man seated alone. He led Lucy around the perimeter of the clearing, checking for evidence of surveillance, before walking over. Only when he was a few feet away did he realize that the man was not his usual handler from Saudi intelligence. He had gray temples and green eyes that seemed to glow in the dark. He looked at the dog in a way that made Coyle shiver.

"I'm sorry," Coyle said. "I thought you were someone else."

He turned to leave. The man spoke to his back.

"Who did you think I was?"

Coyle turned. The man with bright green eyes hadn't moved.

"Who are you?" Coyle asked.

"I'm the one you sold to Saudi intelligence for thirty pieces of silver, along with Nadia al-Bakari. If it were up to me, I'd send you to hell for what you did. But this is your lucky night, Ellis."

"What do you want?"

"I want to watch your face while they put the handcuffs on you."

Coyle stepped away in fear and began frantically looking around. The man at the table gave a half smile.

"I was wondering whether you would accept your fate with the same dignity she accepted hers. I suppose I have my answer."

Coyle dropped Lucy's leash and started to run, but the FBI agents swarmed him in an instant. Gabriel remained in the park until Coyle was gone, then headed down the footpath to MacArthur Boulevard. By noon the following day, he was back in Cornwall.

71

THE LIZARD PENINSULA, CORNWALL

H E WAS A CHANGED MAN when he came back from America; they could see that. The wounds had healed, the siege had been lifted, and whatever calamity he had suffered seemed finally to have passed. After encountering him one drizzly morning outside the old flint church, Vera Hobbs declared him fully restored and suitable for framing. But to whom had he entrusted the job? "Our mysterious friend from the cove isn't the sort to place himself in the care of others," replied Dottie Cox. "If I had to venture a guess, I'd say he propped himself on an easel and did the work with his own hand. That's why he turned out so well."

By then, it was mid-autumn again, and the days were short, a few hours of pale gray amid a seemingly endless night. They would see him in the morning when he came into the village to do the marketing, and again in the afternoon when he walked the cliffs alone. Of meaningful work there was no evidence. Occasionally, they would glimpse him in the gazebo with a sketchbook on his lap, but his easel stood empty in his studio. Dottie feared he had fallen victim to a bout of aimlessness, but Vera suspected the explanation lay elsewhere. "He's happy for the first time in his life," she said. "All he needs now is a couple of little ones to go with that gorgeous wife of his."

Oddly, it was the wife who appeared restless now. She was still unfailingly polite on the streets of the village, but it was clear she was dreading the prospect of the coming winter. She busied herself by cooking elaborate meals that filled the cove with the savor of rosemary and garlic and tomato. Sometimes, if the windows were open, and if one paused in just the right spot, it was possible to hear her singing in Italian in that sultry voice of hers. Invariably, the tunes were hauntingly sad. Duncan Reynolds diagnosed her condition as cabin fever and suggested that the women invite her out for a girls-only night up at the Godolphin Arms. They tried. She turned them down. Politely, of course.

If the restorer was aware of his wife's predicament, he gave no outward sign of it. Fearing the couple was headed for a crisis, Dottie Cox decided to have a word with him next time he came to her shop alone. A week would elapse before she was presented with an opportunity. Appearing at his usual time, half past ten, he took a plastic basket from the stack near the door and began filling it with all the joy of a soldier foraging for supplies. Dottie watched him nervously from behind the cash register, rehearsing her speech in her head, but when the restorer began placing his items on the counter, she was able to manage nothing more than her usual, "Morning, luv."

Something about Dottie's tone made the restorer fix her briefly with a suspicious stare. Then he looked down at the newspapers stacked on the floor and furrowed his brow before handing over a crumpled twenty-pound note. "Wait," he said suddenly, taking a copy of the *Times*. "This, too." Dottie slipped the newspaper into the sack and watched the restorer depart. Then she leaned over the counter to have a look at the paper. The lead story concerned the imminent collapse of the regime in Syria, but just below there was a piece about a recent anonymous donation of a painting by Titian to the National Gallery in London. No one in Gunwalloe imagined there might be any connection. And they never would.

The National Gallery released a vague official statement concerning the donation, but within the corridors of British intelligence there came to exist an unofficial version of the story that unfolded roughly along the following lines. It seemed the legendary Israeli intelligence officer Gabriel Allon, with the full knowledge and approval of MI5, had cleverly manipulated a sale at the venerable Christie's auction house in order to channel several million pounds into the terror network of Rashid al-Husseini. As a result, a newly rediscovered painting by Titian briefly entered the collection of the Saudi heiress Nadia al-Bakari. But upon her death, it was quietly returned to its rightful owner, the noted London art dealer Julian Isherwood. For understandable reasons, Isherwood initially considered keeping the painting but thought better of it after the aforementioned Allon suggested a far nobler course of action. The art dealer then made contact with an old chum from the National Gallery—an Italian Old Master expert who had unwittingly played a role in the initial deception—thus setting in motion one of the most important donations to a public British institution in years.

"And by the way, petal, I still haven't received one red cent from the CIA."

"Neither have I, Julian."

"They don't pay you for these little errands you're always running for them?"

"Apparently, they regard my services as pro bono publico."

"I suppose they are."

They were walking along the Coastal Path. Isherwood wore country tweeds and Wellington boots. His steps were precarious. Gabriel, as always, had to resist an urge to reach out and steady him.

"How much bloody farther do you intend to make me walk?"

"It's only been five minutes, Julian."

"Which means we've already substantially exceeded the distance of my twice-daily trek from the gallery to the bar at Green's."

"How's Oliver?"

"As ever."

"Is he behaving himself?"

"Of course not," said Isherwood. "But he hasn't breathed a word about his role in your little caper."

"*Our* little caper, Julian. You were involved, too."

"But I've been involved from the beginning," Isherwood replied. "This is all new and exciting for Oliver. Lord knows he has his faults, but beneath all that blubber and bluster beats the heart of a patriot. Don't worry about Oliver. Your secret is safe with him."

"And if it isn't, he'll be hearing from MI5."

"I think I'd actually pay to see that." Isherwood's pace was beginning to flag. "I don't suppose there's a pub up ahead. I feel a drink coming on."

"There's time for that later. You need exercise, Julian."

"What's the point?"

"You'll feel better."

"I feel fine, petal."

"Is that why you want me to take over the gallery?"

Isherwood stopped and placed his hands on his hips. "Not next week," he said after a moment. "Not next month. Not even next year. But someday."

"Sell it, Julian. Retire. Enjoy your life."

"Sell it to whom? Oliver? Roddy? Some bloody Russian oligarch who wants to dabble in culture?" Isherwood shook his head. "I've put too much into the place to let it fall into the hands of a stranger. I want it to stay in the family. Since I have none, that leaves you."

Gabriel was silent. Isherwood reluctantly started walking again.

"I'll never forget the day Shamron brought you into my gallery for the first time. You were so quiet, I wasn't sure you could actually speak. Your temples were as gray as mine. Shamron called it—"

"The stain of a boy who'd done a man's job."

Isherwood smiled sadly. "When I saw you with a brush in your hand, I hated Shamron for what he'd done. He should have left you at Bezalel to finish your studies. You would have been one of your generation's finest painters. As of this moment, everyone in New York is trying to figure out who painted that portrait of Nadia al-Bakari. I only wish they knew the truth."

Isherwood paused again to gaze down at the waves beating against the black rocks at the northern end of the cove. "Come to work for me," he said. "I'll teach you the tricks of the trade, such as how to lose your shirt in ten easy steps or less. And when it's time for me to devote my remaining energy to gardening, I'll leave you with more than enough resources to carry on in my absence. It's what I want, petal. More important, it's what your wife wants."

"It's very generous, Julian, but I can't accept."

"Why not?"

"Because one day, an old enemy will make an appointment to see a Bordone or a Luini, and I'll end up with several bullets in my head. And so will Chiara."

"Your wife is going to be disappointed."

"Better disappointed than dead."

"Heaven knows I'm no expert when it comes to long-term relationships," said Isherwood, "but I have a hunch your wife might be in need of a change of scenery."

"Yes," said Gabriel, smiling, "she's made that abundantly clear."

"So come to London, at least for the winter. It will give Chiara the distraction she needs, and it will save me a fortune in shipping fees. I have a panel by Piero di Cosimo that's in desperate need of your attention. I'll make it well worth your while."

"Actually, I may have something in Rome."

"Really?" asked Isherwood. "Public or private?"

"Private," replied Gabriel. "The owner lives in the very large house at the end of the Via della Conciliazione. He's offering me a chance to clean one of my favorite pictures."

"Which one?"

Gabriel answered.

"I'm afraid I can't compete with that," Isherwood said. "Is he going to pay you anything?"

"Acorns," said Gabriel, "but it will be worth it. For Chiara's sake, if nothing else."

"Just try to stay out of trouble while you're there. The last time you were in town . . ."

Isherwood stopped himself. It was clear from Gabriel's expression he no longer wished to dwell on the past.

The wind had torn a hole in the veil of clouds, and the sun was hovering just above the sea like a white disk. They remained atop the cliffs a moment longer, until the sun was gone, then started toward home. As they entered the cottage, they could hear Chiara singing. It was one of those silly Italian pop songs she always sang when she was happy.

AUTHOR'S NOTE

PORTRAIT OF A SPY IS a work of fiction. The names, characters, places, and incidents portrayed in the story are the product of the author's imagination or have been used fictitiously. Any resemblance to actual persons, living or dead, businesses, companies, events, or locales is entirely coincidental.

The *Madonna and Child with Mary Magdalene* portrayed in the novel does not exist. If it did, it would bear a striking resemblance to a similar painting by Tiziano Vecellio, also known as Titian, that hangs in the State Hermitage Museum in Saint Petersburg, Russia. Lot 12, *Ocher and Red on Red*, oil on canvas, by Mark Rothko, is also fictitious, though in May 2007, a similar painting, *White Center (Yellow, Pink and Lavender on Rose)*, fetched $72.84 million at auction in New York, a record for the artist. According to published reports, the buyer was the ruler of Qatar.

The art dealers, auctioneers, and consultants who appear in the novel, along with other books in the series, were created by the author and are in no way meant to be construed as fictitious renderings of real people. There is indeed an enchanting art gallery at 7–8 Mason's Yard in London, though its owner, the inimitable Patrick Matthiesen, shares nothing with Julian Isherwood other than his warmth and brilliant wit. The techniques for the restoration and relining of paintings described in the novel are accurate, including the speed with which a gifted restorer, if necessary, could knock a picture into shape. Deepest apologies to the management of Christie's in London for using an Old Master auction to fund a terrorist network, but I'm afraid operational security required keeping the affair secret.

Students of the global war on terror will no doubt recognize that, in creating the character Rashid al-Husseini, I have borrowed much from the curriculum vitae of the American-born al-Qaeda cleric and recruiter Anwar al-Awlaki—including his Yemeni background, his disturbing connection to two of the 9/11 hijackers in San Diego and Northern Virginia, and his apparent journey from moderation to radicalism and terror. The fictitious Malik al-Zubair was also inspired by real terror masterminds—namely, Yahya Ayyash, the Hamas master bomb-maker known as "the Engineer," and Abu Musab al-Zarqawi, the Jordanian terrorist who led al-Qaeda in Iraq. Ayyash was killed in January 1997 by a small bomb concealed in a cellular phone. Zarqawi, who was responsible for the death of hundreds of innocent Iraqis during the bloodiest phase of the Iraq insurgency, was killed in an American air strike on a safe house north of Baghdad in June 2006.

The border crossing between the United Arab Emirates and Saudi Arabia described in the novel does not exist. The actual crossing is many miles to the north and in recent months has been prone to long backups due to changes in Saudi customs procedures. The spectacular rise and fall of Dubai has been faithfully portrayed, along with the deplorable treatment of its large foreign workforce. Unfortunately, Dubai is not the only Gulf emirate where foreign workers are routinely abused and treated as virtual indentured servants. In March 2011, the Guggenheim Museum under construction in neighboring Abu Dhabi faced a threatened boycott by more than a hundred prominent artists who were outraged over conditions at the site. "Those working with bricks and mortar," the Lebanese-born media artist Walid Raad said in a statement, "deserve the same kind of respect as those working with cameras and brushes."

Financial intelligence, or "finint," has been an important

weapon in the war on terror for many years now. The Treasury Department's Office of Terrorism and Financial Intelligence collects and analyzes transactional data, as does the FBI's Terrorist Financing Operations Section. In addition, the CIA and numerous private companies connected to the vast American national-security complex all routinely track the flow of money through the bloodstream of the global jihadist movement.

Regrettably, a decade after the attacks of 9/11, much of this money still comes from the citizens of Saudi Arabia and, to a lesser extent, the Sunni Muslim emirates of the Persian Gulf. In a secret cable made public in December 2010, Secretary of State Hillary Clinton wrote, "It has been an ongoing challenge to persuade Saudi officials to treat terrorist financing emanating from Saudi Arabia as a strategic priority." In conclusion, Clinton's memo declares that "donors in Saudi Arabia constitute the most significant source of funding to Sunni terrorist groups worldwide."

One would think that Saudi Arabia, the country that produced Osama Bin Laden and fifteen of the nineteen 9/11 hijackers, would do more to clamp down on terrorist fund-raising on its soil. But other diplomatic cables have revealed the House of Saud has been unable or unwilling to shut down the flow of money to al-Qaeda and its affiliates. Militant groups operate front charities inside Saudi Arabia with impunity or simply solicit cash donations openly during the annual Hajj pilgrimage to Mecca. Prince Mohammad Bin Nayef, leader of Saudi Arabia's counterterrorism efforts, told a senior American official that "we are trying to do our best" to stem the flow of cash to extremists and murderers. But, he added, "if money wants to go" to terrorists, there is little Saudi authorities can do to stop it.

Which begs the question: Does the House of Saud, which owes its power to a covenant formed two centuries ago with Muhammad

Abdul Wahhab, truly wish to sever financial ties to a Sunni extremist movement it helped to create and nurture? A tense meeting in 2007 might provide an important clue. According to leaked government cables, Frances Fragos Townsend, a senior counterterrorism adviser to President George W. Bush, asked Saudi officials to explain why the Kingdom's ambassador to the Philippines was associating with suspected terrorist financiers. The Saudi foreign minister, Prince Saud al-Faisal, dismissed Townsend's concerns, stating the ambassador was guilty of "bad judgment rather than intentional support for terrorism." He then went on to criticize an American bank for raising "inappropriate and aggressive questions" about accounts maintained by the Saudi Embassy in Washington, D.C.

While the global terror threat has evolved since the morning of September 11, 2001, one thing remains unchanged: al-Qaeda and its affiliates and imitators are actively plotting to murder and maim on a mass scale in Western Europe and the United States. Dame Eliza Manningham-Buller, the former head of MI5, predicted in 2006 that the struggle against Islamic terror would "be with us for a generation," while other security officials have warned of a "forever war" that will force the West to maintain aggressive counterterrorism programs for decades, if not longer. It is likely that the ultimate length of the global war on terror will be determined, in part, by the seismic events shaking the Arab world at the time of this writing. Much will depend upon which side emerges victorious. If the forces of moderation and modernity prevail, it is possible the threat of terrorism will gradually recede. But if radical Muslim clerics and their adherents manage to seize power in countries such as Egypt, Jordan, and Syria, we might very well look back fondly on the turbulent early years of the twenty-first century as a golden age of relations between Islam and the West.

ACKNOWLEDGMENTS

THIS NOVEL, LIKE THE PREVIOUS books in the Gabriel Allon series, could not have been written without the assistance of David Bull, who truly is among the finest art restorers in the world. Each year, David gives up many hours of his valuable time to advise me on technical matters related to the craft of restoration and to review my manuscript for accuracy. His knowledge of art history is exceeded only by the pleasure of his company, and his friendship has enriched our family in ways large and small.

I am indebted to the brilliant art consultants Gabriel Catone and Andrew Ruth for taking me to the November 2010 Postwar and Contemporary evening sale at Christie's in New York and tutoring me on the tactics involved in purchasing paintings worth tens of millions of dollars. Truth be told, I found the world of the high-stakes auction far more intriguing than the world of spies and terrorists, and the experience had a profound impact on the ultimate course of the novel. Needless to say, Gabriel Catone and Andrew Ruth have little in common with the fictitious Nicholas Lovegrove other than their sophistication and extraordinary knowledge of the business of art.

Several Israeli and American officials and counterterrorism experts spoke to me on background, and I thank them now in anonymity, which is how they would prefer it. Roger Cressey, the director for transnational threats at the National Security Council from 1999 to 2001, has been an invaluable source of information regarding U.S. counterterrorism policy, and an even better friend. For the record, he has no links whatsoever to the firm of Rogers & Cressey, based on Cannon Street in London.

My dear friend, the eminent anesthesiologist Dr. Andrew Pate, advised me about the disorder known as arteriovenous malformation, or AVM. Also, a very special thanks to M, who lifted the veil on certain matters related to data collection. I do not pretend to be aware of all the technology available to American, Israeli, and British intelligence, but I have tried to write about it in a way that both serves the story and does not bore readers. I am confident the true capabilities of the U.S. government far exceed anything I have described in the pages of *Portrait of a Spy*.

I consulted hundreds of books, newspaper and magazine articles, and Web sites while preparing this manuscript, far too many to name here. I would be remiss, however, if I did not mention the extraordinary scholarship and reporting of Steve Coll, Robert Lacey, James Bamford, Ron Suskind, Jane Mayer, Jim Krane, Dore Gold, Robert F. Worth, Scott Shane, Souad Mekhennet, and Stephen F. Hayes.

Having lived in the Arab world in the 1980s, I was familiar at the outset of this project with the stifling oppression faced by far too many of the region's women. Jan Goodwin's seminal work *Price of Honor* was an invaluable resource, as was *Inside the Kingdom* by Carmen Bin Laden. The writer, activist, and commentator Irshad Manji inspired me with her spirit and vision. Dr. Qanta A. Ahmed's luminous account of her time spent working in Saudi Arabia as a physician helped me to better understand the challenges faced by female professionals in one of the world's most conservative societies. Her book's haunting title, *In the Land of Invisible Women*, found its way into the thoughts of my heroine, Nadia al-Bakari, as did the clarity of its vision. If women such as these ran the affairs of the Middle East, I'm sure the world would be a much better place.

ACKNOWLEDGMENTS

Louis Toscano, my dear friend and longtime personal editor, made countless improvements to the manuscript, as did my copy editor, Kathy Crosby. Bob Barnett, Deneen Howell, Linda Rappaport, and Michael Gendler were a priceless source of wise counsel during a very busy year, as were Jim Bell, Bruce Cohen, Henry Winkler, Ron Meyer, and Jeff Zucker. My study partners—David Gregory, Jeffrey Goldberg, Steven Weisman, Martin Indyk, Franklin Foer, David Brooks, and Erica Brown—kept my heart focused on what is truly important, even when my thoughts strayed to the unfinished manuscript lying on my desk. The peerless Burt Bacharach inspired me with his genius and his enduring passion for his work. Jim Zorn gave me friendship and faith when I needed it most.

A heartfelt thanks to the remarkable team at HarperCollins, especially Jonathan Burnham, Jennifer Barth, Brian Murray, Cindy Achar, Ana Maria Allessi, Tina Andreadis, Leah Carlson-Stanisic, Leslie Cohen, Karen Dziekonski, Archie Ferguson, Mark Ferguson, Olga Gardner Galvin, Brian Grogan, Doug Jones, David Koral, Angie Lee, Michael Morrison, Nicole Reardon, Charlie Redmayne, Jason Sack, Kathy Schneider, Brenda Segel, Virginia Stanley, Leah Wasielewski, and Josh Marwell, who profoundly influenced the plot of *Portrait of a Spy* with a single question.

I wish to extend the deepest gratitude and love to my children, Nicholas and Lily. Not only did they assist with research and the final preparation of my manuscript, but they gave me unconditional love and support as I was struggling to meet my deadline. Finally, I must thank my wife, the brilliant NBC News journalist Jamie Gangel. In addition to managing my business, running our household, and raising two remarkable children, she also found time to skillfully edit each of my drafts. Were it not for her patience, attention to detail, and forbearance, *Portrait of a Spy* would not have been completed. My debt to her is immeasurable, as is my love.

ABOUT THE AUTHOR

D ANIEL SILVA IS THE number one *New York Times* bestselling author of *The Unlikely Spy*, *The Mark of the Assassin*, *The Marching Season*, *The Kill Artist*, *The English Assassin*, *The Confessor*, *A Death in Vienna*, *Prince of Fire*, *The Messenger*, *The Secret Servant*, *Moscow Rules*, *The Defector*, and *The Rembrandt Affair*. He is married to NBC News *Today* correspondent Jamie Gangel; they live in Washington, D.C., with their two children, Lily and Nicholas. In 2009 Silva was appointed to the United States Holocaust Memorial Council.